BLOOD
TRUTH

Also by Matt Coyle

BLOOD TRUTH

A RICK CAHILL NOVEL

MATT COYLE

OCEANVIEW PUBLISHING
LONGBOAT KEY, FLORIDA

5|18 BTR

ISBN 978-1-60809-239-0

Published in the United States of America by Oceanview Publishing

Longboat Key, Florida

www.oceanviewpub.com

10 9 8 7 6 5 4 3 2 1

For my brother, Tim Coyle
A person of quiet courage who has inspired me
my whole life

ACKNOWLEDGMENTS

This book was made better by the input and support of many people.

My sincere thanks to:

My agent, Kimberley Cameron, for her supreme faith and guidance.

Bob and Pat Gussin, Lee Randall, Emily Baar, Lisa Daily, and Michael Fedison at Oceanview Publishing for raising the bar and continued support.

David Ivester and Ken Wilson for greasing the skids on marketing.

Carolyn Wheat, Cathy Worthington, Grant Goad, Patty Randall Roe, and Penne Horn from the Saturday group for helping to polish the rough spots.

My family, Jan and Gene Wolfchief, Tim and Sue Coyle, Pam and Jorge Helmer, and Jennifer and Tom Cunningham for listening and continuing to get the word out.

Nancy Denton and Jennifer Cunningham for multiple reads.

David Putnam for inside police information.

Dr. D. P. Lyle and Dr. Sally Kim for help with the cardiovascular system and medical insights.

Finally, a banking representative who wishes to remain anonymous, which makes me think I got some great inside info.

Any errors regarding law enforcement, medical issues, or banking procedures are solely the author's.

BLOOD TRUTH

CHAPTER ONE

I HADN'T BEEN to the house since my father's funeral. Eighteen years. I had to go back ten years before that to find a good memory. At least, one that involved my father. I was nine, and Little League baseball tryouts were a few days away. Dad was throwing me ground balls in the backyard. I'd just mowed the lawn down to the nub, and it was playing fast. We had to do twenty-five in a row without an error, including the throw back to him, before we ended practice. Sometimes it took fifteen minutes, sometimes an hour. Sometimes we had to clip a portable spotlight with a long extension cord to the eaves of the garage to hold back the night.

That day, we were on a roll. Ten in a row. Clean. Fifteen. Clean. After twenty, my dad grabbed a handful of gravel from the walkway between the garage and the concrete slab on the side of the house where we kept the trashcans. He sprinkled the gravel three feet in front of me. He told me bad hops were a part of baseball.

A part of life.

Number twenty-one caught a pebble, took a bad hop, and the ball ricocheted off my chest. I snatched the ball off the ground and fired a strike to my dad's first basemen's glove to beat the clock ticking in his head. Twenty-two missed the pebbles. Clean. Twenty-three hit a pebble and stayed low, but I gloved it and whipped the ball to my dad. Clean. Twenty-four skidded dead right, but I backhanded it and made the throw. Clean.

Twenty-five clipped a pebble and shot straight up into my mouth. I fell to the ground on my back and grabbed my mouth with my right hand. Blood. Tears. Error. Dad hustled over, knelt down over me, and wiped my lip with his handkerchief. It stung and kept bleeding. He helped me up and started to walk me to the house.

I let go of his hand and wiped tears from my eyes and blood from my lip. "We didn't make twenty-five in a row."

"I think we can skip that today." He smiled, towering over me.

"No. We can't quit just because things get hard." I parroted the saying he'd told me since I could first understand words. I believed the words. They were engrained in my psyche, my DNA. But my mouth hurt and the blood scared me and I wanted to quit. More than anything, though, I wanted my dad to be proud of me.

"Okay, but just one more. That one took a bad hop and wouldn't have been ruled an error." He patted my ball cap.

"Twenty-five in a row."

We finished an hour later under the spotlight hanging from the eaves.

* * *

My mother sold the house three months after the funeral. Dad had died years before the bottle finally killed him. After he "retired" without a pension from the La Jolla Police Department, my mother moved to Arizona with the man she began seeing while she and Dad were estranged. I'd been to Arizona twice in eighteen years.

The neighborhood had changed a lot since I'd last been there. Every house but one in the cul-de-sac had either been remodeled or torn down and rebuilt. The lone holdout was the house I'd grown up in. Even that was about to change.

The house was laid bare, stripped down to the studs and concrete slab. New owners had bought it from the family my mother sold it to. Looked like they wanted to make the most of the La Jolla zip code and take the tract out of the tract home I'd grown up in. Bigger. Better. Modern. They'd framed up to two stories so they'd get a glimpse of the bay down the hill two miles away. What was a house in La Jolla without a view?

Just a childhood with some good memories buried beneath the bad.

I got out of my car and walked through the open gate of the temporary chain-link fence that encircled the house. The afternoon sun cast a shadowed grid onto the ground. A couple of construction workers were putting up drywall in the family room. Or where the family room used to be. I walked over to the porch and the front door opening. I knocked on the side of the frame. One of the drywallers stepped back and looked at me. Blond, buff. Probably surfed the daylight hours he didn't work.

"This is a construction site. You can't be in here." No anger, just stating the facts.

"I've got an appointment with the new owner, Bob Martin." I had my own facts.

"Mr. Cahill." A voice came from behind the tar-papered framing of the garage. A tall man appeared. Midforties, short curly brown hair. Wire-rim glasses. Looked like an architect, which he probably was. Tear down, build up, and flip. We shook hands.

"The item I called you about is out in the back."

I followed him through the garage into the backyard. A worker cut wood on a table saw on the lawn where I used to play catch with my dad. There were no eaves to clamp a spotlight. There would be soon. Different eaves.

Bob led me over to a makeshift table of composite wood laid over two sawhorses. Blueprints were spread out next to a wall safe without a wall connected to it.

"Here it is." He pointed at the safe. "Found it in the closet of the smallest bedroom."

My father's den. No one had been allowed in there. Not even my mother. When I was eight or nine, I found my dad's extra set of keys in his bedroom dresser while he was at work. I sneaked into the den and found a ledger with dates and dollar amounts written down in the closet. Nothing else interesting. I didn't remember a wall safe. It wasn't until years later that I figured out that the ledger contained payoff amounts from the mob. Probably for my dad. I'd always held out hope they'd been for someone else, but hope is often just a lie you tell yourself to avoid the truth.

"Thanks." I walked over to the makeshift table.

The safe was about eighteen by fifteen inches and three or four inches deep.

"It was hidden inside a false wall behind a shelving unit." He smiled like he'd just opened King Tut's tomb. I doubted I'd find any treasure inside. "The last owners didn't even know it was there. My realtor found your mother and late father's names as the original owners. Your mother told me to call you."

He did. She didn't. Fine by me. My mother did tell me that whatever was in the safe was mine and she didn't need to know its contents. Through an e-mail. The intimacy of modern technology.

The safe was beige and had a round dial combination lock in the middle of the door. I'd been paid cash out of wall safes a few times for my job as a private investigator. They all had digital keypad locks. This safe was probably at least twenty-five years old, which would fit into my father's time frame.

"Can I pay you for your trouble?" I asked Bob Martin.

"Oh, no." He smiled. "It wasn't any trouble at all. I just hope there's either something valuable in there or a keepsake that will bring back some good memories."

I wasn't sure the safe was old enough to contain any good memories. I thanked Martin and picked up the safe. Heavy. Weighed about twenty-five pounds.

The past weighed a lot more.

CHAPTER TWO

My black Lab, Midnight, met me at the front door of Cahill Investigations' home office. Also known as my home. I was the agency's owner, investigator, and sole employee. Kept complaints about the boss down to a minimum. Business had been good for a while. I'd been the news media hero of the week about a year back and it had been a marketing bonanza. If the media had dug deeper, I could have been the villain of the week. That might have been even better for marketing.

I was between jobs right now, but not worried about making my monthly nut like I would have been a year ago. I had savings. I had options. I had a twenty-five-year-old safe without its combination from my late father's den.

The safe. I knew how to pick a lock on a door, but not a safe. The pick set I kept in the trunk of my car would be of no use. I lugged the safe upstairs to my office. Midnight followed me and found his spot under my desk. My cell phone rang while I checked my mental Rolodex for former clients who could crack a safe. None.

I looked at the incoming call.

Kim.

My ex-girlfriend whom I hadn't talked to in almost two years. Since she'd gotten married.

I answered.

"Rick?" She used to call me Ricky. The only person who'd ever tried. Her voice had a slight nervous waver. My stomach, the same.

"Kim. How's married life?" My voice, cooler than I'd intended, covered up my stomach's nerves. And the pang in my chest.

"Fine." Flat. "I'm hoping you can help me."

"Of course. What do you need?"

"I mean I want to hire you."

"Oh." I had a rule to never fall for a client. I wondered if that included taking on a client who'd I'd already fallen for earlier in life. My life, my rules. "Well, I'm a little, kinda, ah, I could give you contact info for someone who's really good."

"This probably wasn't a good idea. I'll find someone on my own. I hope you're well."

"No, wait." I didn't have a rule that said I couldn't help a friend. "Whatever you need."

"Okay." An inhale. "Could we talk about it in person?"

"Sure." I wanted to see her. But I didn't want to see her. I didn't want to be reminded of the life I let slip away. "I meet with clients at Muldoon's. Turk lets me use a booth if the restaurant's not too busy. Can you meet me there at six tonight?"

"Yes." It sounded like a question. She may have been trying to figure out what she'd tell her husband to get away.

Her husband. Not my problem.

* * *

Muldoon's Steak House sat on Prospect Street, La Jolla's restaurant row. It hadn't changed much in the forty-plus years it held up the north end of the row. Square concrete building in a sea of modern remodels. It withstood the waves of trends that restaurants in the area had tried and discarded. Muldoon's was an old-school steak house, family owned. Run by Turk Muldoon.

My onetime partner. And one-time best friend.

I walked inside the dimly lit entry at 5:55 p.m. Turk manned the hostess station. Still a massive man who was an all-conference line-backer at UCLA twenty years ago. But he looked thinner than the last time I'd seen him. And older. Gray pinched in on his curly red hair around the temples. His once cherubic face now drawn back to finally show his age. Years spent leaning against a walking cane can do that. The fact that he could stand upright at all was a near-miracle. The doctors thought Turk would live the rest of his life in a sitting position when they extracted the bullet wedged against his spine four years ago.

The night he saved my life.

"Rick." He forced a smile. "You here to meet with a client or have dinner?"

"Client." I forced a smile of my own.

"Booth four is available." He pointed his cane toward the dining room. "You know the way."

"Thanks." I started for the dining room, relieved our conversation was over.

"How will I know your client?" His voice over my shoulder stopped me. "Will he ask for you?"

"She." I turned back toward him. "It's Kim. You can just send her back. Thanks."

"Connelly?" Turk's eyebrows rose. He always liked Kim. He never understood why I broke up with her. With each passing year, neither did I.

"Parker."

"That's right. I remember hearing she got married." No mirth in his eyes. Maybe a hint of sadness. He knew better than most how life can change for the worse in an instant.

"Yeah. She got married."

I went into the dining room I used to run four years ago, and hid in booth four.

Kim appeared a few minutes later. She wore a green silk blouse that made her emerald eyes pop. Her blond hair swept off her face, she looked every bit the successful realtor she was. But tired. And worried. And still beautiful.

My breath tightened. I pushed down feelings that didn't belong to me anymore. Feelings I didn't know I still had. Feelings I missed.

I slid out of the booth and stood up. I didn't know whether to extend my hand for a shake or close in for a hug. Kim didn't, either. Finally, we stepped into an embrace. Awkward at first. Then close, warm, and long. And filled with memories.

"You look good, Rick. How have you been?" The smile that caught my eye eight years ago and, through everything since, had never let go. Wide, bright, light sparkling in her green eyes. I realized right then how much I'd missed it.

"Fine. Congratulations on your marriage." Her husband was the biggest realtor in La Jolla. His smiling mug was on every bus bench in town.

Kim looked down at the table. "I didn't know if I should send you an invite."

"It's okay. I'm happy for you." I was. Even as I kicked myself, I was happy for Kim. I wouldn't be able to live with myself if I wasn't.

"I saw you on the news last year." She looked up from the table. "I almost called. I didn't know what to say. I'm glad you're okay."

"Thanks." I remembered hoping at the time she would call. And feeling stupid about it. "Why do you need a private investigator?"

"I hope I don't, really." Her eyes grabbed the table again. "I want you to follow Jeffrey."

"Your husband?" This could turn ugly.

"Yes."

"Why?"

"Why do you think?" She looked up, face tight.

I knew why, but she had to tell me. Not to make her feel bad, but because that's how I ran my business. Everything had to be spelled out. No surprises. When the truth came out hard and raw, I didn't want the client to try and turn the ugliness back onto me. Even if I was just doing a favor for a friend.

"It has to come from you."

"I think he's having an affair." Her lips pinched together and her nose twitched. "Did you have to make me say it out loud?"

"Yes, I did. I'm sorry." My cheeks blossomed heat. "Why do you think he's having an affair?"

"Things could have been different, Rick." Liquid collected in the bottom of her eyes. "You pushed me away. You never let me in."

Kim was right. She never understood that I wasn't good enough for her, and I never saw her as an equal to the idolized memory I had of my late wife, Colleen. No one ever could be. Not even Colleen. But none of that mattered now.

"I'm asking these questions because it's my job. It's how I get to the truth. Sometimes people think their spouses are having affairs when there's an innocent explanation." Not often, and sometimes it's because of some other deceit.

"I found a second cell phone."

"Some people have one phone for personal use and one for work."

"Not realtors. We're on call twenty-four seven. And I found a text message to someone named Sophia."

"What did the text say?" Kim's answer could make this an open and shut case.

"He asked this Sophia if everything was on schedule. She didn't reply."

"That could be about anything." Maybe not so open and shut after all. "Did you ask him about it?"

"No. I can't." She shook her head. "I've already caught him in a lie once. I couldn't stand to see him lie to my face again."

"What was the lie?"

"We were supposed to have lunch together at George's at the Cove a few days ago, but Jeffrey canceled at the last second because he had to show a property in Del Mar to one of our top clients." The unspent tears had dried up, but the angry flush came back into her cheeks. "I kept the reservation and went to lunch by myself. As soon as I sat down, I noticed the client Jeffrey was supposedly meeting sitting at a table twenty feet from me. I went over and asked him if he was meeting Jeffrey later. He said no. When I asked Jeffrey how the meeting went later that night, he said it went okay."

"You're sure it was the same client?"

"Yes."

"But you didn't confront Jeffrey about it?"

"No. I stood there and let him lie to me. I've never felt so small."

"So, you'd rather I get you proof before you confront him? Wouldn't it be easier to tell him about the phone and the lunch and hash things out? It will hurt, but trust me, it hurts less than getting a third party involved taking pictures in the dark."

"I can't. But I need to know right now."

"Okay. I'll look into it. Why the rush?"

"I'm pregnant."

CHAPTER THREE

I'd been following Jeffrey Parker in his white Lexus LS for two days. I hadn't caught him in the arms of another woman, but I had seen some of the grandest real estate in La Jolla. Made me wish I had an extra five or six mil lying around. None of the properties Parker showed had For Sale signs out front. He had a wealth of pocket listings. Luxurious homes where he got first dibs.

Parker and a client emerged from a house overlooking the beach on Sea Lane. Not quite Malibu a hundred fifty miles up the coast, but you still had the ocean for a backyard and even got a front yard as a bonus. I sat in my car and watched Parker from up the block. Gray slacks, white shirt, no tie, navy blazer. Tall, three or four inches over me. Fit. Square jaw. I understood why Kim chose him instead of waiting for me to figure things out. I just didn't understand why she took so long to make the choice.

The client, a thirtyish playboy, drove off in a Maserati. Parker locked up, then got into his car. He headed toward La Jolla Boulevard.

I grabbed my cell phone off the car's console and tapped a number. "He's coming your way."

"Roger. I'll duck and cover and follow after you."

"Check."

Moira MacFarlane had been a PI longer than I had, and was damn good at it. She ran solo, like me, and we sometimes teamed up when one of us had a multiple-day surveillance gig. Two cars gave the subject different looks when he checked his rearview mirror. We both drove newish Honda Accords, the most popular car in Southern California. Ubiquitous on the streets of San Diego County. Even in high-end La Jolla. Moira's was white, the most popular color. I drove black, number two on the list. It blended better with the night.

I pictured Moira ducking below the dashboard and chuckled. She didn't have to duck down too far. She barely stood five feet tall but had an attitude that would fill up an NBA number-one draft pick. We'd met after a lawyer, unbeknownst to me, promised her a job then gave it to me instead. She tracked me down and showed me that attitude up close. We settled things over a couple beers, but every time we met since, she'd still greet me with a giant chip on her tiny shoulder.

I didn't have that many friends. I couldn't unfriend one of them just because she acted like she hated me.

Parker turned right onto La Jolla Boulevard, not left, which would take him back to his office in the village.

I followed him with Moira in tow. He headed south toward Bird Rock, the tail end of La Jolla. Plenty of expensive homes down there with ocean views to show clients. Except he rolled right through, down to Mission Boulevard into Pacific Beach. PB was a few hundred grand lower in zip code than La Jolla, but it still had enough million-dollar homes to interest Parker Real Estate. A rookie agent though, not the boss.

Parker made a right on Missouri Street and drove past apartment complexes and condos. He headed toward the end of the street, which dead-ended at the ocean after a block. My gut turned over. Unless Parker had made a wrong turn or intended to park and stare at the ocean, he had two potential destinations. Both hotels. He turned left into the underground parking lot of The Pacific Terrace Hotel.

"Shit."

"What?" Moira's voice jarred me. I'd forgotten I had her on speakerphone during the drive. Lost in my dread of what a hotel meant. One that was hidden from La Jolla but close enough for easy access. I tried to lie to myself that maybe Parker was just meeting a client from out of town. The lie didn't take.

Jeffrey Parker was meeting a woman.

"Nothing. Bust it into that garage. We have to find out who he's meeting."

I drove to the dead end and parked illegally in front of the low steel barrier that protected the sidewalk from the road. Moira swooped into the underground parking lot. I tugged my ball cap low, hopped out of the car, and ran around to the front entrance of the hotel. I'd never met Jeffrey Parker, but he knew who I was. Years ago, when he and Kim were just dating, they'd had conversations about me. He wasn't a fan. My face had been in the news enough over the past couple years for Parker to find out what I looked like.

I hustled through the upscale, fern-dotted lobby toward the door to the stairwell and went through it. I plugged my earbuds into my phone as I ran up the stairs. The Pacific Terrace only had three stories, but most of the rooms had decks that faced the ocean. Not the normal hookup dive I was used to when I worked the adultery detail.

I guess when you were the King of La Jolla Real Estate, the view outside the sin room was almost as important as the one inside.

"The elevator went up to the third floor." Moira's voice buzzed in my ears as I hit the second-floor landing. My instincts had been correct. Only the top floor for Jeffrey Parker.

"Were you on the elevator with him?" I huffed out the words as I pumped up the last flight of stairs.

"No."

"Go back to your car and wait." I didn't have time for further elaboration.

"Yes, sir. Asshole." She hung up.

I opened the door to the third floor of rooms three inches and peeked out. The hallway was empty, but I heard the click of a door being closed. I walked about midway down the hall and estimated that the sound had come from room 310. I looked up and down the hall to make sure no one could see me, then put my ear to the door. No murmured conversation, just the whooshing equalization of my own eardrum.

I took the elevator down, exited the hotel, and jogged back to my car. No parking ticket. Yet. A spot had opened up a few cars away while I was in the hotel. I jumped in my car and nabbed it before someone else could. Parking spaces in Pacific Beach were as scarce as in La Jolla.

I punched Moira's number.

"Would you mind meeting me out on the street?" I tried to sound pleasant.

"You're an asshole. I'll be right there."

"Could you bring your sun hat with you?"

"Roger."

I opened the trunk of the Accord and unzipped a large duffel bag, then pulled out my tools of deception. A pair of white shorts, a Hawaiian shirt, a Pittsburgh Steelers ball cap, and my Nikon DSLR camera. A lot of PIs used video cameras these days. I preferred the stark, frozen images of life. I got back into the car and changed, then emerged as a tourist awestruck by the beauty of San Diego. The beauty I let slip into the background all too often in my everyday life.

Moira emerged from the parking garage wearing rolled-up Levis, showing off her shapely calves, flip-flops, a tank top, and a floppy sun hat that shaded her silver-dollar brown eyes.

"You're too tan," I said.

"You're not." She looked at my Irish legs. "Besides, women go to tanning booths all over the country. Even here."

"You're right."

I led her over the knee-high barrier at the dead end onto the sidewalk. We took a wooden staircase down to the flat sandy beach below the hotel. The beach was empty save for a few couples walking down by the shore. I glanced over my shoulder up at the third floor of the hotel and saw the balcony of the suite in the dead center. Empty.

Moira and I walked diagonally across the beach cutting in front of the hotel. We headed down to the water, and I took peeks back at the balcony. Still empty.

"Okay. Do your thing." I lifted the camera hanging from the strap around my neck and pointed it at Moira.

She made goofy poses in front of the water, and I pretended to take pictures of her. She moved away from the ocean so she was now between me and the hotel. I aimed the camera above her at room 310's balcony and zoomed the lens. Jeffrey Parker came into view sitting in a lounge chair. Alone. Was he renting the room as a getaway crash pad? Maybe the crown did weigh heavily on the king.

A flash of movement behind him. Someone handed him a glass of wine. I shifted the camera and caught a woman. Thirties. Beautiful.

Wearing a silk robe.

CHAPTER FOUR

My STOMACH SANK, but I clicked the shutter release and took Parker and the woman's photo. Find the truth, no matter what. That was my charge, my mission. Truth was the crucible by which all lives were judged. Without it, life and death had no meaning. Today, *no matter what* meant breaking the heart of a woman whose heart I'd already broken before on my own.

The woman on the balcony sat down in a lounge chair with her own glass of wine next to Parker. Short brown hair. Tan. She slipped one tan leg over the other. I couldn't see whether she wore a bikini underneath her robe or nothing at all. Even from a distance, I could feel her sensuality. A hunger that vibrated off her body. A carnal beckoning.

Parker was still in the clothes he'd worn when he arrived. They hadn't gotten down to business, yet. I snapped off a few more shots.

"Is he with someone?" Moira shifted her pose to hands on hips and I continued to take pictures of the couple on the balcony above her head.

"A woman."

"Bingo."

Moira knew who my client was, but she didn't know my relationship with Kim. This was just another case that we were about to successfully wrap up.

"Yeah." I didn't match her enthusiasm.

"What's wrong?" She put her hand on top of her sun hat and thrust out a hip. "We cracked the case. That's what we get paid to do."

"The client's a friend."

"Oh." She dropped her hand to her side and fell out of character for an instant. Then she spun and looked back at me over her shoulder. Composure regained.

Moira and I had a business relationship. Though I considered her a friend, our conversations almost always avoided the personal. Did that really make us friends? I wondered what she considered me. Now wasn't the time to blur the line.

Moira kept posing and I kept taking pictures. Up on the balcony, Parker's lips moved. The woman laughed and placed her hand on his thigh. Parker smiled and patted the woman's hand. They both wore sunglasses concealing their eyes. Verbal foreplay? I couldn't tell. The woman stood up and led him into the hotel room. I snapped another shot.

The camera couldn't reach into the darkened hotel room, so I couldn't see if verbal foreplay had escalated into the physical. I didn't have to see. I didn't want to see. I didn't want to have to lay the photos in front of Kim and watch her break apart as I had so many other women during the four years of my PI career. It was hard enough to do to strangers. I'd never had to do it to a friend. The other photos I had of Parker and the woman were proof enough for me. I hoped Kim wouldn't want more.

More was always better left to the imagination.

"That's a wrap." I dropped the camera and let it hang from the strap around my neck.

"For the day or the whole case?" Moira let go her pose.

"Everything. I'll send you a check in a couple days." My voice flat under the ocean's revelry. We trudged through the sand to the wooden staircase. A wave broke into whitewater behind us with a rolling hiss.

"Tough news to have to give to a friend." Moira put a hand on the staircase railing and stopped. "Sorry, Cahill."

Her sincerity stunned me. It may have been the nicest thing she'd ever said to me.

"Thanks." I walked up the stairs, Moira at my side.

We split at the sidewalk. She walked over to the garage, and I headed to my car. She stopped at the mouth of the garage and turned toward me. "Do you want to get a beer? I'm buying."

The new nicest thing she'd ever said to me.

"Thanks, but I'm going to hang out here and see how long he stays." I took a step toward my car, then stopped and turned back. Moira disappeared into the darkness of the garage. "I'll take a rain check, though. And I'll buy."

"We'll see." Her sandpaper voice came out of the dark. "But you blew it. You had me in a rare moment of weakness. You may never get another chance."

I didn't have a rebuttal to the truth. I wondered if Jeffrey Parker would.

* * *

Parker's Lexus rolled out of The Pacific Terrace Hotel garage at 4:37 p.m. No passenger. Just him. He'd been at the hotel for about an hour and a half. Plenty of time to do what he shouldn't. I ducked down in my car as he passed. I let him go. I'd gotten what I'd needed, but didn't want. If Parker had a second woman on the side, I didn't have to know about it, and neither did Kim. The truth may be life's crucible, but it didn't have to rub salt in every wound.

I sat in my car looking at the ocean below the horizon, running through scenarios on how best to present Kim the evidence that would confirm her suspicions. There wasn't an easy way. The facts were what they were. The truth would hurt. Kim deserved better.

She'd wasted five years in and out of a relationship with me. When she finally figured out that I'd never figure it out, she went with her second choice. Now it looked like he was a worse choice than me.

Movement in my side-view mirror caught my eye. A silver late-model Cadillac with the license plate PWR BRKR passed by me and turned into The Pacific Terrace Hotel garage.

I knew the car and the license plate. Peter Stone. Power Broker. Turk Muldoon's silent partner in the restaurant and a man who had once tried to kill me. I jumped out of the car and ran toward the garage. Stone was a onetime Vegas casino boss, a present-day philanthropist, and an all-time asshole.

Maybe him showing up at a hotel that housed the woman screwing my client's husband was just a coincidence.

There were plenty of reasons for Stone to visit The Pacific Terrace Hotel. He'd left Vegas behind long ago and had morphed into a real estate developer. He might even be an investor in the hotel. But my experience with Stone had proven that he didn't believe in coincidences. When it came to him, neither did I.

I slipped into the darkened garage in time to see Stone walking toward the elevator with a black leather briefcase in his hand. Expensive, with a leather strap secured through a silver clasp.

I tracked him from a distance, using parked cars for cover. He entered the elevator. As soon as the doors closed, I dashed to the staircase and sprinted up to the third floor. I cracked the stairwell door on the third floor and listened. The ping of the elevator and, seconds later, the swoosh of the doors opening. I crept out of the staircase and inched along the wall. A knock on a door. A woman's voice. I peeked around the corner and saw a profile of gray hair enter a room.

I knew the hair and I knew the room. Peter Stone had business with the woman who had ruined Kim Parker's marriage.

CHAPTER FIVE

I'D JUST PUNCHED my ignition when Stone's Cadillac emerged from The Pacific Terrace Hotel garage. I slid down in my seat and let him drive by. He hadn't been in the woman's room more than fifteen minutes. Sex was off the table. I wondered what had been on it.

Peter Stone. A briefcase. A woman in a hotel room. A lot of possibilities. Not many that a philanthropic icon would want on his resume.

I turned off the ignition and wondered what Jeffrey Parker had gotten himself into and how much I wanted to know. And how much I didn't want to tell Kim.

Two minutes later, a late-model white Corvette Z06 convertible slipped out of the garage. Top down. Woman behind the wheel. Scarf over her hair, tied under her chin. Big round sunglasses. Audrey Hepburn from a 1960s movie.

Except this woman had already starred in my movie. Stop-action still shots from the balcony of room 310. A woman driving an eighty-thousand-dollar sports car wasn't just an extra, existing only to fill up Jeffrey Parker's leisure time and fantasies. She had her own story. Maybe Parker existed just to fill up her leisure time.

Would it matter to Kim? Her husband had broken civilization's most sacred oath. The deed was the betrayal. The partner, unimportant. Except to me. I'd uncovered the sin, but not the whole truth. Especially with Peter Stone involved.

I turned the ignition back on.

* * *

I pulled up behind the woman as she sat at a stoplight. I took a picture of the Corvette's license plate with my phone. The woman turned right on Mission Boulevard. So did I.

I called Moira.

"Too late, Cahill. You had your chance." The husky jackhammer voice. "You need a friend tonight, hug your dog."

"Don't get your hopes up. I need you to run a plate."

Moira had connections at every police department in San Diego County. I had a major disconnect with the La Jolla Police Department that reverberated throughout all the other PDs in San Diego. When I needed to find out who a car was registered to, or any information a cop could give me, I called Moira.

"Another favor? You're a one-way street, Cahill. Give me the plate number."

I texted her the photo of the Corvette's license plate and heard a ping through the phone. "I just texted it to you."

"Thanks, Einstein." That offer of a beer, a distant memory. "You already onto another case? How did your friend take the bad news?"

"Same case. I haven't told her yet."

"Then what's the plate for?"

"Just tying up loose ends."

"You're delaying the inevitable." Her voice softened, but the words were hard. "Quit chasing your tail and tell the woman what she hired you to find out." She hung up.

I followed the Corvette through Pacific Beach and Crown Point as it took the Ingraham Street Bridge over Fisherman's Channel, which connects Mission Bay and Fiesta Bay. The Corvette exited onto Nimitz Boulevard just before the Sea World exit. The woman took Nimitz through Ocean Beach and turned right on Rosecrans, the main road through Point Loma.

Famous for its historic lighthouse and the Cabrillo National Monument, Point Loma is located on a peninsula bordered west and south by the Pacific Ocean and the San Diego Bay to the east. It's a small, sleepy community with pockets of wealth that can match any in San Diego. Point Lomans are just less ostentatious about it.

The Corvette exited Rosecrans up a steadily climbing street, then left, and right again up a San Francisco–style hill. I followed a block back and felt like an astronaut in liftoff position as I climbed the last hill. The Corvette turned into a driveway of a home three quarters of the way up the street. The house was an old, nothing-special midcentury with a multimillion-dollar view of the harbor, airport, and downtown San Diego. It looked like a knockdown and flip waiting to happen. The other homes on the street were all more modern and probably appraised at a million more than the house where the Corvette parked. Still, location, location, location.

I passed by the house just as the woman walked from her car toward the front door. She carried a black briefcase with a silver clasp. Peter Stone's briefcase. What secrets did it hold? Probably just money. Once clean, now dirty or vice versa. But did it have anything to do with Jeffrey Parker? Probably not. Just another sin by people who committed a lot of them.

I U-turned at the top of the street and parked a couple homes above the house on the opposite side of the street. Not for the first time, I evaluated the choices I'd made in my life that led up to me sitting in a car admiring other people's views. Money can't buy you happiness, but it can buy you a view.

I pulled out my phone and logged onto a paid website and ran a deed search on the house across the street. A couple years back, I'd call Kim when I needed to know who owned a property. It had been free and I got to talk to Kim. If I called her now, I'd have to explain why I wanted the address and how it related to my surveillance of her husband. She'd get the bad news about her husband tomorrow. Unless Kim asked for extra details, I'd keep the Point Loma address and Peter Stone to myself. This was just me scratching an itch.

For twenty bucks, the website gave me the owner of the house. Gaia Trust. I tried to dig deeper into the trust, but the website didn't have any details. I looked up Gaia Trust and didn't find anything except references to Gaia who I already knew to be the Greek ancestral goddess of all life. Mother Earth. My phone buzzed. Moira.

"The car is being leased by a Sophia Domingo, age thirty-eight." As usual, no preamble from Moira. "Lives at 1022 1st Place in Hermosa Beach."

"Good work." Hermosa Beach was a couple hours north in Los Angeles.

"I'm not done. Married twice. Divorced twice. No record of employment over the last three years."

"I guess when most of your work is done under the sheets, you keep the employment under the table."

"Clever, Cahill." She hung up before I could thank her.

I watched the house and admired the view for an hour, then drove home. The case was over. The information I had to give to Kim might end her marriage. The only woman I'd ever loved since the death of my wife twelve years ago. Pregnant with the child of the man who was cheating on her two years into their marriage. Thoughts a better man wouldn't allow pulled at the edges of my conscience. Could the destruction of Kim's marriage I'd chronicled for her be the pathway to our getting back together?

What kind of man was I?

CHAPTER SIX

I MET KIM at Muldoon's the next morning at seven thirty. The restaurant only served dinner and wouldn't be open for another nine and a half hours, but the back door was open for deliveries. My agreement with Turk didn't have time restrictions, as long as I didn't interfere with day-to-day business. I nodded at the kitchen manager and led Kim past two steel food-prep tables, the walk-in refrigerator, and the dishwashing station out into the dining room. I tapped the dimmer switch next to the open grill and lit up the raised booths in the corner. Kim followed me up to my unofficial office in booth four.

She wore slacks and a blazer. No sign of a baby bump. Blond hair pulled back for business. This morning's business would be different than any she'd ever experienced. For me, just another one of the dozens and dozens of adultery cases I'd handled over the years. Except that it wasn't.

I kept the folder containing my report and photos closed in front of me on the table. I gave Kim a brief overview of tailing her husband the first day. No bombshells. Then I told her about day two, The Pacific Terrace Hotel, and Sophia Domingo with Jeffrey on the balcony of room 310. I left out Peter Stone, the briefcase, and the house in Point Loma. Parker's sin was enough for Kim. The rest would be an unneeded worry. She had a baby and a broken marriage to worry about. That was enough.

Kim's face tightened, but she held it together.

"Do you have pictures, Rick?" A hint of disdain, now that what I did for a living affected her life. "I know you usually take pictures."

I opened the folder and slid it across the table to her. She looked at the photos one by one, staring at each for thirty seconds or more. Her cheeks flushed red and her mouth pinched flat, but she didn't say anything. Her eyes, clear, dry, angry.

Finally, "Are you holding back pictures that are more revealing?" The disdain more evident now. "I know getting those is your specialty."

I took the insult. The karmic penalty for wondering if showing Kim her husband's infidelity might open a path for us again.

"No. These are all I have. All I took."

"How long was Jeffrey with her?"

"It's all in the report." I pointed at the folder.

"I don't want to read it." Slight glisten in her eyes. "I'm asking you."

"He was there about an hour and a half."

She looked at the photo of the woman in the silk robe with her hand on Jeffrey Parker's thigh for a long time. "Do you think what you've shown me today proves that my husband has been unfaithful?"

"There could be an innocent explanation."

"I need your honest opinion. What do you think?"

"I think they look comfortable with each other." I thought back to Parker and the woman in lounge chairs on the balcony, sipping wine, sharing a laugh. The hand on his thigh. This wasn't their first time. "They're probably having a physical affair. And it's probably been going on for some time."

"So, he's not just fucking another woman, he's in a relationship." Her face twisted into an anger I'd never seen in the eight years I'd known her. And I never heard her use that word before. "That's worse than fucking a different call girl every other night."

"People make mistakes, Kim. For a variety of reasons. Marriages can survive this kind of thing. I've seen it plenty of times."

"Not this one."

"Talk to him before you make any decisions. Don't hurry into anything. Take a breath."

"Stop." She held up a hand. A tear ran down her cheek. "You don't have that right. You gave it up two and a half years ago."

"I still care about you, Kim." The words were true, but they sounded false even to me as they tumbled out of my mouth. "I want you to be happy."

"Please. Enough." She took an envelope out of her purse and handed it to me. "Thank you for finding the truth."

"There's no charge." I set the envelope on the table next to the folder in front of her. "It's on me."

"It's not on you." She grabbed the envelope, threw it at my chest. More tears slid down her cheeks. "That just makes it worse. You don't get to play the hero. You better cash the damn check. This was a business arrangement. I hired you because you're the best PI in San Diego at spying on people having affairs. Not because we used to be friends."

She pushed out of the booth and ran out of the restaurant.

CHAPTER SEVEN

SAN DIEGO SAFE was located next to a couple quick-service restaurants in a strip mall in Kearney Mesa. Squat building painted beige and brown. Probably built before I was born. I lugged my dad's wall safe into the store and set it down on the front counter. A seventyish man in a Dickies work shirt behind the counter eyeballed me over reading classes. The name on the tag above his left pocket read Phil. The owner and the man I'd talked to on the phone.

"I'm guessing you're Mr. Cahill."

People twice my age addressing me as Mister made me feel like an impostor.

I stuck out a hand. "Call me Rick."

We shook. His hand, leathery and strong.

"Well, let's have a look." He spun the safe around like it was on a lazy Susan. "Gardall concealed wall safe, SL4000/F-G-C. Fine product. Doesn't give up its contents easily. I'll have to drill it to open it up. Hate to do that."

"It's okay by me." I wasn't going to use the safe again. I had a gun safe. I didn't have anything more important to conceal than a gun.

"Seems like a waste." He pointed brown eyes at me over his cheaters. "And you said over the phone that you'd tried combinations with numbers that may have had some meaning to your father?"

"Yes." I'd tried his birthday, mine, my sister's, my mother's. Even the date of their wedding. The combination, like the safe, was just another secret that my father took to his grave.

"Well, then, it's going to cost two hundred dollars to drill it out. I have to use a special bit. You think there's anything in here that's worth two hundred dollars to you?"

"I have no idea. Drill away."

"Give me thirty minutes."

"Take your time." My father had been dead for eighteen years. I could wait a little longer to find out what was in a safe I didn't know about until four days ago. "I'm going to get something to eat."

"The safe will be ready for you to open when you get back."

I walked outside. It was still morning and the October sun hadn't shown all of its teeth, yet. The quick-service restaurants in the mini mall didn't interest me. The Original Pancake House was only a mile away. I started walking. I figured the walk back to San Diego Safe after breakfast would be much needed after the heavy carbo-loading I was about to take on.

I bought a newspaper from the box dispenser outside the restaurant, and went inside. Nine thirty and OPH was humming. When Kim and I used to come here for our Sunday morning ritual, there was always at least a twenty-minute wait. Today being a weekday, I only had to wait a couple minutes for a table to open up.

The hostess sat me at a two-top in the noisy restaurant, and I pulled the mini pencil out of the binding of a notepad I always carried with me, and went to work on the *USA Today* crossword puzzle. Kim and I used to tag-team it over our breakfast. Another ritual. Melancholy memories bubbled up, and I set aside the crossword. Memories from happier times. And memories from this morning at Muldoon's.

The pancakes were as good as I remembered. Heavenly pillows topped with butter and warm maple syrup. Halfway through, I regretted my choice of restaurants. Not because of the food or my expanding belly. Because of the memories.

My phone buzzed on the walk back to San Diego Safe. My memories had come full circle. Kim.

"Rick, I want to apologize for how I treated you this morning." A low hush. "You didn't deserve that. I childishly took my pain out on you. I'm ashamed. I'm sorry."

I could almost hear her lash a switch across her own back. It made me uncomfortable because she wasn't alone. I shared in the guilt. Not for anything I did in Muldoon's, but for what I didn't do years ago. Her sentiment at Muldoon's hadn't been wrong, it had just been redirected from an earlier time.

"Kim, you don't have to apologize to me. Ever. I'm sorry how things turned out." With her husband. With me.

"No. I was wrong. Please let me apologize."

"Okay. Accepted." I just wanted to move on.

"I asked Jeffrey about Sophia." Her apology had been sincere, but she also needed a sounding board.

"What did he say?"

"That she was a client. I didn't ask him if he was sleeping with her. I'd told him I'd found his second phone."

"What did he say about the phone?"

"He said that she requested he use a separate phone because she didn't want anyone to know that she was talking to another realtor. She was afraid someone at our office would see their correspondence and word would get out."

"Do you believe him?" It was the worst lie I'd ever heard in an adultery case. And I'd heard plenty. Parker had gotten the other phone to hide his relationship with Sophia from Kim.

"Not really." Exhale, then a pause. "Maybe. I'd never doubted Jeffrey until he lied to me about seeing the client in Del Mar the other day."

All I'd known about Jeffrey Parker before his wife hired me was that he was an upstanding guy. But I'd seen all-American men turn into Italian politicians when the wrong woman gave them attention. Sophia Domingo was the wrong woman.

"I told you from the start that things weren't always as they seemed and that sometimes there were simple explanations." Although, not in this case.

"But you think he's lying, right?"

"I don't know him well enough to make a determination. You should go with what your gut tells you." Kim was pregnant and thought she'd married a good man who would make a good father. It wasn't my place to talk her out of it.

"I don't know what to believe. You didn't actually see them have sex or even kiss. They didn't even hold hands. You just saw her touch his leg once, right?"

"Right."

Silence. Then, "There's something else I didn't tell you about."

The sound of Kim's voice told me it wouldn't be good news.

"What's that?"

"When I found the phone and the texts to Sophia, I found another phone number that Jeffrey had called a couple times."

"Okay."

"I called the number from my phone and a man answered. I recognized the voice from interviews I'd seen on TV." She hesitated. "I'm pretty sure the man was Peter Stone."

"You talked to him?"

"Not really. I asked for Sophia and he said there was no one there by that name. He has a very distinctive voice."

"Did you ask your husband about the calls to Stone?"

"No. I didn't think about it at the time. I was more concerned about this Sophia person."

"Why didn't you mention it when you hired me?"

"I knew about your history with Peter Stone and worried that you wouldn't take the job if you knew he might somehow be involved." She let go a long breath. "Now, I'm worried that Jeffrey might have some connection to him. I don't know what to think. I'm scared."

"Why don't you ask your husband?"

"I can't tell if he's telling me the truth anymore."

I told her what I'd learned about Sophia and Peter Stone, the house on the hill in Point Loma, and Stone's briefcase.

"Why didn't you put all of this in your report?" A tinge of the anger carried over from this morning's meeting at Muldoon's.

"It wasn't pertinent to discerning whether or not your husband was having an affair."

"Then why did you investigate on your own?"

"Seeing Peter Stone with the briefcase changed things." I let out a guilty breath. I'd been keeping my own secrets. "It made things bigger than just an adultery case."

"That's why I still need your help."

"You want me to continue to follow Jeffrey?"

"No. He's going to Las Vegas today for a convention." Silence. Then, "I want you to follow Sophia."

"That's not a good idea."

"Why?"

Seventy-five percent of the surveillance I did involved people cheating on their mates. But I tracked the mates, not their bed buddies. Tailing a private person for another private person was a different game. And sometimes dangerous. Motives were important. Some PIs had unknowingly or knowingly tracked down people who were targeted for murder by their clients.

Kim didn't have murder in her heart, but she was human. She might confront Sophia and things could turn ugly.

"Because she's a private person. She's not related to you or a business partner. It's unethical."

"Rick. I'm about to start a family." Her voice pitched high and cracked. "I need to know what kind of environment I'm bringing this child into. If my husband involves himself with men like Peter Stone, I need to know. If he's a cheater, I need to know. If it's all a mistake, I need to know that, too. I have life-changing decisions to make soon."

"Does Jeffrey know you're pregnant?"

"No. I found out the day after I saw his text to Sophia on his secret phone. I'm not telling him until I discover whether he's still the man I married, or someone else."

Kim had told me she was pregnant, but not her husband. In some ways, that could have made me feel good. I felt awful. How could you start a family with a man you didn't trust?

Start a family. Colleen and I had talked about starting our own before she died. Well, when we weren't yelling at each other those last few months. Before then, when things were good. Other than being married to Colleen for two years, I hadn't felt a part of a family since before my father died eighteen years ago. Kim deserved to feel confident in starting her own.

"I need your help, Rick." Kim's voice softened. "You're the only person I trust in my life right now."

I wasn't sure I warranted Kim's trust, but she'd always had mine. She'd never failed me—even when I'd wished she had, so I could have taken an easier out.

"Okay." I'd pick up her case again—after I closed one that had been with me for over twenty-five years.

CHAPTER EIGHT

PHIL GREETED ME at the counter when I returned to San Diego Safe.

"The safe is ready for you to open." He led me into a work room in the back. The safe sat on a wooden workbench. Unopened.

"Why didn't you open it?"

"It's not my business to look at what people have hidden away from the rest of the world."

Apparently, it was my business to find out what my father had hidden away from the rest of the world, including his family, for at least twenty years.

Phil went out into the showroom and closed the door behind him. I felt like I'd been left alone for a private viewing of a loved one. I guess I had. All that remained from my father, other than his LJPD badge, which sat in my sock drawer, was in this safe.

I put my hand on the handle, but didn't open it right away. My father had died a drunk nine years after he'd been kicked off the La Jolla Police Force. The reasons were never made public, and my father never gave me an explanation. Rumors of him being a bagman for the mob swirled in the winds of whispers behind my family's back. Did the safe hold the verification of the rumors? I'd lived almost three decades not knowing. Did I really have to learn the truth now? Ever? Why squelch the tiny flicker of hope I'd held onto for all these years?

I'd chased the truth my whole life. No matter the cost.

I pulled open the safe door.

The narrow safe had one shelf, forming a lower and upper compartment. An oily rag folded around something sat in the lower compartment. I pulled out the rag and unfolded it like I was unwrapping a deli sandwich. Inside was a gun. Old-timers often stored handguns in the oily rags they used to clean their weapons.

The gun was a Raven MP-25 semiautomatic pistol. A pocket gun that could fit in the palm of my hand. Also known as the original Saturday Night Special. Cheap guns produced in the 1970s after the import of such were banned by the Gun Control Act of 1968. Where there's demand, the free market—and the black one—will supply.

I'd never seen the gun before. My father had had five or six guns that I knew of, but none of them had been a Saturday Night Special. My mother sold them all after he died. I wrapped the gun up in the cloth and put it back into the safe.

The top compartment held two sealed letter envelopes. One a couple inches thick and the other thin. I pulled out the thick envelope and looked for an address or any kind of markings. Nothing. Blank and slightly yellowed. I didn't open it. I knew what was inside. I just didn't know how much.

The second envelope had a slight bump in the bottom of it. I put my fingers on the bump. It felt like a key. I stared at the envelope for a few seconds, then finally opened it. The key was slightly longer than a house key and had square teeth on one side. It looked like it went to a safe deposit box.

Another secret waiting to be revealed.

I ripped open the envelope full of money. It held hundreds and fifties. Too many to count now, but a lot of money. I ran my hands inside both compartments to make sure there was nothing else inside the safe. There wasn't. Thank God. I'd seen enough.

The ledger with the dates and dollar amounts I'd found in my father's den as a kid wasn't in the safe. But plenty more was. A gun, a large wad of cash, and a key to a safe deposit box. The tools and rewards of a cop on the take? Probably. I felt that tiny flicker of hope I'd carried most of my life turn to smoke.

I put the cloth-wrapped gun in my jeans pocket and stuffed the envelopes into the front pocket of my sweatshirt. I opened the door into the showroom, and Phil was waiting for me.

"Did you find what you needed?" He went back behind the counter.

"I guess." A candle bell to snuff out the flame.

"I can repair the hole I drilled and reset a new combination and you'll have a workable safe again."

"No, thanks. I don't have any need for a wall safe." I kept my secrets inside. "You can keep it if you can find a use for it."

"Sure. Thanks. I'll take $50.00 off your bill, so the total is a hundred and fifty." He smiled for the first time that morning. "Will that be cash or charge?"

I had a twenty-year-old envelope stuffed full of cash. I pulled out my wallet and swiped a credit card through the electronic reader. I didn't know where the money in the envelope came from or what my father had done to earn it. But I knew it was dirty.

I'd killed four men and broken plenty of laws in my thirty-seven years. The police had ruled the killings justified or taken credit for them for their own purposes. Or never found a body. I'd taken the law into my own hands, but never for personal gain. I'd done it because I lived by the code my father had taught me when I was a child: *Sometimes you have to do what's right, even when the law says it's wrong.*

Somewhere along the way, my father forgot about the *what's right* part and just focused on the *wrong*.

* * *

Midnight greeted me at the front door and sniffed at the pockets
in my jeans and sweatshirt. He smelled something different on me.
Decades-old sin. He followed me upstairs to my office. I took out the
gun and envelopes and put them on my desk, then sat down.

I opened the envelope full of cash and started counting. Fifteen
grand in hundreds and fifties. The hair on the back of my neck
spiked. The amount stunned me. A fair amount of money now, a lot
twenty-five years ago. When my father had died of cirrhosis of the
liver eighteen years ago, my family was barely getting by. I was on a
full-ride football scholarship at UCLA, but I worked in a restaurant
in the summer and off-season and sent money home to my mom. My
father never held a steady job again after he was fired from the La
Jolla Police Department. Fifteen thousand dollars would have paid a
lot of delinquent bills.

What did he do to earn that much money and why did he keep
it hidden away when it could have helped his family? I had a feeling
the answer to the first question had something to do with the answer
to the second. The possible answers to the questions scared and saddened me.

And, now, what was I supposed to do with the money?

I couldn't pretend the money was a lucky windfall and go out and
spend it on something stupid. Or even something smart. I put the
envelope of cash in a desk drawer. After I finished with Kim's case,
I'd give the money to charity. The only way I knew to make that dirty
money clean.

I opened the other envelope and poured out the key onto my desk.
The key had Diebold Inc, Canton Ohio imprinted on one side of the
tab. The other side had S335. I'd never had a safe deposit box, but I
was pretty sure this key went to one.

My father had banked at Windsor Bank and Trust in La Jolla. He'd sometimes take me there as a kid when he'd cash his LJPD paycheck. I didn't know if he had a safe deposit box. Apparently, he did. If not at Windsor, then somewhere else. But would the box still be active? Safe deposit boxes aren't free. You have to rent them. Someone had to pay the rent, and my father had been dead for eighteen years.

If I somehow found the safe deposit box and it was still active, what would I find inside? More wads of fifties and hundreds? Another Saturday Night Special? Did I really need more proof to confirm what everyone else already knew?

My dad had been a dirty cop.

I put the key onto my key ring. That left the gun. I had plenty of my own guns. All legally registered. Well, all except for a derringer I'd taken from a dead man's gun safe. It had saved my life, so I kept it. I didn't need another pocket gun.

Probably be best just to file down the firing pin and throw the weapon away. I unwrapped the Raven MP-25 and looked at it. A nasty little piece of work. I realized I hadn't checked to see if it was loaded when I found it in the safe. I picked it up and released the tiny magazine. Loaded.

The backstrap of the grip was abrasive in my hand. I grasped the gun by the barrel and examined the backstrap. It had scratches along it. More like file markings. My guess was that was where Raven Arms had put its serial number, and someone had filed it off.

I set the gun down quickly like it was a live snake. Serial number filed off. Untraceable. A criminal's gun. Or a gun a crooked cop carried to throw down at an officer-involved shooting scene in case the crook he shot hadn't had a weapon. There wasn't much difference between a cop and a crook in that situation. Except one might be a murderer.

My stomach turned over and my mouth cottoned up. There wasn't any hope left that my father hadn't been a bad cop. The whispers had been true. It was just a matter of how bad. This was where my father's truth had gotten me.

I picked up the magazine to slide it back into the gun, then stopped. Years of handling guns kicked in and told me the magazine felt light. It held six rounds. I examined the clip. It had a tiny window opening vertically down its middle. I counted the bullets inside. Only four. Two short of a full magazine.

The gun had been fired at least twice before my father hid it away in the safe. Along with the fifteen thousand dollars and the safe deposit key.

What had been in the gun's sights when my father pulled the trigger? And had fifteen grand been his reward?

CHAPTER NINE

I SAT IN my ubiquitous Honda Accord above the house in Point Loma where I'd tailed Sophia yesterday. Her car was in the driveway.

I tried to keep my mind on Kim's problems so I could forget about what I'd found in my father's safe. The one he kept hidden from everyone in his home. Even his wife. After seeing what was in it, I understood why he'd kept it hidden. And who he really was. The money in the envelope bothered me, but not as much as the gun. My father had been on the take. A little graft to afford the house in La Jolla and college for my sister? Maybe. Some twisted altruism to take care of his family. But why hadn't he spent the fifteen grand in the envelope?

The gun was different. Darker. Depths below dirty. Malevolent.

The two missing bullets. Where had they gone? There were plenty of innocent explanations. My father had taken it off a crook or found it on the street as is, with four bullets in the magazine. Or, he'd tried the gun out on the range, went through a magazine or two and stopped before he emptied the last clip. Perfectly reasonable explanations. Except they didn't jibe with the man I knew.

My father always kept his guns loaded. He used to take me to the shooting range when I was a kid, before everything turned to shit. The routine was always the same. All guns were unloaded and put in the trunk of the car with boxes of ammunition. We followed the same procedure after we were done shooting before we left the range. We reloaded all the guns when we got home.

My father thought an unloaded gun was a less useful weapon than a hammer or a baseball bat.

He always said if someone broke into your home, the two or three seconds it took to load your gun could get you and your family killed. He never had access to a gun that was less than fully loaded. Fully lethal.

But, even if I could overlook the MP-25's light clip, I couldn't ignore the most glaring issue. Why had he kept the gun in the hidden wall safe? He kept a Colt 45 in the top drawer of his nightstand when he and my mom went to bed each night. All other weapons were stored in the gun safe in the garage. What made a cheap Saturday Night Special special enough to keep in a hidden wall safe? A Saturday Night Special that had a filed-off serial number and two missing bullets.

The gun, the safe, the cash, the safe deposit key, all wrong. Worse than the rumors that had whirled around my childhood. Could I leave it at that? My father *was* dirty, case closed. Move on with a life that was perpetually stuck in the past. Mine, my father's. Could I live with what I found if I dug deeper? And what if I uncovered a twenty-five-year-old crime? I couldn't bring a dead man to justice. Would anyone care if I tried?

Only if it was for murder.

An untraceable gun. Two missing bullets. Fifteen grand in an envelope. A hit. A murder. A paid assassin. Had my father used the hidden gun to kill someone for money? Or was the money in the envelope from something else? Maybe my father kept the gun because someone else had used it in a murder and he was blackmailing the killer.

The truth was unknown. Buried. Along with my father's credo, I couldn't ignore my own. Find the truth. No matter what.

Movement in the driveway of 3235 Lucinda caught my eye. The white Corvette pulled onto the street and went down the hill. Top down, Sophia Domingo behind the wheel. Alone. I let her go three quarters of the way down before I followed. She hit the bottom of the hill, made a couple turns, and emptied out onto Rosecrans heading east.

I called Moira, who was stationed outside The Pacific Terrace Hotel.

"I've got her in Point Loma going east on Rosecrans. Stay put for now, but be ready to roll. I don't want to be the only car she sees in her rearview mirror all day."

"Roger."

Sophia took Rosecrans all the way east to where it emptied onto either Interstate 8, or I-5. She took 5 North. She could have been heading to The Pacific Terrace Hotel or somewhere else. I buzzed Moira again.

"Hustle through PB to get to I-5 North, but don't get on it unless I tell you to."

"You like giving orders, don't you?" Her voice, gravel going through a lawn mower.

"Just to you."

She hung up.

Sophia drove past an on-ramp into Clairemont and paralleled Mission Bay. A handful of sailboats waiting for wind dotted the small bay. She stayed in a middle lane as she approached the Grand/Garnet exit, which fed into PB en route to The Pacific Terrace Hotel. She wasn't going back to the hotel.

Quick tap on Moira's number.

"Get onto 5 North."

"I'm at the light on Bluffside Avenue about to get on the freeway."

"Stay on the phone and let me know when you're on."

Sophia passed the Balboa exit and continued north toward La Jolla.

"I'm on." Moira.

"Speed up. She just passed Nobel."

Thirty seconds later, I caught view of Moira's white Accord in my rearview mirror. She passed me, and I fell back three cars behind her and five or six behind Sophia.

Moira and I traded places a few times over the next twenty minutes as Sophia Domingo continued up I-5 past Del Mar, Solana Beach, and Encinitas. She finally exited onto Carlsbad Village Drive and drove into downtown Carlsbad. She pulled into a shopping center and parked in front of a restaurant called Fresco. I slowed, but drove past the parking lot. Sophia exited her car and walked toward the entrance of the restaurant.

No briefcase today.

I called Moira, who was a hundred yards or so behind me, after I cleared the mall.

"Pull into the parking lot of Fresco and get some lunch. Lay back in the lounge until Sophia gets seated."

"I've done this before, asshole."

I whipped a U-turn a block down and parked in the shopping center in front of an ice cream parlor with a clear view to Sophia's car. Radio silence from Moira. A couple minutes later my phone pinged with a text.

Moira: *She just kissed a girl and she liked it.*

Me: *What?*

Moira: *She met a woman. They kissed hello. On the lips like they've done it before. A lot.*

CHAPTER TEN

Sophia kissed a woman? The room at The Pacific Terrace Hotel. The kimono and wine in the afternoon. Her hand on Jeffrey Parker's leg. The two of them retreating into the hotel room for an hour and a half.

Could I have read the situation completely wrong? Maybe Sophia was bisexual. Maybe the meeting in the hotel room with Parker had more to do with Peter Stone than Afternoon Delight. I didn't know which would be worse information for Kim. Her husband was having an affair or he wasn't, but was connected to Peter Stone.

I texted Moira: "Order something they can prepare quickly and pay up front."

Moira: *Like I said asshole, I've done this b4.*

Me: *Try to get a photo of the other woman.*

Moira: *Already have three.*

Ahead of me as usual. Didn't mean I wasn't still in charge.

Me: *When they're done, you take the woman. I'll take Sophia.*

Moira: *Roger.*

My phone pinged again. I opened a text from Moira and saw three pictures of the woman who'd had lunch with Sophia. Late forties, natural blond, attractive, fit, power woman's business suit. A sugar momma? The suit said she could afford it.

I sat in my car and eyed Sophia's Corvette while I ran scenarios through my head.

Sophia could simply be bisexual and still be having an affair with Parker. Bisexuality was hardly an oddity these days.

So, what did that leave? Without Stone's involvement, it wouldn't have changed the affair scenario too much. She was bi. She liked men and women and was currently involved with both. But Stone couldn't be ignored. Just like you shouldn't ignore dark clouds gathering behind you on a sunny day.

Stone was now a commercial real estate developer. Mostly hotels and some retail. Jeffrey Parker was the biggest residential realtor in La Jolla and one of the biggest in San Diego County. There wasn't an overlap. Parker facilitated home purchases and sales for private citizens and Stone built hotels for businesses. They both had connections to where people slept, but nothing more.

Why the phone calls between the two on Parker's secret phone? If the calls had been on his other phone, it wouldn't have been a red flag. Parker and Stone were both La Jolla bigwigs and involved in local charities. It wouldn't be surprising if they knew each other and talked every now and then, even if their businesses didn't intersect. Same rarified social stratum.

Could Parker have simply made the calls to Stone on the secret phone for convenience sake? Maybe he'd left his other cell at the office or in another room at home. That could explain outbound calls. I needed to ask Kim if the calls between the two had been outbound or inbound.

Even if there was an innocent explanation for the phone calls, that still left Sophia Domingo. Why had Parker and Stone both met with her at a hotel in close proximity to each other? Stone had given her a briefcase full of something. Probably money. Certainly not the first briefcase full of money he'd given someone in a back room. But why? What could she do for him? She had no discernible job or income, yet drove an eighty-thousand-dollar sports car. All the signs of a high-priced call girl, not a backroom power broker. Right down to the expensive hotel room and liaison with Jeffrey Parker.

The call girl and the ex-casino boss. Not an unusual pairing. Especially when it came to Stone. I knew he'd sampled the professional women whom he'd allowed to work his casino before his partner sold him out to a corporate conglomerate. Stone and his partner had owned the last rumored mobbed-up big casino on the strip.

Now he was clean, his background ignored or polished by those who played the game on the outside edge of the law. A contribution to a lawmaker's favorite charity. Usually their own. Bundled donations to a candidate's campaign. A briefcase full of money going to a slush fund. Stone had gone from gangster to crony capitalist. All with the change of a zip code.

Had he and Sophia somehow hooked Jeffrey Parker into something that not only crossed ethical barriers but broke the law? Maybe the briefcase was a payoff from Stone to Sophia for bringing Parker into whatever game they were playing.

Moira's text kept me from pondering questions I didn't yet have answers to.

Moira: *They're on the move.*

Twenty seconds later, Sophia exited Fresco and got into her car, then headed back to the freeway. I followed, well back.

Moira called as I entered the freeway, four cars behind Sophia.

"Lady who lunches is on foot." The husky voice. "I've trailed her for a block. She's walking fast like she had to get back to her job."

"What was the tone of their lunch, business or pleasure?"

"Hard to say. Aside from the lip-smack hello, the conversation seemed serious. Kind of intense."

"Who was in control?" I spotted a California Highway Patrol cruiser in my rearview mirror and eased back on the gas.

"Pretty even. I'd give the edge to Sophia."

"Did they part civilly?"

"A bit chilly." Moira's breath picked up like she was moving faster. "The woman just went into an office building. I want to see the name of the business she goes into."

She hung up.

The CHP behind me took an off ramp in Encinitas. Probably to cross over to the other side of the freeway and stalk some prey there. Sophia kept a steady pace at seventy miles an hour.

Moira called back.

"The woman went into a business called Dergan Consulting. She's Dergan. Dina." A hint of satisfaction in Moira's voice. "I looked it up online. Their website says they specialize in coastal land use advocacy dealing with the California Coastal Commission."

"In other words, she's a lobbyist."

"Right. And by the looks of the company's office, she's doing very well. Dergan Consulting takes up the whole third floor of the office building."

"Head back to the 5 and drive south. I'll call you back when Sophia lands."

"Roger."

"And, Moira, good job."

"Tell me something I don't know." Having gotten the last word, she hung up.

Sophia drove past all the Del Mar exits. Next up, La Jolla. I followed by rote and let my mind sift through what I'd just learned.

Dina Dergan. A lobbyist who had dealings with the Coastal Commission. The all-powerful unelected bureaucracy appointed by the governor. They had first and final say on any development, commercial, residential, or private, along the California coast. Unelected bureaucrats. Lobbyists. Hotel room briefcase exchanges. Things were starting to add up, and their sum was Peter Stone. Buying influence. Cheating to get what he wanted.

Stone gave a briefcase full of money to Sophia. The next day she meets with a woman who lobbies the California Coastal Commission. There must have been a decision coming up soon by the commission on commercial land use somewhere along the coast.

I called the one man I knew in San Diego who might know.

"Scott Buehler." World-weary, slightly cynical voice.

"You still working for *The Reader*?"

"Cahill. You owe me an interview."

The Reader was an anti-establishment independent newspaper. The establishment being whoever was in charge of local government, right or left. Buehler was its sole investigative journalist, which meant he covered everything. I'd promised him an interview last year if he'd do a little digging for the public interest. But mostly, for my interest.

"I'm old news, Buehler."

"You welch on our deal last year and now you're looking for another favor?"

I had fully intended to uphold my end of the deal. Until I made another deal with someone else that had much greater significance to my well-being. I never told Buehler, because the only two people who knew about it were me and the person on the other end of the deal.

"I haven't asked for a thing."

"You called just to say hello?"

"Well, that and ask for a favor."

"What's in it for me?"

This was tricky. Buehler would happily trade info if it led to getting some dirt on Peter Stone.

I'd be happy, too. But if some of the dirt ended up burying Jeffrey Parker, then I'd betrayed Kim's trust in me.

"You know, you're right. I haven't been fair to you. I should probably stop wasting your time. I'll try the *U-T*."

The *Union-Tribune* was the major daily in town. I had no connections there and nothing to offer them, but I guessed that Buehler hated the idea of giving up a potential story to competition. Especially one owned by a national media conglomerate.

"What do you want?"

Never underestimate the power of insecurity.

"Any major land use decisions coming up for the California Coastal Commission?"

"You don't read our paper, do you, Cahill?"

"Only when there's an interview with me in it."

"Funny." Nothing close to a laugh. "UC San Diego is selling off a portion of Scripps Institute of Oceanography's undeveloped land. The commission is having a hearing today right here in San Diego on whether or not to approve the sale to a developer."

"Who's the developer?" Had to be the Peter Stone Development Company.

"GBASD."

"Who?"

"Green Builders Alliance of San Diego. They are an organization of builders who claim to be green. If you ask me, they're more about greenwashing than the environment."

"Greenwashing?"

"Businesses claiming to be environmentally friendly, but aren't. They may claim to use a few green materials, but the majority of what they use and produce degrades the environment. GBASD has used the green card to get government contracts even though they haven't been the lowest bidder."

"Is Peter Stone Development Company part of GBASD?" Greenwashing would be right down Peter Stone's alley.

"How did you know?"

"Wild guess. If they win the bid, is GBASD going to put up a huge hotel or resort?"

"No. A massive residential development."

Residential? Stone's expertise was commercial. He must have branched out. Whatever the case, once the homes were built, someone would have to sell them.

Jeffrey Parker.

CHAPTER ELEVEN

STONE AND PARKER were connected. The phone calls. Sophia Domingo. Sophia's lunchmate, Dina Dergan, a lobbyist to the Coastal Commission. The residential land sale. Parker could have simply been making moves behind the scenes to advance his real estate business. Maybe Sophia was his entree to meeting Stone. A man who, if the Coastal Commission vote went his way, was about to develop some of the most expensive residential real estate in all of California.

Maybe Parker was using Sophia to get to Stone. Slimy, but not illegal. If sex was involved, laws weren't broken. Only marital vows and Kim's heart. I still had some investigating to do.

Stone's briefcase, probably full of money, was more nefarious. If it was being used to bribe a public official, that was a felony. If Parker was caught up in Stone's machinations, he could go to jail and the security of Kim's budding family was in danger.

Sophia exited the freeway at La Jolla Village Drive and took Torrey Pines Road down into the village of La Jolla. She headed in the direction of Wall Street and Parker Real Estate. My pulse jumped. What if she went into their office looking for Jeffrey and Kim saw her? If Kim confronted her, the game was over. On second thought, that might be for the best. Kim would finally have the frank discussion she needed to have with her husband.

But how would Stone react when word got back to him that Kim had blown whatever play he was planning? I knew Stone to be vindictive and dangerous. I changed my mind on what was best.

The Corvette pulled into the pay parking lot across from the real estate office. Crap. I stopped alongside a car parked next to the curb. Just another idiot in La Jolla waiting for a free parking space to come open. I was really giving Sophia time to park and leave her car before I entered the lot and followed her on foot. I took a couple honks and middle fingers as cars swerved around me, then I parked in the lot.

I exited on foot just as Sophia passed Parker Real Estate. One possible nasty scene with dangerous repercussions avoided. Sophia walked another block and then went inside a nail salon. No need to follow her in there. I figured I had at least an hour to kill. I called Moira.

"Sophia just went into La Jolla Nail Design on Wall Street. How far away are you?"

"Five minutes out."

"Okay. Stake out the salon and call me if Sophia leaves before I come back."

"Where are you going?"

"Back in time."

* * *

Windsor Bank and Trust sat on Ivanhoe where Wall Street T'd into it. It took up the ground floor of a cement and glass building featuring New Orleans–style French Quarter balconies. At four stories the building was one of the tallest structures in downtown La Jolla. The building's architect was the same man who designed the iconic Coronado Bay Bridge.

I walked inside and went to the customer service cubicle in the lobby. The bank had been modernized since I used to go in with my dad when he'd cash his La Jolla Police Department paychecks. I was so proud when he'd walk me up to a teller's window dressed in his LJPD blue uniform. Even as an eight-year-old kid, I could tell the respect the tellers, the bank manager, and the bank's founder, Jules Windsor, had for my dad was genuine. The looks, the smiles, the handshakes.

Respect.

It would all be gone within two years. Replaced with contempt after the whispered rumors that swirled around my dad metastasized into hurricane winds. Nine years later he'd be dead. Killed by the bottle and the shame of losing the respect he'd earned during his twenty-two years on the police force.

Still, before all the wrong that was to come, I wanted to be just like my father when I grew up. The looks, the smiles, the handshakes. The respect. I ended up serving one-tenth as long on the force as my father, and hadn't earned anywhere near the same respect. But after just two and a half years, our law enforcement careers suffered the same fate. Quietly let go without a pension.

The difference: I'd never been on the take. And I'd never murdered someone for money or blackmailed someone else who did.

I asked the young customer service woman who I needed to talk to about opening my late father's safe deposit box. She called the bank manager. I didn't tell her that I wasn't even sure my father had ever had a box there or, even if he did, it probably would have been inactive and its contents sent to the California state treasurer years ago. Our tax dollars aren't enough. The state even gets to keep the dead's forgotten assets.

A woman in a feminine version of banker's attire approached with a smile and an extended arm. Blue pinstriped suit with an open-collared blouse revealing a tasteful silver necklace. No chain pocket watch. Attractive, forties, salon-aided brown hair that fell down to her shoulders.

"Hello, I'm Gloria Nakamura." She grabbed my hand in a firm shake. "I'm sorry for your loss."

"Rick Cahill. Thanks."

"Nice to meet you, Mr. Cahill. If you'll come with me, we'll just take care of some paperwork so you can access the contents of your father's safe deposit box."

She led me to a desk to the left of the tellers' windows. She hit a couple keys on a computer keyboard, then looked up at me.

Pursed lips and raised eyebrows. "What was your father's full name?"

"Charles Henry Cahill."

No reaction. Neither my name nor my father's brought up any ugly headlines in her memory. She must not have been a native La Jollan or didn't keep up on the local news. Or maybe the world didn't revolve around me anymore.

"And the box number on the key?"

"335."

She typed some more on the keyboard. "I've found it. He's had the box here since 1990."

1990. The year my father was kicked off the La Jolla Police Force. "Is it still active?"

"Yes."

Bingo. After all those years, with the key stashed in a hidden safe, my father's safe deposit box still had secrets left to reveal. It made sense that he'd rented a box at Windsor Bank and Trust. He was a man of routine. He drank the same whiskey every night, ate the same meal at his favorite restaurant when he went out, and used the same bank when he hid secrets from his family. And the rest of the world.

"Has anyone else had access to it?"

"Only if they came in with a key like you have today and they had your father's death certificate. Then they'd only be able to look at the contents of the box with a bank representative supervising."

Gloria talked as she typed. "Do you have a copy of the death certificate?"

"No. He's been dead eighteen years."

"What?" She stopped and looked up from the computer screen.

"He died eighteen years ago. He had a will. His limited assets were dispersed back then. I found a safe deposit key in some of his old things and thought I should see what's inside."

"Well, I can certainly understand that." Her eyebrows stayed up. "But unfortunately, under California Probate Code 331, we'll need a death certificate to open the safe deposit box. At that time, you can inventory what's inside, but cannot remove anything without petitioning the court for ownership of the contents. The only caveat is if there is a will and trust instruments inside. In that case, we'll make a photocopy of all wills and trust instruments removed from the safe deposit box and keep the photocopy in the safe deposit box until the contents of the box are removed by the personal representative of the estate or other legally authorized person. Are there other living heirs who could lay claim to the contents?"

"My mother and my sister are alive, but they don't care what's in the safe deposit box. And I think my father's sister is still alive."

I hadn't talked to Aunt Lila in eighteen years. She'd tried to keep our familial bond alive, but I let it wither and die. She was a link to my father. To who he'd become, not who he was back when I was an idolizing kid. After he died, I didn't want to be reminded of either one.

"Well, the laws still have to be obeyed." She tried to soften it with a smile. "Where did your father die?"

"Bakersfield."

He used to take a bus up to Aunt Lila's house every few months to dry out. The last time he made the trip, he never came back. Lila flew his body to San Diego on American Airlines. His body was loaded with cargo into the hold of the plane. Only nine years after he'd been kicked off the police force.

And a lifetime away from the earned respect.

"Well, if no one still has a death certificate, you'll have to contact the Bakersfield County Recorder's office to get a copy. I'm sure you can look them up online."

"Look, Ms. Nakamura. I'll jump through all the hoops as soon as I can and come back to collect whatever's in the safe deposit box. But I'm here right now." I pulled out my wallet and handed her my driver's license. "Here's my ID. Broderick Macdonald Cahill. Charlie Cahill's son. I just want to get a look at what's in the box. Now. So I can figure out whether all the hoop-jumping is worth it."

And to get a quick glimpse to see if there was any other evidence hidden away that explained the Saturday Night Special and the fifteen grand in cash in my father's secret wall safe.

"Well, I'm sorry, Mr. Cahill." No smile now. "I can't grant you access without the death certificate. I'd be breaking the law and I'd lose my job."

She stood up like it was time to go.

I stayed seated.

"I'll play the game and come back with a death certificate to see what's inside the safe deposit box. But I have another question for you." I nodded at her seat. She hesitated, then sat down. Anything to get rid of me. "Like I said, my father died eighteen years ago. Can you explain to me why he still has an active safe deposit box? I know they're not free and my mother closed her and my father's accounts here after he died. Who's been paying to keep it active?"

"That's private information. I'd be breaking bank rules—"

"I know. I know. The world would come crashing down if you told me." I put my hands behind my head and leaned back in the chair. "Is

Jules Windsor in? Maybe he can help me. He knew my father when my father worked for the La Jolla Police Department."

Windsor knew me, too. Not to talk to, but just enough to dislike. I tried to help a woman accused of killing his son a few years back. Things turned around, but the look he gave me at the arraignment told me he'd never forget. Or forgive. Luckily, Gloria Nakamura didn't know about all that. She just knew that I was a pain, had asked for her boss, and that my dearly beloved father had been a cop and a friend of Jules Windsor.

"He's not going to give you any more information than I can."

"Maybe not. Although he might think it's unusual that a man who'd been dead for eighteen years still has an active safe deposit box. If someone else isn't paying for the box, that would mean that my father must have set up an account to have it paid for through an automatic withdrawal. A different account than the one my mother closed after he died."

A hint of pink blossomed across her cheeks.

"All well and good, except that when the executor of my father's will was gathering information on all his bank accounts, she must have missed that one and the safe deposit box." I raised my eyebrows, put my hands on the desk, and leaned forward. "I just can't figure out how, since my father did all his banking here. Wouldn't it be the bank's obligation to divulge that information when they were presented with a death certificate in regard to accessing his accounts?"

"I can't speak to what happened eighteen years ago. I have to abide by the bank's carefully constructed rules that always have our depositors' best interests at heart."

"Well, if the account paying for my deceased father's safe deposit box was set up by him, then the bank has been siphoning off money from it for eighteen years depriving my father's heirs their just inheritance. I know an investigative reporter at *The Reader* who loves to write about corruption involving the ruling class. Scott Buehler. Maybe you've read him."

Gloria Nakamura's face flushed deep pink and her lips twitched, but she didn't say anything.

"Look, I don't care about the money. I just want to know if the safe deposit box is being paid for by an account my father set up."

"There is a checking account in your father's name that pays for the rental of the safe deposit box." She stood up. "If you come back with the proper paperwork, I'll be happy to open the box and have you take ownership of its contents. Is there anything else, Mr. Cahill?"

"Why didn't the bank give this information to the executor of my father's will and why didn't it report my father's death to the state of California? Isn't the state supposed to freeze the account until the will is read and the contents of the account are dispersed?"

"That's the normal procedure." She stared down at the computer avoiding my eyes. "Unless the account funding the rental of the safe deposit box is a joint account."

"A joint account?" I thought my mother had closed her and my father's joint accounts right after he died. "What's the name of the other person on the account?"

"I'm afraid I can't tell you that. It's against banking regulations."

"So is withholding the identity of a bank account to the executor of a will pertaining to the deceased owner of the checking account."

"Not necessarily when it's a joint account."

"We both know the bank messed up and should have informed the executor of my father's estate."

"Mr. Cahill." Gloria lowered her voice to just above a whisper. She walked around the desk and stood in front of me. Fake smile on her face. Not for me, but for anyone who might be looking. "I've given you all the information I'm legally allowed to. I suggest you come back when you have a copy of your father's death certificate and we will show you the contents of the safe deposit box. That's the best we can do."

"That may be the best you think you can do, but it's not enough." I smiled and spoke in a normal conversational tone. "An objective third party, say a newspaper, might disagree with you. It might question Windsor Bank and Trust's unusual management of a dead man's assets. If you give me the other name on the joint checking account, I'm sure we can avoid that."

The bank guard near the door eyeballed me. I doubted he could hear our conversation, but maybe he read the body language of the bank manager.

Gloria's mouth stayed curled, but she squinted angry eyes at me. "Let me walk you to your car."

I let her lead me outside the bank. A couple people stood at a coffee cart near the entrance of the building. A handful of pedestrians walked along the sidewalk. Too many people for Gloria to use the volume she probably preferred when she spoke. She kept the pained smile shellacked on her face.

"I don't appreciate being blackmailed, Mr. Cahill. I've been more than fair with you." The smile broke and she suddenly looked tired and scared. "I've worked hard to earn this position and I don't appreciate you bullying me into risking it just because I'm trying to protect the bank's good reputation. I have a daughter to support."

She was right. I'd pushed her into a corner and threatened her livelihood. I didn't feel good about it. But I could live with myself. I'd done worse. She stood between me and the truth. That's all that mattered.

"I'm sorry you're the one in this position. I can get Jules Windsor to trade places with you, if you like. But somebody's going to tell me the other name on that checking account that's been keeping my father's safe deposit box active for eighteen years after his death. You can tell me now, or you can wait until I've talked to every news organization in town about your bank's practices."

"Go ahead. We've done nothing wrong."

"We'll see what the TV and newspaper reporters think."

"You're a real bastard." Venom holding back tears.

"When I have to be."

"Antoinette King." She swung around and went back inside the bank.

Antoinette King. I'd never heard the name before. What connection did she have to my father? And why did she share a checking account with a dead man that enabled his safe deposit box to remain active? A box that no one had accessed in at least eighteen years.

CHAPTER TWELVE

I WALKED ACROSS the street toward La Jolla Nail Design. No sign
of Moira. But she was good at what she did and wouldn't be standing
right outside the salon. I scanned the block and saw her sitting in
the outdoor seating pen of the Burger Lounge. She sipped something
through a straw from a covered plastic cup. I crossed the street and
headed her way.

"Sophia still in the salon?"

Moira raised her eyebrows, went duck lipped, and tilted her head
to the side. Point taken. I sat down next to her and put my arm around
her shoulder like we were a couple. "What's in the cup?"

"Chocolate milkshake."

We did have something in common other than gumshoe work,
after all.

"Can I have a sip?"

She gave me the same look as when I asked her about Sophia and
took a long sip from the straw. She put her hand on my leg. Just another couple enjoying an afternoon in downtown La Jolla. "Where
have you been? And cut the 'back in time' bullshit."

"I was at the bank."

"I know. I saw you exit it." Another sip and still no offer to share.
"What does a bank you don't patronize have to do with going back
in time?"

"How do you know it's not my bank?"

"You write me checks every once in a while, idiot."

Oh, yeah.

"Why do you suddenly care about what I do?" I asked.

"You're an asshole, Cahill."

Moira ignored me for the next half hour as we watched the nail salon a block away.

She suddenly nodded toward the salon. Sophia had exited it and was heading our way. I turned my head back to Moira, close to her face and away from the sidewalk. She did the same so our faces were hidden from Sophia. Thirty seconds later, I sensed her pass us and I spied her over Moira's shoulder. She walked past Parker Real Estate without even a side glance, then crossed the street and went into the parking lot that held her car.

"You take the lead." I took off my Padres cap and put it on Moira's head. She exited the Burger Lounge sidewalk corral and walked toward the parking lot glancing through store windows like a lookeeloo shopper as she went.

She left her milkshake behind. I took a sip and only got the gurgle of a straw sucking up air from an empty cup. I put the cup down and walked over to the parking lot.

Sophia drove through La Jolla and headed south on Interstate 5, but didn't get off at Rosecrans, the exit back to the house on the hill. She went farther south all the way to downtown San Diego. She took Pacific Coast Highway to Waterfront Park adjacent to the harbor. The park had large swatches of grass, a park for kids, and housed the San Diego County Administration Center. The Center had a view of the San Diego Maritime Museum, the harbor, and the ocean beyond. A parcel of land worth tens of millions of dollars. I guess the bureaucrats deserved a view, too.

Sophia parked in an underground garage a block away and walked over to the Center. Moira and I each parked within eyesight of her car.

I got out of my car and followed Sophia. I texted Moira to stay and watch Sophia's car.

The Administration Center building with its Beaux-Arts/Spanish Revival–style architecture looked like it came straight out of a 1940s noir movie. A sign in the lobby said that The California Coastal Commission was holding a meeting in the Board of Supervisors' chambers. I didn't see Sophia enter the meeting, but figured it had to be the reason she'd come down here.

I wondered if she'd come to the meeting on behalf of Dergan Consulting, Peter Stone, or Jeffrey Parker. Or all three.

The room had a raised platform where the supervisors sat and could look down on the people who elected them and had business before them. In this case, twelve Coastal Commission commissioners, seven women and five men, could look down at the people who weren't allowed to elect them, but who, nonetheless, would still be required under law to abide by their rulings. A podium sat below the commissioners where petitioners were allowed to address the commission.

The chambers were packed with citizens from the seating area to standing room only in the back where I was. I saw Scott Buehler from *The Reader* standing across the room and nodded. Sophia sat in the front row of seated onlookers. I could only see the back of her head, but I knew it was her. I'd spent the last couple days staring at the back of her head. She'd entered the meeting after everyone had already found a seat, yet was able to get a spot right up front. Was the pull all her own or someone else's? No sign of Peter Stone.

The Coastal Commission chairman, a fit middle-aged man from San Francisco who would have looked at home on a yacht, gaveled the proceedings to order. The commissioners spent twenty minutes discussing procedural matters while the crowd standing in the back started to hum with discontent. Finally, the chairman introduced discussion on the Scripps land sale.

The first speaker, a woman from The Sierra Club, made an impassioned speech about maintaining what was left of the pristine land along the coast and the dangers to wildlife of creeping development.

The leader of The San Diego County Building and Construction Trades Council, AFL-CIO followed with his own speech about the sale helping poor and middle-class workers in San Diego find meaningful jobs.

A conga line of private citizens from both sides followed for the next hour. There was some shouting and name-calling and occasional tears, but no violence. Finally, a man in a suit worth more than my monthly mortgage, representing the Green Builders Alliance of San Diego, stood up and walked to the podium. He'd been sitting right next to Sophia Domingo.

The commissioners' posture all improved after they'd slouched and yawned through the last hour. The man echoed what the union boss had said and added that the new development would use green energy and materials. He finished his talk by stating that his group, GBASD, would donate a significant portion from the profit of the development to low-income housing projects and to fund a Scripps Institute of Oceanography study of coastal erosion. He claimed that GBASD was a concerned custodian of San Diego's diverse ecosystems.

A few of the no-growth crowd booed, but much of the audience nodded in silent support. After he finished, Sophia Domingo rose from her chair, did a quick scan of the commissioners, and left. The chairman adjourned the meeting to vote and said the commission would return in a half hour with a decision.

A half hour? Didn't leave much time for discussion. Maybe the verdict had already been determined and the meeting was just for show. I'd be shocked—shocked—if the commission hadn't come to the meeting with an open mind. Is that why Sophia left without waiting for a decision? Maybe she was just grabbing a snack.

I exited the Board of Supervisors' chambers fifteen seconds behind Sophia. She walked by a couple vending machines in the hallway and exited the building. I watched her head to the parking garage and called Moira.

"She's on her way back to you. You're going to be solo for a while."

"Why?"

I explained the meeting and the vote to her.

"You really think it's that important to find out how the commission votes?" she asked.

"I'm not sure about anything, but my gut tells me that Parker, Stone, and Sophia are all connected through this land sale."

"Maybe you should start doing some sit-ups and your gut won't do so much talking."

"Check in when she lands somewhere."

"Roger."

* * *

Stone's kind of game. Rigged. He and the house had the edge back in his casino days, and he still had it in his reinvented corporate life. But the Coastal Commission was hardly pro-growth. They'd even been known to prevent private citizens from adding on to homes they already inhabited. Okaying new development on pristine land above the ocean in La Jolla would be like threading a camel through the eye of a needle.

Fifteen minutes later the commissioners returned to their chairs. Stoic like a death penalty jury. It took the chairman a few gavels to quiet the crowd. The chairman finally spoke.

"The charge of this commission is to be a good steward of the eight hundred and forty miles of California's magnificent coastline. I can tell you every single commissioner you see up here takes that responsibility very seriously. Along with that stewardship, the health of each coastal community has to be taken into consideration, as well."

The environmental crowd read the tea leaves and began to murmur its discontent.

"With that sacred responsibility, we make sure that any coastal development balances the needs of the environment against the needs of the community. We feel the sale of parcel 1655 to Green Builders Alliance of San Diego perfectly balances both needs. The vote passes seven to five."

A rich man just made it into heaven.

The crowd erupted into protest, and I slipped out the chamber doors and hustled to my car. Sophia Domingo and a briefcase had gotten Peter Stone what he wanted. And probably got Jeffrey Parker the listings to the most expensive new residential development in all of San Diego County. Maybe he'd bedded Sophia, maybe not. But he most likely just guaranteed that the child growing inside Kim would never want for anything.

Family. The biological imperative. Could you fault a man's means when the end was his child's security?

* * *

I called Moira as I walked to my car.

"Where is our girl headed?"

"She just got onto Via Capri in La Jolla and is going up the hill."

"Stone."

"What?"

"She's going to Peter Stone's house."

"How do you know?"

"I know where he lives. In a mansion on Hillside Drive." I got into my car. "Don't follow her when she turns right onto Via Siena. In fact, you can head home or onto your next job. This one's over." I told her about the Coastal Commission vote and my theory about the briefcase and Peter Stone's involvement.

"So all of this was about real estate and not about cheating hearts?"

"There still might be a cheating heart or two, but that may have just been a spin-off from the main show." I got onto I-5 and headed north. "I'll send you another check in the next couple days."

"Roger. When do you want me to start helping you with the other thing?"

"What other thing?"

"Windsor Bank and Trust. Going back in time."

"I don't know what you're talking about."

"Don't be an asshole." A hard word, but her voice, surprisingly soft. "I saw you talking with that woman in front of the bank. Neither one of you looked happy. You're up to something, and I don't think it's another case. I think it's personal. Call me when you need me on it. You won't have to send me a check for that one."

She hung up.

Moira was smart. Smarter than me. That didn't surprise me. But the fact that she cared did. I couldn't shrug off the warmth that tingled along my spine. But as much as I valued Moira's abilities, I had to tackle the mysteries of my father's past alone.

CHAPTER THIRTEEN

I MET KIM at her office at Parker Real Estate at one p.m. the next day. The receptionist led me through a lobby that was shiny white and blue with a slight colonial vibe, into a large open room with a covey of fifteen wood and glass cubicles in the middle. Eight or ten real estate agents in the cubes talked on the phone or studied computer monitors. White-wood paneled glass offices circled around the perimeter. Kim's office was in the back-left corner. She pointed me toward a chair and closed the door.

"Thanks for meeting me here." She sat behind her desk. Blazer, slacks, white blouse. Professional, beautiful, but tired. The circles under her eyes I'd seen the other day had nested a little deeper and hued darker purple.

"Sure, but I don't understand why we couldn't meet at Muldoon's." I looked through her glass wall out into the covey of cubicles. Heads whipped back to their computer screens. "Word will get back to your husband that I was here."

"I don't care anymore." She pushed a piece of paper across the desk in front of me.

It was a contract for a 10 percent partnership in Parker Real Estate. The new partner's name, Sophia Domingo. The date of the contract was two days ago. The day Jeffrey Parker met with Sophia in her hotel room at The Pacific Terrace Hotel.

"Hmm."

"You're damn right, 'hmm.'" Kim snatched the contract and put it in a desk drawer. "I don't even own ten percent."

"How did you find the contract?"

"I snooped around in Jeffrey's office. It was in a locked drawer in his desk. I found his extra set of keys in his assistant's desk early this morning before anyone else was in. Now I know why I don't have keys to his desk."

"Did you talk to him about it?" I asked.

"No. He can talk to my lawyer when he gets back. My divorce lawyer."

"This may not be for the reasons you think."

"What are you talking about?"

I handed her a manila folder like the one she'd just slid across the table at me. This one contained everything I'd learned about Sophia Domingo. The lunch with Dina Dergan, the woman she kissed on the mouth who owns the Coastal Commission lobbying firm, Peter Stone and the Green Builders Alliance of San Diego, and about the commission's vote yesterday at the San Diego County Administration Center.

She read the report and then looked up at me.

"So you're telling me a lesbian screwed my husband?"

"I don't know whether she screwed him or not. I think their meeting might have had more to do with the Coastal Commission's vote than sex."

"You think that's why he gave her ten percent of the company?" Her cheeks flushed red beneath the purple circles under her eyes.

"It would make sense if she got Jeffrey partnered with Stone in the Scripps development. Did he mention it to you?"

"No. But he's been pretty buttoned up lately about the business. We just talk about our individual home sales and not the big picture. He spent a lot of money opening up offices in Del Mar and Rancho Santa Fe, and they haven't done well. We're losing money in both areas and are stuck with five-year leases on the offices. The people who live in those towns are very proprietary. They're not very open to outsiders."

"The Scripps development would more than offset any losses Parker Real Estate is having with the rest of the business."

"Yes, it would, but none of that matters to me anymore." Kim opened a desk drawer and pulled out a checkbook and scribbled on a check. "I'm paying you with a company check. Double your normal fees. Jeffrey can discuss this with my divorce lawyer if he has a problem with it."

Kim held onto the anger, but I saw cracks around her eyes. The wall was about to come down and tears would follow. I didn't want to see her cry. I've made her cry before on my own. She deserved better. Better than Jeffrey Parker. Better than me.

I stood up and she came around the desk and hugged me. Hard and long. I hugged her back and regretted how good it felt and how it reminded me of everything I'd lost. We separated and tears pooled in the bottom of Kim's eyes. The selfish part of me wondered if she felt the same way I did.

"Thank you, Rick." She kissed me on the cheek. "I know this has been hard for you, too. Maybe it wasn't fair to ask you to help me. But you were the only person I could really trust. I knew you'd look out for me."

I nodded and left her office. Glad to be done with the case. Sad to be done with Kim. Now wasn't the time to see if a path between us could be reopened. There might never be a time. You can't always correct your mistakes from the past.

CHAPTER FOURTEEN

THE CROSS ATOP Mount Soledad National Veterans Memorial rises forty-three feet above the highest point in La Jolla. The memorial has a panoramic view of La Jolla eight-hundred feet below, the Pacific Ocean, San Diego, and even Mexico beyond.

I liked the view, but I went up there to look into the past. My father used to take me to The Cross to honor veterans. He had me read the plaques of men he'd served with and those of veterans of long-ago wars. The Cross was special to him. It had been special to me, too. When I was young and believed in my father. I still went to the Cross after I stopped believing in him. To face my own truths and decipher the past.

I sat in my car and looked out over La Jolla. The sun danced off the ocean far below, and a gentle breeze slowly pushed scattered clouds around the blue sky. Idyllic. Paradise. But always just out of reach.

I pulled out my phone and googled Antoinette King, the woman who had a joint checking account with my father at Windsor Bank that funded the rental of his safe deposit box. I scrolled through the listings. Most had links to Facebook or Twitter. None that I could tell had any connection to my father, or even La Jolla, or San Diego. I went onto a people finder pay website and couldn't find a single Antoinette King listed in San Diego.

The Antoinette King I needed to find was a ghost.

I dialed the phone number my sister, Beth, had texted me earlier that day. She and I talked on the phone once a year. She called me every Christmas morning. Told me how her two sons were doing in sports. Occasionally, she made one of them get on the phone with me. They were in their early teens now. I couldn't remember what they looked like. They could barely remember who I was. Still, I looked forward to the yearly call.

The last time I called the number my sister gave me, it had been on a landline—iPhones hadn't been invented yet. The number was written down in an address book I'd thrown away long ago.

"Hello?" The voice hadn't changed in eighteen years. Young when she was forty-six. Young at sixty-four.

"Lila, it's Rick." Five seconds of silence. I broke it. "Cahill."

"I know."

"Maybe I shouldn't have called."

"Maybe you should have answered when I called you for two straight years after your father died." Anger I'd never heard in her voice as a kid.

"You're right. I apologize."

"Why are you calling now?"

Aunt Lila had been a free spirit when my sister and I were kids. She'd play football with us in the backyard and laugh the whole time. I couldn't wait until she'd come down from Bakersfield and visit every summer. She once told me that if she ever had a son, she hoped he would be just like me.

She had three girls, but I think by now she'd changed her opinion about me as a son.

"I need a death certificate for my father."

"Don't you mean, 'Dad'?"

"Yeah. Dad."

"He's been dead eighteen years. Why do you need a death certificate now?" She took a deep breath. Could have been a drag off a
cigarette. Or a joint. She'd done both back in the day. "You didn't
seem to care too much about Charlie's death when he died. Why the
interest now?"

She was wrong about that. I'd cried in private for days after my dad
died. But never in front of anyone else. I'd truly been my father's son
at his funeral. Stone-faced, emotions hidden.

"Turns out Charlie had a safe deposit box at Windsor Bank that
nobody knew about. At least, I don't think anyone knew about it.
You were the executor of his estate. Did you know about the box?
Was it somehow overlooked when you were putting together all the
paperwork?"

"No. How did you find out about it?"

"The people who bought the old Parkview Drive house tore it
down and found a hidden wall safe in Dad's den." I wasn't ready to
talk about the fifteen grand and the gun. Not until I discovered the
truth about them. And maybe not even then.

"Did Elizabeth know there was a safe in the den?"

Elizabeth. My mother. Another subject I didn't want to broach.

"No. And she doesn't want anything to do with it. Neither does
Beth."

"I'm not surprised." She spit the words at me. "Your mother quit
on Charlie when there was still time to save him."

"He quit on himself." Lila was right, but my mother was blood.
"Do you know a woman named Antoinette King?"

"No. Who is she?"

"She and Charlie had a joint checking account that has been paying for the rental of this safety deposit box all these years. He never
mentioned her during that last visit with you?"

"I just told you I never heard of her. Do you think he was having an affair with this woman?"

"I have no idea. I know as much about her as you now do. I couldn't find anything online. Nothing on social media. It's as if she doesn't exist."

"As far as I know, he was loyal to your mother until the end. Unlike her. She gave up on your father and found herself a sugar daddy."

"She loves the guy." I'd give her that much. "They've been married for seventeen years."

"Seventeen and a half. She couldn't even wait a full year after your father died to make it official."

"She stayed with Dad longer than anyone else would have." I'd tried to separate myself from his memory sooner than that. Tried. "Are you going to send me a copy of the death certificate?"

"What's your address?"

I gave it to her.

"You sure the letter with the death certificate won't come back to me unopened like all the other letters I sent you after Charlie died?"

"Yeah. I'm sorry about the letters, too."

"Even the one I sent to you after your wife died came back unopened."

"I should have read that one. That was wrong." I even knew that at the time. "I could have handled things differently, but I didn't want to hear about what a great guy my dad had really been. I'd lived with him for eight years after he got kicked off the force. I knew who he was."

"See, that's where you're wrong. If you'd read the letters I sent you, you'd know that." Her voice didn't sound young anymore. It sounded old and broken. "It was hard enough trying to stop my brother from drinking himself to death and then watching him die. I lost my husband because of it. But that's fine, I made a choice. My first family came first. What wasn't fair was losing my brother, my husband, and then my favorite nephew. I don't know if you blamed me for your dad's death or you just didn't want to be reminded of it. Either way, it was fucking unfair. I'll put the death certificate in the mail today."

She hung up.

I couldn't blame her. If I'd been her, I would have hung up as soon as I heard my voice. I treated Lila horribly after my father died. I'd only thought of myself and tried to pretend that my father had never existed. Lila hadn't done anything wrong. In fact, she'd done everything right. She'd taken care of Dad and tried to get him straight after my mother turned her back on him. After I did, too. Aunt Lila was my father's sister. A reminder of the man I'd sworn to forget. It had never crossed my mind that Lila was losing me, too.

I was my father's son.

The last few years, Dad had slept in my sister's room while she was in college up at Berkeley. I remember the last time I put him to bed in that room. My mom was in the master bedroom. Door closed and locked, like it was every night for the final three years of my father's life. I'd walked the old man over to the twin bed, keeping him upright with my shoulder. I dropped him more than set him down onto the bed. I pulled off his boots, and his pants, and his shirt, and rolled him under the covers. He smelled of all-day whiskey and three days without a shower. I'd put him to bed, but I wouldn't bathe him. That would have been too much of an indignity for both of us.

I thought he was already unconscious in a boozy sleep, but he grabbed my wrist when I straightened up over the bed.

"People will disappoint you, Son." The words thick on his tongue. He'd long ago forgotten the meaning of irony. He looked up at me through half-closed, watery bloodshot eyes, "But you have to forgive them. Otherwise it will eat you up. Destroy your soul. I've forgiven them. And I've forgiven myself, but it's too late. Too late."

My father's eyes closed all the way and he fell into a whiskey sleep, already snoring with the first jagged intake of air. The next day, the last day of summer, I drove him to the Greyhound bus station in downtown San Diego and put him on a bus to Bakersfield. For the last time. Five months later, Aunt Lila flew his body back to San Diego in the cargo hold of an airplane.

CHAPTER FIFTEEN

FEDEX DELIVERED MY father's death certificate to my house at eight thirty the next morning. I didn't know what point Aunt Lila was trying to make, but I was glad she'd spent the money on Next Day Saturday A.M. delivery. I wanted to solve the mystery of my old man's hidden safe and secret safe deposit box as soon as possible and put it behind me. Put my father behind me forever. If I found another fifteen grand in my dad's safe deposit box, I'd send Lila a check for the postage. I might even send her the whole fifteen grand.

Jules Windsor and Gloria Nakamura met me at the customer service cubicle at Windsor Bank and Trust. Windsor looked like he'd aged double the four years since I'd last seen him at the arraignment for the woman accused of murdering his son. The death of a child can do that no matter how odious the child had been. His gray hair had receded further back on his head, and his face was a bit more red. He wore the classic three-piece blue pinstripe banker suit. Nakamura wore a smart business dress and trim jacket. No necklace today. Maybe Windsor didn't approve.

I'd called her at the bank earlier to tell her I'd be coming in with my father's death certificate and that I wanted to see the contents of his safe deposit box. She hadn't told me that the bank's namesake and president would be there. Either my father's safe deposit box rated his presence or I did. I wasn't sure what to think about either. Except that, whatever the reason, it probably wasn't one beneficial to me.

Neither Nakamura nor Windsor smiled upon greeting me. No hands were extended to shake. I guessed a bro-hug would have been out of the question. Nakamura led me over to the same desk she had the other day. Windsor walked into the bank vault without a word.

"May I review the death certificate?" Nakamura held out her hand.

I pulled it out of my jacket pocket and handed it to her. She examined the death certificate like it was a fake driver's license and I was an eighteen-year-old kid holding a six-pack of beer. Finally, she handed it back to me. "Follow me, please."

Nakamura led me past the open, round, three-foot-thick steel vault door and into the vault. Windsor was waiting in front of a wall of safe deposit boxes. Silent as death.

The doors to the lock boxes where Windsor stood looked to be about three by five inches, the smallest safe deposit boxes in the vault. I wondered how many envelopes of fifty- and hundred-dollar bills could fit in a box that size. Or how many handguns.

"Mr. Cahill, may I have your key so I can open the safe deposit box?" Nakamura asked.

I handed her my key. She put it into one of the two locks on the safe deposit box, then stuck another key in the other lock. She turned each key and opened the little door and pulled out the thin two-foot-long metal box that was inside. Windsor studied me as Nakamura tucked the container under one arm and removed both keys from the door. I didn't know what he was looking for, but I gave him nothing. Nakamura handed me back my key and stuck the other one in the pocket of her blazer.

"Now we'll all proceed to a viewing room and examine the contents of the box," she said.

She carried the box in front of her in two hands and waited for
Windsor to open a door next to a bank of safe deposit boxes. He
opened the door and we followed Nakamura in. She set the box down
onto a thin table in the middle of the small, narrow room and pulled
open the box, which had a hinge about three inches from the back.

A small manila coin envelope sat in the safe deposit box. Nothing
else. I looked at Windsor, then at Nakamura. She spoke first.

"You may open the envelope and examine its contents, but you
can't remove anything from the bank. As we discussed, if you find a
will, you can take it with you after we make a copy."

"Yes, I remember what I can and can't do with my father's last
earthly belongings."

I took out the coin envelope and felt the outline of two small cylin-
drical objects with my fingers.

I set the envelope back down into the safe deposit box.

"You're not going to open it, Mr. Cahill?" Nakamura asked.

"No."

"Well, now that the box has been opened, the bank needs an inventory of its contents." She reached around me for the envelope. I put
my hand on her arm to stop her.

"I'll do it."

I took out my key chain from my pocket and opened up a blade
from the little Swiss Army knife attached to it. I held the envelope by
its sides and carefully slit it open, then turned it upside down. Two
empty shell casings clattered down into the metal safe deposit box.
Twenty-five caliber. Just like the two missing bullets from the gun in
my father's safe.

CHAPTER SIXTEEN

GLORIA NAKAMURA'S FACE turned as red as Windsor's resting tone. His didn't get any redder. Gloria looked at him for guidance, but he gave her nothing. His attention and scowl were lasered on me.

"I trust that, as we've followed all the regulations under the law, we don't have to worry that you'll go crying to the newspapers that we've treated you unfairly and are stomping on the rights of the ninety-nine percent."

I nodded. Windsor shifted his scowl to Gloria Nakamura and held it on her for a cringing five seconds, then left the viewing room without another word.

I realized my antics the other day had put Gloria in deep water with her boss. My quest for the truth sometimes left collateral damage. It didn't have to with Gloria. Shame I hadn't felt in too long crept up the back of my neck.

I pulled out my cell phone and took one picture each of the shells, then I stuck the Swiss Army knife's blade into an empty shell casing and dropped it into the small envelope. Then did the same with the other one.

"Why didn't you just pick them up with your hand and put them back into the envelope?"

"Old habit."

I didn't want to smudge or overlap any fingerprints or DNA that might have been left behind. By my father or someone else. But I couldn't tell Gloria that or anyone else. If it was evidence from a crime, LJPD had a right to it. But not until I found out what it all meant. Then, I might give them a call.

Depending upon what I discovered.

"I've witnessed a lot of death certificate safe deposit box openings over the years, but I've never seen two empty bullet shells before." Gloria Nakamura gave me a nervous smile. Almost like a pressure release now that her boss wasn't still in the room glaring at her. "I've seen guns and bullets, but never empty shells. What do you think it means?"

"I don't know." Not exactly. "Does Windsor make a habit of watching people open up their dead relatives' safe deposit boxes? Seems like he'd have something more or less important to do. Especially on a Saturday morning."

"No. I've never seen him do it before."

"I guess that makes me special."

She raised her eyebrows.

"Do you think I'm stupid, Mr. Cahill?"

"Rick." I smiled. "Not so far."

"Well, Rick." She didn't smile back. "It looks to me like your handling the contents of your late father's safe deposit box like it's some sort of evidence. Is it?"

"I'll answer one of yours if you'll answer one of mine," I said.

"If I can."

"I'm not exactly sure what these are. Could be some weird keepsakes or, a remote possibility, evidence in a crime. So, I handled everything as little as possible, just in case." Mostly true. I closed the lid of the safe deposit box and handed it to her. "My turn now, right?"

"Okay."

"Why did you tell Windsor about me and the safe deposit box?"

"That's my job." She made a big show of looking me in the eyes and not blinking.

"Really? You just told me you'd never seen Windsor watch a relative open a dead person's safe deposit box before. Why would you tell him about this one? You clearly have the authority to handle this alone without even alerting him about it."

"I told Mr. Windsor about your visit the other day and the unusual situation of your father's safe deposit box and joint checking account. He told me to call him when you contacted the bank again." She raised up the safe deposit box. "Now, can we return the box to its locker?"

"The other day, my father's safe deposit box and joint checking account were normal business practices. Remember? Now they're unusual."

"A little out of the ordinary, but the unusual thing was you threatening the reputation of Windsor Bank and Trust. Mr. Windsor and I take that very seriously." She lowered her eyelids to half-mast and pushed up her lower lip. "Please open the door and follow me back into the vault."

I opened the door and Gloria pushed by me. She did the dual key thing and locked up the safe deposit box. She handed me back my key.

"As we discussed earlier, the only way to claim the contents of your father's box is to go through the courts. Once you do that, we will turn over the contents to you."

"Don't hold your breath."

What would I do with evidence that was probably from a shooting and possibly a murder scene? Give it to the police? Maybe. Or maybe keep it away from the police.

Gloria turned to leave the vault, but I touched her arm to stop her.

"I'm sorry I got you into trouble with your boss." I shook my head. "I wasn't really going to go to the newspapers. It was a bluff. That wasn't fair."

Gloria took a deep breath, closed her eyes, and pinched her lips. Finally, "You jeopardized my job on a bluff? What kind of a person does that? You'll do anything to get your way. Well, you won. Congratulations."

She left the vault and went to her desk without looking back.

Gloria was right. I knew it before she dressed me down. I knew it when I pressured her for information the other day. I'd tried to convince myself that my quest for the truth, for justice, as I saw it, was more important than anything else. Even more important than other people's hopes, dreams, ambitions. Maybe because I didn't have any more hopes, dreams, and ambitions of my own left. All I had was a quest, made up or real, to fill the emptiness left by broken dreams.

CHAPTER SEVENTEEN

I LEFT THE bank and sat in my car watching people pass in front of the windshield, living their lives while I stayed stuck in the past.

The contents of the safe deposit box hadn't solved the mystery, just verified the premise. The money and gun in my father's hidden safe and the empty shell casings in the safe deposit box spelled murder. Either committed by my father or someone else he'd blackmailed after the fact.

Murder. The one crime with no expiration date.

Could my father have crossed that line? If so, why would he keep the evidence that could have put a needle in his arm or send him to prison for life? My father had been kind and a man of honor most of his life. He hadn't gotten mean until after he was no longer a cop. Until then, he'd never raised his hand to me in anger. Afterward, the beatings were rare, brief, but full of rage.

But murder? I didn't think so. Not unless I never really knew him at all. The wall safe, the safe deposit box, the joint bank account with a woman other than my mother all proved that I didn't know him. At least not the man he'd become the last years of his life.

Mean, violent, capable of murder, or not, my old man wasn't stupid. If he'd used the Saturday Night Special in the safe to kill someone with the bullets from the empty shells inside the safe deposit box, he would have gotten rid of the evidence. He must have collected the gun and the empty shells to blackmail someone. Thus, the fifteen grand in the safe. The money he'd never spent. But why hadn't he spent it?

I'd never know unless I found out who was murdered sometime between twenty and thirty years ago and by whom. That shouldn't be too hard to find in La Jolla where the city averaged three or four murders a year. Broadening out to San Diego would be a lot more difficult. Like finding a bloody needle in a haystack.

With the murder weapon missing from a crime scene and the fifteen grand paid to my father for the murder or as blackmail money, I figured the crime had never been solved.

I pulled out my phone and Googled unsolved murders in La Jolla from 1980–2000. A bunch of pages came up, but only a handful specifically about La Jolla. One was on the Crimestoppers website referencing an unsolved murder on the campus of UCSD in 2009. My father was long gone by then. Another was from the *San Diego Union Tribune* about a 1992 unsolved murder on the La Jolla Indian Reservation out in the East County of San Diego, far from the town of La Jolla.

The last one was a La Jolla city government website with cold cases from 1951–2000. Only four unsolved homicides were listed, and just one of them fit the time line of my father.

The website listed a synopsis of the crime: *On November 24, 1989, an officer responded to a report of a traffic accident on Coast Boulevard in La Jolla. Upon arrival, he discovered the victim, Trent Phelps, unresponsive and seated in the driver's seat of his green Ford Mustang that had crashed into a parked car. At first Phelps' injuries were believed to have been caused by the collision, however, a secondary examination revealed that Phelps had suffered two gunshot wounds to the head. He died a short time later.*

Two gunshot wounds to the head. A chill ran through me. Could the murder weapon have been a Raven MP-25? The report didn't list the ballistic evidence. The website didn't give the name of the officer who responded to the scene, either. November, 1989. Five months before my father was kicked off LJPD. Coincidence? Maybe. I needed to find out who the responding officer was. I wouldn't be able to find that information online. Too long ago and not high enough profile.

I drove a few blocks over to the La Jolla Library on Draper Street and, not for the first time, was struck by the mismatched architecture. The front of the library had a Spanish hacienda look, low slung with brown tile roof. A calming SoCal look. Attached to its left end was the annex that Peter Stone had donated and built with his development company. That was two stories and contemporary with an A-frame façade and a little balcony facing the street. Peter Stone Library Annex was spelled out in bold brass letters. Stone left his mark on everything he touched.

I went to the front desk tucked around the corner from the lobby. A middle-aged woman gave me a flat stare. I gave her a smile back.

"Hi. Do you have a microfiche machine and archives?"

"Yes." No smile. "It's on the second floor in the history room. The archives are there, too. Do you know how to operate a microfiche reader?"

"No."

"Hmm." A micro-shake of her head. "I'll send someone up."

I walked upstairs and found the history room off to the right. I went inside and saw a table with a large square monitor on it. The microfiche reader. A tall, thin file cabinet sat next to the table. I opened the top drawer and found rectangular slides, color coded on the top edge. I couldn't tell what I was looking at or where to find what I needed.

"May I help you?" A woman in her late forties, dark hair, high cheekbones under horn-rimmed glasses smiled at me.

"Yes. Thanks. I'm trying to find articles from the *San Diego Union Tribune* for November twenty-fifth through the thirtieth in 1989. For the front page and local section."

"You'll actually want to see slides for both the *San Diego Union* and the *Evening Tribune*. San Diego used to have two competing dailies until they merged in 1992. There was also a San Diego edition of the *LA Times* back then, too. Now we're down to just one paper." She sighed. "Things change. I can get the slides for those dates for the *Times*, too."

"That would be fantastic. Thanks."

The woman grabbed about ten or so slides from the file cabinet, set them down onto the table, and slid one into the rectangular holder on the microfiche reading machine. She showed me how to maneuver the holder to go from one page to another. I thanked her, and she left me alone in the room. I took out my notepad and pencil and started reading.

The first slide she'd set up was from the front page of the *San Diego Union* from November 25th, 1989. The day after Trent Phelps had been found dead in his car on Coast Boulevard. No mention of him, a car accident, or murder. I maneuvered the reader and found the Metro section for the same day. Its front page had a story about Phelps' car accident and death, but no mention of a homicide. No mention of the officer responding at the scene, just a quote from an unnamed police spokesman who said the preliminary report was a single car accident resulting in a fatality. I wrote the reporter's name down on my notepad. Jack Anton.

I replaced the slide with one containing the *Union*'s next day's edition. Nothing about the accident on the front page again. The Metro had a follow-up article by Anton on the accident. It echoed the report

I'd found on the city government website about Trent Phelps' death. Cause of death hadn't been due to injuries sustained in the accident, but instead from two gunshot wounds to the head. The bullets recovered from Phelps' body were too degraded to make a definitive determination of the murder weapon. However, according to Homicide Detective Ben Davidson, the gun was believed to be a small-caliber weapon.

Small caliber. The Raven MP-25 I found in my father's safe was a twenty-five caliber. A small-caliber weapon. Every new piece of evidence pointed to the Saturday Night Special in my father's safe as the murder weapon. Detective Davidson was quoted as saying that LJPD had no suspects at that time. Davidson and Elmer Wilkes were listed as the investigating detectives.

I remember the detectives' names from my childhood. My father had introduced me to them when he gave me a tour of the police station, known by cops as the Brick House because of its white brick façade. I'd only been eight or nine, but I could still remember the flattop crew cut that Davidson wore. And his basketball gut. I don't remember what Wilkes looked like except that he was tall and African-American.

The paper still had no mention of the patrolman who first responded to the scene. Damn.

I wrote down the detectives' names and searched the slides for the paper's next five editions. Nothing more on Trent Phelps. Next, I viewed the *Evening Tribune*'s articles on the crime. The articles were similar to those at the *Union*.

The San Diego edition of the *Los Angeles Times* didn't have anything new to add.

I opened the microfiche file cabinet and found slides that contained the editions for the next two weeks following Trent Phelps' murder. I scrolled through each and found one article each in the

Union and the *Tribune* following up on the murder. Neither had any new information.

A twenty-eight-year-old unsolved murder. Three newspaper reporters. Two police detectives. I wondered how many of those five people were still alive. And how many of them would be willing to talk to me.

CHAPTER EIGHTEEN

I WENT HOME to my office and searched the two detectives and three reporters on a people finder website. Only retired LJPD Detective Ben Davidson and former newspaper reporter Jack Anton were still alive.

Ben Davidson was seventy-seven and lived in Poway, a mostly well-to-do town in San Diego's East County. Home to many of San Diego's professional athletes. The late Tony Gwynn being the most famous. I tried the phone number listed. A woman answered. The search info on Davidson had him divorced with three grown daughters. The woman sounded younger than seventy-seven.

"May I speak with Ben?"

"Who's calling?"

I'd expected him to answer, not a screener. If I gave my name, complete with Cahill, would he be more or less likely to answer? I gambled.

"Rick Cahill."

Silence. Finally, "He's busy. Call back another time."

"Tell him Charlie Cahill's son is on the phone. Maybe he'll make time for the son of a deceased brother in blue."

"He's very busy. Try another time." She hung up.

Worse than I expected. The woman, probably Davidson's younger girlfriend or maybe one of his daughters, had frozen when she heard my name. Presumably my last name gave her the chill. My father had been dead for eighteen years and hadn't been a cop for twenty-seven. Had this woman been around long enough to remember him and now didn't want his son to upset Davidson? Maybe my father had such an impact on Davidson that he'd talked about him over the years and the woman knew better than to bring Davidson to the phone.

I didn't like either scenario and I wasn't going to let Davidson or his gatekeeper ignore me. I had his address. It would be harder to ignore me when I knocked on his front door.

Next up, Jack Anton. The one newspaper reporter left alive. He was sixty-eight and lived in La Mesa, a small incorporated city ten miles east of downtown San Diego. The listing said he had a wife named Barbara, sixty-five. I called the number and again a woman answered.

"May I speak with Jack?"

"Just a second, hon."

She'd either mistaken me for someone else or was a nice person. I wish she had a clone who lived with Ben Davidson. Of course, she hadn't heard my name yet.

I could hear the woman's voice away from the phone. "Jack, phone. Get off the computer and talk to a human being." Her voice had a tease in it talking to her husband.

"He'll be right with you, hon."

Just a nice lady. I didn't meet enough of them in my line of work. I didn't meet enough of nice anybody.

"Jack Anton." Clipped. No nonsense.

"Mr. Anton, my name's Rick Cahill. I'm investigating a murder you reported on twenty-eight years ago in the *San Diego Union* and I wonder if I could ask you a few questions."

"Rick Cahill, huh?" He clucked his tongue like he was calling a horse. "You were just a kid twenty-eight years ago. Why are you

investigating a murder that cold? You didn't join one of the local police forces, did you?"

He knew me. He'd been a reporter, it made sense. I'd been in the
news enough over the past twelve years. He probably knew my father,
too. But how did he know that the murder case was cold?

"No. Let me buy you dinner and I'll explain."

"I tell you what, you come by here tomorrow at noon and we'll
talk." He gave me his address. "I have all my old files here so eating out
doesn't make any sense. Besides, why eat out when you can eat better
at home? Barbara makes a mean grilled cheese."

"Okay." Someone willing to cooperate. There had to be a but in
there somewhere. Or maybe Jack Anton was non compos mentis and
wanted someone other than his wife to babble at. I'd take my chances.
"Thanks."

"I'll have the Phelps murder file ready when you get here."

My gut flipped over.

"How did you know I was investigating the Phelps murder?" I
asked.

"You said a twenty-eight-year-old murder and you're Charlie
Cahill's son. It has to be Phelps."

"Why?" There was nothing wrong with this guy's mentis.

"It was the only murder I reported on that year that went unsolved."

"What does my father have to do with it?"

"Come by tomorrow and I'll show you the file." He hung up.

Jack Anton just might have the answer to my father's riddle. If
he did, why hadn't he reported it twenty-eight years ago? I was too
young back then to read the Metro section of the morning paper, but
my mother did. And so did the parents of my friends and kids I went
to school with. The story would have trickled down to me, instead of
just rumors of some never-defined mob connection.

Whatever it was, I'd find out tomorrow.

* * *

My cell phone rang while I wrote out a check to Moira for her help in
the Parker affair. Maybe the wrong word. Or maybe the right one. I
checked the cell phone screen. Unknown.

I hoped it was a new client. I'd just worked the last week for free,
paying Moira but not myself, out of a sense of honor. At least that's
what I told myself when my conscience told me it was out of pride.
Pride goeth before and after the fall.

"Hello?"

"Rick, so wonderful to hear your voice again." The warm-butter-
over-pancakes voice that always had a dagger hidden underneath. "I
have a job for you. It's right down your mean-streeted alley. In fact,
you're already familiar with the subject to whom it pertains."

Peter Stone.

"Not interested, Stone." Not if I was starving.

"I need you to track down a missing person. The retainer will be
well worth your while. You might even be able to finally get yourself
a real office instead of a pretend one in my restaurant."

"Turk's restaurant."

"Tomayto, tomahto."

"Why don't you contact the police? I'm sure if you look in your
pocket, you'll find a few cops in there."

"I do miss our little chats, Rick. It's been too long." He let go a
breath. "But, unfortunately, I don't have time for the everyday hero
banter. The subject's name is Sophia Domingo. You followed her all
over San Diego a couple days ago."

Sophia missing? Missing to Stone may have been hiding out from
him to Sophia. And probably countless others. But how did Stone
know I'd been following her? Had she spotted me or had Stone already had a tail on her who did? Either way I'd blown my cover. Had

it altered her behavior or had she just gone about her business and laughed at me in her rearview mirror?

"I'm not familiar with the name."

"Well, a 2016 black Honda Accord with the license plate 3UZB657 followed Miss Domingo from Carlsbad to the San Diego County Administration Center downtown two days ago. And one of those friends I keep in my pocket told me that car is registered to you. Coincidence?"

"How long has she been missing and who is she to you?"

"Are you taking the case, Rick? Shall I wire funds into your checking account?" The pleased voice of a man used to bending people to his will.

I didn't know what game Stone was playing, but I never did. In my earlier dealings with him, I'd stared all day at a flat checkerboard while he'd moved pieces around in a three-dimensional game of chess that I couldn't even see.

Until the end.

Stupidity had nearly gotten me killed. Persistence had saved my life.

"I'm trying to get some background so I can make a decision. How long has she been missing?" One thing I was sure of, if Sophia really was missing, Stone wanted to find her before the police did. The why to that was a frightening thing. Something I'd never be a part of.

"Less than twenty-four hours."

"Have you checked with your old friends in Las Vegas? She might be there." Maybe Jeffrey Parker had company on his trip to Sin City.

"That's the one place where I'm sure she isn't."

"Maybe you should check your house, because she went there two days ago at around five thirty."

"See, I knew I'd come to the right man. Job well done. You certainly earned your wages that day." The pleased tone in his voice never portended well for me. Or anyone else. "I very well may have been the last person to see Sophia that day. However, when I talked to her on the phone last night, she informed me she was just about to have a meeting with someone."

He wanted me to ask who the meeting was with. He was certain I would. Just as he was certain about the reactions of every person he manipulated. I waited. Even pulled the phone away from my face and hovered my thumb over the end call button.

Finally.

"Who was she meeting?" I danced on the end of his string.

"A woman named Kim Parker."

A cold finger itched across the back of my neck. Kim? Meeting with Sophia? No. Stone had found my weakness and was probing just for fun. Life was a video game and he held the controller. He had to be lying. I'd met Kim at her office the afternoon Stone said Sophia called him.

Kim had just found out that her husband had given Sophia 10 percent of Parker Real Estate. Shit.

I needed to talk to Kim. I hadn't spoken to her since the meeting in her office.

But first, I had to try to figure out Stone's angle. And how sharp it was.

"Why haven't you called the police if Sophia is that important to you?"

"Maybe I have and you're just for insurance. A backup. Kind of like your relationship with Kim Parker. Waiting on the sidelines to get into the game if the starter, her first pick, messes up."

I'd forgotten how many eyes and ears Stone had out in the world. Assets to extract information from when he needed leverage and a crowbar was just too blunt. Pawns in that three-dimensional chess game. But he was wrong about Kim and me. I'd been her first choice. She'd gone with number two only when she finally figured out that I'd never be able to give her all that she gave me. But right or wrong,

Stone's jab was more defensive than a frontal assault. Trying to keep me away from his own weakness.

"I don't think so, Stone. You can't go to the police. They're for your fake life. The one where you're an upright citizen. A philanthropist donating wings to libraries. You know, the façade. The barrier that keeps people from seeing the real you behind it. Where briefcases change hands in hotel rooms and a fixer like Sophia Domingo gets you a cut of the richest real estate deal in the history of San Diego."

"You're clever, Rick. Much more so than an ordinary second-stringer." A chuckle. His only form of a laugh. It says he's in control and you exist for his amusement. "Maybe there's still time for dear Kim to discern that and put you in the game."

"Why me, Stone? I seem like an odd choice for you to hire, being a second-stringer and all. And there's also the fact that I can't stand you and know who you really are."

"Because you're honest, Rick. Maybe not with the police, but with people who matter. I know Kim Parker matters to you and you know that if she's mixed up in something illegal that I have the money and the connections to help extricate her from the situation."

"What situation are you talking about?" Still dancing on the end of his string. But, he was right, Kim mattered to me. I'd do anything to keep her safe. Even play Stone's game.

"Hopefully not one that has windows with bars on them in her future. Find Miss Domingo, and everything will turn out okay."

"Except for Sophia. What does she have that you want and are afraid she'll give to someone else?"

"I'll wire the fifteen thousand dollars into your checking account. That should cover the first week. Shouldn't it?"

Fifteen grand. The exact amount my father had received for killing someone or for blackmailing someone else who did. Was Stone paying me for the former? I find Sophia so one of his hitters can murder her. And pin the blame on me? Only if I let him. If I found Sophia, I'd warn her about Stone and she could decide what to do. If Stone's men beat me to her, I'd go to the police and tell them everything I knew. First, I had to make sure Kim hadn't done something stupid or gotten herself into a situation that only a man like Stone could get her out of.

"Cash. I'll come by your house tomorrow at nine a.m. I don't want anything on paper that says we're somehow connected." I wouldn't touch my father's murder or blackmail money, but I'd take Stone's dirty money every day of the week. I just wouldn't get dirty for it.

"The world-weary PI, and yet, sometimes so naïve. You didn't really think the wired money would come from my account, did you? I want a paper trail between us even less than you do. Cash is fine. Make it eight tomorrow morning." He hung up.

Time change and last word to show he was still in control. Stone hadn't changed in four years.

That's what I was afraid of.

CHAPTER NINETEEN

I called Kim's cell phone. Voicemail. Her office phone. Voicemail. Home. Voicemail.

I left my office, went into my bedroom next door, and grabbed my Ruger SP 101 .357 Magnum from the nightstand. Peter Stone was deeply involved. I, and everyone I cared about, needed protection now. I found a pancake holster in my sock drawer and slipped it onto my belt. A wooden box caught my eye as I started to close the drawer.

It held the one thing of my father's that I'd kept all these years. His LJPD badge. Tarnished by time and by his reputation. I let the box lay and closed the drawer.

I slid the Ruger into the holster and grabbed a windbreaker from my closet for concealment.

Midnight walked into the room, sat next to the bed, and stared at me. He tried to engage me in a game of blink. The stare was also an accusation that I couldn't deny. I hadn't taken him down to the Fiesta Island Dog Park in over a week. I hadn't even taken him for a long walk for days. He'd been relegated to roaming the backyard and lifting his leg to all too familiar bushes.

I owed him. He'd get his time to unleash his ancestral imperative and swim in the bay and run with other pack dogs soon. But not until I knew that Kim was safe. I called Moira on my way downstairs to my car.

"What do you need my help on now, Cahill?"

"Peter Stone claims Sophia Domingo is missing."

"Why should we care?"

"It's complicated." I went into the garage and got into my car.

"When isn't it with you?"

"I need you to contact one of your sources on LJPD and SDPD and find out if anyone's reported Sophia missing." I pushed the garage door remote. "There's a lot of money in it."

"Stone's money?"

"Yeah. Why do you care?" I pulled out onto the street.

"I don't. I thought you did."

"Not anymore. Check the Pacific Terrace Hotel first."

"Roger. What about the other thing?" she asked.

"There is no other thing."

"Liar!" She spat the word through the phone. "If there wasn't, you would have asked, 'What other thing?'"

She wouldn't let go of her assumption that I was investigating something on my own. She was right. Her smarts and Pitbull-with-a-bone attitude were what made her such a good investigator. But the closer I got to finding the truth about my father, the further away I was from telling anyone about it.

"Call me when you learn something." I hung up.

I tried all of Kim's phone numbers again as I drove toward La Jolla. All went to voicemail. I Googled the main number for Parker Real Estate and called it. Open on Saturday. The receptionist told me Kim was out of the office. I asked if she was showing a house and if I could have the address. The receptionist wouldn't budge.

Kim and Jeffrey Parker lived above La Jolla Shores. I'd never been to their house. I'd never been invited. But I knew the address. I shouldn't. I should have forgotten all about Kim when I found out she'd gotten married. But a few months ago, with too much idle time, and too many people-finder capabilities at my fingertips, I'd found her address.

The house was on Calle Del Oro. High enough up the winding hill to have a view of the ocean a half mile away, as a seagull flies. Modern ranch house design. Large, but not massive. Stylish, but not ostentatious or garish. Classy, unlike some of the recent teardown and rebuilds in La Jolla. It fit Kim, even though Parker had owned the house before she moved in. I'd give him credit for his taste in architecture and women. At least the woman he married.

I sat parked at the curb, surveying the house in the afternoon sun. No cars in the driveway, but the home had a three-car garage. The house's windows gave no hint of movement.

My phone buzzed in my pocket. Moira.

"Nothing about Sophia missing from either PD. She checked out of the hotel last night. I'm heading over to Point Loma now."

"Thanks."

"What's this all about?"

I told her what Stone had told me, complete with his claim that Sophia had said she was meeting Kim last night.

"What's Stone after?" Moira asked.

"I don't know, but I doubt he has good intentions."

"Then why are you helping him?"

"I need to know how Kim's involved and, right now, Stone's an enemy I need to keep close."

"Rick, Peter Stone is not the kind of man you play games with. You of all people should know that."

I couldn't remember Moira ever calling me Rick before.

"I'm not playing a game. I know Stone. Better than I'd like to. He contacted me because he can't go to the police, even though he's got cops on his payroll. His weakness is daylight exposing who he really is to the public. I'll go to the police if I feel I have to."

"Be careful." Softer than I'd ever heard her voice. "What else do you need me to do?"

"Go down to the hotel and see if she or Sophia's car's there."

"Roger."

I got out of my car and walked up to the front door of the Parker house and rang the bell. No response from inside. I knocked loudly on the door and waited. Ten seconds later the door opened. Jeffrey Parker stared out at me. He wasn't smiling. Neither was I. I hadn't expected him to be back from Las Vegas yet. Although, flights to and from Vegas ran all day and were only an hour and a half tarmac to tarmac. He could have left in the morning or as late as two hours ago.

"What are you doing here?" Parker wore jeans, polo shirt. Loafers. No socks. Casual day at home, but for the wisp of hair gel spiking his bangs. He looked ready for a GQ photo shoot except for a nick on his jawline he must have gotten shaving. Nobody's perfect.

"Is Kim here?"

"Why is that a concern of yours?" He bit the words off hard, one at a time.

Parker didn't try to hide it. He hated me. A lot of people in La Jolla did. They hated me because of some rumor, true or false, that they'd heard about my father. Or because they thought I'd killed my wife in Santa Barbara twelve years ago and gotten away with it. But Parker's reasons were different from the rest. He hated me out of jealousy. A man with Hollywood good looks, a four-million-dollar home, and a wife who'd once been my girlfriend whom I still loved. But he knew she chose him only after I wouldn't let her choose me.

Or he could have just hated me for me.

"I need to talk to her. Is she here?"

"That's none of your damn business." He puffed out his chest and balled his hands into fists, popping veins along his well-muscled forearms. "Get the hell out of here."

If he wanted to go, I could take him. Unless he was a black belt in some martial art I'd never heard of. Even then, he'd have to knock me out to stop me. And after everything he'd done behind Kim's back, I had extra incentive. But LJPD hated me more than everyone else in La Jolla. I had a gun on my hip that, even though I had a license to carry, could make me a guest in a room without a view in the Brick House. But my read on Parker was that his physique was for show, not for go.

"Asshole, I want to make sure your wife is okay." I invaded his space. "Tell me if she's here or I'll check myself."

"Why wouldn't she be okay?" His face squinted into a sneer. "You think I'd hurt her?"

Parker whipped his right arm back. I shot a fist into his solar plexus. Hot tuna breath exploded into my face and Parker crumpled down onto the floor of his foyer. I stepped over him and entered the house.

"Kim?" I looked in the kitchen, the dining room, the family room, and started down the long hall for the bedrooms. First one empty. "Kim?"

"I'm calling the police!" Parker's voice echoed down the hall.

"Go ahead!" I shouted. "We can all sit down and have a talk."

A bluff, but it was all I had. I didn't know if Parker had broken any laws in his dealings with Sophia. Even if he had, I was still sworn to secrecy to Kim. A contract with a client was an oath to keep their secrets even after the case was closed, unless they broke the law. With Kim, it was more than that.

If LJPD showed up, I was going to jail.

Parker didn't respond, but I didn't hear his voice on the phone talking to the police. Probably mulling his options. They must not have been very good. What the hell were he and Sophia up to?

I checked the rest of the bedrooms. All six of them and the seven bathrooms. Empty.

When I returned to the foyer, Parker was hunched over, hands on thighs, like he'd just finished a triathlon. He sucked in short breaths.

"Where is she?"

"I don't know." He finally straightened up to his full height, three inches taller than me. But the fight was out of him. "I called her an hour ago, and she hasn't called me back."

"Is that unusual?"

"A little. She usually returns calls within a few minutes. She's probably showing a house and has a lot of walk-ins." His face pinched tight. "Is Kim in danger?"

"I don't know. Probably not. When was the last time you saw or spoke to her?"

My phone buzzed in my pocket. Parker stared at me as I pulled it out. Kim's name on the screen. I answered.

"Why all the phone calls?" Kim asked. "Is something wrong?"

I wasn't sure how to answer that question in front of her husband.

"I just wanted to make sure you were all right." I looked at Parker who pulled out his phone and punched a phone number.

"I just got out of a meeting with my divorce attorney," Kim said.

"Hang up with him!" Parker shouted at my phone. He'd figured out who I was talking to.

"Why are you with Jeffrey?" Anger in Kim's voice. "What did you tell him?"

"Nothing. Call me after you talk to your husband." I hung up.

"What the hell's going on, Cahill?" Parker looked at me and then back at his phone, silent in his hand.

"I don't know. Yet." I left the Parker house.

CHAPTER TWENTY

I PULLED INTO my driveway and noticed a Spectrum cable van a couple houses down. Good luck. A lot of the homes had satellite dishes on their roofs like mine. After a taste of satellite, I wasn't coming back. I doubted my neighbors would, either.

I got inside the house a few minutes after four o'clock. Midnight was waiting for me. I owed him. Dog park, Fiesta Island. We still had a couple hours of sunlight. I wasn't getting paid by Stone until tomorrow morning, so I wasn't officially on the clock yet. Even if Moira was.

I went upstairs with Midnight on my heels and stored my gun in the nightstand next to my bed. We hustled back downstairs and I grabbed Midnight's chest harness and leash out of the closet. He sat in front of me and placed his front legs into the loop one at a time. I snapped the connector over his back, then tossed the end of the leash over his head. He snatched it out of the air, snorted, and danced in place.

It had been too long for both of us.

* * *

Fiesta Island sits in the east end of Mission Bay. It's really a man-made peninsula with a tiny strip of road connecting it to the rest of Mission Bay Park. Sea World is a couple Tiger Woods drives across the bay.

Fiesta Island's biggest claim to fame is that it holds the world-famous Over The Line tournament for two weekends every July. The rest of the time, most of the island is ruled by dogs on the largest off-the-leash dog park in San Diego. Or probably anywhere else.

I parked in the dirt parking lot and Midnight howled out the window in the backseat. He always did. A call back to the wild. I let him out of the car and walked him through the parking lot and down into the sand fronting the bay.

I watched Midnight run and bark and swim for an hour. An hour I wouldn't trade for anything. An hour for both of us to be free. To follow nature's mandate. To feel joy.

I needed more of those hours.

* * *

We got back home just as the sun gave up the day. I washed Midnight in the backyard. After I dried him off, we bull-fought with the towel for a while then I went inside and took my own shower.

I settled into my recliner in front of the TV in the living room and reached for the remote control on the side table, but stopped. I studied the bookcase built in around the TV. Something was wrong about it. The books all seemed to be in place. What was it? More of a feeling than something I could point at.

Then I saw it. The clay sculpture on top of the bookcase that Kim had made for me after we'd been dating about a year. It was supposed to be me in the image of Rodin's *The Thinker*. The likeness was pretty good for someone who'd only taken a class for two months. The body was more sculpted than mine had been since college football, but I guess a girl could dream. I'd praised the gift and truly liked it, but had always seen it as a subtle push. For me to get out of my head and get on with the two of us. Of course, I never did.

What caught my eye tonight was the angle of the sculpture. I'd placed it at about a forty-five-degree angle on top of the bookshelf when I'd moved into my house three years ago. Now it looked to be slightly more square to the room. My imagination? Maybe. But I sat in that chair almost every night and numbed out to the TV. The background had always looked the same. Until tonight. Maybe Midnight or I bumped into the bookcase and jostled the sculpture sometime when we were playing. Possible.

Except the sculpture was heavy and hadn't even moved when a medium-size earthquake rolled through a year ago.

I stared at the sculpture. It had definitely been moved. I got up and walked over to the bookshelf and rose up on my tiptoes so my eyes were just above the top of it. A small black rectangle less than an inch long and half the width of a D battery was snugged up against the base of the sculpture.

An audio recording device. Probably Wi-Fi connected to a receiver somewhere close by.

My face flushed, but cold sweat blistered the hairline on my neck. Someone had breached my house. Invaded my sanctuary. I was vulnerable and hadn't even known it. But who and how? Midnight was always in the house when I was gone. Nobody could get past him without feeling teeth. Then I got it.

The Spectrum cable van on the street when I left for Fiesta Island. Hiding in plain sight. Waiting for me to leave with Midnight so an operative could get inside and bug my house. That still left the who and why. I didn't have any information worth listening to or sharing with someone else. Not yet, at least. Maybe someone wasn't taking any chances with what I might learn and who I might tell it to. Someone who always had to have the odds in his favor no matter the cost.

Peter Stone.

What did he think I already knew about Sophia Domingo that would help me find her? Maybe this was just his standard operating procedure when he hired a PI. Bug them in case they don't tell you everything. Or learn the whereabouts of a missing person before they give it to you so you can get to that person before anyone else. And then do what? The options Stone might employ sent a shiver through me.

Still, I left the audio recorder where it was and turned on the TV. Whatever Stone was up to, I didn't have to let him know I was onto it. Yet.

CHAPTER TWENTY-ONE

STONE'S LAIR HUNG off the side of a hill on Hillside Drive. Thus, the name of the street. You could see the house from below as you wound up the hill. Swirling glass and cement, it loomed like sets of giant grinding gears waiting to pulverize anything or anyone who got too close.

I knocked on the hand-hammered bronze front door that rose to the sky. The last time I'd been there was four years ago. Stone hadn't expected me then. He'd opened the door in a bathrobe. I was the one holding an envelope that time. And a gun.

This morning he answered the door in a suit that was worth more than my whole wardrobe. Dressed for business. So was I. Without a gun this time.

"Rick." He eyed my jeans, bomber jacket, and ball cap. "You look exactly the same as the last time I had the pleasure. Your earnest lateral progression continues. Bravo."

He looked the same, too. Midsixties, but could pass for fifty. Tall. Lean. Sculpted good looks without a surgeon's aid. Gray widow's peak sharp as a knife point aimed at my face. No, he hadn't changed on the outside. But his insides churned the picture of Dorian Gray.

"Well, it beats continued descent. How far down are you now, Stone? The Seventh Circle?"

"Ha!" A genuine laugh without the usual condescension. A first. "You actually opened a book in college during those grueling hours of jock study hall. Come on in."

He pulled the door open. I entered and swiveled my head, checking for bad guys out of habit.

"It's just us today. No need to worry. Follow me down the hall to my office." He smiled an executioner's grin. "That's right, I almost forgot, you know the way."

His house didn't look any more lived in than it had four years ago. Stylish, sharp-edged furniture straight off the staging set from a *Million Dollar Listing* television show. It looked like it could cut you if you caught a corner. The living room had an entire wall of glass that revealed a ten-million-dollar view of La Jolla and the Pacific Ocean. The other walls still had framed mirrors of every size. The better for Stone to gaze at himself twenty-four hours a day.

I followed him down a hallway with photos of A- B- and C-list celebrities. All shaking hands with Stone back in his casino days. Some featured Stone in his remade La Jolla life with local politicians, athletes, and cops. A change of address, money, and lies can buy you a new spotless reputation.

Stone stood behind a huge mahogany desk with the same view from the living room behind him.

"Please, sit." He sat down and I did the same in a white leather chair across from him. A letter envelope sat on the desk between us. About the same width of the one I'd found in my father's wall safe. He looked at the envelope, then at me. "That's yours, Rick. Fifteen thousand dollars, tax free. That's the real reason you don't want it wired into your account or via a check, isn't it? Keeping the Tax Man from grabbing his share."

"I'll declare it as income, but your name won't be anywhere near it."

"As I mentioned yesterday, I want our names intertwined even less than you do." He laughed again, but this had the usual condescension hanging off it. "However, if just a whiff of our collaboration got out to San Diego who's whos, you'd have more clients than you could ever handle. And you wouldn't have to hold your breath hoping your new clients' checks would clear. So, spare me the holier-than-thou outrage. We both know your virtue is transitory."

"You're right." I stood up, grabbed the envelope off the desk, and shoved it into my coat pocket.

"I just don't want to be close enough to be hit by debris when that Stone façade comes tumbling down."

"You'll never escape my reach, Rick." The self-amused mirth left his eyes and the inner malevolence took over. "No one has yet."

Stone's "yet" went back to his casino days in Las Vegas where there was plenty of desert to dig holes for people who tried to outrun his reach. I suddenly wondered if that reach had a hook on the end of it when it came to Sophia.

"If you're looking for a spotter so you can line up Sophia for a kill, you've misjudged how transitory my virtue is." I took out the envelope and dropped it onto the desk.

"I want Sophia alive more than you do. You can walk away right now if you don't believe me. I'll find some other discount gumshoe to take your place before you make it back to your utilitarian Honda Accord. The only memory I'll have of you is that you chose to go against me. That puts you and what few friends you have on the wrong side."

I still didn't know if Kim had met with Sophia the night before Stone claimed Sophia disappeared. All I knew was that Stone and Sophia were connected and so were Sophia and Jeffrey Parker. I could handle being on the wrong side of Stone, but I didn't want Kim to be there, too, because of me.

I picked up the envelope and put it back in my pocket.

"Has someone tried to find Sophia up in Hermosa Beach? That's where she owns a home."

"Hermosa Beach is covered." Stone's face pinched up like I'd asked a stupid question. "You handle San Diego. Call me tomorrow with an update."

I almost told him that I'd just speak out loud in my living room and he could listen in through the "hidden" recording device one of his other stooges had put there. But I'd hold onto that information for now.

"Sophia checked out of The Pacific Terrace Hotel Friday night. Consider that tomorrow's update."

"That's a start." He lifted up the receiver of the phone on his desk and raised his eyebrows. "We're done."

My phone pinged the arrival of a text on the walk back to my car.

Kim: *Can we meet at Muldoon's in a half hour?*

Me: *Yes.*

I wondered if she wanted to tell me that she'd filed for divorce. I wasn't sure how I'd feel if she did.

I called Moira. She started right in without a hello or preamble.

"Sophia wasn't at the Point Loma house. I've called eight local hotels and asked to be connected to Sophia Domingo's room. Zero for eight. Another hundred or so to go. Of course, she probably wouldn't use her real name, but I have to check the easy boxes first."

"Great. I've got an envelope with fifteen grand in my pocket. Half of it is yours."

"Is this your idea of foreplay, Cahill? Because it would take at least the whole envelope to get me interested."

I laughed. She hung up.

I wound down Via Capri into the back end of La Jolla. The marine layer, gray overhead. The briny ocean air sifted through it. An overcast morning in La Jolla was just about as good as a sunny one anywhere else.

I turned onto Prospect Street with too much time to spare, so I detoured over to Parker Real Estate to see if Kim had been at the office when she called me. It was a Sunday, but real estate agents are on call twenty-four seven. After the talk she must have had with her husband yesterday, I figured she might want to get out of the house early this morning. I wondered if Kim was already looking for a new job or if she'd fight for a piece of Parker Real Estate in the divorce. Kim's car wasn't parked out front. I drove up the ramp to the parking lot on top of the building. Just one car was parked up there. A white Corvette Z06 convertible.

Sophia Domingo's car. Empty.

Well, I'd already earned some of Stone's money. I found the car. That was a start.

Maybe I shouldn't have been surprised to see Sophia's car in the parking lot of Parker Real Estate. After all, she was now a 10 percent partner in the company. Except that she'd been reported missing going on two days now. At least by Stone.

I parked next to the Corvette. Its top was up, so I looked through the passenger-side window. No purse or briefcase or any personal items that I could see. Maybe Sophia already had a key from her partnership agreement and had gone into the office. A stairwell thirty feet away in the corner of the roof led down to Parker Real Estate. It had a gated cage around it. All I had to do was verify that Sophia was in the office and call Stone with the good news. I'd found her. It wasn't my job to detain her until Stone arrived. That would be kidnapping. It *was* my duty as a human being to warn Sophia that Stone was looking for her. I'd be done with Stone and Sophia and ready to move on.

I got out of my car and walked over to the caged stairwell. Locked. I wondered if Sophia would come to the front door if I knocked.

Worth a try. I checked my watch. Fifteen minutes until my meeting with Kim at Muldoon's. Of course, there was a simpler way to get into Parker Real Estate. But putting Kim and Sophia in the same office building wasn't a good idea.

I walked back toward my car. An ocean breeze blew another layer off the morning haze. I glanced at the back of the Corvette and stopped walking. Tiny flecks of something dark sprinkled the white paint just below the trunk. It looked like dried blood. I bent down and got a closer look. Something sickeningly sweet and putrid at the same time seeped through the seal of the trunk.

I'd smelled the odor before.

I didn't have to worry about Sophia and Kim running into each other in the office anymore. Unless someone else was in the trunk of her car, Sophia Domingo wouldn't run anywhere ever again.

CHAPTER TWENTY-TWO

HAD STONE BEATEN me to Sophia? The smell seeping through the trunk of the Corvette told me Sophia had to have been dead for at least a day. Probably longer. The temperature yesterday had been warm. Decomposition of the body may have been somewhat accelerated in the trunk of the car, but I doubted so much so that I'd be able to smell it through a sealed enclosure after less than a day.

If Stone had murdered Sophia or had someone else do it, he'd done it before he called me yesterday. If so, why hire me? To set me up for the murder? No. Stone may have been playing three-dimensional chess while I played checkers, but hiring me to find a woman he murdered didn't make sense on any level. Two-dimensional or three.

If not Stone, then who? That was the police department's job to figure out. I took my phone out of my pocket and tapped a phone number.

Kim answered.

"Change of plans. Meet me at your office. I'll be waiting out front."

"Why?" I could hear road sounds in the background.

"I'll tell you when you get here." I hung up.

* * *

I hadn't decided if I'd call the police and report the Corvette and the smell of death. I had to talk to Kim first. According to Peter Stone, she may have been the last person to see Sophia alive. Except for the killer.

My heart told me she couldn't be both.

I drove down the ramp to the street and parked in front of Parker Real Estate. Spaces were starting to fill up as people arrived to eat the best breakfast in La Jolla at The Morning Cup, a block down. On any other Sunday, I'd join them. Not this morning. I'd lost my appetite.

I got out of the car and waited in front of Parker Real Estate.

Kim pulled her BMW into a space next to my Honda Accord. Our lives had gone in different directions since we stopped dating years ago. The next five minutes would tell me in what direction they'd each go from that moment forward.

Kim didn't smile when she got out of the car. She looked worried. That made me worried.

"Why are we meeting here? Jeffrey always comes to the office on Sundays. He'll be here soon."

"We won't be here long." I hoped. "Open the door, so we can talk inside."

"What's going on, Rick?" She unlocked the door and opened it. "What's this all about?"

"Just trust me." I followed Kim inside and walked back to her corner office, shifting my eyes between the floor and wall looking for blood. Clean. Thank God. Kim followed me into her office and sat in the chair behind her desk. I stood across from her. Her eyes were round with concern and her hands fidgeted in her lap.

"Did you have a meeting with Sophia Domingo anytime between Friday and now?"

"What's this about, Rick?" She squinted at me.

"I'll explain in a minute. Please just answer the question."

She looked down at her hands. I wasn't going to like what she said next.

"Yes. We met here Friday night."

The wind left me like I'd been sucker punched in the gut. I'd been ready for her answer. Knew there had to be a simple explanation to clear her of guilt. But the time line and ramifications of the body in the trunk shone like a spotlight in my eyes that I couldn't blink away.

"What time?"

"About seven thirty."

"Why didn't you tell me you were going to meet her?" Anger crept up my neck.

"Because it wasn't any of your business, Rick."

"Bullshit!" I slammed my hand down onto the desk. Kim blinked and straightened up in her chair. "You'd had me follow this woman. You know you should have told me about the meeting."

"You're right. I was afraid you'd be mad and try to talk me out of it." She looked afraid. Afraid of me? Or afraid that I'd found Sophia Domingo?

"What did you talk about?"

"Her involvement with Jeffrey and the partnership deal with Parker Real Estate."

"What did she tell you?" I asked.

"That she and Jeffrey weren't in a sexual relationship."

I didn't care anymore whether that was a lie or the truth. It was a distraction from the main issue. Sophia, Stone, and Parker's business relationship.

"What about the ten percent partnership?"

"Rick, I appreciate all you've done and your concern for me. But the partnership and Parker Real Estate are private matters that I shouldn't discuss. I didn't hire you to spy on the business."

"You hired me to spy on your husband and then on Sophia Domingo. They relate to the business. You think I give a shit about Parker Real Estate? I only care about protecting you." My throat tightened. "What did Sophia do to get the partnership?"

Kim let out a deep breath and looked down at the desk. "She put Jeffrey in touch with Stone. She has connections to the California Coastal Commission. They control any development along the coast. She helped get the Scripps sale through the Commission. It will earn fifty million for the real estate firm that gets the listings. PRE is going to be that firm. This is life changing."

She was right about that. It had already changed one person's life. Permanently. But she wasn't talking about Sophia. She meant her and Jeffrey and their soon-to-be family.

"So, you're staying with Jeffrey?"

"Yes. I asked him about Sophia and he swore to me that they just had a business relationship."

She held my eyes daring me to question her decision. I did, but it was her decision to make. Not mine. I'd made mine by not making one years before. Still, I wondered if it was the fifty million or her husband's denial of a sexual relationship that was the reason she was sticking with him. I wouldn't have wondered a week ago. Before there was a dead body in a car on the roof and Kim was the last person who'd seen the body breathing.

"What time was the meeting over?" With Jeffrey or not, I still cared about Kim. More than anyone else in my life. She had Jeffrey and a growing family, but she needed me right now. Whether she knew it or not.

"Probably around eight. Why? When are you going to tell me what this is all about?"

"Soon. Where was Sophia's car parked?"

"What? Why?"

"Just tell me."

"I don't know." She shook her head and gave me the squint again. "I walked her to the front door and locked it behind her."

"You didn't leave the building together?"

"No. I went back to my office and worked for about a half hour. Why?"

"Was there anyone else in the office when you and Sophia met?" I asked.

"No."

"Was her car still on the roof when you left that night?"

"I don't know. I didn't even know she had parked on the roof. I'd parked out front that morning. I was at the office all day. You have to tell me what's going on. Now." She wrapped her arms around her chest, hugging herself. "You're making me nervous."

Wait until she talked to the police.

"Sophia Domingo's car is parked on the roof of this building. There's something dead in the trunk and I'm pretty sure it's her."

"What?" She shot back in the chair and her eyes went wide. "How do you know? What?"

"Did you see anyone on the street when you let Sophia out of the office? Think back. Friday night is a busy night on this street."

"I don't know. No. Why? Do you think the police will think I had something to do with . . . her, with this?" She hugged herself tighter.

"If you were the last person to see her that night, they'll ask a lot of questions to eliminate you as a suspect. I just want you to be ready."

"Are they coming now?" Her tongue ran along her lower lip. "Did you call them?"

"No."

"Are you going to? What should we do?"

"One of us needs to call the police."

"What do you mean, 'one of us'?" she asked.

I told her about Stone hiring me.

"Why would you work for Peter Stone? You hate him."

"It's complicated."

"What do you mean? Now you're the one holding back information. Tell me, Rick."

"He said that Sophia told him she was meeting you Friday night and then she went missing. He said he could help you if you ended up needing it."

"What kind of help?" Her mouth dropped open. "You think I had something to do with Sophia's death?"

"Of course not." I didn't now, after seeing her body language during my Q and A. But the possibility had itched at the back of my brain. I loved Kim. She was the best person I knew. But people surprise you. Even the ones you love. My father had proven that a long time ago.

"Who do you think did it?"

"I don't know, but we need to get out in front of this. I found the body. I'll call the police."

The Brick House was just a couple blocks down the street. I wanted to have our story straight before the police got there. "You and I agreed to meet here to have breakfast together at the Morning Cup. I got here early and checked the parking lot on the roof to see if you were here. I saw the car, got out to look inside, and saw dried blood below the trunk. Then I smelled . . . death."

That left Stone. Did I call him or the police first? Common sense said to call the police.

Survival said something else.

CHAPTER TWENTY-THREE

IF SOPHIA WAS dead in the trunk of the Corvette and I called in the suspicious smell, the cops would check my cell phone records during the investigation. I didn't want a record of me calling Peter Stone two minutes before I reported the Corvette to the police. There was still a pay phone in front of the Post Office right across the street from Parker Real Estate. I crossed my fingers that the phone still worked. It did.

Stone picked up on the third ring.

"I found Sophia's car. Ninety percent certain that she's dead inside it."

"What do you mean?" No cool façade now. "Why do you think she's dead?"

"The stench of decomp is coming from the trunk. Someone's dead in there. We both know it's her."

"Pop the trunk and find out. I'm sure you have the tools to break into a car."

I did. But not for him.

"I'm not disturbing the crime scene. I thought it was only fair to tell you before I called the police. I won't tell them you hired me to find her. That will stay just between us. I'll give you back half of the money since I didn't find her alive."

"I don't care about the money, you simpleton." Anger vibrated the phone. "Open up that damn car and search it for a black Lexar USB flash drive and then bring it to me."

"No. I found her. I fulfilled our agreement. The rest is on you." I hung up the phone.

A computer flash drive. What was on it that was so important to Stone and why did he think Sophia had it? She must have stolen it from him when she went to his house after the California Coastal Commission vote. Why? Whatever was on that drive, I had no doubts that Stone would kill for it. But if he'd killed Sophia, why didn't he already have the flash drive back in his possession?

I'd done my duty for Stone. He was no longer my concern.

Kim was.

I walked across the street and up the ramp to the parking lot on the top of Parker Real Estate. I didn't drive my car back up there because I didn't want it to be stuck in a roped-off crime scene and have to wait for God knows how long to get it back. The white Corvette was still there. No miracles today. I walked over to the Corvette and stood behind the trunk. The decomp smell was still there, too.

It seemed a bit stronger, but maybe because I already knew it was there. Once you've smelled death, you never forget its scent. I pulled out my cell phone and called the La Jolla Police Department. I knew the number by heart. They probably still had mine memorized, too.

I told the dispatcher what I'd found and gave her my name, address, and phone number. She kept me on the phone and told me to wait until the police arrived. I stayed on the line, even though the urgency of the situation left with the last breath that Sophia Domingo took. Four minutes later, an LJPD cruiser rolled up the ramp with light bar on fire, but no siren. A plain-wrap detective car followed right behind it. Both cars stopped twenty feet behind the Corvette.

A Dick and Jane patrol team got out of the cruiser and stood next to it, letting the lone detective who got out of the plain wrap to take the lead. I didn't recognize the uniforms or the detective. The best news of the day. No cops I'd insulted or tangled with in the past. Rare. A fresh start. The detective ambled over and stopped three feet in front of me. I didn't know whether he could smell the stench of death seeping through the seal of the trunk. He didn't seem to be in any hurry to pop the lid.

I hadn't expected a detective to show up right away. As far as I knew, LJPD still only had three teams of two homicide detectives. I figured Sunday's team would be on call at home with their families at nine a.m.

"Mr. Cahill?" The detective was tall, thin, younger than me. He wore black horn-rimmed glasses favored by hipsters nowadays, but they made him look like a professor or grad student working on his thesis. He had a pleasant smile that didn't say anything but nice to meet you. I hadn't seen a smile like that on anyone at LJPD since my dad had been a cop in good standing there.

"Yes."

"I'm Detective Sheets." He opened his sport jacket to reveal a gold shield clipped onto his belt. "Can you run me through the events of this morning that caused you to call the La Jolla Police Department?"

"Sure." I played the upstanding citizen, I guess because, for a change, I was one. Sort of. "I was meeting a friend for breakfast at the Morning Cup. She works at Parker Real Estate. I didn't see her car out front, so I checked up here in case she'd parked here and decided to do some work. That's when I saw the Corvette." I grimaced and nodded my head. "This is where things get a little strange. I'm familiar with the car and the woman who drives it. Her name is Sophia Domingo."

"How do you know her?" Calm. We were still all friends.

"I'm a private investigator and Ms. Domingo met with the subject of an investigation as well as the person who hired me."

"Who were the client and the subject?" The smile remained on Detective Sheets' face, but his big brain was working behind his bespectacled eyes.

"I'm sure you can understand, Detective Sheets, that I take the confidentiality of my clients very seriously. That's why they hire me."

Still being the upstanding citizen.

Sheets rubbed his chin. "Why do you think Ms. Domingo is dead?"

I stepped away from the trunk of the Corvette and nodded at it. "You don't smell that?"

Sheets took a step forward toward the trunk. He leaned down a bit. I didn't hear an inhale, but at that distance he'd smell the death inside without even trying. He looked to be studying the dark specks of dried liquid that had to be blood. Finally, Sheets straightened up and looked at me.

"Will you excuse me for a second, Mr. Cahill?"

"Sure." Hidden in his good manners was the message to me not to go anywhere. I understood. The quicker he checked the necessary boxes, the quicker I could get on with my life.

Sheets walked over to the two uniforms and spoke to the woman with sergeant stripes on the arm.

Tall. Sturdy. Forties. Brunette. Her partner was a young African-American kid. Tall. Athletic. Snap-creased uni. Chest out. Chin up. Jacked on the power of the badge. He eyed me like he hoped I'd rabbit so he could take me down. I remembered the feeling. I'd still been riding the wave two and a half years into the job before everything changed. It will change for him, too. It does for everyone. Just not as drastically as it did for me.

The kid's sergeant said something to him, and he got back into the cruiser and sat behind the laptop computer locked in a stand attached to the dashboard. Either running a warrant check on me or running the plate of the Corvette to see who the car was registered to. Or both. Sheets stuck his head into the open door of the cruiser and spoke to the patrolman. He straightened up and pulled a cell phone out of the front pocket of his slacks, then made a call. Probably calling a deputy district attorney to try and get a telephonic search warrant from a judge. Sheets put his phone back in his pocket and walked over to me.

"I'm waiting for a judge to okay a search warrant, then the officers and I will open the trunk and see what's inside. I'd like you to stick around while we do that, Mr. Cahill. If there is indeed a body in the trunk, I may need you to help with a preliminary ID. Then we'll have to go into more detail about your relationship with the woman."

"I'll stick around and ID the body if it's her and tell you all I know. But I didn't have any kind of relationship with her. She just popped up in the middle of a case I was working."

"We'll get to all that. But first, we have to find out if there is really a body in there."

Sheets walked around the car and peeked in the windows. He stepped back after he finished, folded his arms, and stared at the car. I don't know what he was looking at and seeing or not seeing, but it had all his attention. His phone rang a minute into his meditation. He answered it.

"Yes, sir. Thank you, Your Honor." He hung up and put the phone back in his pocket. "Sergeant Meyers, Judge Whitney has given me a telephonic search warrant to search the car and any personal items I may find inside. Please protect the scene while I proceed."

Sheets took out a pair of black nitrile gloves from his coat pocket.

"Sir?" The sergeant looked at me with her hands on her hips. "You're going to have to exit the parking lot. Officer Gains will—"

"Mr. Cahill can stay for now." Sheets looked back over his shoulder at Sergeant Meyers. "He may help in identification."

Sheets walked over to the driver's door and tried the handle. Unlocked. He opened the door and scanned the inside of the Corvette, then stuck his hand under the steering wheel and found the trunk release.

The trunk popped open, but just a couple inches. The smell of death flowed out to find fresh air. Not enough to make me gag, but enough to know what we'd find inside.

I stepped back from the trunk. Sheets came to the back of the car.

"Mr. Cahill, okay for me to ask for your assistance, if needed?"

"Yes."

Sheets slipped his nitrile-gloved hands under the lid of the trunk and lifted it up. Death rushed out in an invisible cloud. My hand whipped up and pinched my nose shut on its own. Sheets grabbed his nose and shifted backwards. Just a few inches.

I forced myself to move to the right and peek around Detective Sheets' body.

All I could see was the shape of a crumpled naked body. Pale with green splotches and black blood crusted slits in its skin.

"Sergeant Meyers, call in a 187 and make sure forensics gets up here right away," Sheets said.

Meyers called it in on her cruiser's car radio.

"Mr. Cahill?" Sheets turned and looked at me. He didn't look like a college student anymore.

"Could you step over here and verify that the decedent is, ah, was the woman you call Sophia Domingo?"

I walked over to the car.

Sheets stopped me with an arm across my chest. "Please be careful not to touch anything."

"Sure." He didn't have to worry. I didn't want to touch anything. I didn't even want to see anything. But I needed to confirm for Stone and for myself that the dead body in the trunk was Sophia.

I'd seen death as a cop and I'd seen it as a civilian. Too much of it. My own wife. People I'd considered friends. People I'd killed myself. I hadn't gotten used to it. I prayed I never would.

I felt Detective Sheets' eyes on me. Probably getting a read on my reaction. The real reason he had me look at the body. I held my breath and peered into the trunk of the Corvette. The body had been a woman in life. It was naked. Thirty or forty stab wounds pockmarked it. The body's neck had been slit wide, exposing the larynx. Its eyes open, once human, now two marbles in a death mask. Its mouth agape, a miniature twin of its neck. In life, she had been Sophia Domingo.

Bile rushed up my throat. Then I spotted something else in the trunk that hit me like smelling salts.

Behind the body, sitting upright, a briefcase. I'd seen it before. In the hands of Peter Stone, then in the once living hands of Sophia Domingo.

CHAPTER TWENTY-FOUR

"THAT'S HER. SOPHIA Domingo." I didn't volunteer my knowledge of the briefcase next to her body. Maybe later. Maybe not.

I spun around from the horror and took a deep breath. Death still clung to the air around the car. I started walking toward the ramp that led down to the street. I would have run, if I could have trusted my legs. I wouldn't have stopped until I hit the ocean a half mile away.

"Mr. Cahill." Detective Sheets' voice stopped me. "I'd like to ask you some questions so we can get this investigation kick-started. Are you up for that?"

"Yes."

"Sergeant Meyers, could you escort Mr. Cahill down to the street and wait for me there? I'll be down as soon as forensics arrives. Officer Gains, please secure the scene with crime scene tape and start a log to check in all personnel who arrive."

"This way, Mr. Cahill." Meyers grabbed my arm like I might pass out any second and led me down the ramp. Either that or she was making sure I wouldn't flee. She didn't have to worry. My legs weren't yet ready for the dash to the beach.

"I'm okay, Sergeant." I looked at her hand clamped around my arm, then at her face. "I appreciate the concern, but I'm not going to fall over."

"Okay." She smiled and let go. "Just don't keel over and then sue me and the department."

"No need to worry." I smiled back. "If I wanted to sue LJPD, I would have done it a long time ago."

"I know who you are, Cahill. Let's keep things civil." She hooked her thumbs under her Sam Brown duty belt and flared her elbows.

"That's always my first option." Mostly.

A white van with La Jolla Crime Lab stenciled on the side rolled by and turned around the corner. Would the techs find enough evidence to target the killer?

A knife. The massive number of stab wounds. The slashed throat. Frenzy. Overkill. Personal. My bet was that the killer knew Sophia. Even if Stone was maneuvering me in a game I'd never understand, I didn't think he killed her. The crime was too hot. I'd seen Stone angry up close. Scary, but under control. He was petty and vengeful. But he processed grievances and slights like a computer collating data. When he struck, it was cool. Efficient.

Stone hadn't killed Sophia. Not by his own hands or by a hired killer's. Too much anger. Too much blood. Then who? Sophia's female mouth-kissing lunch date? Jeffrey Parker's claim of innocence or not, Sophia had spent her afternoons in a robe and nothing else behind closed doors with men in an expensive hotel. That could get her girlfriend's blood up.

Parker was supposedly at a convention in Las Vegas. Easy enough to check out.

Of course, there was Kim. Someone screwing your husband and stealing a chunk of the family business would enrage anyone, even Kim. Her body language during our talk in the office told me that she didn't know anything about Sophia's death. But, I'd misread people I cared about before.

Detective Sheets turned the corner on the sidewalk. "Thank you, Sergeant Meyers. I'll take it from here."

Meyers walked back toward the crime scene.

"Mr. Cahill, can you run over the events of this morning again?" He pulled his cell phone out of his pocket and tapped the screen a couple times. "Do you mind if I record this conversation? It's much easier than taking notes and lets me be fully engaged in our talk."

He could call it a conversation, but I knew it would be him asking questions and me answering them. His engagement would be solely directed at my body language. That was fine. I didn't have anything to hide. Well, nothing pertaining to any potential guilt by me.

"Fine."

He tapped the cell phone screen one more time, then put the phone in the top pocket of his blazer. I gave him the same story I'd given him on the roof. Including that I'd occasionally observed Sophia Domingo's movements over the last week and that I had tried the doorknob to the staircase on the roof. Only leaving out my and Kim's motivations for this morning's meeting.

"What were you investigating that brought you into contact with the woman in the trunk?"

"That's confidential between my client and me."

"I did a little homework on you while I was on the roof and found out that you work a lot of adultery cases."

"Among other types of investigations." But his quick research had been good. After trying to do anything but, I still handled more cheating cases than anything else.

"But the odds are, Mr. Cahill, that Ms. Domingo was in the middle of one of your adultery investigations. Correct?"

"I had a talk with my client earlier, and she's willing to discuss my investigation with you. After you talk with her, I'd be happy to elaborate on the case. I have a reputation to protect, Detective. I can't break confidentiality until after you talk to my client."

"Yes. I learned a fair amount about your reputation in the last few minutes." This time he tried on his cop glare. The grad-school smile was more authentic. "Did you ever talk to Ms. Domingo while you were investigating her?"

"I didn't say I was investigating Ms. Domingo."

"You know what I mean."

"I never talked to her or came in contact with her in any way," I said.

"During your investigation, you must have seen Ms. Domingo encounter other people, correct?"

"Yes."

"I'd like you to make me a list of those people."

"You should talk to my client first."

"I don't understand you, Cahill." He finally dropped the deferential mister in front of my name. "You were a cop. So was your father. Don't you want to help me put the monster who butchered that woman behind bars?"

"Yes. After you talk with my client. Her name is Kim Parker and she's right inside this office." I nodded at the building.

"Hopefully, she'll be more cooperative than you." He turned and pulled on the handle of the front door to Parker Real Estate. It was locked.

I knocked on the glass. Kim unlocked the front door and opened it. Her eyes big. Mouth tight. Worried.

"Kim, this is Detective Sheets and he wants to ask you some questions," I said.

"I'll take it from here." Sheets turned toward me. "Please stick around. I may have more questions for you after I talk with Mrs. Parker."

I didn't want her to be alone with Sheets when he questioned her. Not because I was worried about what she'd say, but because I wanted her to lean on me if she needed to. Most people will never be questioned by the police in their lifetime. It can be unnerving, no matter how innocent you are. You never get used to it. Even hardened criminals get nervous, but they know how to hide the nerves better than most. Just like me.

"I'd prefer to come inside as Mrs. Parker's representative."

"You're not an attorney, Cahill." Sheets' face turned red again. This time with anger. "Are you stating that she needs one? If that's the case, maybe we should take this interview down the street to the station, and I can take turns questioning each of you at my leisure. Or maybe I should just arrest you for obstructing a police investigation."

The obstruction threat would have been a bluff from any police department but LJPD. They'd follow through just out of spite and put me in a cell for twenty-four hours. I wouldn't be of any help to Kim there. I wasn't any help to her now either. She hugged herself and color leaked from her face.

"I'll wait out here," I said.

"Thank you for your cooperation, Mr. Cahill." Sheets entered the building and pulled the glass door shut behind him.

I paced in front of the building, worried for Kim, but also for myself. I paced some more, then decided I had to rip the Band Aid off the scab. I went into my car and found a few more quarters in the console. Sheets had been talking to Kim for five or six minutes. Now or never. I went across the street to the pay phone and looked back at the roof of Parker Real Estate. The view was blocked by a large pepper tree. I couldn't see the cops up there, so they couldn't see me. I dropped two quarters into the pay phone and dialed the number.

"Sophia's dead. The briefcase you gave her was in the trunk of her car with the body. The police are about to question me, and I'm going to have to tell them the truth."

"What's the truth?" Stone's voice, a dry ice hiss.

"That you met her at The Pacific Terrace Hotel and gave her a briefcase and that she went to your house the night before she disappeared."

"What about our arrangement?"

"I haven't decided yet. If they ask me a direct question about it, I'll have to answer truthfully."

"Why did you call to tell me this?"

"You gave me a lot of money to find Sophia. I did. I figure it's only fair that I give you a heads up about how things ended."

"The blue-collar honor? Is that it, Rick?"

"Yes." Sweat pocked my forehead. "And I'm hoping that since I've been up front with you, you won't do something stupid."

"Dear, dear Rick." The default cool menace from our earlier conversations returned to his voice. "I thought you knew me better than that. Whatever I do, it won't be stupid." He hung up.

CHAPTER TWENTY-FIVE

DETECTIVE SHEETS OPENED the door of Parker Real Estate and leaned his head out. "Would you come inside, Mr. Cahill?"

Back to grad-school student deference. I got off the bench and walked inside. Kim stood in the lobby, arms still crossed, but her face less tight.

"You okay?" I asked.

"I'm fine." She gave me a weak smile.

"Are you releasing me from our confidentiality agreement?"

"Yes."

"Mr. Cahill, Mrs. Parker has allowed us to use her office while we talk." Sheets smiled like we were all friends again. "This way."

I followed him down the hallway while Kim stayed behind. Sheets waited inside the office and closed the door behind me after I entered. He went behind Kim's desk and sat in her chair. I sat down opposite him.

Sheets spoke into the top pocket of his coat that held his cell phone, identifying who was in the room and the date and time.

"Tell me how you first encountered Ms. Domingo."

Kim had released me from confidentiality and we'd both agreed to tell the cops the truth. Still, I felt uncomfortable giving the police the specifics of a case. Especially this one.

"I was following Jeffrey Parker when he met Sophia at The Pacific Terrace Hotel." I gave him the date and time.

"What did you observe at the hotel?"

I told him about snapping photos from the beach of Sophia and Parker on the balcony of the hotel. The kimono, the wine, the hand on the leg, and the retreat into the hotel room.

"Do you think Jeffrey Parker and Sophia Domingo had sex in the hotel room that afternoon?"

"I don't know." I didn't, but I had my suspicions, which hadn't diminished just because Parker told Kim he and Sophia weren't having an affair.

"Of course, you can't know for sure unless you were there." Sheets glanced through the window in the door, then leaned toward me like he was sharing a secret. "But's what's your professional opinion tell you? You've worked a lot of these kind of cases. You must have drawn your own conclusion."

"I don't know."

"Okay." Sheets leaned back in Kim's chair and nodded. "Who else did you observe Sophia interact with in the course of your investigation?"

"Peter Stone went up to her room in the hotel after Parker left." I feared that Stone and I had different definitions of what stupid meant. "He had a briefcase with him when he entered, but not when he left. Later Sophia left the hotel with the briefcase."

"The same Peter Stone whose name is on buildings all over San Diego?" Sheets crooked his head and smiled.

"Yes."

"Would you recognize the briefcase if you saw it again?"

"Yes."

Sheets pulled out his phone and tapped the screen then reached it out across the desk for me to look at.

I put up my hand. "If you're trying to show me a crime scene photo of the briefcase in the trunk of Sophia's car, I don't need to see it." Sophia's body slashed to death was now forever etched in my memory. Just as my wife's body on a coroner's table was. And the dead bodies of friends I'd discovered. And every dead body I saw as a cop in Santa Barbara. And the four people I'd killed since. "I'm ninety-nine percent certain the briefcase in Sophia's trunk next to her body is the same one Stone gave to her."

"Did she meet with anyone else while you were observing her?"

"Yes. Last Thursday she had lunch with Dina Dergan at Fresco in Carlsbad."

"Who is Dina Dergan?"

I told him what little I knew about Dergan Consulting.

"One other thing, Dergan and Sophia kissed on the lips when they greeted each other at lunch."

"Maybe they're sisters."

"It wasn't that kind of kiss." I was relying on Moira's assessment, but she'd been pretty adamant about the intimacy of the kiss.

"Oh."

I told him about Sophia attending the Coastal Commission meeting.

"After the meeting, she went to Peter Stone's house around five thirty."

"Did you follow her anywhere after that?" He was already working the possible time of death in his head.

"No. My work for Mrs. Parker was complete."

"Anything else I should know?"

Stone. The last person who hired me to follow Sophia. After she was already dead. But there wasn't a paper trail to prove it. What if Sheets thought Stone hired me to find Sophia before she died? I'd be in his crosshairs along with Stone.

"No. I think that's everything."

"Okay. Thank you, Mr. Cahill." Sheets stood up and handed me a business card across the table.

"Call me if you remember anything else about Ms. Domingo or anything at all. Twenty-four seven. That's how I'll be working this case."

"I never had a doubt." I walked over to the door to leave, but Sheets' voice stopped me.

"Oh, one last thing. Where were you Friday night from nine p.m. on?"

"Home."

"Alone?"

"Yes."

"Thank you, Mr. Cahill. We'll be in touch if we have any more questions." Cop smile. Closed mouth and squinting eyes. "Or if we need some clarification."

I walked down the hall and felt Sheets' eyes on my back. He could look all he wanted. The only thing I was guilty of was taking a job from Peter Stone. If he found out, I'd take it from there. Even if Sheets never found out, I'm sure I wouldn't escape punishment for it. But the punishment wouldn't come from LJPD.

It would come from Stone.

Kim stood in the doorway to the lobby talking to someone. The wall dividing the lobby from the offices blocked my view. Kim saw me and stopped talking. I cleared the doorway and saw Jeffrey Parker.

I nodded to him. He glared at me. Detective Sheets' voice behind me interrupted our greeting.

"Mr. Parker." He stepped through the doorway and extended a hand. "Thanks for coming down to talk with me. Let's go back to your wife's office."

Parker gave me one last mean mug, looked at Kim, then followed Sheets down the hall.

"You okay?" I asked Kim.

She looked down the hall at her office, probably to make sure the door was closed. She spoke in a low voice just above a whisper. "What did you tell the detective about Sophia?"

"Just that she came up in an investigation I was performing for you." I kept my voice low. "That I'd seen her and Jeffrey at the hotel."

"You didn't tell him anything about her becoming a partner in the business, did you?"

"No. He didn't ask and I didn't volunteer it. I don't have enough information to talk about the subject."

Kim let out a long breath. "Thanks."

"It's going to come out, Kim. It would probably be better to volunteer it now than explain it later."

"I'll think about it. Thanks, Rick." She walked around the receptionist's desk and sat down. I'd been dismissed without a hug and even a handshake.

"Does the money really mean that much to you?" I stood in front of the desk and looked down at Kim.

"What do you mean?" She asked the question, but her eyes told me she knew what I was asking.

"You never had any money until you got your real estate license and started working for PRE. But you could have made as much anywhere else. You've earned your way, Kim. You can do it again. You don't have to cover for Jeffrey."

"I'm not covering for Jeffrey, and it's not about the money, Rick. It's about family."

"You finally told him you're pregnant?" Her husband, father of her child, the man she chose instead of holding out for me. She told me first, then him. But she was staying with him.

"Yes. He cried. I've known him for four years and I've never seen him cry before. Jeffrey really wants to be a father. I'm going to have a baby. We're going to be a family." She crossed her arms, not to comfort herself this time. As a shield against me. "I'm not going to let anything get in the way of that. Not the police, not . . . anyone."

I was now *anyone* in Kim's mind. A threat. Right there with the police or anyone else who'd try to get between Kim and her husband and, soon, child.

I left without another word. Back to my life of almosts.

CHAPTER TWENTY-SIX

JACK ANTON AND his wife lived in a quaint little green house with white lattice on Fourth Street in La Mesa. A short woman in her sixties answered the door. Fit. Natural shoulder-length gray hair. Crow's feet creeping in on cornflower-blue eyes. She wore yellow slacks and a powder-blue blouse. A smile that would light up any room she entered.

"Mr. Cahill?"

"Yes. Please call me Rick."

"Then you call me Barbara. Now come on in, Rick."

I walked into a living room with original hardwood floors and twenty-year-old furniture. Instead of looking old and dingy, everything worked together. Norman Rockwell's Americana. Tomato and basil smells wafted in from the adjoining kitchen. Tomato soup and not Campbell's. Homemade. Even if I didn't get anything of significance from Jack Anton, I'd get a nice lunch from his wife.

"Cahill." A balding man in cuffed khakis and a short-sleeved light-blue dress shirt stood up from a beige sofa. Late sixties. A couple inches under six feet. Slight paunch. The man looked vaguely familiar to me, but I had no idea why. He walked over and grabbed my hand in a firm grip. "Jack Anton."

"Thanks for seeing me."

"Sure, sure." He released my hand and walked down a short hall. "Let's go into my office."

"Lunch in thirty minutes, boys." Barbara's voice followed us down the hall as we entered Anton's office.

The office was cramped, but neat. The walls were covered with framed newspaper articles, plaques, and family photographs. Snug against the wall to the left of Anton's desk was a massive steel file cabinet. Somehow the laptop and printer on his desk surprised me. I guess I'd expected to see a Royal typewriter and rotary phone. Anton sat behind his desk and I sat in a wooden captain's chair opposite him.

"I was in such a hurry to get back here that I didn't offer you a drink." Anton raised his hands up in the air, open-palmed. "Water? Beer? Glenlivet?"

Glenlivet. The scotch my father drank on special occasions. Until he couldn't afford it after he lost his job on LJPD. In the end, he was drinking whatever he could get his hands on, via whatever means. I wondered if Anton knew my father had drunk Glenlivet. Made me wonder why he'd been so accommodating in meeting with me.

"I'm good. Thanks."

"Fine. Down to business." He opened a manila folder next to his laptop. "I made copies of all the articles I wrote on the Phelps murder. You can have them." He handed me a thin stack of letter-size papers that were photocopies of newspaper articles.

"You do this with all your old articles or just the ones on unsolved murders?" Or just the ones that had something to do with my old man?

I called Anton out of the blue yesterday and today he already had old articles copied and ready for me. Too easy? Too prepared?

"I have the original articles for every piece I've ever written in every newspaper I've worked for going back to my junior year at San Diego

State and the *Daily Aztec*." He got up and walked over to the huge file cabinet, then bent over and opened the bottom drawer. He pulled out a sealed plastic bag with a slightly yellowed cut-out newspaper article in it. "Care to read about the game Dennis Shaw threw for nine touchdowns against New Mexico State in 1969? I was a sports reporter way back then."

"That's okay. My dad told me all about the old-timers when I was a kid. Don Coryell with the Aztecs and Chargers." Maybe Anton was just a pack rat who was eager to show anyone his life's work at the drop of a hat.

I scanned the copies of the articles he gave me. The first two were the ones I'd already read at the La Jolla Library. There were only two more. One was a week after the crime, the other marking its one-year anniversary.

The week-old article had some new information on the murder. Detective Davidson said that Phelps was shot twice in the right side of his head and that he believed the shooter had been sitting in the passenger seat of Phelps' car when he fired the shots. Phelps was last seen alive at 9:15 p.m. at his Pacific Beach laundromat by his manager. The manager said Phelps left to go check on his laundromat in La Jolla. He also stated that he'd seen a transient hitchhiking in front of the laundromat parking lot when he returned from dinner at 9:00 p.m. A police sketch of a twentysomething Caucasian accompanied the article. The suspect looked like a thug straight out of a Hollywood B movie. Crew cut, square chin, curled sneer, and angry slits for eyes.

The article quoted Detective Davidson as saying that Phelps was believed to have had connections to organized crime and his murder may have been a professional hit. All leads were being investigated. The article added that Phelps was survived by his wife of twenty-two years and his seventeen-year-old daughter, Calista, who was a senior at La Jolla High School.

I wondered how Phelps' surviving family felt about his being rumored to have mob connections. I didn't like hearing it about my father, and his never made it to the newspaper.

The one-year-anniversary article uncovered one new fact. LJPD sent the bullets that killed Phelps to the FBI lab in Quantico, Virginia. The FBI was able to identify the bullets as twenty-five caliber. The same caliber as the bullets missing from the handgun I found in my father's safe.

Too many coincidences. Why did my father have the murder weapon?

The hole in my gut where I'd carried my father's shame opened up. I took a deep breath and read on.

The standing theory that Phelps had been killed by someone in organized crime remained, although there were no suspects. Detectives Davidson and Wilkes now worked the case when they had time between new cases, but it had basically gone cold. At that time, the Phelps murder was the only unsolved murder in La Jolla in the last forty years. The article said Mrs. Phelps had recently moved to Northern California. The daughter's whereabouts were unknown.

Neither article mentioned my father or the first officer on the scene. That made a total of seven articles in three newspapers that hadn't mentioned the first cop on the scene, much less list his name.

I put the copied articles back in the folder and set it down on Anton's desk, then looked across at him.

"I called you on the phone yesterday and you guessed correctly that I was interested in the Phelps murder. You implied that my father had some connection to the investigation. But he's not mentioned in any of your articles or anyone else's." The years of mistrust and mystery about my father crept up along my spine and down into my hands, balling them into fists. I leaned toward Anton. "What kind of game are you playing, Anton? Somebody put you up to this?"

"Settle down, son." Anton put up his hands. "You can flip to scary in a blink, just like your old man."

I'd only seen scary in my father the last nine years of his life. Never while he worked as a cop.

"You don't know anything about my father. He's not even in your articles."

"I did know your father, Rick." Anton put his hands down on the desk. "Both before and after."

"Before and after what?" But I knew what he meant.

"When he was a cop and after he wasn't anymore."

"Let's start with how the hell he's connected to the Phelps murder and then we can walk down your memory lane." I sat back and let my fingers unfold. "Was he first on the scene of the Phelps murder?"

"I don't know."

"What?" I bit the "T" hard. This was getting old. "Why not? I thought you were a reporter."

"Detective Davidson stated that Officer Reitzmeyer had been first on the scene. However, Detective Wilkes told me a week later that your dad was there first."

"That doesn't make sense. They should have both been there together. They were partners."

"They usually were, but LJPD had had some retirements at that time and was on one of its famous hiring freezes. One partner rotated every month while the other rode with a rookie."

That much seemed true. I remembered the last ride-along I ever took with my father. He'd had a cruiser to himself.

"Why was neither version mentioned in the paper?"

"Detective Davidson always wanted to be the only contact on cases he worked. He didn't like anyone else's name in the paper to confuse matters."

"Well, this matter seemed pretty confused already. What about freedom of the press? Why didn't you print it anyway?"

"Davidson would have frozen me out. Things were different back then."

"What's so important about the case regarding my father besides two detectives confused about which patrolmen arrived first on the scene?"

Anton picked up a small notepad off the desk that had been next to the Phelps folder. The notepad was similar to the one that I always carry with me when I work a case. The one I had in my back pocket right then, but had not yet pulled out to take notes.

"Hear me out and I think you'll understand." Anton opened his notebook, flipped over a few pages, then appeared to read some notes. "I had a police scanner on in my car twenty-four seven back then. I'd listen to it instead of the radio. That was back when newspapers produced their own content instead of getting everything off the wire services like they do now." Anton shook his head. "Or from Twitter. Anyway, Barbara and I were going through a rough patch back then, so I'd gone to a movie alone at the Cove Theater in La Jolla, after interviewing the LJPD Chief of Police about the growing drug problem in La Jolla. You remember the Cove Theater?"

"Sure. I went to movies there as a kid."

"Yeah. A grand old theater." Anton leaned back in his chair as he went back in time.

"And?"

"Right. I was on the 5 going south to the I-8 when I hear a call go over the scanner for a possible fatal car accident on Coast Boulevard. I was twenty minutes away and I needed a story because La Jolla Police Chief Edwards hadn't given me anything I could work with. So, I headed back up the 5 to La Jolla. I got there right before Detective Davidson did and was the first reporter on the scene."

"You mean Detectives Davidson and Wilkes, right?"

"No. Wilkes was already there. Davidson got there about five minutes after me."

"They were on call at their homes and not rotating out of the Brick House that night?"

"The Brick House, huh? You are Charlie Cahill's son." Anton smiled briefly then went back to reporter face. He scanned his notepad. "Davidson was taking a paid day off. Even though they worked Robbery/Homicide, this was La Jolla and you didn't have too much of Robbery or Homicide back then. One detective could usually handle working on his own from the office."

"Except for that night."

"Right. Anyway, Davidson came from his home and took over lead on the investigation. He was always lead. Wilkes just put up with it instead of making waves."

"My father?"

"I got an anonymous call the day after the accident. A kid down on the beach heard the car crash and later saw the first policeman on the scene take something out of the passenger side of the car and put it in his jacket pocket before the other policeman arrived."

The first policeman on the scene. According to Detective Davidson, Bob Reitzmeyer. According to Detective Wilkes, my father. Wilkes had gotten to the scene before Davidson. His information should be more accurate.

What had my father taken out of the car? The murder weapon and the shell casings. Then he stashed them in a safe deposit box and a hidden safe at home along with fifteen grand in hundred-dollars bills.

Could Wilkes have been wrong and Reitzmeyer had actually been first on the scene? My late father or my former boss and mentor.

"Did you get a description of what the cop looked like? Or what he took out of the car?" My father was three inches taller and thinner than Bob Reitzmeyer. A difficult distinction to discern at night.

"No. It was dark. All the caller could see was that the man wore a uniform and that he reached into the car and put something in his pocket."

"Why the hell wasn't this phone call in your follow-up article?" Anger crept up the back of my neck. "Did you tell Davidson about it?"

"I couldn't put it in the article because the anonymous caller wouldn't come forward. He was a sixteen-year-old kid who was smoking weed down on the beach when he was supposed to be babysitting his twelve-year-old sister."

"He seemed to tell you a hell of a lot about his life. Didn't you get a name and follow up? Why not print it as an anonymous lead?"

"That's not how things worked back then. Maybe now, but not then. It would have never gotten past the editor. And the kid never gave me his name." Anton shifted in his chair.

"What did Detective Davidson say about it when you asked him?"

"That wasn't the kind of thing you could go to Davidson with. He'd say you were trying to make cops look bad and blackball you."

"You certainly were a timid reporter." I threw my hand at the wall. "How did you get all these awards being such a pushover? Are they all for friendliest reporter?"

"I earned every one of those with damn good investigative reporting." Anton squeezed his hands together and his cheeks went rosy. "If I was a get-along kind of reporter, I might still be working at the paper."

"Then why didn't you tell Davidson about the call?"

"I told Wilkes about it instead of Davidson because I knew where to go to get answers." He let go a long breath and released his hands. "Wilkes pretended that Davidson big-footing all the leads on cases didn't bother him. He was the first black homicide detective in LJPD history and didn't want to make waves. But down deep, Wilkes resented the hell out of Davidson. When I told Wilkes about the anonymous call, he told me that your father had been first on the scene. Wilkes heard the call come into dispatch at the Brick House and decided a fatal car crash was better than sitting on his ass at the station. Your father was already there."

"What did he say when you told him about my father supposedly taking something out of the car?"

"He said the kid must have been stoned out of his mind, because Charlie Cahill was the straightest cop on the job. The best, too. That's the way I'd always seen your father, as well. Rock solid."

"This is a lot of smoke for nothing, Mr. Anton. What the hell does some kid's made-up story have to do with my father?"

"Because two months later, the best cop on LJPD, Mr. Rock Solid, was tainted with a story of mob connections that no one would deny, on or off the record. Four months after that he retired short of his full benefits."

"He didn't get any benefits." That much of my father's story I knew. I worked in Muldoon's every summer to help pay the family bills.

"Yeah. I heard the rumor that your father hadn't gotten any benefits, but no one would ever confirm that either. The official story was that he'd retired eight years short of receiving his full benefits. I guess that meant no benefits at all."

"That's what it meant." I scribbled down a summary of what Anton had told me so far on my notepad. "So, you think the Phelps murder was the beginning of my father's downfall?"

"I'd bet this house on it."

"Did you investigate the mob angle about my father? How come there was never anything about it in the paper? I thought that's the kind of shit the press eats up. The fall from grace of a once proud police officer. And don't give me that bullshit about how things were different back then. The press has been tearing people down for hundreds of years."

"That's not how I see my job, son." The red face and the gripped chair arms came back. "My job is to report the facts. Facts that can be verified. Not cheap innuendo. I investigated the facts around your father's retirement and couldn't verify anything other than what the

LJPD hierarchy doled out. Other assignments came up, and I had to put your father on the back burner."

"The stories I heard on school playgrounds as a kid about my dad being a bagman for the mob, where did they come from? Ten-year-old kids aren't smart enough to make that shit up out of thin air. They had to have heard them from their parents, and their parents had to have heard them from somebody close to LJPD."

Anton exhaled and relaxed his grip on his chair. My insults of him and his profession must have taken a backseat to the thought of a kid growing up hearing cruel things said about his father. Everything in my young life took a backseat to that.

"There were leaks coming out of the Brick House. I never printed them, but they made their way around the gossip circles in town. La Jolla was a smaller town back then. Much more insular than it is now."

"Who was leaking?"

"I got it as secondhand information. Confirmation only. Nothing for attribution."

"From whom?"

"Son, I wouldn't give up a source then, and I won't now."

"This was thirty years ago, Anton." I stood up, planted my hands on the desk, and leaned forward. "Chances are the person's dead or no longer a cop. You invited me down here to tell me what you knew about the Phelps murder. You just told me the Phelps case was the beginning of my father's downfall. I didn't come here to learn half-truths. I've been living with them my whole life. Who told you about my father being a bagman for the mob?"

Anton rubbed his mouth. I remained standing and leaned harder into my hands.

"His partner. Bob Reitzmeyer."

CHAPTER TWENTY-SEVEN

BOB REITZMEYER? MY father's best friend. The man who saved his life in Vietnam. The only cop from LJPD who showed up at his funeral. The man who'd been my mentor and whom I still respected. Even if he no longer respected me. I didn't believe it. I didn't want to believe it.

"What did he say to you?"

"Just that there was a ledger with payoffs listed to your father and he'd seen it."

So had I. A ledger I'd found in the closet of my father's den the one time I sneaked in there. I didn't know what it was at the time. Just a leather-bound book with dates and dollar amounts listed. I was nine or ten years old. It wasn't until I was older that I figured out what it was. But still, I'd clung to the hope that there'd been an innocent explanation that I never demanded to hear from my father.

"You got your confirmation. Why didn't you print the story?" I said.

"Reitzmeyer wouldn't go on the record. He said your father had already lost enough."

My father's code, the one I still lived by.

Sometimes you have to do what's right even when the law says it's wrong.

Had he twisted that to cover his own shame? Done errands for the mob and justified his crimes by trying to convince himself that he was just taking care of his family? A father's biological imperative? Had he grabbed the gun and shells from the dead man's car to cover for a mob hit?

The blood receded from my head. Cold sweat blotted my forehead. My mouth sucked dry. My breaths, quick and shallow. The rumors I'd avoided my whole life, and held out a sliver of hope that they were lies, were true. The man I worshiped as a kid, loved more than any person in my life but my late wife, even now, was a criminal.

The truths I'd built my whole life around were lies.

I stood up and lurched around Anton's desk, hunched over, grabbed his wastebasket, and retched into it.

Again.

"Son? Are you okay?" I felt Anton's hand on my back.

I held the wastebasket close to my face, unable to control my heaving body. The stench of hot bile assaulted my nose. The rot I'd held in all my life exposed to the air. My teens. College. Two and a half years on the Santa Barbara Police Force. My life at Muldoon's. Working for Reitzmeyer. Now, on my own. The shame of my father, the truth of my blood, had churned unseen inside me waiting for the one remaining strand of childlike belief to break.

Today it did.

I straightened up and kept the trash can at my waist.

"Sorry."

"It's okay, son." Anton put his hand down to his side, not sure what to do. Probably the first time someone had puked in his trash can.

"Be right back."

I whipped open the office door and went into the bathroom next door down the hall. I turned on the cold water in the sink and rinsed my mouth out. Over and over. Then I cupped water in both hands and splashed it onto my face. The color came back and my breaths were deeper.

Luckily, the wastebasket had been empty before I tried to fill it up. I ran a little water into it from the faucet, then flushed the contents down the toilet. Five more rinses and I got rid of the smell.

Barbara Anton's voice greeted me from the kitchen when I exited the bathroom.

"Lunch will be ready in five minutes!"

Anton was seated back behind his desk when I reentered his office. I set the trash can down in its spot.

"Sorry about that. Breakfast didn't sit well with me. Probably should skip lunch." I pointed at the trashcan. "I washed it out. It doesn't smell."

"Don't worry about it, son. Sit back down."

"I think I got what I needed. I'm going to head out. Thanks. Please apologize to your wife for me."

My father had taken evidence from the scene of a murder to cover for the mob. The fifteen grand was probably payment. Maybe he'd never spent the money because the reality of who he'd become finally caught up with him when he'd gotten kicked off the force. Maybe he thought spending the money would have been the ultimate betrayal after LJPD didn't arrest him. Maybe he kept the gun and the shells to convince himself that someday he'd do the right thing and give the evidence to the police. When he sobered up. Of course, he never did.

Now he'd left the evidence to me. What was I supposed to do with it? Give it to the police so they could prove what I'd already proven to myself? My father was a criminal. Maybe they could finally close the twenty-eight-year-old cold case. Trent Phelps owned some laundromats. A business with large amounts of cash. The mob has used laundromats for years to clean things other than clothes. Money. The cash goes in dirty and comes out clean in the form of profits. Phelps was probably skimming off the top and got caught. Mob justice. Society still had the right to dole out its own justice. I guess that meant I'd call someone down at the Brick House and tell them about the evidence.

Sometimes you have to do what's right even when the law says it's *right*.

"Just sit down and hear me out for a couple minutes." Anton pushed a hand toward the empty chair.

Anton had more to tell. I'd already puked in his wastebasket. I guess I owed him an ear for a few more minutes. I sat down.

"Like I told you earlier, I knew your father before and after all this. I knew what kind of a man he was."

"So did Bob Reitzmeyer. He knew my father better than you, better than my mother, better than me. He gave you your confirmation. You going to tell me now that you don't believe it?"

"I'm not sure what I believe, but Charlie Cahill's story has followed me around for the last three decades. I pull out the old articles and my notes and read through them every couple years. I've never been able to quite believe your father would betray all he believed in for a few pieces of silver. When you called yesterday, I thought now would be a good time to look over everything again. This time with a partner."

"Sorry, Anton. Your notes and articles tell the whole story. My father did sell his soul for the few pieces of silver, got caught, then dealt with his Judas guilt by living inside a bottle until the booze and the guilt killed him. That's your story. Just another fall from grace. Nothing special about it. Write the story if you want. I don't care. Just don't make my father out to be a hero. Only a ten-year-old kid would believe that."

"Think it all the way through." Anton leaned into his desk, his hands agitated. "Your father died a poor man. If the mob had been paying him off, where was the money?"

Fifteen grand of it had been in a safe hidden in a wall. But that would remain my secret until I shared it with the police and no one else.

"After he was kicked off LJPD he didn't have any more value to the mob." Or anyone else. "Why would they continue to pay someone who could no longer give them anything of value?"

"Still, there had to have been some evidence of the extra money you saw as a kid. An expensive new car, a boat, a vacation home. Something. The Charlie Cahill I knew never showed anything but a solid middle-class guy. Does anything from your childhood stick out in your mind?"

"No." Except for the fifteen grand. "That doesn't mean he didn't have it stashed away somewhere or spend it some way other than on his family."

Like on another woman. Antoinette King. The woman who, eighteen years after my father's death, was still paying the maintenance on a safe deposit box in my father's name. I wondered how much mob money she siphoned off while my father was alive.

"You think he gambled?" Anton asked.

"I don't know. There's a lot about my father I never knew." I ran a hand through my hair and let go a breath. "Thank you for showing me the old articles and sharing your notes. I appreciate your trying to defend my father. I spent most of my life doing the same thing. Even to myself. But I got what I came for. Maybe not what I wanted, but what I needed. If there's a way for me to do you a favor sometime, let me know."

A knock on the office door. "Lunch is ready, boys."

"Your stomach still bothering you, son?" Anton gave me sad eyes. "My wife went to a lot of trouble today to make us a nice lunch."

After emptying its contents, my stomach now had a void. My nausea had passed after I accepted the truth about my father. I was suddenly hungry. To fill the void. And to start a new life now that I finally knew the truth about an old one.

I stood up. "Let's eat."

* * *

I got onto I-8 and headed west toward the 805. Barbara Anton had sent me home with a tub of the best tomato soup I'd ever tasted and Jack had slipped a file under my arm containing copies of the old newspaper articles and his typed notes. I planned to eat the soup for dinner. I didn't have any plans for the file. I'd already gotten the confirmation I needed from Anton, just as he had from Bob Reitzmeyer. Only, Anton wouldn't take it for the truth it was. He still held out hope that my father had somehow remained the man everyone thought he was. I didn't. Of course, I had more information.

Hope can be a dangerous thing. It gives you an excuse not to see the truth. Without the truth, life's a lie. I'd lived a lie long enough, even as I'd claimed the truth as my life's mission years ago.

I had one truth now, my father's. I owed it to Trent Phelps' family and the police to help them find their own truth.

I pulled out my phone and hit the phone number for LJPD.

CHAPTER TWENTY-EIGHT

"Detective Sheets, please." I'd left Sheets' business card with his direct number at home before I visited Jack Anton, so I called LJPD's main phone number.

"Who may I say is calling?" A woman's voice.

"Rick Cahill."

"And what is this regarding, Mr. Cahill?"

"I'll tell Detective Sheets what it's regarding when he answers the phone." No need to broadcast my father's involvement until I talked to Sheets.

"Humph." I made another friend at LJPD. I heard the click of my call being transferred.

I only knew one other homicide detective down at the Brick House. Detective Denton. A disciple of former police chief Tony Moretti, who was now a congressman in Washington, DC, Denton hated me almost as much as her old boss had. Sheets would be busy with the Sophia Domingo murder, but I figured he'd take what I had to give him on my father and add it to the cold case file they had on Trent Phelps. LJPD was too small to have a team of detectives dedicated to cold cases, but they didn't have many unsolved murders anyway. Sheets or some other detective would get to the Phelps case after he arrested the murderer of Sophia. And I could clear my conscience, if not my father's name.

Hopefully, whoever Sheets arrested for Sophia's murder wouldn't be anyone I knew. Unless it was Peter Stone.

"Detective Denton." Same matter-of-fact voice I'd heard two years ago.

Shit. I didn't say anything and was about to hang up.

"Cahill?"

The operator must have given my name to Denton when she picked up Sheets' phone.

"Hello, Detective Denton. I was trying to get through to Detective Sheets."

"He's out of the office. I'm his partner." She hit the "P" in partner hard. "Whatever you were going to tell him, you can tell me. Is this about the Domingo homicide investigation that you're right in the middle of?"

Sheets had obviously gotten her up to speed. I doubt he had me "right in the middle" of the investigation, but Denton would love to put me there. They had a hard time moving on down at the Brick House. They carried grudges like they were skin rashes. Always ready to flare up with just the slightest scratch. Chief Moretti may have left for a larger throne, but his attitude remained.

Or maybe it was just me.

"I'm not in the middle of anything, Detective Denton. I wanted to talk to Detective Sheets about something that has nothing to do with the Domingo murder."

"What is it concerning?"

I wanted to give the police the evidence my father had hidden away decades ago and move on with my life. But I was still in neutral. Giving the evidence to Denton would be like giving it to Moretti.

Ammunition to prove that my father was dirty and, thus, I was dirty by blood. Just like they'd always believed.

"It can wait."

"Are you withholding evidence in a murder investigation, Cahill?"

"No." Probably. Just not the investigation she and Sheets were investigating. "I'll talk to Sheets another time."

"You're risking being charged with obstruction of justice."

"Get back on the leash, Denton. Moretti's not around to try to impress anymore." I hung up. A mistake. Maybe. But Denton hated me whether I played nice or not. Besides, my way was much more fulfilling. For a while.

I probably should have waited a bit to call Sheets anyway. He had plenty on his plate and the Phelps case had been cold for twenty-eight years. I was the only one trying to warm it up. And that was just because I was in a hurry to clear my conscience and get on with my life. My lateral progression could wait a few more weeks.

CHAPTER TWENTY-NINE

MIDNIGHT GREETED ME at the front door. He did the dance in place like I owed him another trip to Fiesta Island. A couple hours there would do us both some good. Me as much as him. I walked over to the sliding glass door and let him outside for now. I went into the kitchen and put the tub of Barbara Anton's tomato soup in the refrigerator. I pulled out Jack Anton's file on the Phelps murder from under my arm and thought about tossing it into the trash. What more was there to learn? My father's criminality was now confirmed. I didn't need Anton's file lying around as a constant reminder.

I set the file down on the kitchen table and opened it. One look before the trash. I'd already read the newspaper articles. They hadn't produced anything different from what I already knew. I put the articles aside to throw away after I read the notes Anton had slipped into the file. He'd read me his notes on the stoner kid seeing a cop take something out of the car at the accident scene, but the file contained dozens of pages of other notes.

Most of the notes were later cleaned up and printed in the newspaper articles. I read the ones Anton had written about Trent Phelps' journey the night of his death. The manager at his laundromat on Grand Avenue in Pacific Beach had said he left at 9:15 p.m. to go to

his La Jolla store located on Pearl Street. I remembered that laundromat. A few buddies and I had gotten drunk a couple times when we
were in high school and taken turns seeing how long we could cycle
in the dryers. I won. I won a lot of stupid competitions back then.
Anything to keep me from going home and listening to my parents
fight. The laundromat was long gone now.

Anton's notes said the first call to LJPD reporting the accident
on Coast Boulevard was at 9:57 p.m. Presumably, the accident had
been reported within a minute or two from the time it occurred. The
accident must have happened around 9:55 p.m., forty minutes after
Phelps' PB manager said he left for La Jolla. Even with traffic, which
wouldn't have been stop and go, the drive wouldn't have taken more
than twenty minutes. Really closer to ten or fifteen.

But why had Phelps even been on Coast Boulevard? The quick-
est way to the laundromat would have been via La Jolla Boulevard to
Pearl Street. Coast was out of the way, in the opposite direction of
Pearl. Maybe Phelps went for a drive by the ocean after he stopped by
the laundromat. I scanned Anton's notes. The manager at the Pearl
location said Phelps never arrived at the laundromat that night. He
could have made the drive by the beach before he planned to go to
the laundromat.

No way of knowing. Probably didn't mean anything, but it twitched
along the back of my neck nonetheless. I sat back in the kitchen chair
and looked at Midnight through the paneled glass of the door to the
backyard. He looked at me. Fiesta Island on both our minds.

I looked back down at Jack Anton's notes from the night he claimed
everything started going wrong for my father. I'd become convinced
the downward slide had been my father's own doing. Anton wasn't
sure. What did he see that I didn't? We'd both believed my father had
once been an inherently good man. Somewhere along the way, he'd
made choices that he couldn't unmake, which had sent him spiraling

downward. It was there in Anton's notes and in my father's secret safe and safe deposit box. Anton didn't know about the safe and safe deposit box. Would he still hold out hope for my father's goodness if he did? Had he learned things about my father over sipping scotch that told him Charlie Cahill couldn't be tainted under any circumstances? Even if the proof was right in Anton's own notes?

I'd never sipped scotch with my father. He'd stopped sipping and started chugging the cheap stuff by the time I began paying attention. But I still owed the man I'd once so admired who'd broken my soul a deeper look into the night that changed his life irreparably. And my family's.

Fiesta Island would have to wait.

I read through the notes that were for the article a week after the murder and those for the one-year anniversary piece. The last couple pages of notes were paper clipped together and had a yellow sticky attached to the top page with Charlie Cahill written on it. According to the notes, Anton and my father met for drinks at the Whaling Bar in La Jolla on October 22, 1990. The bar used to be attached to the La Valencia Hotel, the grand dame of old money hotels in La Jolla. An overnight stay there cost a Bill Gates inheritance. The Whaling Bar, which had a mural of a whale hunt over the bar, was much more accessible than its big sister hotel. It had since closed and been remodeled into an upscale French bistro. Because La Jolla didn't already have enough of those.

Raymond Chandler and Gregory Peck were among the locals known to drink at the Whaling Bar.

And apparently, years later, my father and Jack Anton did, too. According to the notes, Anton had asked my father out for drinks to talk about the cold Phelps case. The date was eleven months after the Phelps murder. The notes said my father was working as a security guard for a strip mall in La Jolla at the time.

I remembered seeing him leave for work at night in a blue uniform. Only this one said security on it instead of La Jolla Police Department. He always had a frown on his face when he left for work instead of the smile I remembered seeing when he left for his job as a cop.

The notes were in the form of a conversation, so Anton must have audio-recorded them. He probably edited while he transcribed them because the conversation jumped right in without any preamble or hellos.

"Did Detective Wilkes ever tell you that I told him I received an anonymous call two days after the murder stating that the caller saw a police officer take something out of the front seat of the car and put it in his coat pocket?" Anton asked.

"No. But whoever told you that was lying."

"Were you first on the scene?"

Cahill stared at me, then took a long sip of his scotch and said, "Whatever the police report said."

"I never saw a police report. The Brick House won't release it because the case is still open.

"Davidson said that Reitzmeyer was first on the scene, but Detective Wilkes told me off the record that you were."

"Don't believe what everybody tells you. You can get into trouble that way," Cahill said.

"Are you telling me that Wilkes was lying and that Reitzmeyer was first on the scene?"

"I'm telling you that you can't always believe what people tell you, anonymous or otherwise. Thanks for the drink. Good luck with your story."

"Let me buy another round."

"Okay, I'll go one more. I'm sure the love of my life can bear to be without me another half hour or so."

I remembered my mother screaming at my father almost every night about coming home late with alcohol on his breath. He came home late a lot the first year after he lost his job at LJPD. Even when he wasn't working security at a strip mall. After two years, my mother stopped caring and locked herself in what had once been my parents' bedroom. The room where I used to play with my toy train while they tried to sleep in on Saturday mornings. Dad would crawl out of bed and sit down on the floor and play with me and Mom would laugh at us both.

I outgrew the train and my parents grew apart. And shouting took the place of laughter.

"Are you surprised that LJPD seemed to lose interest in the Phelps murder fairly quickly?"

"That seems a little editorial for a reporter. Did you ask Detective Davidson that?"

"Not in so many words. This whole conversation is off the record, Charlie, just like I told you earlier. No attributions go into the article unless you want them to. Why do you think LJPD stopped working the case?"

"I don't know. I wasn't around very much longer."

"What really happened with your retirement? I don't believe the rumors that you had some connection to organized crime. That's not the Charlie Cahill I know. You were the best beat cop they ever had down at the Brick House. What happened? Why didn't you fight for your job?"

"Just because you don't believe the rumors doesn't mean you have to believe the myth. Good-bye, Jack."

"Charlie, tell me the whole story. I'll get it on the front page of the paper and you'll be able to clear your name and get your reputation back."

"Talk to Judas about my reputation. He sold it for thirty pieces of silver."

"What do you mean?"

Cahill left without responding.

Judas? He must have meant Bob Reitzmeyer who'd spread the rumors of my father's fall from grace to Anton. But my father had gotten it wrong, he'd taken the thirty pieces of silver for himself and left it in his hidden safe.

The last page of Anton's notes looked to be a summary, possibly written up just recently for me. Anton said he never talked to my father again, despite him calling and leaving numerous messages. He said he attended my father's funeral and was saddened that the only cop or ex-cop there was Bob Reitzmeyer.

That's why Anton looked familiar to me. I didn't remember him from the funeral, but I must have seen him there and my mind imprinted his image without knowing what to do with it. I wasn't surprised I didn't remember Anton. The funeral was eighteen years ago, and I spent most of it staring at the ground. A priest said a few words, but no one else spoke for my father.

Not my mother. Not Bob Reitzmeyer. Not me.

We just put him in the ground and laid a plaque over him:

Charles Henry Cahill
Husband, Father, Veteran
Dec. 6, 1945–Oct. 3, 1999

Husband. Father. Veteran. That would be enough for most men. But my father had been so much more for most of his life. He'd been a cop for twenty-two years. The best cop anyone had ever known until the truth came out. The truth that Jack Anton refused to believe, but for which I had proof. The gun and the empty shell casings that he'd taken from Trent Phelps' car the night of the murder. Protecting the mob killer and getting fifteen grand in return. He never spent that money, but what about the other money I'd seen listed in the ledger I found in his den as a kid?

How long had he been on the take? When did he transform from the best man most people ever knew into the scumbag he became? A cop on the take. Did it start with one bad decision or had he always had a dark soul that he'd kept hidden from everyone? Even those who loved him most and knew him best.

Jack Anton's notes hadn't provided that answer. Maybe his old partner would.

CHAPTER THIRTY

BOB REITZMEYER DIDN'T return my call at nine o'clock the next morning. Or the one at ten thirty. I set him aside and took Midnight to Fiesta Island. A bonus for him. Twice in one week. The sun pushed through the last bit of marine layer and washed the bay in orange and blue. Midnight hurtled himself into the water after the ball and paddled it back to shore. Over and over. He chased dogs up and down the beach, unfettered joy in his eyes and dangling tongue under a California sun in America's Finest City.

I tried to get lost in that joy. Too hard. Forcing it didn't give me the relief, the decompression I'd hoped for. Too much had happened in the last few days. The tension pressed tighter. Sophia Domingo's murder, Kim's recommitment to her husband, the proof of my father's sins. They all wound together into a tight ball at the base of my neck. Fiesta Island was Midnight's sanctuary, but it would take a Swedish masseuse, an acupuncturist, and a fifth of whiskey to relieve the knot my body had become. Or, a different life.

I warmed up Barbara Anton's soup after I returned from Fiesta Island. Midnight fell asleep at my feet while I sipped the soup, his legs reenacting his runs on the beach as he slept. The soup did its best to relieve the knot. Creamy, sweet, herbaceous. On most any other day, it and Fiesta Island would have eased me out. Not today. Not this week.

I called Reitzmeyer at two. He wouldn't take the call. I couldn't wait on him all day. Sitting still made me think. I didn't want to think. I needed movement, action. Not thought.

Retired La Jolla PD Detective Ben Davidson lived in a rural area in the southeasternmost part of Poway just off Scripps Poway Parkway and Highway 67. Davidson's house sat on a rocky bluff with no neighbor within ten acres. The house itself was modern and probably around thirty-five hundred square feet. Not huge, but not small for a retired ex-cop with no wife and no children in the home. The house had a three-car garage. No cars were in the driveway.

I hadn't called ahead because I didn't want to run into Davidson's gatekeeper again. Unless Davidson's car was in the garage, it looked like my gamble hadn't paid off. I parked in the middle of the horseshoe driveway across from the front door.

I rang the doorbell and waited. No one came to the door. No movement that I could discern from inside the house. I'd heard the doorbell, so I knew it worked. I rang it again and knocked three times loudly and waited some more. No one. I went back to my car and opened the door just as the door to the house opened. An elderly man stood hunched over a wheeled walker.

"Are you here to try to sell me something?" The man's voice quavered and his mouth fell open when he was done speaking.

"Are you Ben Davidson?"

"Who else would I be?"

I closed the car door and walked back to the house. The man was emaciated, but nicely dressed in slacks and a button-down sweater that were both a couple sizes too large. Gray wisps of hair crisscrossed his mostly bald head. The years had eaten away at Ben Davidson. I didn't recognize any portion of the stout beer-bellied man I'd met at the La Jolla Police Station almost thirty years ago.

"I'd like to talk to you about my father."

"Is he Jesus Christ?" Davidson showed me yellow teeth in an opened-mouth smirk. "You gonna try and sell me some religion? You're a little late."

"No. My father was Charlie Cahill. He worked at LJPD while you were there."

"Charlie Cahill?" He straightened up a bit, but still steadied himself with the walker. "I haven't thought of that poor schmuck in years."

"He's been dead for almost two decades. I just want to ask you a few questions about him." I put out my hand. "I'm Rick Cahill."

"Yes, yes. Rick Cahill." He gave my hand one weak shake then dropped it. "I remember reading about you. They said you murdered your wife. That's the last time I thought about Charlie. Reading about you made me think of him. I guess he wasn't any better at being a father than he was a cop."

My blood rose and percolated under my skin. The blood my father gave me. I let it simmer. At least Davidson was talking and without his gatekeeper.

"Maybe we could go inside and you could explain to me why he was a bad cop."

"I guess they couldn't prove it."

"Prove what?"

"That you murdered your wife. Or else you'd be in prison."

"I didn't kill her. That's why I'm not in prison." I smiled. One ex-cop to another. "Now, are you going to invite me in?"

"Sure, sure." He took a couple backward steps from the door holding onto the walker. "Won't be the first time I've sat across from a murderer."

He was enjoying himself. That made one of us.

I walked inside, closed the door behind me, and followed Davidson down a dark slate-tiled hall. He was unsteady on the walker, but kept up a quick pace. Living dangerously above a hard, hip-breaking floor.

He led me into a living room with the view of a pool outside and a rocky hillside beyond. Davidson dropped down into a white wing-backed upholstered chair. A photo of a middle-aged couple sat on a side table next to his chair. The woman bore a resemblance to Davidson in the eyes. Cold. I sat across from Davidson in his chair's twin.

"Now, what would you like to know about your father?"

"How well did you know him?"

"I knew him as well as anyone else at the Brick House." He shifted his weight and winced. "I made Homicide Detective, and he didn't get past patrolman after twenty years on the job, but I knew him. LJPD was a small force, just like it is today. You couldn't hide your true self from men who were trained to uncover secrets."

"What was my father's true self?"

"Don't you already know that, son? Your father thought of himself as high and mighty, but he was just as corrupt as every . . . as a common criminal."

"Just as corrupt as everybody else? Is that what you meant to say?"

"Don't go putting words into my mouth, boy." He gave me a look that had probably been nasty enough to put a scare into someone under the white lights in an interrogation room twenty years ago. "Just as corrupt as every criminal I put behind bars in my thirty-year career. The brass at the Brick House didn't have the stones to arrest him for being on the take. They made your father the poster boy of LJPD for years, so when the truth came out they kept everything quiet to avoid a public relations nightmare."

"And that truth was?"

"Your father did favors for what was left of the Italian Mob in La Jolla and San Diego back then. He looked the other way here, covered something up there. Whatever they needed."

"Do you have proof for any of this?"

"I know your father kept a ledger of his payoffs."

"Did you ever see it? How do you know he wasn't collecting evidence on someone else?"

"I have it on good authority." Davidson's face flushed pink. "Did you come here to learn the truth or argue against it?"

"The truth. But I haven't heard anything convincing yet."

"How about fifteen grand in a brown paper sack? Is that proof enough for you?"

"You saw it?"

"Hell, yes I saw it." A noise came from the front of the house. "You're going to have to leave now, sonny."

"Pop?" A woman's voice. "Whose car is in the driveway?"

"You better move along." The pink evaporated from Davidson's face and he looked more gaunt than when I arrived. "Gina doesn't like me having visitors."

I stayed seated. A woman clacked down the tile hall toward me. Tall, broad through the shoulders, attractive in a masculine way. The woman in the photo next to Davidson's chair.

"Who are you?" The voice on the phone from the gatekeeper call. She put her hands on her hips and splayed her legs.

"Rick Cahill." I stood up and offered a hand. She ignored it.

"Did you invite him over, Pop?"

"No." Davidson shrunk further into the chair. "He just showed up."

"You're going to have to leave. My father's ill and is not supposed to have visitors."

"Okay. But one last question." I looked down at Davidson. "Why did you put in the police report that Bob Reitzmeyer was first on the Phelps crime scene when it was really my father?"

"Phelps?" Davidson's jaw went slack. "What do you know about Phelps?"

"Am I going to have to call the police, Mr. Cahill?" The daughter pulled a phone from her purse and punched the screen. "I know you have some experience at being arrested."

"Things started going downhill for my father the night he discovered Phelps' body." I kept my eyes on Davidson. "Why?"

"Yes, I'd like to report an unwanted intruder in my father's home." Gina spoke into the phone.

"I'm leaving. We'll talk again, Mr. Davidson." I turned and walked down the hall. The clack-clack of Davidson's daughter behind me.

"He's about six feet tall, two hundred pounds, brown and brown. He's been menacing my father."

I opened the front door.

"Cahill."

I turned to look at Gina. She now had the phone down at her side.

"You got what you wanted. I'm leaving."

"My father is dying of cancer." There was still anger in her eyes, but maybe pain, too. "I can't have people coming by and upsetting him."

"He didn't seem upset until you arrived."

"You can't hurt me any more than my father's illness has. He's lucid now, but he'll have nightmares tonight." Her brown eyes blurred with liquid. "My father deserves to die with dignity."

I left the house and got into my car and thought about my father dying without dignity or anything else he'd earned in his life.

CHAPTER THIRTY-ONE

LA JOLLA INVESTIGATIONS hadn't changed much in the two years since I'd left there. The headquarters was still on the first floor of a ritzy La Jolla law office building. Shiny and sharp-angled copper and bronze. The car in Bob Reitzmeyer's parking spot was still a BMW. Just a newer model than the last one I'd seen there.

The receptionist was new. Blond and pretty like the last receptionist. A prerequisite to work the phones for Bob. She smiled like she meant it. Bob wouldn't when he found out who was in the lobby.

"Rick Cahill for Bob Reitzmeyer."

"Do you have an appointment?" A smile like it was a reasonable question. She'd been answering my calls all day and telling me Bob couldn't talk to me. She knew I didn't have an appointment.

"No, but he'll see me. Just tell him I'm here to talk to him about my father."

She smiled, but with less sincerity, picked up the phone, and told Reitzmeyer I was there to see him. The look on her face said Bob told her he wouldn't see me. I peered over the counter at her office phone and read Speaker upside down below a clear plastic button. I shot my hand over the counter and pushed the button.

"I'm here to talk about my dad. Remember him, Bob? He used to be your best friend."

The line clicked to a dial tone.

"You're going to have to leave, sir." The receptionist's face flushed an angry red. "You can't interrupt a call like that. Please leave or I'll call security."

"You're right. I apologize. You can call security, but Bob will be out here in a few seconds to personally escort me to his office."

She picked up the phone's handset again just as Bob appeared in the lobby. A little grayer than the last time I'd seen him, and his face redder than I've ever seen it.

"What do you want, Rick?" He strode across the lobby, his teeth clinched in a snarl.

"Should I call security, Mr. Reitzmeyer?" The receptionist had her hand poised over the keypad.

"Not yet, Eva." He put a hand in her direction and stared me down through blue eyes. "Well, Rick?"

"Let's go back to your office and talk about my father."

"What about your father?"

"About his last few months at the Brick House. You want me to hang a line for the laundry out here or do you want to talk in your office?"

He glared at me some more and pinched his lips. Then he turned and started down the hall to his office. A few heads prairie-dogged over the cubicles where investigators used office computers to access the investigative websites I now have to pay for a la carte. I recognized one of the faces eyeing me suspiciously. I nodded. The face frowned and slipped down below the gray wall of the cubicle. I hadn't made too many friends in my two years at LJI.

I followed Bob into his pebbled-glass office. He thumped the door shut behind me, then went and stood behind his desk. His face still red, a stark contrast to the gray Van Dyke anchoring his chin.

"You're lucky I didn't have security throw you out on your ass. Is this how you operate on your own? Bursting into people's workplaces and interrupting private phone conversations?"

"When I have to."

"It won't get you very far, Rick."

"It got me into your office."

"Your father's memory got you in here. Just like it got you the job here in the first place. And then you fucked that up."

I was way past insults. You had to break the skin to hurt me now.

"Let's talk about my father's memory."

"What about it?" Reitzmeyer threw up his arms. "What angle are you working now, Rick? What piece of the past do you want to dig up and make another mess of this time?"

The last piece I'd dug up had cost me my job at LJI. And some people their lives.

"When did you know, Bob?"

"Know what?"

"That my father was on the take?"

Reitzmeyer tilted his head and squinted at me. "Is that what this is about? The rumors?"

"Rumors don't start out of thin air. They come out of someone's mouth."

"Wherever they started, they were never proven." Reitzmeyer finally sat down.

I remained standing and noticed all the police and PI commendations on the wall behind Reitzmeyer. My father had had a wall full, too. But he kept his hidden in the den where no one else was allowed. My mother boxed them all up along with the rest of his belongings and was going to give them to Goodwill. I took them instead. In place of the good memories I no longer had. As if the items could fill up the void my father left in my life. The void that started well before his physical death. Beginning nine years before he was kicked off the police force and the man I'd copied my life on died a little, one drink at a time.

I was in college at the time and had no place to put my dad's stuff, so I rented a space at a storage facility that I could barely afford. Years passed, the memories faded, and my dad's belongings became junk no longer worth the monthly rental. I fulfilled my mother's intentions and donated my father's belongings to Goodwill.

The only thing I kept was my dad's LJPD badge. Only because he'd given it to me himself when I was eleven. LJPD hadn't let my father take the badge with him when they pushed him out, but the man sitting across from me had used up favors and gotten it back for my father.

I thought of the badge, Bob and my father's friendship, and where Jack Anton had told me he heard the rumors about my father's fall.

"But you believed the rumors, didn't you, Bob?" I put my hands on his desk and leaned in. "In fact, you helped spread them."

The red splashed back across Reitzmeyer's face. Embarrassment from being called out? Maybe. Anger? Definitely.

"What the fuck are you talking about?"

I wouldn't give up Anton after he and his wife invited me into their home and fed me. But I'd use his words. If Bob figured out where they came from, I could live with it.

"The ledger with the payoffs listed. You told just enough people that you'd seen it and you were convinced my dad was dirty." Retired LJPD Detective Ben Davidson being among them.

"Who told you that?"

"It doesn't matter. It's been twenty-seven years. My father's dead. Most of the people in La Jolla today have never heard of him. His taint died with him quietly in the dark a long time ago. Nobody knows or cares about it anymore. Not even my mother. My father never existed to her now." I took my hands off the desk and straightened up. "Just you and me. We're the only people who give a shit about the legacy of Charlie Cahill. All I want is to hear the truth come out of your mouth. Just like it did in whispers twenty-seven years ago."

"Your father was a good man, Rick." The red left his face and took some life with it.

"Was. I know. But he didn't die that way. He died a broken man who'd taken money from the people he was supposed to protect the rest of us from. I just want to know how and when it started. Who showed you the ledger?"

"I found it myself." Reitzmeyer let out a breath. "We were riding together and had just finished grabbing lunch. Your father was still inside the restaurant using the john. I went out to grab a quick smoke, so I looked for cigarettes in your father's duffel bag in the trunk of our cruiser. I found a little brown notebook in there. I opened it. I thought maybe your father was trying to be the next Joseph Wambaugh and writing notes about the job. He was a literary guy. The smartest, most well-read cop I ever knew. I wanted to read his notes so I could needle him. Then I saw the dates and the dollar amounts and the street names—Grand Avenue, Cass Street, Turquoise Street, Pearl Street, Genesee Avenue—in your father's handwriting."

I remembered seeing the boxy letters when I'd found the ledger in my father's den. I didn't know what it was then, but I'd recognized my father's handwriting.

"Couldn't he have been keeping records on someone else?" A reflexive vestige of hope that I no longer believed.

"I wish, Rick. I wished that then and I wish it now," Reitzmeyer said, his head down. "All the dates with dollar amounts next to them were shifts when your father was alone driving an L car and I had a boot riding with me."

"So, the ledger had dollar amounts only on days when my father was working shifts alone?"

"Right."

"How far did the dates go back?"

"I don't remember."

"Did you find the ledger before or after the Phelps murder?" I asked.

"Phelps? What the hell does Phelps have to do with anything?"

"Because my father was pushed out of the Brick House within six months of him rolling first on the scene of that murder."

"I don't remember exactly when I found the ledger." Reitzmeyer straightened up in his chair. "How the hell did you come across Phelps?"

I thought about telling him the truth. Bob and I were close once. He'd been a mentor and a man I respected more than any other alive. Our rift was over an old case from LJPD. Nothing else. I'd lost some respect for him, and he'd probably never trust me again. But the actions we'd both taken had lived up to my father's credo. We both did what we thought was right even though the law said it was wrong. Just different actions at different times. I wanted to tell Bob about the gun. I wanted to tell someone. Holding it in, being the only person alive who knew my father probably had concealed the murder weapon used in an unsolved murder made me feel dirty. Guilty. A coconspirator.

My father's son.

"By accident." Trust ran both ways. Reitzmeyer and my father were like brothers. Maybe he already knew Charlie had taken the gun from the car. Maybe I wasn't the only coconspirator. "It got me interested, though, and I did some research. An unsolved murder that LJPD thinks is mob related and six months later my father is exposed as a bagman for the mob. Seems a little coincidental, doesn't it?"

"Not unless you're looking for conspiracies that aren't there." Bob rubbed his hand over his Van Dyke. "Your father was the godfather to every one of my children and the best man at two of my weddings. He took me under his wing when I was an eighteen-year-old kid in Vietnam and became a big brother to me. I joined LJPD because of him. I loved him. I still do. But somewhere along the way, he took a wrong turn. I doubt it had anything to do with Phelps. It doesn't matter now. It's done. Charlie's gone."

I couldn't argue a single point, but I still wanted answers.

"Charlie was first on the scene at the Phelps murder, right?"

"I think so." Bob shrugged. "What does it matter?"

"I'm not sure." Except that it verified that my father had been the cop the anonymous caller saw take something from the crime scene. Probably the murder weapon.

"Did LJPD ever find the murder weapon?"

"Not that I know of."

"Twenty-five caliber handgun, right?"

"I think so." Bob squeezed his eyes down on me. "Why?"

"I've just been reading old newspaper articles on the case. Just trying to get the facts right."

"The Phelps murder doesn't have anything to do with what happened to your father." Reitzmeyer put his hands together on the desk. "I know you're searching for answers. Sometimes there just aren't any. Your father was a good man who went bad. We'll never know why, but down deep you know it's true."

Maybe Bob didn't have to know why, but I did. And I needed to know who my father was protecting when he took the murder weapon from the crime scene.

I turned to leave, but thought of something. "Do you know a woman named Antoinette King?"

"No." No blinks. No obvious deception. "Why?"

"Just a name I came across in some of his old things." Reitzmeyer didn't need to know about the joint checking account that funded my father's safe deposit box at Windsor Bank and Trust. I didn't think he was lying about Antoinette King. But maybe he just didn't know her name.

"What about other women?"

"What about them?"

"We've established that my father was a crooked cop. Was he a crooked husband? Did he have women on the side?"

I knew Bob understood all about women on the side. He'd been married and divorced three times. When I worked for him, I'd seen him go off to lunch with his girlfriend and later that evening invite one of the attractive lawyers we shared the building with into his office and close the blinds after hours. More than once.

"Hell, no."

"You don't have to cover for him, Bob. He's dead. It doesn't matter anymore."

"The truth matters, Rick." His blue eyes a stone wall. "Your father went wrong, but not that way."

So my father kept one oath before God. That still left the question of Antoinette King and the joint checking account that funded the safe deposit box with the spent shells.

Maybe I was looking at the Phelps murder from the wrong end.

CHAPTER THIRTY-TWO

DUSK PUSHED TOWARD night as I turned onto my street. I spotted it right away. A Spectrum cable van. Parked in front of my house. I whipped my car into the driveway. Midnight barked from inside the house. I started to walk to the front door when I noticed movement on the right side of the house. A man in a Spectrum work shirt holding a metal clipboard emerged from behind the hedge. My height. Thinner, but fit. Late thirties. All-American good looks. He smiled at me then looked down at his clipboard.

"Mr. Cahill?"

I didn't say anything. My right hand instinctively went to my hip for the Ruger in the pancake holster. I remembered even before I touched my belt that I wasn't wearing it. Investigating a twenty-eight-year-old cold case hadn't called for a gun. Dealing with someone who broke into my house did. I spread my feet a few inches to widen my base.

"You're the next person on my list." He walked toward me. "I was just checking to see if you still had a cable hookup. We'd really like to get you back in the Spectrum family."

"Checking the transmitter?"

"I'm sorry?" He tilted his head like he didn't know what I was talking about. Emmy worthy. He kept walking toward me. "I was checking the cable hookup like I said. We'd really like to get your business back."

"Maybe we can figure it all out after I call the police." An empty threat, but he didn't have to know that. Even though I wasn't working for Stone anymore, I wasn't going to get the police involved.

Never a good idea to poke the bear. Or the great white shark.

"The police?" He stopped in front of me holding his clipboard to the side. No bulge in either pocket. He looked unarmed.

"Yeah. We can wait inside until they get here and then you can explain the listening device on top of my bookshelf and the wireless transmitter you just checked on the side of my house. We can look inside your truck and see if you have cable or surveillance equipment in there."

"I don't understand. Your name's right here on the list of potential customers." He lifted up the clipboard as if to show me. But I was ready.

He swung the clipboard at my face. I blocked the blow with my forearm and shot a straight right to his nose. He staggered backward. Blood trickled from his nose. He threw the clipboard at me and charged in. I ducked the board and caught him with a left hook to the rib cage as his punch glanced off my shoulder. Air and a groan exploded out of him at once. My hand stung. The back door of the van burst open. I spun toward it and caught a fist in the face. Right in the eye socket. Stars. A dark form behind them. I slipped the next punch and fired back a right that caught the man in the ear. Something banged off the back of my head from behind. I stumbled and went down.

I rolled over and saw the black man run around the van to the driver's side and the white one whip open the door and jump into the passenger's seat. The van peeled out and sped down the street, its back door wide open. It disappeared around the corner. I didn't give chase. I'd talk to their boss soon enough.

I rolled onto my back and took a couple deep breaths. My left eye throbbed and poured out a stream of tears. I didn't even try to open it. The back of my head ached. I ran a hand over it and felt a small, mushy lump below the crown. The faux cable man's metal clipboard lay next to me on the ground. It now had a bend in it that would have fit perfectly around my head. He had to choose metal. What was wrong with plastic or even particleboard?

I sat up and everything throbbed harder for a few seconds then settled back into pulsating aches. I scaffolded up to my feet. My cell phone rang in my pocket. I didn't even make the effort to answer it and let it go to voicemail.

Midnight greeted me at the front door. He licked my hand, probably more concerned with the changing color of the skin under my eye than his dinner. But when I filled his bowl, he went right at it.

I grabbed the bag of ice I kept in the freezer for aches and beatings and found the couch. I wished I'd had the foresight to visualize that violence sometimes leaves more than one sore spot and kept two ice bags available. The eye hurt most, but the head was more vital. I held the ice to the lump on my head with one hand and fished my phone out of my pocket with the other.

I figured Stone had made the call I ignored after his men reported to him what happened at my house. He probably wanted to gloat, complain, or feign ignorance. Mostly, he'd want to get information. He must have sent his men by to check their surveillance system because it hadn't been transmitting conversations from any phone calls. That's because I'd been making them outside. I checked the screen. No name. I didn't recognize the number. It had a local area code.

I weighed returning the call to find out who'd made the original. Stone's listening device was still on top of the bookshelf. The ice helped, but my head still ached and so did my eye. Getting up and going outside to make a call didn't promise a big enough return against the discomfort it would cause. I could call the number later or let the listening device pick up my voice and feed it to the receiver. Stone would get a freebie, but at this point I didn't care. The equipment would be returned to sender tomorrow and I couldn't imagine a phone call where Stone would hear anything either to his advantage or detriment.

I tapped the number on the screen of my cell phone. The line picked up after two rings.

"Detective Sheets." Maybe I'd been wrong about letting Stone listen in.

"Rick Cahill returning your call." I set the ice bag down on the floor, slowly stood up, and walked toward the sliding glass door to the backyard. Midnight sidled up next to me. The recorder on top of the bookshelf wouldn't pick up my voice through a sliding glass door.

"Actually, I was returning your call." The grad student voice. "Hailey said you had information I needed to hear."

Hailey. Detective Denton.

"I just had some questions about a cold case." I slid the door open and stepped outside.

"I thought this was about Sophia Domingo's murder."

"No. I tried to explain to Detective Denton that it was about a cold case. It can wait."

"What's the case and what's the information? Maybe one of the other teams is working on it during their down time."

Could I really rat out my father? My blood? I wanted Trent Phelps' killer to pay for his crime. I wanted the Phelps family to get their justice. I'd learned about justice from my father. He'd sworn an oath and given twenty-two years of his life in the pursuit of it. I'd grown up believing that, aside from his family, justice was the most important thing in my father's life. But he'd proven that wrong.

"It's not important. Sorry to waste your time." I wasn't ready to convict my father yet. There was still one holdout juror looking for indisputable truth. Me.

"If you're withholding evidence in a criminal investigation, you can be charged with obstruction of justice." The cop voice. "I'm sure you're aware of that, Mr. Cahill."

Justice. Obstructed. Upheld. My father had done both. So had I.

"I am. I just wanted to get a copy of a police report of a cold case. I'm investigating something on my own and thought you could help."

"I don't know what kind of game you're playing, Mr. Cahill. Detective Denton warned me about you, but I like to form my own opinions. I'm forming one now." Sheets hung up.

I didn't know what kind of game I was playing either. Just that I wasn't playing it well.

CHAPTER THIRTY-THREE

THE PETER STONE Development Company was located on the twentieth floor of the Wells Fargo Building, the bronze and glass monolith on B Street in downtown San Diego. A woman straight off the cover of *Glamour Magazine* greeted me from behind a glass desk. Severe haircut, stunning eyes, Slavic cheekbones. She shot a quick glance at my black eye and then focused on my good one.

I played the same game that I'd played with Bob Reitzmeyer's assistant yesterday. Rick Cahill. No appointment. He'll see me. She made a call and twenty seconds later, her sister or beach volleyball teammate appeared and greeted me.

"Mr. Cahill?" She was six-two in heels, had a slight Russian accent, and wore a wraparound chocolate dress like a second skin. She looked me straight in both eyes and I almost forgot I had a black one. "Please follow me."

I would have followed even without the please. She led me down a hall with glass offices that had glorious views of downtown and the harbor beyond. People were in discussions and examining what looked to be blueprints and architectural designs. This was a real business, not a façade. Energy vibrated through the walls. Dirty money or clean, Stone was a successful businessman. Which made his off-the-books exercises even more despicable.

The hall dead-ended at a brushed-copper door that reminded me of the drawbridge that allowed egress into Stone's fortress on the hill in La Jolla. Stone liked what he liked and had the wealth to buy it.

"This way, Mr. Cahill." The woman opened the door and ushered me into an office that matched the square footage of my entire house. I followed her in and didn't even check behind the door for a thug this time.

Stone stood up from behind a massive desk. A panoramic view of the harbor took up the back half of the office. He flashed a smile that made it all the way to his eyes. The first friendly looking smile I'd ever seen from him. A vein in my neck throbbed.

"Thank you, Svetlana."

"May I prepare you an espresso, tea, a beverage?" Svetlana pointed the question at me and glided her hand toward a bar area in the corner of the office. I looked at Stone, and he raised his eyebrows echoing her question.

"I'm fine. Thank you."

Svetlana left the room and I couldn't help but watch her do so. Then I remembered where I was and turned to face the predator cloaked in civility. He still wore the same friendly smile.

"Rick. Please. Have a seat." The baritone voice rolled out smooth like a fruit smoothie. Not an ounce of condescension. He pointed to a leather chair in front of his desk. I sat and so did he. "What happened to your eye?"

The vein in my neck kept throbbing. I waited for a trap door to open under my chair. This was the Peter Stone the public saw. The successful businessman who used his wealth to fund charities.

I did a quick scan of the room. No one else was there.

"You can drop the act, Stone. It's just you and me."

"I hope you're here to tell me you have a flash drive in your possession that you took off Sophia's body before you called the police

Sunday." Hard edges closed in around his eyes and his smile went cobra. "If that is the case, I'll forget your intrusion into my office."

"Sorry, Stone. Sophia didn't have a flash drive on her. She was naked when someone butchered her." I thought of the gaping wounds, the dried blood, and the dead eyes. Nausea circled in my stomach and threatened to rise up. I fought it back. I wasn't there about Sophia. LJPD could handle that on their own. "The only thing in the car was your briefcase in the trunk next to her body. I have no idea what was in it. The police have it now."

"I've talked to the police, Rick. So, if this is some remedial attempt at a shakedown, you're wasting your time. And mine."

"I'm returning your equipment." I pulled the audio recorder and the transmitter from my coat pocket and tossed them onto the desk. "I'll overlook this one and the assault from your surveillance guys." I pointed at my eye, then leaned over the desk and stared him in those dead eyes. "But if you ever send someone to break into my house again, I won't come down to your office in the middle of the morning and talk about it over an espresso. I'll come to your house in the middle of the night while you're sleeping and I won't ring the bell first."

Stone looked at the surveillance equipment on the desk then back at me. I'd just threatened him and meant it. I expected to see malevolence straining on a leash. I saw uncertainty instead.

"Someone attempted to bug your home?" A real question. No venom. No smirk. No sign that he was enjoying my troubles.

"Yes, but I found it right away. Then yesterday I caught a couple guys dressed as Spectrum reps checking the transmitter they'd hidden outside my house." I studied his face for a tell. "You're telling me they weren't yours?"

"No. When did they plant the listening device?" Life in his eyes. At the molecular level and primitive, only concerned with self-preservation. He was telling the truth and he was worried.

Why?

"Saturday afternoon." If Stone hadn't bugged my home, who did?

"Before or after I called you?"

"After."

"How can you be sure?"

"When I got home late Saturday afternoon, a Spectrum cable van just like the one with the two dudes who jumped me yesterday was parked on my street. I took my dog down to Fiesta Island for an hour and a half. When I got home the van was gone, but I noticed something had been moved on my bookshelf. I looked and found the mini recorder." I pointed at the device I'd tossed on his desk. "They'd been waiting for both me and my dog to be out of the house at the same time."

"And you didn't come to my home until the next morning." He seemed to be talking to himself.

The always-composed veneer was gone. Stone was spooked. Normally, I'd have been elated. Now it just made me nervous. Whoever could spook Stone had to be dangerous. And lethal.

"Right. What's going on?" Did I really want to know? I had my own problems, but if Stone's problem was someone bugging my house, then his problem was mine, too. "Who's behind this, Stone?"

"How long was it between our phone call and the cable van showing up on your block?"

"How 'bout you answer my questions first?"

"Answer my question." He snapped the words off. His ever-present spearmint cool melted. "How long?"

I thought back to Saturday afternoon and Stone's veiled threat about Kim. I'd gotten off the phone with him and drove right over to Kim's house, punched her husband, searched the house, and came back home.

"An hour at the most."

Stone's eyes rolled up to expose his whites. The eyes of a Great White when it was about to strike prey with a kill shot. But Stone wasn't preparing to attack, he was thinking. So was I. Probably about the same thing.

An hour.

Not enough time to scramble a surveillance team from a dead stop and get them to my house in cover uniforms and a vehicle. Not even the CIA could do that from scratch.

"An hour's not enough time." I walked back and forth in front of Stone's desk. "And the catalyst would have to have been the phone call you made to me. That would mean that either one or both our phones are bugged, or wherever you made the call from is bugged. And if they're listening to our phone calls, why even bother with a bug that needs a Wi-Fi transmitter nearby? None of this makes any sense."

Stone stared at me through his predator eyes. The spark of life I'd seen earlier was gone. The computer in his head was running numbers, scenarios, assets and liabilities. My life's worth may have just been calculated down to a spreadsheet or a pie chart. Someone had bugged my house. I might know something, even by accident, that could hurt Stone. Was I worth more to Stone alive so he could use me to draw someone out—or dead on the chance that I might know something?

An asset or a liability?

"Think it through, Stone. The timing doesn't work. The bug doesn't have anything to do with you."

"You might be right." The smirk. He was back in control. "And you might be wrong. Did you know that I started in the, let's just call it the business, as an odds maker?"

"You mean a bookie."

"Your word, not mine."

"No, I didn't know you were, ah, an odds maker." I didn't like where this could go, but at least I was back on familiar ground. The dangerous man behind the hundred-million-dollar mask. "I'll bet your charitable foundation friends don't either?"

"If they bothered to look hard enough, they could find out. But they wouldn't want to risk stopping my checks from coming in." He swiveled his chair around looking at the view to remind me that he was wealthy, in case I'd forgotten. "Anyway, my proficiency at calculating the odds for some of my friends in the business helped me climb all the way up the ladder to a partnership in a casino."

"Your point?"

"Either someone bugged your house because of your connection to me or because of something else." He steepled his fingers and raised his eyebrows. "Either way, the odds are not in your favor, Rick. Enjoy the rest of your day."

CHAPTER THIRTY-FOUR

I CHECKED MY rearview mirror the whole drive home. No one was following me. Yet.

I could have just left the bug disabled or destroyed it and gone on with my life. But I had to prove to Stone how smart I was, and in doing so, I'd proven how stupid I was, instead. And vulnerable.

Stone was afraid of somebody, and I'd put myself right in the middle of his fear. And put a target on my back. Yet, I still believed the bug didn't have anything to do with him. I could only hope that Stone would come around to sharing my view. Before he looked at his asset and liability spreadsheet one last time.

Midnight greeted me at the front door. I knelt down and scratched his neck. He delicately sniffed around my black eye, then licked me on the cheek. I still had somebody in my corner. I let him outside and went into the kitchen to grab a water out of the refrigerator. The folder with the information about the Trent Phelps murder that Jack Anton had given me was still on the kitchen table.

Phelps. My father. The safe deposit box.

A chill started along the back of my neck and echoed in my stomach. I sat down at the table.

An hour hadn't been enough time to get a surveillance team to my house, but how about four or five hours? That would be enough time.

Start with a white van the team already had. Paint the Spectrum logo on it. Two, three hours max. An hour to dry. Drive over to my house, knock on the door to see if anyone's home. They hear Midnight bark from inside the house, go back to the van and wait. They got lucky that I came home and took Midnight to Fiesta Island. If I hadn't left, maybe they would have tried to use a sales pitch to get inside the house. One guy distracts me with some questions in the kitchen while the other plants the bug in the living room.

One hour, no. Four or five, yes. Subtract back five hours from when I returned from punching Jeffrey Parker at his house. Around ten a.m. About the time I was in Windsor Bank and Trust looking at the contents of my father's safe deposit box. With Jules Windsor and Gloria Nakamura. Two spent twenty-five-caliber shells. In Charlie Cahill's safe deposit box that had been kept active for over twenty-five years by a joint checking account with Antoinette King.

The spent shells were the catalyst. Two small-caliber gunshot wounds to Trent Phelps' head in a twenty-eight-year-old unsolved murder. I read about it myself in the old newspaper articles. Gloria Nakamura would have been no more than ten to fifteen years old twenty-eight years ago. Jules Windsor owned the oldest private bank in town then, just as he did now. He knew my father. He knew the goings-on in La Jolla, the hometown of his customers. Surely, he knew about the only unsolved murder in La Jolla in the last fifty years.

The unproven speculation by the police was that the murder had been a professional job. Phelps owned five laundromats around San Diego. An all-cash business. Organized crime like all-cash businesses. Perfect places to hide their ill-gotten gains. The Mafia started the practice of money laundering by buying actual laundromats. A place to hide dirty money and comingle it with legitimate income and make it come out clean. Once clean, some of the money would go into a bank. Windsor owned a bank, but he was a pillar of society. So were a lot of bankers who got caught up in the savings and loan crisis of the eighties.

The facts were that Windsor saw the spent shell casings in my father's safe deposit box Saturday morning. Saturday afternoon someone bugged my house. Coincidence? Possibly. Maybe I'd just let my imagination off the leash and my ingrained paranoia ran alongside it. But someone bugged my house. I hadn't imagined that. And they'd done it five hours after Windsor and Gloria Nakamura had seen the spent shells from the same caliber of gun that killed Trent Phelps. I hadn't imagined that either. The police had verified that the murder weapon was a twenty-five caliber.

The only case other than Phelps that I'd been investigating the past week was Jeffrey Parker's sexual and work habits. Yes, he'd somehow gotten connected up with Peter Stone and Sophia Domingo and Sophia had been murdered. But she was already dead when someone put a bug in my house. I was convinced the Stone/Sophia connection had nothing to do with someone bugging my house.

It had to be connected to the Phelps case and the first connection had to be Jules Windsor. Had he hired the team to bug my home or had he called someone else after he saw the contents of my father's safe deposit box? Who? An old mob connection? Maybe.

Even if it was the mob who sent two men to my house, they wouldn't use the Spectrum employee ruse to bug my home. If they wanted information, they'd beat it out of me. The surveillance team smelled like specialized independents to me. Probably PIs, but they only do electronic surveillance. Specialized freelancers.

So, if the mob hadn't bugged my house, who sent the team that did? The only person I knew who could answer that was Jules Windsor.

* * *

Moira knocked on my door at eleven a.m. Time to split Stone's fifteen grand. Midnight wagged his tail when I let her in and she scratched him behind the ear. She'd liked Midnight from the first time they'd met. The jury was still out on me.

"You want some coffee?" I'd have to make it. I didn't drink coffee, but I always kept some around for guests, on the rare occasion that I entertained. Probably too old and stale now for someone who could tell the difference.

"What happened to your face?"

"Caught somebody who bugged my house." I led her to the kitchen table. "Sit down. I'm taking that as a no to coffee."

"No coffee." She sat down and only her head and shoulders showed over the edge of the table. "Who were they? Did they have something to do with Sophia?"

I'd called Moira Sunday after I'd discovered the body. Wanted her to know about it so she wouldn't be surprised if the police contacted her.

"I don't know who they were." I sat down at the head of the table next to her. A letter envelope sat on the table between us. "They got away, but I don't think Stone hired them or that they had anything to do with Sophia."

"Then who?"

"I don't know, yet, but I'll figure it out. No need to worry." I worried enough alone.

"Didn't say I was worried." The staccato unfiltered cigarette voice.

"Seventy-five hundred courtesy of Peter Stone." I picked up the envelope that was full of hundred-dollar bills and handed it to her. "Thanks for the help on the Parker case. Hopefully, this helps make up for all the license plate and felony checks you've gotten me from the police pro bono over the last couple years."

"We're even, Cahill." She stuffed the envelope in the back pocket of her Levis. Her big brown eyes were even bigger than normal. With concern. "What about the guys bugging your house? Are you working another case already? Something dangerous?"

"No." Probably. "It's under control."

"When have you ever had anything under control?" She had a point.

I stood up like it was time for her to go. She got up, scratched Midnight, and headed for the front door. I followed her like a good host who kept stale coffee around for his guests. Moira stopped in front of the door and whipped around to face me.

"It's the other thing, isn't it?" Moira's eyes electric with the chase.

I didn't have a single person on my side of this errant knight's errand I'd taken up to verify the truth I already knew about my father. Someone smarter than me and just as tough was sitting on the sidelines ready to help.

"Yeah. It's the other thing."

"Tell me what's going on, Rick." She thrust her hands out from her sides. "I can help."

"I can't tell you what it's about, Moira. Not now. Maybe never." I shook my head. "But I could use your help. If you can work under those conditions, I'll pay you double your rate."

"I offer to help you out of friendship and you insult me like that?" Her round eyes split in half and red bled through her tan cheeks. "I don't want your money, you asshole."

My Adam's apple tightened up. "When did we become friends?"

"When I realized that you needed to have at least one in your life." The anger left her face. "Keep your stupid money. I've got seventy-five hundred in my back pocket and some free time. What do you need me to do?"

"Try to find out who the surveillance team is that bugged my house. Two men. White van made up to look like a Spectrum vehicle. White guy, late thirties, brown hair, good looking, lean, my height. Black guy, same age, bulkier, but in shape, short cropped hair."

"A black guy can't be good looking?"

"He could have been, but I mostly just saw his fist and his backside as he and the other guy ran to the van and took off."

"Okay. I'll see what I can find out."

* * *

Gloria Nakamura didn't even try to hide her anger when she saw me standing at the information desk in Windsor Bank and Trust. She strode so quickly toward me that the girl behind the desk shot her eyebrows up.

"Do you have a court order for the contents of your father's safe deposit box, Mr. Cahill?" She folded her arms across her chest. "Otherwise, I can't imagine why you are here."

"To talk to Jules Windsor."

"He's not here, so I guess you can leave."

The woman sitting at the information desk pretended to concentrate on her computer monitor.

"Then I need to talk to you."

"I'm afraid that's not possible." She shook her head. "I'm very busy."

"Walk outside with me. This will only take a minute."

"I told you. I'm busy."

I looked at the woman at the information desk, still staring intently at her computer monitor even though she hadn't touched her keyboard since Gloria came over. I kept looking. The woman's face turned pink.

"I can wait here in the bank until you're not busy anymore. Then we can talk."

Gloria walked over to the door to the bank and went outside. I followed. She planted herself under the overhang just outside the door and spun to face me.

"Do you ever make it through a single day without threatening someone to get what you want?"

"I wouldn't consider telling someone I'd wait until they weren't busy a threat."

"You know damn well what I mean." She pointed a finger at my face. "You were going to try to embarrass me until I talked to you."

"You're right. I apologize." I lifted my hands up, palms facing me. "I know you have a job to do, but I need some help. If I was smarter or nicer, I'd have approached you in a different way. But you saw the empty bullet shells in my father's safe deposit box. You know this is serious."

"Then why don't you go down the block to the police station if it's that serious?" Her tone softened down to annoyed.

"When the time comes, I will. But right now, I just need you to answer a couple questions. That's all. No threats about going to the newspaper. No making you look bad in front of Windsor. Just a couple questions."

Gloria looked around like she'd suddenly realized we were outside. She squeezed her hands together in front of herself. Finally, "What do you want to know?"

"What did Windsor do after I left the bank the other day?"

"I don't see how that's relevant or any of your business."

"Come on, Gloria." I was more tired of this dance than she was. "Answer a couple questions and I'm gone. What did he do?"

She let go a breath and shook her head. "He went back to his office. Does that solve your great mystery?"

"Did he make a phone call?"

"I don't keep track of his every move." She threw her hands up.

"But you did keep track of his moves that day because you were afraid he was upset with you and you wanted to smooth things over. Didn't you?"

Gloria looked me dead in my good eye. For about five seconds, then her eyes found the ground.

"Did he make a call?" I asked.

"Yes." Her face flushed, but not out of anger. "I went into his office after you left to apologize for him having to deal with an asshole like you, and he was on the phone. But so what? Bankers make phone calls like everybody else. That's hardly a crime."

She was right. Bankers made phone calls like everyone else. But I think this call went to the person who hired the team to bug my house. The team broke in. That was a crime.

"Did you hear any of the call?"

"No. He asked me to leave his office and told me that he'd talk to me after he was done with the call."

"What did he say to you after he was done?"

"I've answered enough questions, Mr. Cahill. I'm not going to tell you about personal conversations I had with my boss."

"You told me that it was unusual for Windsor to witness the opening of a deceased's safe deposit box. You know that there's something not quite right about this whole thing. You're too smart not to. What did he say?"

She looked at her shoes again. I waited. She didn't make a move to go back inside. She wanted to tell me. I just had to shut up and let her.

Finally, "He told me to call him if you ever contacted me or came in again."

"Do me a favor and wait about an hour before you call him."

"Why should I do you a favor?" This time she didn't have any problem holding my eyes. "All you've done since I met you is cause problems."

"I'm irritating, I know. But I'm guessing Jules Windsor doesn't ask you to call him every time an irritating customer comes into the bank." My eyebrows went up in case my words weren't strong enough on their own. "All I've done is be a squeaky wheel, jump through the bank's hoops, and examine the contents of my late father's safe deposit box. Because of that, the president of the bank shows up to witness a common banking procedure, something he's never done before, and then he makes a phone call after he sees what's inside the box, and a couple guys . . ."

I left it there, touched my black eye, and let her fill in the blanks. Gloria had been right. I'd do anything to get my way. Relying on sympathy, included.

"Someone attacked you?" Her eyes went big and she put her hand over her mouth. Violence wasn't a part of everyday banking life.

"A couple of someones. And I'm pretty sure they did so as a result of the phone call your boss made the day we opened my father's safe deposit box. Something's not right about the whole thing. I just need an hour head start to find out what it is."

"Maybe you're right, but my daughter depends on me staying employed." She turned and opened the door to the bank.

"Just give me an hour. Please."

Gloria entered the bank without saying another word.

CHAPTER THIRTY-FIVE

JULES WINDSOR DIDN'T have an ocean view, but he had his own little hill and about an acre of La Jolla real estate to look out over. The estate took up three lots on La Jolla Rancho Road, a mile down the shadow of Mount Soledad. A sprawling ranch house, more stately than modern, sat on a crest of the hill. Old money. Old La Jolla banking money. I stared up at the house through a closed wrought-iron gate. A Bentley sat on the crown of the red brick driveway in front of the house. The license plate read Windsor BT. You didn't have to be a private investigator to figure out the car belonged to Jules.

I pushed the button on the intercom built into the gate's brick stanchion. No chance for a ruse to get inside the gate and surprise Windsor with a knock on his front door. The closed-circuit camera staring down at me from atop the stanchion nixed that idea.

"Yes?" A woman's voice.

"Rick Cahill to see Mr. Windsor."

"One moment, please." Ten seconds later, the woman came back on. "I'm sorry. Mr. Windsor is busy. Perhaps you could call ahead next time and make an appointment."

"Okay."

Her side clicked off. I pushed the button again.

"Yes." A slight hiss on the end of the "S".

"This is Rick Cahill. I'd like to make an appointment with Mr. Windsor for the next moment he's available. I'm nearby and can be there in a moment's notice."

"Please leave or I'll be forced to call the police." She clicked off.

I wasn't ready to see LJPD again. Yet. Now I'd never know if Gloria Nakamura gave me that hour or ratted me out. Didn't matter. I wasn't getting inside.

I'd parked my car in front on the street below the gate. The camera was focused on the gate area.

The fence that surrounded the estate was covered in ivy, à la Wrigley Field. You couldn't see in, but they couldn't see out, either. The entrance gate and the gate that opened to the driveway twenty yards in the other direction were the only vantage points in or out. I scanned the top of the fence for other cameras. Just one pointed down at the driveway entrance. None pointed at my car.

I peeked through the opening between the gate and stanchion. Windsor's house had a four-car garage. His Bentley was parked out front. If he was in for the day, the Bentley would be in the garage. It was a Bentley, not a Chevy SUV ready for another load of kids. Bentleys don't stay out at night. Windsor would be heading out sometime before the end of the day.

La Jolla Rancho Road didn't have sidewalks or even curbs. The estates' boundaries just rolled right out to the street. No other cars were parked on the street. If you came to visit, each home had plenty of driveway to accommodate you and all your friends.

Staking out Windsor and waiting for him to leave without being noticed wouldn't be easy. I got into my car and decided to do a quick reconnaissance of the area. A black Jeep Grand Cherokee rolled up and angled in front of me before I could pull out. La Jolla Private Security in white paint along the side. Tinted windows.

Windsor hadn't called LJPD. He'd called his own police force. I punched the ignition off and waited for an ex-cop or a couldn't-make-it cop to jump out of the Jeep and bring his attitude over to my window. I didn't have to wait long and I got a bonus.

Two men with balloon chests stretching the seams of black La Jolla Private Security uniforms, beach volleyball Ray Bans, and Sig Sauer pistols strapped to their sides exited the Jeep and took cop vehicle stop positions. One circled behind my car on the passenger side and the other circled around me to stand behind my left ear, making me turn to look at him. Neither had pulled their Sigs. Highlight of the day.

I thought back to my father's days as a security guard after he left the force. He didn't drive around in an expensive late-model war wagon wearing a new custom-fitted uniform patrolling neighborhoods full of luxury homes. His twenty-two years on the force couldn't get him that kind of job. The rumors of his corruption were in the coastal breeze that blew across La Jolla. No one of Jules Windsor's stature would allow a bent man like Charlie Cahill to patrol his neighborhood. The best he could do was pace up and down a strip mall located on his old beat, protecting a liquor store, a frozen yogurt shop, and a Chinese restaurant. No gun. No badge. No dignity.

I was only ten at the time and didn't understand why he'd changed uniforms and jobs or why Uncle Bob never came over for dinner anymore. I asked him once why he no longer wore a badge.

He told me, "I don't wear one on the outside anymore, but I still wear one inside, close to my heart."

That heart shrunk over the next nine years as he drank more and more and lost job after job until he just gave up.

The rent-a-cop standing next to my window didn't wear a badge either. But he acted like he did.

"May I ask what you're doing parked in front of this residence?" Buzz cut. Hoarse voice caught in his throat.

"I don't think so."

"In fact, I can. La Jolla Private Security has been contracted by residents in the area to provide them with round-the-clock security. Under the law, we are able to question and hold suspects who pose a threat to the residents until the police arrive."

"Considering the only things posing here are you and your partner, I'm free to leave. So, move your wannabe-cop SUV out of my right to the road or we can all talk to lawyers."

"Why don't I call someone down at LJPD instead, and we can all wait here until they arrive and then you can explain why you're harassing Mr. Windsor."

"Go ahead. Make the call." All in on a semi-bluff. My cards weren't great, but I gambled that they were better than the rent-a-cop's. "If you're not going to move your toy truck, I've got plenty of time. Maybe you should check with old Jules before you make the call, though. He may not be as eager as you think to discuss with the police why I want to talk to him."

That one stunned him. No quick retort. I couldn't see his eyes behind his Ray Bans, but they were probably whirling in thought. Finally, "Wait here."

He walked to the back of my car and conferred with his twin. The twin nodded and stared at me while the leader pulled a cell phone from his pocket and made a call. He had a conversation with someone that I couldn't hear. He put the phone back in his pocket and walked over to me.

"You and your car are now on file with us as a possible threat to this neighborhood. If you harass Mr. Windsor again, or anyone else in this neighborhood, or are even found loitering in the area, there won't be a discussion the next time we stop you."

I let him have the last word. What I'd learned from our encounter was worth the hassle. The twins got back into their Jeep and backed up behind me. I drove away slowly. They trailed behind me for a few hundred yards, then whipped an illegal U-turn and sped off in the opposite direction to enforce the will of the wealthy elite of La Jolla.

I waved good-bye in my rearview mirror. I should have blown them kisses. Windsor knew my reputation with LJPD. He knew if he'd let the La Jolla Private Security guard call the police, LJPD would make the rest of my day, and possibly night, miserable. That would have been the most obvious and effective way to stop me from bothering him. But he passed. Because he was afraid what I might say to the police about why I wanted to talk to him. I didn't even know what exactly it was he feared that I knew.

But I was certain he was hiding something. And that he, or whoever he called after I left the bank the other day, had hired the crew that bugged my house.

Whatever Windsor was hiding had something to do with my father, the contents of his safe deposit box, and the twenty-eight-year-old murder of Trent Phelps.

* * *

Moira called me on the drive home.

"Got 'em."

"Who?"

"The assholes who bugged your house and gave you the black eye, dummy." A little lightness to her voice. More bongos than snare drum. Maybe this was what friendship sounded like.

"Who are they?"

"Edward Armstrong and Jamal Ketchings. They go by Discreet Investigations. They're out of Fairbanks Ranch. They don't even have a website. Strictly word of mouth."

"Any criminal records?" I asked.

"No. They both spent over a decade in the Army. Must have been how they met. Get this—they were both in military intelligence."

"Military intelligence covers a lot of ground. They could have gathered intel for troop movements or worked as spooks. Nice prerequisite for spying on people and planting bugs. How did you find them?"

"I've been at this game for fifteen years." Back to the snare drum. "I've made a lot of friends along the way. Friends who know things. You should try making a new friend every once in a while."

"I don't have to. I have you. Especially now that we're friends."

"You're pushing it, Cahill."

"Give me the address of Discreet Investigations. I want to go make some new friends."

She gave me the address.

"You want to come with me?" I asked.

"I have a better idea."

"Why am I not surprised?"

"Shut up and listen." She let out a breath. "These guys are ex-military. They probably have an arsenal at their office."

"They didn't seem like rough and tumble types to me."

"You mean when they gave you a black eye and got away from you?"

"Sneak attack. Two against one," I said.

"Whatever. You don't have to be tough to pull a trigger. Listen, how about I hire them for a job. We have them come to my house. I tell them that I think my boyfriend is cheating on me and I want them to bug the house we share because I have to go away on business. That way, we get them on our turf. Fewer guns. You can surprise them and threaten to go to the police for breaking into your house. Some leverage to get them to spill on who hired them."

"That's why you have seventy-five hundred in an envelope in your back pocket. You're smart."

"You forgot charming."

"Yeah. That, too. When are you going to set this ruse up?"

"Ah, I already did." Not the usual staccato voice. "Tonight at seven."

"Who's running this investigation?"

"Me."

"I guess you are. Thanks for including me." Another call buzzed my phone. "See you tonight."

"Roger."

I checked my screen for the incoming call. La Jolla Police Department. I should have known.

After good news, there's always some bad to follow. I answered.

"Mr. Cahill, this is Detective Sheets." The grad student voice. Friendly. "I'm hoping you can come down to the station and talk. It shouldn't take long. Could you make some time today or tomorrow?"

"What do you want to talk about?"

"We just want to tie up some loose ends about your discovery of Sophia Domingo's body."

"I can be down in ten minutes." I'd learned over the years it's best to take bad news head-on. Or maybe I just had a hard head.

CHAPTER THIRTY-SIX

THE LA JOLLA Police Department was in an old white brick building that had once been the La Jolla Library. Not much had changed on the outside of the building known as the Brick House in the twenty-seven years since my father had worked there. Maybe a paint job or two, but it still looked the same as when my father brought me to work for the last ride-along I took with him when I was nine. Everything in our lives would change within a year later.

My sweat glands went Pavlovian as soon as I entered the building. Not from what happened to my father. I had my own history with the Brick House. A woman in a starched blue uniform with sergeant stripes sat behind the raised desk in the lobby. Blond, younger than me, intelligent eyes. She actually smiled. An improvement to the young and old flattops and pointed attitudes I'd had to deal with in my other Brick House encounters.

Even so, sweat still slid down from my underarms.

"Rick Cahill to see Detective Sheets."

"One moment, please." She picked up a phone and told someone I was downstairs. "Detective Sheets will be right down."

Still smiling. She must not have known my and my family's history with LJPD. I thought they taught a class on it at the police academy. Detective Sheets came down the stairs from Robbery/Homicide holding a leather portfolio. He thanked me for coming, and we shook hands like we were new friends, then he led me up the stairs to the Homicide division. The sweat pump under my arms, which had fallen back to neutral, slammed into overdrive as soon as we turned down the hall leading to the interrogation rooms.

Sheets stopped at the nearest room on the left, pushed open the door, and flipped the light switch. The small room went white from two buzzing fluorescent light bulbs above. A small table with three chairs in the corner. One chair facing the door and the camera hanging over it. My chair. I'd sat in it a couple times over the last four years and mostly told the truth. Today I didn't have anything to lie about. Still, the sweat pumped.

I followed Sheets in. He left the door open, signifying I could leave at any time. But I knew if I left before Sheets got what he wanted from me, I'd probably end up back in the same room again. And the door would be closed the next time.

"Have a seat, Mr. Cahill." Sheets pointed at the seat I already knew to take. A bottle of water sat on the table in front of me. I hoped I wouldn't stay long enough to get thirsty. Sheets sat down kitty-corner to me and set the portfolio on the table. He didn't open it. Good. I didn't need to see crime scene photos of what I'd seen in person and still saw in my dreams at night.

"Call me Rick. Let's keep it friendly." I turned off my phone to show him how he'd get my full attention. Friendly like.

The red light on the camera over the door lit up. Action.

"Sure, Rick." A smile, but no offer to call him by whatever his first name was. "So, tell me about how you first came in contact with Sophia Domingo."

"I never really came into contact with Ms. Domingo. Like I told you the other day, she interacted with a target of my surveillance. I never spoke with her or ever got closer than fifty feet from her."

"Did you ever follow her and make her the target of your surveillance?" Sheets made the question sound like a friendly aside.

"Yes."

"Why was that?"

"Now we're getting into client confidentiality."

"As you know, I've already spoken with Kim Parker, your client." Sheets smiled and leaned in. "I know she hired you to follow her husband because she was afraid he might be cheating on her. Why did you begin following Sophia?"

"Jeffrey Parker met her at The Pacific Terrace Hotel, so I figured I'd follow her and see what I could find out about her."

"And what did you find?"

"That she was somehow affiliated with real estate in La Jolla and San Diego. I thought I already told you all this the other day."

"Just trying to be thorough." A smile. Half grad student, half homicide detective. "You said Sophia was affiliated with real estate in La Jolla. Did she have a business relationship with Jeffrey Parker?"

"You'd have to ask him." My chair suddenly felt uncomfortable. Kim wanted to keep Sophia and Parker's new partnership quiet. Kim wasn't a client anymore, but she was still a friend.

"I'm asking you as a professional PI. What's your take?"

"My take is I'm not in the real estate business and don't know very much about it." Flattery works on the vain. I'm many things, but not vain.

"Okay, let's talk about something you know a lot about." Full cop smile. I knew what was coming. "Cheating spouses. That seems to be your specialty. Do you think Jeffrey Parker was having an affair with Sophia Domingo?"

"I think they probably had sex the day I followed him to The Pacific Terrace Hotel." I'd cover for Kim on Sophia's professional relationship with Jeffrey. Not her sexual one. Kim had made her choice.

This wasn't personal. Sheets was right. This was my specialty. "And my guess would be that they'd done it before."

"How did Kim Parker react to this information?"

"I told her what I saw, which was Parker and Sophia drinking wine on the balcony of the hotel room. I didn't offer an opinion on what it meant." Not a lie. I gave an opinion, but only after Kim prodded me.

"Yes, and how did she react?"

"Calmly."

"Really, Mr. Cahill?" Sheets put his hands on the table and an edge on his voice. "You give Mrs. Parker proof that her husband is cheating on her and she's calm?"

"I didn't give her proof of anything. I told her what I saw."

"I understand." Sheets leaned back in his chair. "You don't want to say anything that could put her in a bad light. I know you and Mrs. Parker had a relationship in the past."

"I'm just giving you the facts, Detective Sheets." In a light I thought appropriate.

"Okay, let's go back to the morning you found Sophia Domingo's body." He leaned forward and the front legs of his chair hit the floor with a thud. "You and your ex-girlfriend decided to meet for breakfast in La Jolla on Sunday morning, the very same morning that Sophia Domingo, the woman who'd been having an affair with Kim's husband and who she'd hired you to follow, is lying dead in the trunk of her car on top of Kim and Jeffrey's place of work. Is that about right?"

"Friends having breakfast together doesn't seem very unusual, Detective. I can't speak to the rest of your scenario."

"Friends and business associates. You were under her employ, remember?"

"Not at that point. We'd already concluded our business."

"Oh, so this must have been a debriefing meeting where she paid you for a job well done." His eyebrows went up like he'd scored a point.

"No. Friends hoping to have a nice breakfast."

"How did Jeffrey Parker feel about your and his wife's friendship?"

"I don't know. You'd have to ask him."

"Does any of the rest of what you call a scenario seem a bit coincidental to you, Mr. Cahill?" He rolled his eyes. "The odds of you stumbling upon the body of a person you were investigating on your way to an innocent breakfast with the woman who hired you are astronomical. Now, if you somehow already knew the body was there, then everything would make more sense."

"What makes sense is that someone left Sophia's body on the roof of Parker Real Estate for a reason." The sweat under my arms was matched by some along my hairline. "And I doubt if Kim Parker had had something to do with Sophia Domingo's death, she'd plant the body on top of her own building."

"And neither would you, right?"

"Is there a more direct question you'd like to ask, Detective Sheets? 'Cause the gotcha game is played out."

"As a matter of fact, I do." He grinned and slapped the table. "Would you mind if I take a sample of your DNA?"

Not the question I'd expected.

"Why do you want my DNA? I told you I tried the door handle to the staircase on the roof, but I didn't touch anything else."

"We just want to eliminate you as a suspect. Then you and I won't have to have too many more of these talks."

"Sure. I'll give you a sample." My heart kicked over. I thought back to Sunday morning and the Corvette and Sophia's body in the trunk. Could I have accidentally touched something aside from the door to the staircase and not know it? Did I get close enough to her body when I identified it to have a tiny piece of me slough onto what was once her? No. The DNA would absolve me and the police could concentrate on finding the real killer.

Detective Sheets opened the portfolio and pulled out a large envelope and set it on the desk. He then pulled some nitrile gloves from his pocket and put them on.

"Have you eaten in the last hour, Rick?" Rick. We were friends now. I guess it's better to be friends when you ask someone to open their mouth so you can stick something into it.

"No."

"Could you take a sip of water and slosh it around in your mouth for a few seconds?"

I did as asked and Sheets opened the envelope and took out a printed form, a long thin packet, and a box about the size of a toothbrush. He ripped open the packet and pulled out two long cotton swabs with cotton on just one end.

"Please open your mouth. I'm going to rub two swabs on the inside of each cheek for about thirty seconds. It will seem like a long time while I'm doing it, but please be patient."

I opened my mouth, and he pushed the swabs at me like the airplane going into the hangar. Without the turns and sound effects. He rubbed the swabs inside my mouth long enough for us to go steady. He slid the swabs into the little toothbrush box and closed it. He put the box down on the table, then slid the form across to me. I read the form. A search warrant for my DNA.

"Please sign the search warrant and you'll be on your way."

I signed the form and slid it back to Sheets.

"Thank you for your cooperation, Rick. We'll contact you if we need anything else." He stood like it was time to go.

I stayed seated.

"Why the DNA, Detective? What kind of evidence was found on the body?"

Sophia's murder was LJPD's case, not mine. I'd spied on her for a couple days while she probably cheated on her lover by having sex with a married man, had a more dangerous business coupling with Peter Stone, and probably helped cap a sleazy land deal by paying off someone on the Coastal Commission. I'd surveilled worse people. But they hadn't ended up naked and slashed to bits in the trunk of their cars. She was someone's daughter. There was someone somewhere who would grieve her loss. I needed to know if my spying on her had in any way abetted her destruction.

"Now you're the one crossing into confidentiality, Mr. Cahill." Sheets smiled. "I'll contact you if I need anything else."

"I think I'll wait until you have my DNA samples all sealed up, if it's okay with you."

"Are you insinuating I'd falsify evidence?" Sheets' face blew pink.

"Just following my own routine procedures, Detective. No offense." I didn't have anything against Sheets, yet, but LJPD had something against me and my father. I was willing to make one more enemy to be sure my DNA didn't get mistaken for someone else's. Or vice versa.

"I guess everything I've heard about you is true, Cahill." The color faded from his cheeks. He must have defaulted to the LJPD institutional knowledge about who I was. Facts in the place of emotions.

"That I'm a cautious man?"

"No. That you're always working an angle, can't be trusted, and only care about yourself." He locked eyes onto mine that looked more cop than at any time since I met him two days ago. "Just like your father."

"You don't know anything about my father, Sheets." I stood up by reflex. A residual from the molecule of hope I'd carried inside me all my life and knew now to be folly. Still, my father, my blood. I'd defend them until the end of my life even though I knew both were tainted. I pointed at the cotton swabs. "Are you ever going to put the swabs into the envelope so I can get out of here?"

Sheets stared at me and I stared back. I was ready to piss all over the interrogation room if I had to. More DNA to test. Sheets finally picked up the box and sealed it in the envelope.

I left the room without another word and hustled down the stairs and out of the Brick House before my sweat had a chance to dry.

CHAPTER THIRTY-SEVEN

I'D NEVER BEEN to Moira's house before. She'd never invited me. Even though we were now friends, this wasn't a social visit. She owned a California Craftsman bungalow on Fay Avenue in La Jolla, a couple blocks down from the high school. The La Jolla address surprised me. She was much better at this private investigative stuff than I was.

Moira must have read my mind when she opened the front door and greeted me on the wooden porch.

"The home my late husband grew up in." She waved me inside. "Don't get any ideas that you can latch onto a sugar mama. I'm house wealthy and everything else just getting by."

Moira wore a white tailored pantsuit with a plunging neckline revealing more cleavage than she'd ever shown before. At least to me. She usually wore jeans and floppy sweaters or sweat tops. She wore makeup that made her large eyes and lips pop. I'd always found her attractive in an unconventional way. Tonight, she was exotic. Stunning. Staged for our guests.

"You're too old for me anyway." I winked at her and set down the garment bag I brought with me on her sofa and unzipped it.

"Thus, I have the wisdom to know that you'd never be able to satisfy me." She clucked once like she was calling a horse. "Where did you park?"

"Down by the high school, off the main drag." I pulled out a windbreaker and hung it on a clothes hook by the front door and dropped a pair of my tennis shoes on the floor.

"Good. They should be here in forty-five minutes." She pointed down the hall. "Go hang the rest of that stuff in the closet in the bedroom and use the top left drawer of the bureau for the socks and underwear. Make it look like a man lives here or as close as you can come to one."

I staged the bedroom and then went back into the living room.

"Which one did you talk to, Armstrong or Ketchings?"

"Neither. These guys are all about secrecy. The number you call is only a voice mailbox. You request their services and they text you back on a line which won't allow you to return the text."

"They'll talk to us tonight. Even if they need convincing." I opened my jacket to show her the shoulder holster with the Smith & Wesson .357 Magnum.

"Yep." Moira stood up, turned, and flipped up the back of her jacket revealing her own holster housing a Ruger snub nose .38. She had just enough of a teapot behind to allow the jacket to lay flat without revealing a bulge. A genetic endowment that served as a target whenever Moira turned her back on men.

"You sure you're up for this?" I closed my coat. "You can let them in and then leave while I do what I need to."

"You need backup, Cahill. Two of them, one of you. Even you know that math doesn't add up."

"Yeah, but we may have to pull these guns to intimidate them, and things could go sideways. We'd be looking at kidnapping with a deadly weapon."

"They'd never press charges. They don't want the police to know they even exist." She shook her head. "Besides, they broke into your house and assaulted you. I'm in, Cahill. For whatever."

Seven o'clock came and went. Seven thirty. Still not here. Moira called Discreet Investigations' phone number at seven thirty-five and left a message on their voicemail. No new text. We contemplated scrapping the ruse and planned to drop by their office unannounced tomorrow. Finally, a knock on the door five minutes later. Moira checked the peephole and then nodded at me. I tiptoed down the hall and slipped into the first door on the left. The bathroom. I closed the door and put my ear up against it.

I heard Moira's muffled voice, but couldn't make out all of her words. Then a man's. Same thing. The voices got louder and a little clearer.

Moira's voice, ". . . late."

Male voice, ". . . ran long."

Moira, ". . . two-man team."

Male voice, ". . . a one-man job."

Moira, louder. Closer. "Our bedroom is down the hall. I guess that would be the best place to start." Reluctant. Meryl Streep in character. "I pray that I'm wrong and this is all just my imagination."

Male. "Hopefully, it is and the recorded record will give you the peace of mind you're hoping for."

Recorded record. That's what they called spying on someone. Made it sound like they were historians instead of spies and breaking-and-entering artists. The voice sounded like the white guy who'd cracked me on the head with the metal clipboard. I was going to enjoy our conversation.

"Where's the best place to put a camera . . ." Moira's voice trailed off, probably as she went down the hall into her bedroom.

I waited a couple seconds, then slowly opened the bathroom door and eased out into the hall. Moira stood in the doorway of her bedroom with her back to me.

"I'll put one in this light fixture that will get a fish-eye view of the whole bedroom." The man's voice from inside the bedroom.

I pulled the Smith & Wesson from its holster and held it against my leg as I walked down the hall. I touched Moira on the back and she walked into the room toward the opposite wall. When she settled there I stepped into the room, keeping the gun at my side. The white guy from the Spectrum truck stood in the opposite corner, his nose swollen from my fist. A briefcase sat open on the bed facing him.

"Which one are you, Armstrong or Ketchings?" I gave my wrist a quick twist so that he noticed the gun.

The man whipped wide eyes at me, then down at the briefcase.

"Don't move!" Moira had her gun out and pointed at his chest. "Hands up and step back from the briefcase."

The man froze with his eyes still on the briefcase.

"Step back." I aimed at center mass with a two-handed grip. He put his hands up and took a step backward. I kept my gun trained on him and advanced.

The man's eyes fell back to normal and a tiny smile creased his lips.

"Turn around. Hands against the wall. Spread them," I said, then turned to Moira. "You got him?"

She had her gun still trained on him in a two-handed grip, left foot forward in a Weaver combat stance. She nodded without taking her eyes off the man. She'd never been a cop like I had, but studied tactics and spent a lot of time at a shooting range.

The man slowly turned and pressed his hands against the bedroom wall. I pulled the briefcase toward me and spun it around. It held well-organized surveillance equipment and one item that didn't belong. A 9mm Beretta pistol in a custom holster fashioned to the inside lid of the briefcase. I picked it up, made sure the safety was on, then stuck it in my waistline behind my back. I closed the briefcase and pushed it to the far end of the bed.

I stuck my gun between the man's shoulder blades to remind him there were two guns against him, then quickly holstered it and patted him down. No other weapon. I pulled out a set of keys, a medium-size Swiss Army knife, a wallet, and a cell phone from his pants' pockets. I tossed the keys, the knife, and the phone onto the bed. I opened the wallet to the clear plastic sheaf that held his driver's license.

Edward Haines Armstrong.

I threw the wallet onto the bed with his other stuff and put my gun on him again.

"Hands on top of your head and turn around, Edward. Or do you prefer Eddie?"

Armstrong turned around and showed me a larger smirk than when I'd made him face the wall. He didn't say anything. Just the smile.

"What's so funny, Eddie? Breaking and entering and assault? Keep smiling. They like pretty boys up at Chino."

"I'm the one being held at gunpoint by two people and had my licensed firearm stolen."

"Why don't we call LJPD and we can get this all straightened out." I had no intention of calling the police. At least not the ones who worked out of La Jolla. Armstrong and his partner's crimes against me had taken place at my house in San Diego PD's jurisdiction. But the police were my bargaining chip. "Or you can tell me who hired you to bug my house. You do that and we can call it even. No harm done."

"I'll take my chances." The smirk.

"Was it Jules Windsor or someone else?" I watched his eyes for a tell. Nothing. Just the smirk that I wanted to pistol whip off his face.

"You're not as smart as you think you are, Cahill." He nodded at Moira. "You think I'm just going to show up at some house without doing research? We're called discreet for a reason."

"You're here, aren't you?"

He ignored my question and told me how smart he was.

"According to the county assessor, this home belongs to a Moira Jocelyn MacFarlane, who happens to be a private investigator. The woman who called us claimed to be Joan Brown, but the photo we found for Moira MacFarlane looks a lot like the woman standing in the corner pointing a gun at me. It seemed strange that a private investigator would hire someone to spy on her cheating boyfriend when she could do it on her own for free. So we dug a little deeper and found that you two have worked together before."

"If you figured all that out, why did you show up?"

"Maybe we *can* work something out. How about we go back into the living room and talk about this?"

"We're fine here. Start talking. Who hired you to bug my house?"

"Like you said, Jules Windsor." Armstrong looked me straight in the eye.

"When?"

"Last Saturday."

"What time did he call you?"

"I don't remember the exact time. Late morning." Still looking at me in the eye. Hadn't blinked yet.

Too easy. First he was defiant when I mentioned the police, now he was giving me what I wanted without trying to bargain it for something else.

"Why did Windsor want you to bug my house?"

"We don't ask that question."

"What does Windsor do for a living?"

He still kept his eyes on mine, but they went blank for a millisecond. "My arms are getting tired. Can I at least put my hands down?"

"Keep them up."

"That's not a fair deal. You're keeping me hostage in this bedroom in the back of the house and holding guns on me while I tell you the whole story."

The hair spiked on the back of my neck. Too late. A hissing sound came from the front of the house. Moira spun her weapon toward the hallway just as a smoking canister landed in the bedroom. Tears bled from my eyes. I fought to keep them open. I spun from Armstrong and aimed my gun at the bedroom doorway. Coughs erupted from my mouth as my throat closed up. I couldn't breathe. My eyelids snapped shut. Face on fire. Gun hit the floor. Hands to my face. Eyes, nose, and throat burned. No air. I lunged blindly at the doorway fighting to find oxygen. A noise. Pushed to the floor. Armstrong's gun ripped from my waist.

CHAPTER THIRTY-EIGHT

"EDDIE! PUT THIS on!" A muffled voice.

Footsteps and vibrations next to my head. I pushed off the floor. Fire down my throat as I gagged for air. My eyes welded shut. I yelled Moira's name, but all that came out were hacking coughs. No air on the intake. I stumbled forward and banged into something. Moving. Human. I clawed at it and felt hair. A woman's. Moira. I grabbed around her waist and we stumbled forward. Blind. Tears. Snot. Coughs. A breeze on my face. I pushed us toward it. Stronger. Forward. Stairs. Midair. Hard landing. Face on the ground. Cool. Grass.

I rolled onto my back and forced one eye open. Night. Stars shimmering through my tears. Coughs racked my chest. I found wisps of air after each hack. More coughs. Not mine. I rolled onto my side and forced my other eye open. Moira on all fours coughing and dry heaving into the grass.

"Water. Hose." I managed real words.

She pointed one hand behind her toward the front of the house and a flower bed. I crawled toward the flowers and found a coiled hose connected to a faucet. I grabbed the end of the hose and turned on the faucet. Water roiled out. I turned the hose on my face. Relief. My eyes still stung and my face was still on fire, but the heat had been turned down. I forced my eyes to stay open and poured water into them one at a time. More relief.

I climbed to my feet and ran over to Moira with the hose. She was still on all fours coughing and retching into the lawn. I pushed her over and sprayed her face with the hose. She coughed and rolled back onto all fours. I sprayed her in the face some more as I coughed and coughed. I put the hose in my mouth, then spit out the water. Again and again. Some relief. I did the same to Moira as she tried to push me away.

I continued the outdoor shower for five minutes. Ten? Fifteen? I don't know how long, but Moira and I were soaked through and her entire front lawn was a puddle by the time I turned off the water.

Moira lay on her back on the soaked lawn taking big gulps of air and only coughing after every fourth or fifth breath.

"You ruined my best outfit," she said between coughs. "This is going on an expense report."

"I didn't know you could expense stuff on a pro bono job."

"I will now."

I reached down a hand, which she grabbed, and pulled her up to her feet. We sloshed up the stairs onto the porch and looked through the open door of the house. An empty canister lay on its side in the living room, a mate to the one that Armstrong's partner had tossed into the bedroom. The second man, probably Ketchings, must have set it off right before he threw the other one into the bedroom. Maybe that's why the tear gas took effect so quickly. The entire inside of the house must have been one big gas cloud. Moira and I stood on the welcome mat and sniffed for the smell of any lingering tear gas.

"I'll go in and open all the windows so we can air the place out." I looked down at Moira and saw my arm around her shoulders. I didn't remember putting it there. "You shouldn't stay in there until we're sure all the tear gas has dispersed."

"I have to get out of these clothes. I'm cold. Let's go in and grab something to wear and change out here."

"Deal."

We held our breath, rushed inside, and ran to the windows first. My eyes stung again. Not as badly as before, but bad enough to want to get the hell out of there. We threw open all the windows in the living room and darted back to Moira's bedroom. She opened the window over her bed, and I grabbed a pair of slacks and a button-down shirt I'd hung in the closet to dress the room for Armstrong and company. Moira grabbed a couple things out of her dresser and running shoes from her closet, and we hustled back to the front of the house. I picked up the tennis shoes I'd dropped near the door and the windbreaker off the hook near the door and bolted outside.

We both let go of our breaths and sucked gasps of air like we had when we'd tried to recover from the tear gas. Moira looked at me and giggled and I started laughing. We sat down in a love seat on her porch and laughed until we cried. The stinging in our eyes made it easy. We stopped and I patted Moira on the back. We looked at each other like we never had before. The danger. The pain. The moment. We leaned toward each other. She shot her lips against my cheeks, then pulled backward.

"What are you trying to do, Cahill? Kill our blossoming friendship in the crib?"

"I don't know what you're talking about." I released her hand, which I had somehow been holding. "Let's get out of these wet clothes."

I walked to the far side of the covered porch and kept my back turned on her. I took off my shirt and put on the one I'd taken out of the closet. I started to button it. My skin stung. I ripped the shirt off and threw it onto the ground.

"Moira!" I turned and saw her naked back. "Don't put the clothes on. They have tear gas on them."

She dropped the sweatshirt she'd had in her hands.

"What the hell am I supposed to do, go to the store naked and buy some new clothes?" She turned toward me with her arms crisscrossing her chest, a hand over each breast.

"I've got some clothes in my car." I always kept a quick change in my trunk for long surveillance jobs to have a different look. "Wait here."

She went back to the love seat and sat down, keeping her chest covered. I went through the gate of the white picket fence and jogged the two blocks to my car without a shirt. I hopped in and drove back to Moira's and parked in front. I grabbed a duffel bag out of the trunk and took it up to the porch. I pulled out a pair of sweatpants and a hoodie and tossed them to Moira. She let them hit her and fall to the ground.

"You hoping I'd catch those so you could cop a peek, Cahill?"

I turned my back to her and looked out at the darkened street.

"Let's go to my house while your place airs out. Take a hot shower. Figure out what just happened."

"Roger."

CHAPTER THIRTY-NINE

WE DIDN'T TALK on the drive to my house. Both lost in thought. I wondered whether the information Armstrong had offered was valid. And why he'd come if he knew the job was a setup. I pondered what the hell almost happened on the porch with Moira, too. The danger we'd survived had jacked our adrenaline and other hormones had gotten caught up in the rush. Heat of the moment or hidden feelings? I had too much danger in my life already to even consider exploring those feelings.

I glanced over at Moira. She stared out the window in the passenger seat, bundled up in my sweats four sizes too big like she was wrapped in a blanket. She had to be wondering if the offer to help me was worth a home invasion and maybe more turmoil to come. I doubt she'd ever held a gun on someone before. It was an unsettling experience the first time. Wondering if you could pull the trigger if you had to. I already knew the answer to that question. Four times.

Midnight greeted us at the door. He sniffed my wet jeans and sneezed. He backed up, crooked his head, and looked at me. The faint residue of tear gas on my pants had already attacked his powerful nose. I led him to the sliding glass door in the living room and put him outside.

"Bathroom with a shower is upstairs. First door on the right. I'll try to find you something that fits better."

"Thanks, Cahill."

I followed her upstairs and went into my bedroom after she peeled off into the bathroom. I went into the master bath and kicked off my shoes, jeans, and underwear, and put on the terrycloth robe that hung from a hook on the door. Moira needed something to wear. There was only one option that would come close to fitting her. I opened the bottom drawer of the dresser in the bedroom. A plastic clothes bag sat in the drawer. Nothing else. I hadn't opened that drawer or the bag in it in years.

I pulled out the bag and opened it and found a pair of blue and gold UCLA running shorts. I'd bought them for Colleen the day after I met her when I was still a Bruin and she was down visiting from UC Santa Barbara where I would follow her via a transfer the next year. We got married three years later.

I pulled out a green t-shirt with a Lake Tahoe logo from the bag. From our honeymoon. There was a hairbrush in the bag, too. With long whips of blond hair intertwined in the bristles. I left the brush in the bag and took the shorts and shirt down the hall and hung them on the doorknob of the bathroom where Moira was already in the shower.

I went back into my bathroom when I heard the water stop and took a shower. The hot water felt good, except for my face, which still burned from the tear gas. I turned off the hot water and let the cold run on my face to take some of the sting out.

When I went downstairs, Moira was sitting on my couch in Colleen's clothes. She'd let Midnight back inside and was scratching his head. I sat in the recliner opposite her.

"He wanted to keep me company," Moira said.

"Feeling better?"

"Yes. Thanks for the clothes." She pulled her shirt and let it go. "You keep a set of women's clothes around for situations like this?"

"No."

Moira studied my eyes and read something in them. "I'll make sure you get them back, Rick."

"Thanks." I smiled at her kindness. "Beer? Something harder?"

"Someone just gas-bombed my house. What do you think?"

"Exactly what you're thinking."

I went into the kitchen and grabbed a bottle of Bushmills off the top of the refrigerator and two rocks glasses from the cabinet. I left the rocks in the freezer. I set the glasses down on the coffee table between Moira and me and poured two fingers in each.

"Here's to gas masks and hot showers." Moira held up her glass. I sat down, grabbed my glass, and clinked it off hers.

I took a sip and my body warmed. In a good way. Not like burning tear gas.

"Sorry about tonight," I said.

"Me, too." Moira took her second sip of Irish whiskey.

"I'll pay for any cleaning expenses or new clothes you have to buy."

"That's not what I'm sorry about."

"Then what?" I drained the Bushmills from my glass, afraid of what Moira would say next.

"I'm sorry you don't trust me enough to tell me what this is all about."

"Aside from Midnight, I trust you more than anyone else in my life right now."

"That's sad." She looked down at her glass. "You should have at least one person in your life who you can tell secrets to."

"Who's yours?"

"My son."

Her son, Luke, was a sophomore at Cal Poly San Luis Obispo. I didn't know the two of them were that close. I guessed I didn't know Moira as well as I thought.

"The stories he could tell." I poured more whiskey into my glass and topped off hers.

"He'll never tell, Cahill." She smiled. "He shares my blood."

Blood. Inescapable. The secrets it hid.

"Why do you think Armstrong came to your house if he smelled a setup?" I had a theory. I wanted to see if Moira's was a match.

"I think he wanted to learn what you knew." She leaned forward on the couch. "I think he had a bug on his body and his partner was listening in while you questioned him."

"Me, too. His partner was listening live, but I'm sure he was recording it for whoever hired them." I leaned forward, too. Eager to have someone to throw ideas at even if I couldn't tell her the bigger story. "Armstrong gave me Windsor because I mentioned his name first. When I pressed him to see what he knew about Windsor, he signaled his partner. Time to abort."

"So Windsor didn't hire them?"

"No. Not directly, at least."

"But you think he's somehow involved in ... in whatever this is that you won't tell me."

"Yes." I hit my drink and avoided her eyes. "I promise, I'll tell you what this is all about if I ever find the truth I'm looking for."

"You're telling me the president of the largest independent bank in La Jolla is involved, but you won't tell me how?"

"Not yet."

"I know you're new to the concept of friendship, Cahill. Here's a tip. It goes both ways." She squinted the round out of her eyes and pressed her full lips into a straight line. Heat turned her tan cheeks maroon. "I volunteered my services and my house to help a friend.

Now I'm wearing borrowed clothes, my house is a wailing wall, and I've probably made an enemy of one of the most powerful men in La Jolla."

She was right. I didn't know how to be a friend. I knew how to be an ex-lover still carrying a torch and play hero for a woman who had moved on, but I didn't know how to be a real friend. Moira did. For some reason I hadn't figured out yet, she'd chosen to be one to me. And she'd already sacrificed for the one-way friendship.

I finished off my fourth finger of Bushmills and set the glass down.

"You've probably heard about my father."

"I know he was a cop. Is he still alive?"

"No. He died eighteen years ago."

"Does all this have something to do with him?" She spread her hands out, as if encompassing the whole world.

"Yes. He was a cop until he was pushed off the force. The rumor was he was doing favors for the mob."

"I heard about that when a friend at LJPD tried to talk me out of working with you on the Randall Eddington thing a couple years ago."

"Maybe you should have listened."

"Maybe, but that's my decision to make." She wagged a finger at me. "Nobody else's."

"Okay." I shrugged. "Anyway, I stumbled onto some evidence that probably proves the rumor to be true."

Moira looked at me, then shook her head. "So all this is about proving your father was a dirty cop?"

I'd opened the door, now I didn't know when to close it.

"It's about finding the truth."

"Where does Jules Windsor come into your truth, Cahill?" Her staccato voice had a harder edge than usual.

"I found a key to an active safe deposit box my father had at Windsor Bank that no one seemed to know about."

"How is that possible if he's been dead for eighteen years? Doesn't the bank have to report those to the state authorities after a year or so?"

"If the box is left abandoned. His box has been paid for by a joint account he had with a woman named Antoinette King."

"Who's she?"

"I haven't been able to find out yet. There's no trail of her anywhere online that I could find."

"What was in the safe deposit box?"

How long could I leave that door open? Long enough for her to learn that my father may have hid evidence in an unsolved murder? My father, my blood. Our secret.

"That's not as important as what happened after I opened the box in Windsor's presence." A lie. How many lies had I told in the last week? "He made a phone call and five hours later Armstrong and Ketchings bugged my house."

"You're not going to tell me what was in the safe deposit box?"

"Not right now."

"Dammit, Cahill!" She slammed her hand down on the coffee table. Midnight bolted up to all fours. "How the hell am I supposed to help you if you don't tell me what's going on? I guess you haven't been paying attention. I'm pretty damn good at investigating things and figuring them out."

"You're the best. I know." I stared at my empty whiskey glass. Waiting to refill it with courage. Or amnesia. "It's between my father and me right now. Blood. Like the secrets you and your son share."

"Your father is dead and I've never pointed a loaded gun at someone over a secret Luke told me."

"I know. I'm sorry about all of it. You are released from helping me and you can report what happened tonight to the police, if you want."

"Gee, thanks for your okay, Cahill. What part would you like me to report? That I held a man captive in my home at gunpoint or that I invited him over to my house under false pretenses so I could lay in wait to hold him captive?"

"I guess not."

"Who do you think hired Armstrong and Ketchings?" She cocked her head and gave me the big eyes. "Or is that a big secret, too?"

"I honestly don't know. The only thing I'm fairly sure of is that Windsor called someone involved in an incident that happened twenty-eight years ago that began the process of getting my father kicked off the police force."

"But you won't tell me what that incident is?"

"I . . . I can't."

"You can, but you won't." Her cheeks glowed a brighter maroon.

"I can't explain everything right now. I'm sorry."

"But you might never tell me what's really going on, right?"

"Maybe. I don't know yet."

Moira popped off the couch and hustled upstairs. Two minutes later she came back down wearing the sweatshirt from my car I'd lent her a while ago. She didn't retake her spot on the couch. She stood in front of the recliner I sat in and looked down at me.

"I'll send you a bill for the housecleaning, the dry cleaning, and the hotel I stay in tonight." She turned and took a step then stopped and turned back to me. "And I'll clean the clothes you lent me and get them back to you."

"Let me at least give you a ride." I stood up and fumbled for my keys in my pocket.

"An Uber driver is five minutes away. I'll wait outside."

"Cancel the pickup. This is ridiculous, I'll take you."

"No thanks." She headed for the front door. "I'd rather pay to get a ride from a stranger than take one from someone who doesn't know how to be a friend. Call another friend the next time you need help. Good luck, Cahill."

She left and slammed the door behind her.

CHAPTER FORTY

I STARED DOWN at a bowl of stale, soon-to-be-soggy Cheerios. I
didn't have the energy to make something more substantial for breakfast. I'd slept around three hours. And that had been in multiple shifts.

Moira had broken the law for me last night. She'd helped me. Out of
friendship. True friendship that I hadn't had in my life for a long time.
And I'd thrown it away because of pride. Blood pride. Family pride. For
a family that had long been split apart. I had no family. My wife was
dead. My father, dead. I hadn't seen or talked to my mother in years.
I spoke to my sister once a year in an awkward Christmas phone call.

How many more friendships would I have in my life?

I grabbed my phone and tapped a number. Moira surprised me by
answering. I'd thought I'd have to leave an apology on her voicemail.

"I just saw it on the news," she said by way of greeting. She didn't
even sound angry. What had changed my luck?

"Saw what?"

"The two unidentified bodies, one white, one black, each with two
bullet holes in their heads, found in a white van parked in the Coggan
Aquatic Complex parking lot early this morning."

"What's the Coggan Aquatic Complex?"

"The pool at La Jolla High School two blocks from my house."

"Holy shit!"

"Holy shit is right." Her voice went from tenor to soprano. "That's not why you called?"

"No. I called to apologize and to tell you the whole story about my father."

"Considering what I just saw on the news, you need to tell me everything. Now."

"I will. All of it." Finally.

"Pick me up at the Lodge at Torrey Pines in a half hour. I'm just finishing an Eggs Benedict breakfast in my room. I couldn't pass up room service. I'll add it to the cleaning bill for the house and the clothes."

"The Lodge at Torrey Pines?" One of the most expensive hotels in all of San Diego.

"Yeah. You pissed me off last night, Cahill. And I decided to make you pay. Literally."

"I'll be there in thirty."

"Roger."

* * *

I pulled up in front of the rustic but oh-so-expensive Lodge at Torrey Pines, which overlooked Torrey Pines Golf Course and the Pacific Ocean beyond. Moira stood out front, still wearing the Bruin shorts I'd lent her, but holding the sweatshirt I'd pulled from my trunk in her hand. She wore a brand-new Lodge at Torrey Pines sweatshirt. The cost for my sins continued to rise. She hopped into my Honda Accord.

"Nice sweatshirt."

"You're lucky you called when you did, Cahill." She smiled. "I was about to order an in-room massage."

"I get the feeling you're a bad breakup." I pulled out of the parking lot and onto North Torrey Pines Road.

"Actually, I usually walk away quietly. There's always someone else. You really pissed me off."

"I figured that out."

I drove down Torrey Pines into the village of La Jolla. By the time I parked in front of Moira's house, I'd told her everything. The ledger, the safe, the gun, the envelope full of cash, the safe deposit box, the shell casings, the Phelps murder case, newspaper reporter Jack Anton, Jules Windsor, Bob Reitzmeyer, Ben Davidson, Antoinette King. All of it.

We sat in the car next to the curb in front of Moira's house. Two blocks away, there was, no doubt, still a crime scene being investigated by LJPD that had come about because someone had found a hidden safe in the house I grew up in. And I chose to investigate it.

"All of this has to do with your father and a twenty-eight-year-old unsolved murder?" Moira finally said after I'd stopped talking.

"I can't come up with any other explanation."

"And now Edward Armstrong and Jamal Ketchings are dead because of it."

"Yes."

"And we have targets on our backs." Moira's eyes went rounder than normal and her voice lost some of its usual confidence.

"I don't think so." I squeezed her hand. "I think we'd already be dead. Whoever hired Armstrong and Ketchings must have been listening to the live feed from the bug on Armstrong last night. And from somewhere very near here. Whoever it was probably killed Armstrong and Ketchings right after they left your house. Or very soon thereafter if they had a set rendezvous at the pool parking lot. They could have very easily shot us while we were lying blind, coughing our lungs out on your front lawn."

"But maybe they were afraid one of my neighbors would see them. They had cover in the pool parking lot when they shot Armstrong and Ketchings. Maybe they were waiting for a chance to ambush us."

"I don't think so." I continued to hold her hand. "They could have followed us to my house last night and shot us there. The only reason Armstrong showed was because he'd been sent by whoever hired him to try to find out how much we knew. Armstrong must have called the person who hired him to bug my house when you called him and he found out we were connected. They figured out it was a setup and that I'd be there to try to get information out of Armstrong. They planned to turn the tables on me. Find out what I knew. Whatever the shot caller heard last night must have been enough to convince him that we weren't onto him."

"I wish I had as much confidence in your judgment as you do." She eased her hand from mine. "You've been wrong before."

"I know. That's why we're going to the police. I'm not taking any chances. It's time to pull this thing out of the dark and let someone else look at it."

"I'm glad you said that, Cahill. Because I was going to the police with or without you." She opened the door to the car. "Let's check out the house and then go over to the pool."

If I hadn't gotten Moira involved, I'd investigate more on my own before I went to LJPD. But, I wasn't a lone wolf on this one. I couldn't make decisions that would put other people in danger. Still, it was LJPD. Nothing good had ever come from any interaction I'd had with them. Maybe Moira would change my luck.

We walked up onto the porch and sniffed. No nose or eye irritation. Moira unlocked the front door and we slowly entered the house. All the open windows seemed to have done the trick because neither of us felt any irritation. I followed Moira back to her bedroom. Still no irritation. She walked over to where she'd been standing when Ketchings lobbed the tear gas canister into the bedroom. She bent over and picked up her Ruger .38 revolver. She put it on the top shelf of the closet.

I walked around to the other side of the bed and found my Smith & Wesson on the floor. I didn't remember dropping it. When the tear gas hit, my body defaulted to survival and all actions redlined to finding clean air. To live. I picked up the gun and put it in the pocket of my coat.

Moira pulled a pair of jeans off a hanger from her closet, pressed them against her face, and inhaled.

"You may have been saved from a dry-cleaning bill. I'll check the house more thoroughly later. I'll change into these and then we can go over to the pool and talk to the police." She looked at me and I nodded. "Get the hell out of my room while I change. We're not in a war zone anymore, Cahill. Some privacy, please."

I picked up the tear gas canister off the floor and went into the living room. I grabbed the other canister and put both empty vessels on the table in the kitchen. I didn't throw them away because I might need them as evidence to back up the wild story Moira and I were about to tell the police. I'd handled the nozzles on top so as to leave undisturbed any fingerprints the police might find on the canisters. Armstrong and Ketchings had spent time in military intelligence. They were probably familiar with tear gas and knew where to obtain it. I doubted the person who hired them had any connection to the tear gas. Still, I did my best to preserve any evidence, just in case.

Moira came in to the living room wearing jeans and a green sweater.

"I'll wash the shorts and t-shirt you lent me and get them back to you." She gave me a small closed-mouth smile. "I'll take good care of them, Rick."

"Thanks." She was pretty good at this friendship thing. I still had a long way to go.

CHAPTER FORTY-ONE

I PUT MY gun in the trunk of my car. I had a conceal carry license, but I was going into enemy territory. I didn't want to give LJPD a reason to act first and ask questions later.

We drove the two blocks to the high school. La Jolla High School sat below a bluff that held Muirlands Middle School. The northernmost end housed the Coggan Aquatic Complex and parking lot. The lot was roped off with yellow crime scene tape. A white van was parked behind the tape. It looked like it could have been the same van Armstrong and Ketchings painted a Spectrum logo on and drove to my house. Today, it was just white. A white-coated evidence tech had the passenger-side door open and was examining something. I couldn't see who was on the other side of the van.

Four LJPD cruisers surrounded the scene along with two plain-wrap detective cars. Five TV news vans formed a phalanx beyond the police cars. A double homicide in La Jolla was big news. Bigger than a drive-by shooting in Southeast San Diego would ever be. A gaggle of reporters and cameramen formed a semicircle around someone. Probably a police spokesman. There were too many media types in the way to get a good view.

My stomach tightened up and my mouth went dry. LJPD was bad enough. Add the media and flop sweat and nausea were sure to follow. The media swung both ways with me. Sometimes they wanted to make me a hero, but mostly they chose villain. I'd had enough cameras and microphones stuck in my face for a lifetime. Accusations in the form of questions usually followed.

I parked at the opposite end of the lot.

"Maybe you should talk to the detective in charge and I'll wait here," I said.

"You know more about the cause for all this than I do, Rick." She looked at me and tilted her head. "Are you okay?"

"I'm fine." She was right. The story was mine. If I stopped tackling things that had bad memories attached, I'd stay home and watch *Seinfeld* reruns all day.

Moira and I approached the crime scene and were stopped by my old friend Officer Gains who'd been first on the scene when I discovered Sophia Domingo's body. He stood ten or so feet outside the crime scene tape. I gave him a nod of recognition. He gave me nothing.

"I'm afraid you'll have to leave, folks." He held up his hands in a double-barreled stop sign. "This is a crime scene."

"We need to talk to the detective in charge of this investigation, Officer Gains." I matched his business glare. "We have information that may be pertinent to the case."

"You can give it to me and I'll relay it to the appropriate personnel," Gains said.

"If that's the way you want to play it, Officer." I nodded toward the crime scene. "I'm sure the lead detective will be happy that you took over his job and decided who he should talk to and when."

Gains scowled at me. I scowled back. Two chances with him in less than a week, and I'd yet to make friends. I'd better hold onto Moira for as long as I could. Gains finally put his hand up to his shoulder and pushed the call button on the radio clipped to his uniform.

"Sergeant?"

"Gains." A woman's voice crackled over the radio.

"I have two civilians here claiming to have information about this investigation. One of them is Cahill."

Cahill. I didn't even get a first name or a mister. Just Cahill. Probably not even capitalized. A common annoyance. Like, "I'm not feeling well. I think I caught a cahill." Or, "Get the swatter, there's a cahill buzzing around." That's what I got for being a good citizen, "cahill."

"Be right there." The voice on the radio didn't sound happy either.

I scanned the crime scene and surroundings looking for the sergeant. A woman in dress blues and sunglasses appeared from behind the semicircle of media. Sergeant Meyers. Gains' superior from the Domingo crime scene. The cameras and reporters all kept their places when Meyers left the gaggle. She wasn't the face of this crime scene. Made sense. The cameras and microphones were probably all pointed at the lead detective on the case. That ruled out my pal Detective Sheets and his partner, Detective Denton. They were busy working the other murder I had a faint connection to. Good.

Sergeant Meyers marched toward us with a scowl that matched the one Gains still wore. She probably taught it to him during training.

"You claim to have information regarding this crime scene?" Meyers didn't look at or acknowledge Moira. I had all of Sergeant Meyers' attention.

"Yes." I nodded at Moira again. I was being polite. And happy to have someone to share the blame. "We'd like to talk to the lead detective."

"Well, the lead detective is talking to the press right now and the other detective is inside the tape investigating the scene with the crime scene techs." She folded muscular forearms over her chest. "You're just going to have to tell me what you think you know."

"Your call, Sergeant," I said.

"Yes, it is." She took off her sunglasses and narrowed her eyes on the sun and me. "Are you sure the information that you just had to deliver at the crime scene doesn't have something to do with all the TV cameras here?"

A lot of people in La Jolla who thought they knew me well didn't know me at all.

"I'm certain." I bit off the words.

"A little free publicity for your PI agency?"

"Do you want to hear what we have to say, Sergeant?" Heat crept up the back of my neck. "Or should we just keep it to ourselves and go home?"

"You'll stay right here and tell me what you know. Let's step behind this police car so we don't perk up interest from the reporters. Wouldn't want them to think you were on some glory run." She walked around a police cruiser that was parked twenty feet behind us. Moira and I followed. The heat from my neck spread around to my cheeks. Moira looked at me and stepped in front to shield me from Meyers before I could say something we'd both regret.

"Hi, Sergeant. I'm Moira MacFarlane." Moira smiled. Soft and friendly. She stuck out a hand and Meyers gave it a half-assed shake. "Do you have identification on the two victims yet?"

"What do you do for a living, Ms. MacFarlane?" Meyers actually took out a notepad and pen from her back pocket.

"I'm a private investigator."

"What a surprise." She pinched her lips and shook her head. "Your partner here, being an ex-cop, knows that we don't release the names of murder victims until their loved ones have been informed."

"Of course." Moira stayed patient. Much longer with Meyers than she'd ever been with me. "Well, if the victims are Edward Armstrong and Jamal Ketchings, we know their whereabouts last night from about seven forty to eight o'clock."

Meyers put her sunglasses back on. We'd been correct about Armstrong and Ketchings. They were the dead bodies in the van. Finally, Meyers said, "And where was that?"

"My house—7312 Fay Avenue. Two blocks from here."

"What were they doing there?"

I jumped in. "We were interviewing Armstrong to find out who had hired him and his partner to bug my house."

"You're telling me someone put a listening device in your home?"

"Yes. The two dead guys."

"And they went to Ms. MacFarlane's house on their own accord to be interviewed by you?"

Meyers air-quoted "interviewed" with her fingers.

"I used a ruse to get them there. Only Armstrong showed up, but Ketchings came to the house about twenty minutes after Armstrong arrived."

I caught Moira drop her head and stare at the ground out of the corner of my eye. Seemed like she was for the truth, the whole truth, and nothing but the truth. I wasn't going to volunteer that we'd held Armstrong at gunpoint. That made us suspects number one and two, if we weren't already.

"A ruse?" Meyers asked.

I told her about discovering the bug in my home and finding Armstrong and Ketchings in front of my house with the fake Spectrum cable van. Then Moira's call as a wary girlfriend checking up on her boyfriend. I held back everything about my father and my suspicions about Jules Windsor. That was for the detective in charge. I didn't know if Sergeant Meyers was a gossip, and I didn't want the story getting around the Brick House. My father had already suffered enough from Brick House gossip. I didn't want his memory to be further sullied. Until it had to be.

Meyers cocked her head when I was done. "You're either leaving something out or making a lot up, Cahill. Why?"

"I told you the truth, Sergeant." Some of it.

Meyers turned to Moira. "Is this how you remember things, Ms. MacFarlane?"

Moira looked at me and then at Sergeant Meyers. I held my breath. I wouldn't blame her if she told Meyers all the stuff I'd left out. Even us holding guns on Armstrong. She had to know that she wouldn't be charged if she rolled over on me. I was the prize for LJPD. She'd get a pat on the back for wrapping a bow around me.

"Yes." Moira looked Meyers in the eye when she answered. Instead of being happy or relieved that she backed my story, my stomach turned over. I'd gotten Moira involved in holding a man at gunpoint and now she'd lied to the police because of me. Friendship.

"You two stay right here." Meyers wagged her index finger in our faces, then circled around the PD cruiser and walked back toward the crime scene. I watched her go, then turned to Moira.

"If it becomes necessary, I'll take full responsibility for holding Armstrong at gunpoint."

"I think we should just tell Sergeant Meyers what really happened right now before we make things worse for ourselves than they already are." She bit her lip.

"This is my responsibility. You got involved because of me. The only other people who know you had a gun last night are dead. There's no reason to confess to something that had no bearing on the outcome of events. I held a gun on Armstrong. No one else. You got it?"

"Meyers is back." She raised her eyes over the car. "With someone else."

I turned around and looked over the police car at Meyers and the someone else.

LJPD Detective Hailey Denton stared daggers at me that I could feel through both our sunglasses, even though I couldn't see her eyes. She and Sergeant Meyers circled the car and stood in front of us.

Brown hair, longer than I remembered. Tan sports coat, blue slacks. All business.

"Cahill, Sergeant Meyers tells me that you were the last person to see the deceased in that van over there alive." She looked over her shoulder. I followed her eyes. The media who'd been interviewing her before were now heading our way. "Maybe we should talk about this at the station."

"Aren't you working the Sophia Domingo murder?" I couldn't believe my luck.

"Not anymore. Made an arrest and handed it off to the DA and their investigator this morning."

"An arrest?" I didn't think LJPD even had a legitimate suspect as late as a couple days ago.

"Who?"

"That's not public knowledge yet." She looked at the approaching herd of media, microphones and cameras in hand. "But it will be soon, so I guess there's no harm. We arrested your old girlfriend's husband this morning, Jeffrey Parker."

CHAPTER FORTY-TWO

JEFFREY PARKER? THAT couldn't be right. He had an alibi. He'd been in Las Vegas the weekend of the murder.

"Really?"

"Yes, Cahill. Really." A lot of breath in her voice. "Now, if it's alright with you, we'd like to try and solve these other murders, too. So, could you follow us down to the police station where we can talk without the media listening in?"

"We'll be there in five." I turned and walked back to my car. Moira caught up to me as I got in.

"Jeffrey Parker?" Moira looked at me after she slid into the passenger seat and closed the door behind her.

"I guess he wasn't in Vegas when Kim thought he was." I was surprised Kim hadn't called me. She must be frantic. She'd need a friend. That used to be me. I pulled out my cell phone and tapped her number as I turned right on Pearl Street. Voice mail. I didn't leave a message. I didn't know what to say.

"Do you think he did it?" Moira asked.

"I don't know." It didn't matter what I thought. Only what LJPD thought. But I knew from experience that they could be wrong. "But I don't think so."

We beat Detective Denton to the Brick House. She walked into the foyer from around back while Moira and I waited near the sergeant's desk.

"Please follow me upstairs." Denton motioned to the staircase. "We'll talk up there."

She went up the stairs and we followed. It had only been a day since my last interview in a white light room, and I'd survived that one. Still, the familiar sweat started to percolate under my arms and my breath shortened. Denton stopped in front of the door to the interrogation room where Detective Sheets had questioned me yesterday.

"Ms. MacFarlane, would you mind coming inside?" Denton opened the door to the room. "I'd like to hear what happened from you first. Mr. Cahill, please have a seat on the bench. I'll hear your version next."

She pointed at a wooden bench across the hall and followed Moira into the interrogation room and shut the door. I wondered how Moira felt now about choosing me as a friend.

* * *

Thirty-five minutes since Moira went in with Denton. I paced the hall. My phone buzzed in my pocket a couple minutes later. Kim.

"They arrested Jeffrey." Tears in her voice. "I don't know what to do."

"Have you hired an attorney yet?" I'd hold her hand if needed, but practicality came first. It had to if she wanted to get her husband out of jail. The best way to help was to go through the needed steps to get someone out of jail after they've been arrested. I knew the steps. I'd been arrested for my wife's murder and I'd helped other people who'd been arrested. "Has a bail hearing been set yet?"

"Yes. We have a lawyer."

"Who?"

"Alan Fineman."

"Good."

Fineman was the best criminal defense attorney in San Diego. Various talking head gigs on television had given him a national reputation. He deserved it. He'd been the lawyer for someone I once cared about who'd been arrested for murder. The case never went to trial because I discovered the real killer. Clumsily, mostly by accident.

"The bail hearing is tomorrow."

"I'll be over as soon as I can. I'm stuck in the middle of something right now that I can't get away from. It will probably be an hour or so. Everything is going to be okay." I didn't know that, but Parker had the best lawyer in town and the assets to buy whatever experts and tests Fineman needed to offset the state's case. Justice was blind, but not deaf, and money talked.

The door of the interrogation room opened, and Moira came out followed by Detective Denton.

"I gotta go," I told Kim. "I'll be there as soon as I can."

"Mr. Cahill, I'm ready for you, now," Denton said. "Ms. MacFarlane, please stay available as we may need to talk again. Soon."

I looked at Moira. She held my eyes for a second then looked at the floor. I didn't know if that meant she had or hadn't confessed to holding a gun on Edward Armstrong on the night he was murdered.

I followed Detective Denton into the square room with the white lights. She closed the door behind me, and I sat in my favorite chair facing the door and the red-lighted camera above it. Denton sat down at the table kitty-corner to me. Sans sunglasses, I could see the gold flecks in the irises of her brown eyes. It gave her eyes a faint glow. No glowing smile to match as she stared at me across the table.

"Do you know how many murders we had in La Jolla last year?" she said.

"No."

"One."

"Okay." I knew where this was going, but didn't want to kick-start it.

"And now we have three in less than a week that you are somehow involved in."

"I'm not involved in any of them." The sweat trickled down under my arms. I concentrated hard to even out my breathing. "I contacted LJPD in both instances to give whatever information I could to help you solve the crimes." Mostly. Enough for them to find the truth without hurting innocent people along the way. I didn't know yet if I'd succeeded in the Sophia Domingo murder. I didn't know if Jeffrey Parker was guilty or innocent.

"Yes, I know. I'm nominating you for the Citizen of the Year Award." She tilted her head and frowned. "Where were you between seven and midnight last night?"

I told her the same story I told Sergeant Meyers an hour earlier. The same one Moira must have told her five minutes ago. I left out the part about holding a gun on Armstrong. I hoped Moira had, too.

"So, Mr. Armstrong just stood there and complied when you questioned him? Why didn't he just leave?"

"I was between him and the door." True.

"So, you were holding him against his will?"

"No. He may have felt that way. I'm not a mind reader."

"But his partner had to teargas Ms. MacFarlane's house to extricate his partner."

"I could only speculate it was his partner. I couldn't open my eyes."

"You're missing the point, Cahill. Jamal Ketchings had to use tear gas to get his partner away from you and out of the house. Sounds like he was being held against his will. Were you holding a gun on Armstrong?"

"Ketchings chose to use tear gas. He didn't have to." The glow from Denton's eyes seemed to grow brighter. "I'm licensed to carry a concealed firearm and I had one during our meeting. Armstrong and Ketchings had broken into my home and hidden listening devices and then, later, assaulted me. I didn't want to take any chances of being assaulted again."

"I'm impressed with your ability to spend a minute not answering a simple question. You should run for mayor. However, if you don't answer my question right now, I'm going to fulfill a wish I've had for the last two years and arrest you."

"Armstrong was probably aware that I had a gun. Go ahead and arrest me if you can trump up some charge. I'll be out on bail tomorrow." I smiled like there wasn't sweat running down my underarms. "You seem to be unusually concerned with the press. They'll be hanging around when I make bail. I'm sure they'll want to know why you arrested me. They may come to the conclusion that you have a vendetta against me."

A bluff. I'd never volunteered anything to the press. They'd asked me lots of questions over the years and, occasionally, I answered them. But I never sought them out. I liked the press about as much as I liked Denton, but she didn't know that.

Denton's mouth pinched tight, and I could almost feel the heat from the gold flecks in her eyes. She let go a long exhale like she'd been holding her breath for two minutes. She stared at me some more then finally spoke again.

"How did you come across Edward Armstrong and Jamal Ketchings initially?"

I told her about finding the bug on my bookshelf and then the incident with the fake Spectrum van in my front yard.

"And why didn't you report this to the police? You didn't have to deal with anyone here. You live in San Diego PD's jurisdiction."

"I thought Armstrong and Ketchings were involved in something I was investigating on my own. I didn't want to get the police involved until I had more proof."

"Proof of what?"

The moment of truth. I'd already given Moira the okay to tell the police what I'd told her about my father. The fifteen grand, the Saturday Night Special, the empty shell casings. Once I'd told her the truth and saw how it led to Armstrong and Ketchings' death, I knew Moira had to tell the police. There were killers somewhere out on the street who had to be caught. Moira telling what she knew about my father would help that cause. Me telling it would feel like a betrayal.

To my father whom I already knew to be guilty?

Blood. Family. Hope. I'd hoped I could still find a scenario where my father wasn't guilty. Of something. Taking money from the mob. Looking the other way. Covering up evidence of a murder. But I couldn't. Everything I'd found out in the last week had done just the opposite. My father had been guilty. Of everything. Still. My father. My blood. LJPD, where he'd served with distinction until he went wrong. Where the rumors started. Where justice was served on him quietly in half measures. An organization I knew to be corrupt. Not just because of my father. The corruption may have started with him, but it didn't end there. It lived on.

"I'm investigating a twenty-eight-year-old murder. I uncovered some evidence that got me too close to the truth and somebody hired Armstrong and Ketchings to bug my house to find out what I knew."

"Cahill playing hero again. Going lone wolf and leaving more dead bodies in your wake." The glow in Denton's eyes turned into laser beams. "Do you ever consider the possible ramifications of your actions before you decide to throw on your cape? You're a human wrecking ball without a conscience. What's wrong with you?"

I wished I knew. I could blame it on my father's blood, but that would be declaring that I had no choice. I had choices. Sometimes I made the wrong ones. But I had good intentions while I paved the road to hell.

"You want to hear what I have to say or do you want to play Doctor Phil?"

"I want to put you behind bars or force you to move to Alaska. You're a menace." She leaned back in her chair and her jacket flipped open revealing the gun on her belt. I guessed a practiced move meant to intimidate. The gun didn't scare me. The badge that said LJPD on her other hip did, and the white light room did. "Until I can do either, I guess I'll have to listen to your story."

"Do you know anything about the Trent Phelps murder case? Happened in November 1989."

"I ask the questions in here, Cahill. You've been in one of these rooms often enough to know that. You came to us claiming to have some story to tell. Start telling it."

I told her what I knew about the Phelps murder, that my father had been first on the scene. And that his life started going downhill shortly thereafter. I told her about the empty shell casings in his safe deposit box, but not about the hidden wall safe or what was in it. If it had been another detective, any other detective, I might have spilled all of it. Denton reminded me of what the Brick House had been and still was. What would she do with the information I had to give her? Would she investigate or hold onto it until she could use it as a bludgeon against me? It may not even matter. Moira might have already told Denton everything I'd told her about my father.

"Your late father keeps some shell casings in a safe deposit box for God knows how long and you're trying to tie it to the death of a couple surveillance experts you claim bugged your home?" Denton leaned forward into my space. "That's quite a jump. Even for you."

Moira hadn't told her about the gun in my father's safe. Neither would I.

"The shells were .25 caliber. Check the murder book on Phelps. The murder weapon was a .25. Two shots to the head," I said.

"Even if that's true, it's still a leap."

"Five hours after Jules Windsor saw those shells in the safe deposit box viewing room, I found a bug in my house after seeing a fake Spectrum cable van in my neighborhood. A couple days later, the van came back and Edward Armstrong searched for the receiver he'd planted outside my home. I confronted him and he and Ketchings attacked me and then escaped. Check with my neighbors. I'm sure one of them spotted the van in the neighborhood."

"A Spectrum cable van in a residential neighborhood. How unusual."

"You think I like dealing with LJPD, Detective? You seem to know my history here. Why the hell would I want to tangle with anyone at the Brick House if I didn't think it was absolutely necessary?"

"We're just your first stop. The media is next. You get to tell them how you came here and told us how to do our job. More publicity for your backwater little agency."

"I guess we're done here." I stood up.

"Sit down."

"Are you arresting me, Detective? Otherwise, I'm free to go. I came here to tell you what I knew but you don't want to hear it."

CHAPTER FORTY-THREE

I WALKED TO the door and opened it. Detective Sheets stood in the doorway. He must have been watching the live camera feed from another room. He smiled. I didn't.

"Detective, you're in my way," I said.

"Rick, would you mind giving me a couple minutes? No more than ten, I promise." He held up his hands. "Then you can go."

"I can go right now if I want to, Detective." I shifted my gaze from him to Denton.

"I know." He pushed his glasses up his nose. "This would be a personal favor to me. Just you and I will talk."

Denton got up and squeezed by both me and Sheets and left the interrogation room. The bad cop exited, time for the good cop. LJPD was behind on modern interrogation techniques. Nowadays you bond with the subject right away. Any badgering comes later. Sheets was a little late with the friend approach. But he was the closest thing to a clean cop I knew at the Brick House.

Armstrong and Ketchings were dirty, but they didn't deserve to die. And if their deaths were related to Trent Phelps, there was still a murderer free, walking the streets for twenty-eight years. He'd killed again. He knew I was asking questions. How long before he pointed his gun at me?

I retreated into the room and sat back down.

"You were watching the feed. You already heard what I told Denton."

"Yes." Sheets sat down in the chair Denton had vacated. "Why do you think Mr. Windsor is somehow involved?"

I told him what bank manager Nakamura had told me about Windsor never being present for the opening of a dead relative's safe deposit box before and that she had seen him making a phone call right after he left the viewing room.

"Do you know of any connection he may have had with Trent Phelps twenty-eight years ago?"

An LJPD cop engaged in finding the truth instead of breaking hard on me. A ploy? Maybe, but I'd ride it as long as it took me closer to finding out the truth about my father.

"No, but I'll bet Phelps banked at Windsor Bank and Trust. If Windsor didn't hire the guys who bugged my house, he knows who did. Find them and you'll find who killed Armstrong and Ketchings. And probably Phelps. Have you checked Armstrong and Ketchings' offices and computers yet?"

"No." Detective Sheets shook his head.

"That would be a good place to start." I guess I *was* there to tell the police how to do their job.

"We can't. There was a fire at their office last night. It destroyed everything."

Whoever killed Armstrong and Ketchings were smart, thorough, efficient. Yet, they'd left Moira and me alive when it would have been easy to kill us the same night they killed the surveillance specialists. They didn't take unnecessary chances. We weren't a threat to them. Yet. If they found out I'd gone to the police, I might be.

"You can still get their phone records from their provider, as well as e-mail records," I said.

"They had their own server. We're working on getting phone records." Terse, like I'd brought up a bad memory. He let go a long
breath and his shoulders dropped half an inch. "Is there anything else
you can tell me about Armstrong and Ketchings or your father and
the safe deposit box?"

"No, but Windsor sicced some private security goons on me when I
went by his house to ask him some questions. He's hiding something.
I'm sure it has something to do with Trent Phelps' murder. Check his
phone records and find out who he called last Saturday at about ten
fifteen or ten thirty a.m. That number will lead you to whoever hired
Armstrong and Ketchings. And probably their murderer."

"Rick, I've got two more people murdered." Sheets leaned across
the table and touched my forearm. His eyes held sadness that belied
his age. "They're my responsibility. I have to tell their families that
they've been murdered. I owe it to Edward Armstrong and Jamal
Ketchings and their families to find their murderers. I know that you
know what it's like never to at least have that closure. I need your help
so I can give it to someone else."

Sheets knew my story. Knew my wife had been murdered and the
case was never solved. He was the first cop to take my side and see me
as a victim left in the killer's wake instead of the killer. Of course, it
could be a con to get me on his side.

"I'm trying to help, Detective. That's why I came down here." He
might find the killers and bring them to justice, but that wouldn't
bring closure to the family. A murdered loved one was a hole in your
gut that could never be filled.

"I know. I appreciate that. But I don't think you're telling me everything. Detective Denton was right. Finding empty shell casings in a
safe deposit box and tying them to a decades-old murder is a stretch.
A huge one. What are you not telling me? What else do you know?"

"It's not a stretch, Detective. Like I said earlier, my father was first
on the scene at the Phelps murder scene. Phelps was shot twice in

the head with a twenty-five caliber handgun. My father opened a safe deposit box soon after the murder. That box contained two twenty-five caliber empty shells. Five hours after Windsor and I discovered the shells, someone bugged my house and now the men responsible are dead."

"Are you telling me your father murdered Trent Phelps?"

"No."

"Then why else would he have the empty shells from the bullets you claim killed Phelps?"

"He was first on the scene. Someone saw a cop take something from the car at the murder scene and put it in his pocket before any other cops arrived."

"What?" Sheets turned pink. "Where the hell did you hear that?"

"From a newspaper reporter who covered the story twenty-eight years ago."

"He reported in the paper that a police officer removed something from the car before the scene was secured and crime techs were there?"

"No. It was an anonymous call and his editor wouldn't let him put it in a story without corroboration. Look in the murder book. See if any spent shells were found at the scene."

"Rick, do you understand what you're saying? You're telling me that your father took evidence from a crime scene and withheld evidence in a murder."

"Yes."

What I couldn't say out loud yet was that he'd taken the gun used in the crime and had probably been paid fifteen grand to do so. That was too personal. Too revealing. Too much to confess about the blood that ran through me. Not at the Brick House. LJPD. The police force my father served and honored. Until he disgraced it. To tell it all would be too much of a betrayal even after my father had betrayed my belief in him.

"Give me this reporter's name."

I did and also gave him Jack Anton's phone number. Sheets wrote down the information in a notepad. Then he shook my hand and thanked me for talking with him. I put my hand on the door to leave, then turned around.

"I think you made a mistake arresting Jeffrey Parker for Sophia Domingo's murder."

"Why?"

"He was in Las Vegas at the time of the murder. I checked with the hotel. He checked out Saturday morning. Sophia had to have been murdered Friday night at the latest. You saw the decomp starting on the body."

"His hotel room was booked until Saturday, but he didn't physically check out. He had the do not disturb sign on his door the whole time he was supposedly in Las Vegas. The last time he used his keycard to get into his room was Thursday night. No one at the convention remembers seeing him after Friday morning." Sheets exhaled through his nose. "Looks like your old girlfriend is going to be available again soon."

CHAPTER FORTY-FOUR

KIM WRAPPED HER arms around me when she answered the door. The whites of her green eyes were stained red. Her hair was pulled back in a messy ball. I walked her inside her house and closed the door behind us. I stroked her matted hair. I let her pain ooze into me. I felt her hurt. But something else, too. Something wrong inside me felt her warmth with the pain. Wanted to be able to hold her again without the pain. Hold her as I had when we'd been a couple.

"I don't know what to do." She stepped back out of my arms, maybe sensing my selfish desperation pushing against her pain. "What if he doesn't get bail?"

"You've got the best defense attorney in San Diego. He'll get Jeffrey bail." I eased my hand around her bicep and walked her into the living room. She sat down in an off-white upholstered luxury sofa. I took the matching armchair next to it.

"I don't know." Fresh tears welled in the bottom of her eyes. "It depends on how much the bail is."

My eyes did a quick survey of the classy, expensively appointed living room. I wasn't an interior designer, but I'd been in enough La Jolla homes to know that the furniture in the room, when new, had to have been worth close to a hundred thousand dollars. I didn't imagine it would be that difficult for Kim to get together two hundred and fifty grand for a $2.5 million bail.

"Let's see what happens at the hearing first, then go from there. Fineman may get the bail down lower than you expect."

"I hope so. We could barely afford to hire him as an attorney."

"Kim, your financial health is none of my business." I raised my hands palms up and let my head follow my eyes around the room this time. "But this has to be a three- to four-million-dollar home. Jeffrey owns the most successful real estate agency in La Jolla. I'm sure you have the finances for him to get the best defense anyone could hope for."

"That's what I thought until I talked to Jeffrey's accountant today." She looked down at her hands and a tear rolled down her cheek. "The investment in the offices Jeffrey opened up in Del Mar and Fairbanks Ranch spread our resources thin. We're losing a lot more money at each location than I thought. Jeffrey had to take out a second mortgage on the house to hire Fineman."

"I guess being the in-house real estate broker on the Scripps development deal would have pulled Jeffrey out of the hole he was in?"

"Yes." Her answer was like a question. Like she was wary of where the answer might take me.

"Was the partnership with Sophia Domingo contingent upon PRE getting the Scripps' listings?"

"I don't know, but the partnership agreement was already signed when we found out that we didn't get the bid." Kim suddenly stood up and started pacing. "And the partnership with Sophia was only for the La Jolla office. The only office making money and the one that helps offset some of the losses of the other two."

I didn't know if LJPD had any physical evidence against Jeffrey Parker, but they had a stronger case than I was aware of before I came to Kim's house. A strong motive. Sophia dupes Parker into giving her

10 percent of the La Jolla office with the promise of the Scripps windfall. The Scripps deal falls through but Sophia still gets ten percent of
the profitable business. Then ends up dead before she can collect on
the deal.

"Rick." Kim stopped pacing in front of my chair and looked down
at me. Green eyes, swollen but still stunning. "I know I've already
asked a lot of you, but I need your help again."

"Whatever you need."

"Would you investigate the . . . Sophia's . . . her death? I can't pay
you anything for a while, but I will when I can. I promise."

"I don't want any money." I stood up. "But your lawyer won't like
me sniffing around. I'm sure he's got the best investigators in San
Diego working the case."

"I don't know them." She grabbed my hands. "I trust you, Rick.
More than anyone else in my life right now. I know you'll find the
truth."

That's what I was afraid of.

CHAPTER FORTY-FIVE

My phone buzzed as I drove south on La Jolla Shores Drive. The afternoon sun had melted the morning haze and washed the day in bright. Everything but my mood. What would I tell Kim when I found the same proof that LJPD had that her husband had killed Sophia Domingo? I answered my phone hoping for a distraction from reality.

Jack Anton's name displayed on the screen.

"Rick, I just got a call from someone at LJPD about the Trent Phelps murder."

"Detective Sheets?"

"No. Detective Dixon. He wants to go over my notes from the stories I wrote about the murder. Did you talk to the police?"

"Yes, but I talked to Sheets and Detective Denton. I don't know who Dixon is." I took the exit out of La Jolla onto the 52 heading home. "Should I have not mentioned you?"

"No. That's fine. I don't know a Detective Sheets, but the name Dixon rings a bell somewhere in my memory. Maybe he was a beat cop back when I covered crime. Anyway, I'm happy to help however I can. Maybe they can finally solve the murder and give the Phelps family some closure."

There was that word again. Closure. As if finding the killer could bring back a loved one. There was no closure. Only justice. And maybe revenge.

"Maybe. Wherever they are."

"Ingrid, the wife, lives in San Diego."

"Really? How do you know that?"

"We've kept up an erratic correspondence over the years. I interviewed her a few times during the first couple years after the murder."

"In the article about the one-year anniversary, you wrote that she'd moved to Northern California."

"She did. Then she remarried and moved back to San Diego ten or twelve years ago. That's when we restarted our correspondence via e-mail." He chuckled. "That newfangled technology."

"Do you think she'd talk to me?"

"I don't know. I can ask. What do you want to talk to her about?"

"Her husband." I paused. "My father. If there was any connection between the two of them."

"Okay. I'll ask her if she'd mind me giving you her contact information."

"Thanks."

"You're a lot like your old man, Rick."

That statement hadn't been a compliment for almost thirty years.

"In what way?"

"Whatever happened at the end of his career, I always knew Charlie Cahill to be a man who tried to do the right thing and always sought to find the truth, no matter the repercussions." He took a sip of something. Maybe something hard from his desk drawer. "You're the person who got the ball rolling again on the Phelps murder. If you hadn't been persistent, Phelps would still be an uncleared cold case sitting in a file cabinet in the basement of the Brick House."

And Edward Armstrong and Jamal Ketchings would still be alive. My father had only covered up one murder. I'd been the catalyst for two more.

"Yeah. A regular chip off the old block."

I set an appointment to meet with Jeffrey Parker at the jail. I lied and said Kim would be with me to get his approval. I needed to talk to him alone and didn't want to wait until he was out on bail. I wanted Parker to still be caged. Smelling the stink of desperation and fear, his own and others. Hearing the clanging of doors shut on freedom and the roar of caged men's anger bouncing around 360 degrees of cement and steel.

CHAPTER FORTY-SIX

LA JOLLA HAD its own Police Department and criminal court, but no jail. The county jail held what few La Jollans needed incarceration. The San Diego County Jail was on Front Street in downtown San Diego. A twenty-plus-story boxy cement edifice that reminded San Diegans that, even though we lived in paradise, there was still evil among us, and we needed a place to house paradise's lost.

I sat on a steel stool bolted to the cement floor in front of a thick glass window framed by a steel counter and steel dividers halfway up the window affording those on my side of the glass a slice of privacy. A phone handset hung on a lever on the plank on the right side. Parker sat down and picked up the receiver off the counter on the other side of the glass.

Parker wore orange jail scrubs and looked like he'd aged five years since I'd seen him last. His skin matched the gray cement wall behind him. Purple circles hung under his eyes. The scrubs were two sizes too big or he'd shrunk after half a day in jail.

I was 70 percent certain that Parker killed Sophia. The percentage rose the more I learned. If he did it, I wanted him to pay. No second chances on the one *thou shalt not* that only God could forgive. But looking at Parker now, only a few hours in a cage and already a deteriorated version of his free self, I felt sorry for him.

"I thought Kim was coming with you." He cupped his hand around the speaking end of the receiver to try to grab an inch of privacy in a building built of bars where there was none.

"Change of plans."

"What do you want, Cahill? Haven't you inserted yourself into Kim's life enough?" Color returned to his face. Red. "Or did you just want to see me in jail to take the sting out of the fact that Kim chose me over you?"

"I'm here because Kim asked me to do her a favor." My phone vibrated in my pocket. I left it there. "She believes you're innocent. She also chose to believe you when you told her that you and Sophia didn't have a sexual relationship."

"I still don't know what you want, Cahill."

"Kim asked me to help save your life. I want to know that she's not throwing her life away on a lying cheater." I leaned toward the glass and zeroed in on Parker's weary eyes. "How many others were there before Sophia?"

"There wasn't anyone and Sophia was strictly business."

"Listen, asshole, you lie to me again, and I'm walking away, straight to the police." I leaned toward the glass and gripped the handset tighter. "Kim can choose not to believe what her eyes told her in the photos I took of you and Sophia at the hotel. I can't. You and Sophia were working on more than business. Was she the first or were there more? Don't fucking lie to me."

Parker's head and shoulders slumped and his eyes glistened early tears. "There was no one else. Just Sophia."

I'd expected a lie, but his body language told me he spoke the truth.

"If I could only go back in time." His eyes gave way to tears and his voice came out hoarse. "Sophia had an aura. She was beautiful and sexy and she came on to me. It wasn't just her. It was everything wrapped up together. The Scripps development, the money, the way to save my business. Kim and I had been having problems. I know it's not an excuse. I'd do anything to take it back. I almost lost the love of my life. She's the best person I've ever known. We're going to start a family and I've blown everything."

"Why did you leave the convention in Las Vegas early without checking out of your hotel? To set up an alibi for when you killed Sophia?"

"No." He wiped a tear away and shook his head. "Sophia called me and told me that GBASD wasn't going to give me the listings for the Scripps development. So, I drove back to San Diego to meet with her and to see if we could salvage the agreement."

"Maybe you tried to salvage more than just the agreement. You didn't check out of the hotel so Kim would think you were still in Vegas while you cheated on her. Again."

"It was going to be the last time. The guilt of cheating on Kim was tearing me up inside. I needed the Scripps listings to save my business."

"But you weren't going to get them. You figured out that Sophia had used them as a lure to get you to give her ten percent of your business, so you killed her."

"No I didn't." He slammed his free hand down on the steel counter on his side of the glass. "I'd already almost ruined my marriage because of Sophia. Kim is the best thing that ever happened to me. I wasn't going to spend the rest of my life in prison and lose her for good."

"Well, you may have to anyway."

I wasn't any more convinced that Parker was innocent of killing Sophia than when I walked into the jail. But I was convinced that he loved Kim.

As much as I did.

* * *

The phone call I'd received while I was in the jail was from Jack Anton. He'd left me the phone number of Trent Phelps' widow, Ingrid. Now Ingrid Samuelson. I called the number as I headed north on Interstate 5 out of downtown San Diego.

The woman who answered had a Scandinavian accent and didn't sound old enough to be Phelps' wife twenty-eight years ago and the mother of a now forty-five-year-old daughter. I asked to speak to Ingrid. The woman said I was talking to her.

"Jack Anton gave me your number."

"Yes, he told me you wanted to talk to me about Trent's murder."

"Can we do it in person?"

"Well, my husband's at a business dinner. Can you come over now?"

"Yes."

She gave me a Carmel Valley address, and I told her I'd be there in a half hour.

Carmel Valley was east of Del Mar across Interstate 5. No ocean views but huge parcels of undeveloped land, horse country, and gated communities. I punched in Ingrid's address on the keyboard at the gate and the massive wrought-iron barrier swung open to the gated community.

Ingrid's home had a horseshoe stone paver driveway in front of a five-thousand-square-foot home that looked like it had been built, stone by stone, from an English castle complete with a turret at the entrance. Across the highway in Del Mar, the house would be worth five to six million dollars. My recollection was that Phelps had lived in Pacific Beach. It had taken a while, but Ingrid had married up. Or she'd found a career that paid better than doing laundry for the mob.

I rang the bell and an attractive woman in a flowing Mumu opened the door. Silver hair swept back from a perfectly symmetrical face accented by rounded cheekbones and blue eyes. She would have been stunning at any age, but, doing the math, I knew she had to be at least in her midsixties.

"Mr. Cahill?" The lilting Scandinavian accent I'd heard on the phone.

"Yes."

"Please come in." She opened the door into a spotless foyer with travertine floors and a soaring ceiling. Ingrid led me into a living room that had a grand piano in the corner with plenty of room for a sing-around, and an L-shaped sofa that was as big as the patio in my backyard.

Ingrid sat at one end of the sofa. I sat halfway down from her to still be within hearing distance.

"May I get you a refreshment? Wine? Lemonade? Water?"

"No, thank you."

"So, Jack tells me that you're investigating my late husband's murder."

"Yes. But the police seem to be interested now."

"According to Jack, only because you stirred things up, right?" A high-wattage smile.

It would be too difficult and too personal to explain the safe, the safe deposit box, and the dead surveillance crew.

"I guess so. Have the police contacted you?"

"No, and I doubt they will."

"Why do you say that?"

"They never really seemed interested in finding the truth twenty-eight years ago, I can't imagine why they would be now." She cocked her head to emphasize her disdain. "They interviewed me and my daughter one time and never followed up." She laced one leg over the other exposing a tan ankle. "I told them who killed Trent, but they didn't listen."

"Who?" I edged forward on the sofa.

"Whoever was blackmailing my husband. Someone at the police department."

My stomach dropped into a bottomless well. If she was right, my father wasn't just guilty of hiding evidence in a murder. He was the murderer.

"Your husband told you he was being blackmailed?"

"He didn't call it that. I did. Someone on the police force was extorting money from him. The police officer called it a surtax to allow my husband to stay in business."

"Who?" Ingrid knew my last name. She had to know the familial connection.

"He wouldn't tell me. He didn't like to talk about it. He didn't talk much about the business."

"Did he ever report it to the police or the FBI?"

"He couldn't." She frowned and suddenly looked close to her age.

"Why not?"

"My husband borrowed money from the wrong people to start his business when he couldn't get a loan from a bank. They made him do things. He didn't really own the laundromats. They did—and they cleaned more than just clothes."

"Did your husband tell you that?"

"Not at first. I did the books for the business the first few years we were open. I started asking questions when things didn't add up quite right. Trent made me quit and hired a bookkeeper after that. But the bookkeeper was a cousin of one of the men Trent borrowed money from."

"How did you find out about the police extortion?"

"I didn't. My daughter did."

"How?"

"Callie used to walk to the Pearl laundromat after school and do her homework in the office until Trent was done with work. Then he'd drive her home for dinner. She—"

"I thought you lived in Pacific Beach. That would be a long walk."

"We lived in PB, but we used Trent's parents' address in La Jolla as our residence so Callie, I mean Tonya, could go to the La Jolla schools."

"Who's Tonya?"

"It's Callie. The same." A sad smile. "She changed her name after her father died because of everything in the papers about Trent being connected to organized crime. I agreed with her decision because I thought her real name might hurt her chance to go to a good university. Everyone calls her Tonya now, but she'll always be Callie to me."

"Sorry for the interruption. Please, continue."

"It is not a problem." She flashed the Nordic queen smile again. "One day Callie was doing homework when she heard shouting outside the office door. She listened against the door and heard a man say that Papa, I mean Trent. Callie called him Papa. The man said that he was late with the tax. If he didn't pay the next day, there would be consequences. Then the man left. Callie looked out the office window and saw a police car drive away."

"Did she recognize the police officer or describe what he looked like?" I held my breath hoping not to hear that he had brown hair, blue eyes, and a square jaw. Anything but a description of my father.

"No. She just saw the police car drive away." Liquid sparkled in her blue eyes. "Callie wasn't like most teenagers. She still believed her father was perfect. Strong. A good man. She loved him more than anything in the world. More than me. When she walked out of the office, she said Trent looked scared, beaten. He wouldn't tell her what happened when she asked. She told me about it when she got home.

I pestered Trent for days until he finally told me about the loans from the mob and the policeman extorting him."

"But he never gave you the name of the cop?"

"No."

"Did Callie ever see the policeman again?"

"No."

"How close was this in relation to Trent's . . . death?"

"You can call it murder, Mr. Cahill." Her eyes steeled. "That's what it was, and the person who killed Trent is still free."

"Call me Rick." I nodded my head. "That's right, it was murder, and I want to help find the killer." Even if it was my father. "Was this years or months before Trent died?"

"Months. Less. He was murdered six or seven weeks after Callie heard the conversation."

"Did you tell the police what Callie told you about the cop demanding money?"

"Yes." Her eyes and lips squeezed down, showing the flip side of a Nordic queen. "The fat detective took notes and nodded his head like what I told him mattered, but he never questioned me again."

"The fat detective? There was only one?"

"No." She shook her head. "Two. The fat one, Detective Davidson, told the black one to interview my daughter."

"Where's your daughter now?"

"She's a linguistics professor at UCSD."

"Do you think she'd talk to me?"

"I'll ask her. She doesn't like to talk about those times. She likes to remember her Papa as the man she thought he was, not the man he became."

Callie Phelps and I had at least one thing in common. I was just a bit further along in facing reality.

"Please give her my phone number. Maybe learning who killed her father will eventually make it easier to remember her father at his best."

"I would like that. She's had a hard life. She never recovered from her Papa's death. I had to find a job to keep us going. It forced me to move forward and leave the past behind. I found love again and started a new life. Callie never did. She's smart, works hard, but she has no husband. No one to love. She was a happy child. After her father died, she was never happy again."

"Is there anything else you can think of that could help me find out who killed your husband?"

"No. You find the policeman who extorted money from Trent and you find the killer."

"Why are you sure they are the same person? Why would the cop extorting your husband kill a source of income?"

"Because Trent was going to stop paying and go to the police. He knew one policeman he could trust. Three days after he told me he was going to talk to the police, someone murdered him."

"What was the name of the policeman he was going to tell?"

"I don't know. He wouldn't tell me."

Could it have been my father? A man Phelps thought he could trust, but who may have gotten him killed.

CHAPTER FORTY-SEVEN

THE AUTUMN EVENING had pulled the sun down early and it was dark by the time I got home. A black Hummer sat in front of my house when I pulled into my driveway. A man got out of the driver's-side door and walked toward my car. Tall, fit, bald. Black skinny-legged suit. I got out of my car and walked back to the trunk. Where I kept a gun.

"Mr. Cahill, someone would like to speak with you." An accent. Slavic, maybe Russian.

I popped the trunk with my key fob and reached in for the holstered Smith & Wesson .357 inside.

"Don't move." A different Slavic voice. Behind me.

My hand stopped six inches short of the .357. Cold steel against the back of my neck. Fight or flight buzzed along my nerve synapses and my internal radiator hit radioactive. The hand not holding the gun patted me down, then grabbed my collar and pulled me backwards. I didn't resist. Fight or flight weren't options, just instinct.

"This way." The driver waved toward the Hummer. "Don't keep the boss waiting."

The person behind me pulled the gun from my neck and let go of my collar. I walked toward the Hummer. It had tricked rims and chrome finishes. The driver opened the backseat passenger door. I stepped up into the car and sat down on a black leather seat under the flash on the ceiling light.

A woman stared at me from the other seat. Long goth black hair. Jutting cheekbones. Black leather everything including knee-high boots. Raccoon-eye makeup and black lipstick. Underneath the makeup, she may have been attractive and may have been twenty-five or thirty-five.

"You have something that belongs to me. Give it to me and we'll become friends." Just a trace of her friends' accent hiding under an American millennial disinterested lilt.

I noticed a man in the front passenger seat turned toward me just as the ceiling light went dark.

He held a gun with a silencer screwed into the barrel. Pointed at me.

"I want to be your friend." I smiled in the dark and tried to keep my voice from cracking. "But I don't have anything that belongs to you."

"This isn't a good start, Rick." She slung a leather boot up into my lap and pushed the heel into my crotch. Hard enough to know it was there, but not so hard to kill offspring I'd yet to have.

"Why don't you tell me what you think I have so I can solve the misunderstanding?"

"What you took from Sophia." She ground her heel deeper. The pain sucked the breath out of me. I would have punched her in the face if not for the guy with the gun. And the other guy with the gun outside.

"I didn't take anything from Sophia. I never even spoke to her." The woman pushed harder. I groaned. My eyes adjusted to the dark. Front Seat still had a gun pointed at me. The Hummer's windows were tinted, so the boys on the outside couldn't see inside.

She ground harder. I groaned and doubled over, sliding my hand against my pocket until I found the outline of the key fob. I pushed against what I thought was the upper button. The alarm on my car chirped and flashed yellow lights. The man in the front seat moved his eyes from me toward my car outside.

I sprang at him and grabbed the gun's barrel. The woman leaped at me, and I got a knee up just in time to fend her off. Pain shot into my right thigh. I slammed the top of my forehead into the man's nose and kicked the woman in the face as she stabbed a knife at me again. The man's grip on the gun loosened. I yanked it free and hit him in his bloody nose with it then whipped it on the woman. She swung the knife wildly missing me by a foot. I grabbed her arm, yanked her toward me, and slammed my elbow into her temple. She slumped back against the door. The knife dropped onto the car seat. I grabbed it and pointed the gun at the man in the front seat. He leaned against the dashboard groaning like a sedated bear.

Someone outside tapped on the woman's window. Shit.

"Don't move or say anything," I said to the man in the front seat.

The woman was unconscious. I gently slapped her cheek a couple times. More taps on the window.

"Boss?"

The woman's eyes blinked open. They stared at me, but looked confused. Her bottom lip had puffed up where I kicked her.

"Do you know where you are?" I made sure she saw the gun.

She nodded and the gun brought her eyes into focus.

"Boss." Another tap on the window. "Are you okay?"

"Do as I say or I use this." I rolled my hand holding the gun. "You understand?"

She nodded. No panic in her eyes. Just a calm hatred.

"Open the window an inch and tell your man to stop bothering you. If you show him anything but your eyes, the gun goes off." I glanced at the man in the front seat. He still had his head in his hands against the dashboard.

The woman tapped the window button in the arm of the door and nothing happened. Shit.

"Boss!" Outside.

I hit the door lock button and all the doors clicked locked. The man outside pulled on the door hard enough that I could feel the Hummer tremble.

I grabbed the woman by the lapel of her leather jacket and pulled her toward the opening between the two front seats.

"Push the ignition button."

She pushed the button on the dash. I yanked her back into her seat. Pounding on both the passenger- and driver-side windows now.

"Boss!"

"Crack the window." I pointed the gun at her and leaned back against the opposite door.

She opened the window an inch.

"What?" she shouted.

"Are you okay?" The voice from outside.

"Don't bother me. I'm playing with my new toy." The last sentence came out as a purr. She closed the window and looked at me. "Okay. Now what?"

The adrenaline vibrating my body cinched down a notch. My leg stung to life. I glanced at my thigh and saw a hole and dark splotch on my Levis. If she'd hit the femoral artery, I'd already be woozy if not unconscious on my way to bleeding out. Alive, but in pain, still leaking blood, and would need medical attention soon.

"What's your name?"

"Tatiana."

"Okay, Tatiana, you and I have to figure out how to get out of this without guns going off and feelings getting hurt."

"You already hurt my feelings, Rick." She touched her lip then looked at the man in the front seat. "You hurt Petrov's, too."

Hearing his name, the man in the front seat leaned back from the dashboard and looked at me. His nose had a hump in it and blood circled his lips like a war paint Fu Manchu.

"You stabbed me in the leg, so we're even." I nodded at my thigh. "I don't know what you're looking for and I don't care what it is. But, isn't it possible that, now that Sophia's dead, the police found whatever it is when they searched her car and where she was staying?"

"The police don't have it. Trust me." She smiled a nasty jag. "But you already know that."

"No I don't. And if you keep thinking that, we're never going to become friends and we'll all die inside this Hummer."

"You can't live forever." She gave me the smile again. "Let's try it this way. How much do you want for the flash drive? Maybe we can work something out."

Sophia? Flash drive?

The goth psycho had to mean Peter Stone's flash drive. Stone was hooked up with the Russian Mafia. No wonder he was worried. I shouldn't have been surprised. He owned a ten-million-dollar home in La Jolla. There had to be some dirt in all that clean money he donated around town. No matter how many crony capitalism contracts he secured. He'd gone from one mob in Las Vegas to another one in San Diego. Only this one was more dangerous.

"I don't have your flash drive. I don't have anything that belongs to you or anyone else. I'm not in that kind of business."

"Peter Stone might think differently."

"Stone?" I played dumb out of instinct. Preservation. Even with a gun in my hand.

"Yes. Peter. I know you two had an arrangement concerning Sophia."

"He hired me to find her." Dumb didn't work with people who knew the truth. My leg throbbed. "And I did, but she was already dead. I never went into her car. I never went into her home. The closest I ever got to Sophia was tailing her in my car."

"Well, that leaves your ex-lover and her husband, then. Jeffrey Parker. He must have the flash drive. If he does, he's putting his wife in danger. You have seventy-two hours to get me back the drive. If you fail, you'll be responsible for what happens."

Kim.

I waved the gun in front of Tatiana. "You forgot who's holding the gun."

"You have the gun. I have the power." She showed me teeth. "You can kill everyone here tonight. Nothing will change. You and your friend will be dead in less than twenty-four hours. There will be no one to mourn you at your funeral. How sad."

Tatiana reached into her jacket pocket.

"Hold it!" I tightened my grip on the gun. She froze her hand. The man in the front seat's eyes went wide.

"I'm just taking out my phone."

I leaned forward and put the gun against her forehead and slid my free hand into her pocket on top of hers. I felt something metal and rectangle. A cell phone. I took it out and leaned back against the door opposite her.

"Why do you want the phone?"

"To text you my contact information. You're going to need it when you call me to tell me you have my flash drive."

I glanced at the phone, then back at her.

"You can call the police, Rick." She read my mind. "That might keep you alive for an extra day, but it won't save Kim."

I'd negotiated the best I could, which wasn't much of a negotiation at all. Tatiana was right. I had the gun, she had the power. The Russian Mafia didn't make idle threats. I accepted her terms or died, along with Kim. I tossed the phone into her lap.

I started to recite my phone number.

"Rick, you're such a foolish boy. I already have your number." She turned toward the window and swept her arm across it like Vanna White. "Look where we are. I know everything I need to know about you. And your ex-girlfriend. The one you still love."

She punched something into her phone and my cell chimed in my pocket. No need to look at Tatiana's contact information tonight. Hopefully, I'd have a reason to in the next three days.

CHAPTER FORTY-EIGHT

As soon as Tatiana and I made nice, I got into my car and headed to the emergency room at Scripps Hospital in La Jolla. La Jolla. I couldn't avoid it. That's where my insurance dictated I go. The road started to get blurry and the night closed down around my car. Nausea. I'd lost more blood than I realized. Shock had set in and my body was shutting down.

I made it off the freeway and up the hill to the hospital. My hands were numb on the steering wheel. Luckily, I'd been to the emergency room before. Once for me, once for someone else. My vision had squeezed down into a tunnel. I could only see what was directly in front of me. I parked in front of the emergency room and got out of the car. And landed hands first on the pavement, just in time to keep from face-planting. I tried to stand, but my bleeding leg gave way again. The tunnel narrowed. I saw the bottom of the automated glass-doored entrance and started crawling.

The tunnel closed in on itself.

* * *

"Are you with us, Mr. Cahill?" Blurry-bodied voice.

"Mah legged."

"Yes." The nurse came into focus. A nice smiling face welcoming me back to the living. I liked the face. I liked being alive. "A surgeon operated on your leg and we've given you blood and now you're on an IV drip so you can get more fluids back into your body."

"Thakou . . . Thank you."

"You're welcome." She patted my hand. "We're happy to have you back."

"Where did I go?" I looked over my left shoulder and saw the IV bag on a stand connected to my arm. I was in a hospital room with the curtain pulled between me and the next bed.

"A nurse found you just outside the emergency room door. You were in shock and you'd lost a lot of blood." She put her hand on my shoulder. "What happened?"

"I had an accident."

"With a knife?"

"Pretty stupid, huh?" I smiled to hide the guilt I felt about lying to this nice lady who'd helped keep me alive. "I couldn't find a screwdriver and was using a knife to screw in a screw in a picture frame and it slipped."

"You must have been pushing pretty hard on the screw." She removed her hand from my shoulder and folded her arms across her chest. "You nicked the superficial femoral artery. If the nurse hadn't found you, you would have bled to death in another twenty minutes. You're very lucky."

"I feel lucky. And stupid."

"Are you sure there isn't something else about how you were injured that you'd like to tell me? Would you like me to call the police?"

The police. I thought about the goth psychopath, Tatiana, and her threat. No, not a threat, a promise. To kill me. And Kim. I looked at the clock on the wall. Eleven twenty-seven. I had less than seventy-two hours to find a flash drive that may no longer even exist. I couldn't go to the police. They'd just get in the way and the clock would keep ticking.

"I'm sure. When can I leave?"

"The doctor wants you to stay overnight so we can monitor you. The artery had to be surgically repaired." The sweetness had left her voice. "We need to keep you here and put more fluid in you."

"How many more bags?" I nodded at the IV bag above me.

"At least one more after this one."

"Would you mind getting my phone?" I asked. "I need to let somebody know where I am."

She opened a wooden wardrobe against the wall and took out a white plastic bag and handed it to me.

"Your personal items are in the bag and your clothes are in the closet. Your pants are in there, too, but they're ruined. We had to cut them off."

"Thanks. What about my car? I think I left it in front of the emergency room."

"I believe an orderly parked it in the parking structure. I'll check and make sure." She stood staring down at me with her arms still crossed. "You're not planning on trying to leave tonight, are you, Mr. Cahill?"

"No. I just like to know where everything is."

"Okay. I'll give you a little privacy and find out about your car." She left the room.

I fished my phone out of the bag and called the one person I could rely on to help me tonight.

"Rick? Now what?" The pebbles in a clothes dryer voice. Moira. The last time I'd been injured and in the hospital, I'd called Kim. I couldn't rely on her for help anymore. She had more than enough troubles of her own.

I hadn't talked to Moira since we'd both been questioned by the police down at the Brick House. A lot had happened since. No one on LJPD had arrested me for holding Edward Armstrong against his will on the night he was murdered, so Moira must have lied for me in the white square room. Being questioned by the police can be unnerving. Lying to them had to be frightening for someone who'd never done it before. It still scared me and I was a veteran at it.

Now I had to ask her for another favor.

"Are there still some of my clothes hanging in your closet?"

"You're calling to talk about clothes after what happened at the police station today?"

"We can talk about that later. I promise. Right now, I need your help."

"Of course, you do." She paused, but I could hear her breathing. "I'm afraid you'll have to find someone else this time. And every other time going forward. Good-bye, Rick."

She hung up.

Another bridge pulled up and burned. Right in front of me. I couldn't blame Moira. I'd put her in a couple of untenable spots in a period of less than twenty-four hours. She'd helped me out of friendship. What had I given her back? Nothing. Not even a thank-you for lying to the police for me. I'd been too caught up in trying to right decades-old wrongs and playing savior for Kim one last time.

I set my phone down on the nightstand and stared at the blank TV bolted to the wall. An incoming text pinged my phone. I picked up the phone. The text was from Tatiana. It was a photo of the front of Kim's house with the current time stamped on it.

CHAPTER FORTY-NINE

I SAT IN my car in front of Kim's house. No black Hummer. No knife-wielding goth Mob Boss. No gun-toting bald foot soldiers. The text had been a warning only. It had served its purpose. The clock was ticking.

I turned and looked over my left shoulder between the headrest of my seat and the door of the car at the IV bag I'd hung from the hand grip above the backseat window. The liquid still followed gravity from the bag down the tube through the needle stuck into my arm and into my vein. Sizzling pain began to push through the meds the anesthesiologist must have pumped into me while the surgeon mended the injured artery in my leg. The nurse had called in a prescription for Percocet at an all-night pharmacy before I sneaked out of the hospital. I hadn't had time to stop and fill it on my way to Kim's.

I reached across and opened the glove compartment and found a Subway napkin left over from long hours of surveillance in the car. I folded the napkin into a little square and pulled the IV needle out of my arm. I put the napkin over the hole then wrapped it in duct tape I kept in the glove compartment. It held the napkin in place along with the hair on my arm.

I opened the car door and maneuvered my good leg out onto the pavement and grabbed the wooden cane I'd stolen from my sleeping roommate before I staggered out of the room with an IV bag—still connected to my vein—hidden inside my jacket. I left forty dollars on the chair next to the man's bed. I hoped that would cover the cost of a new cane. It wouldn't the inconvenience.

Pain stabbed at my wound like a psycho goth chick with a knife all over again as I leaned on the cane and slid my leg out of the car. Sweat washed down my face. Nausea crawled back up my throat. I took a deep breath and a tiny step. A breeze tousled the flap of denim that had once been a pant leg.

Someone in the emergency room had cut the pant leg from the bottom up through the waistline. I'd closed the gap at the waist by cinching my belt tight, but it had opened a little with each halting step to my car when I fled the hospital. Now a three-inch-wide vent exposed my skin from my hip bone to my ankle.

I stopped at the bottom of the stairs in front of the house and texted Kim that I was outside. It was after midnight and I didn't want to frighten her by knocking on the door. I also wouldn't mind help getting up the stairs.

Twenty seconds later the front door opened and light flooded out of the house silhouetting Kim in the doorway.

"Rick?"

"Yes."

"What's wrong?"

"I'll explain inside."

"Okay." A quaver in her voice. She opened the door wider, waiting for me to ascend the stairs and enter the house.

I teetered on the cane and my good leg and hoisted the bad one onto the bottom step. And dry heaved. I hadn't eaten since breakfast. I was running on empty and empty came up.

"Rick, what's wrong?" Kim scampered down the steps toward me.

"I..." I bent over and puked up stomach acid. My skin went clammy and my hands went numb.

Kim stroked my back as I spit the last of the acid from my mouth.

"Here." She put her arm around my waist and her neck under my arm. "Let's sit down for a second."

"Okay."

We shuffled a couple feet from the puddle of bile I'd left on the stairs, and Kim and the cane guided me to a gentle landing on the other side of the staircase.

Kim straightened up and looked at me through the splash of light coming from the house.

"What happened to your pants?" She threw her hand up to her mouth. "And your leg?"

"I'll tell you inside." The nausea hadn't gone away. It was scraping my stomach for more ammunition. "Can I have some water?"

Kim ran up the stairs and into the house. Despite the nausea, I needed some food. Whatever painkillers they'd given me while they stitched up my leg had burned through my adrenaline and were now working on my empty stomach. If I could keep it down, food would make the nausea go away. Kim bolted from the house and down the stairs three at a time. She handed me an open bottle of water, and I took a long sip.

"Thanks." I took a heartier gulp. The nausea was swimming in the water looking for an exit. "I need something to eat. Can you help me inside?"

"Of course." Kim grabbed me as she had earlier and we glaciered up the stairs.

Once inside, she steered me into the kitchen and sat me down at a rustic wooden table. Bile floating on water rose up my throat. I hyperventilated and fought it back down.

"Can I have a piece of bread?"

Ten seconds later Kim put a piece of freshly cut sourdough in my hand. I took a small bite and swallowed without chewing. Then another, using my teeth this time. My stomach settled and blood returned to my skin. My fingers tingled. But the pain in my leg spiked and reminded me how I'd gotten in this condition.

"The color is coming back into your face." Kim stood over me with a hand to her cheek. Green eyes wide. "I have some spaghetti from a couple nights ago. Do you want some?"

"Please."

Kim warmed the spaghetti on a Wolf six-burner range with a built-in flattop. Range envy supplanted the nausea. She stood over the pot and stirred silently, saving her questions until I had some real food in me. She sipped from a big glass of red wine. The bottle, opened before I staggered into her house, sat on the counter two-thirds empty. She was still in the very beginning of her first trimester and life had been pitching her high and tight lately.

She put a plate of spaghetti in front of me that, right then, smelled as good as anything I'd ever smelled. The taste didn't disappoint. Kim sat down diagonally from me with her own plate. She looked like she hadn't eaten or slept since the police questioned her on Sunday morning. We sat quietly and ate for a few minutes. Me in large fork-spun mouthfuls, her one noodle at a time.

"Are you going to tell me what happened?" She looked at me over the glass of wine she held in front of her mouth.

"Somebody thought I took something of theirs from Sophia."

"Who?" Kim asked.

A lie or the truth?

"Tell me, Rick." She'd read my pause for what it was. "Don't lie to me to try to make me feel better. I'm not going to feel better until Jeffrey's trial is over and he's home safe."

She might not be able to feel better, but she could feel worse.

"I'm not sure, but I think it's the Russian Mafia."

"What?" Her eyes and her mouth went wide. "Why would they think you'd take something from Sophia?"

She hadn't asked me if I'd taken what the Russians wanted. The thought hadn't entered her mind. I loved her in that moment as much as I ever had for her unconditional faith in me. In her belief that, underneath the scars and the darkness, there was goodness in me. I'd disappointed her too many times to count. She'd chosen another man over me. But she hadn't lost her faith in me. The one thing in the mess of a life I'd made that I still strove to live up to.

And she didn't deserve to hear the truth I had to tell her.

"I don't know." I put my hand on hers and gently squeezed. "But it gets worse. It's some kind of flash drive, and since I don't have it, they think Jeffrey does."

"Why do they think that?" Fear rode out on her voice.

"Process of elimination."

"How do they know the police didn't find this flash drive when they searched her car?" She pulled her hand from mine and bit her lower lip. "They must have searched the hotel room, too."

"I don't know how they know, but I can guess. They have someone on their payroll at LJPD. It wouldn't be the first time." I thought of my father and his betrayal.

"Do you think these people killed Sophia over the flash drive?"

"Maybe."

Tatiana stabbed me. Someone stabbed Sophia. The thought that the stabber may be the same person had crossed my mind. The surgeon who operated on my leg would have the wound measurements as evidence against the knife Tatiana used on me. Maybe the wounds matched those on Sophia. Or maybe Tatiana used a different knife. Or maybe Jeffrey Parker used his own knife. Right now, it didn't matter. Finding the flash drive did.

"Then we have to go to the police." Kim stood up. "They stabbed you. They wanted something from Sophia. They have the weapon and the motive. This will get Jeffrey out of jail for good."

"We can't go to the police." I pulled out my phone and showed her the photo of her house that Tatiana texted me. "They'll kill you, they'll kill me, and they'll kill Jeffrey. They aren't afraid of the police. They'd trade one of their soldiers to do life in prison for making an example of us."

Kim sank back down into her seat, eyes wide and mouth slack. "What are we going to do?"

"We have to find the flash drive."

"How?"

"We have to search the house and Jeffrey's office."

"He doesn't have it." She spit the words at me. "Besides, the police already searched all over this house."

"They were looking for something that would incriminate him in Sophia's murder, not necessarily an anonymous flash drive."

"But why would he take it? Just tell the Russians he didn't take it. Make them understand."

"They don't want to understand, Kim. They want the flash drive."

"The police took his computer." She put a hand to her forehead.

"What else?"

"I don't know. I was in shock. Some clothes. Some knives from the kitchen."

"Flash drives?"

"I don't know. I signed some papers, but I didn't read everything they took."

"Show me Jeffrey's office." I stood up with the help of the cane. The pain in my leg doubled, but I stayed upright. The food hadn't helped the pain, but I felt steadier. Stronger.

Kim led me down the hall to Jeffrey Parker's converted bedroom office. It took a while, but I made it on my own. We searched his desk. No flash drives. We searched the closet. Nothing. No safe hidden behind a façade that held a flash drive or decades-old secrets.

We searched their bedroom, the spare bedrooms, every room in the house. Each new search a little more frantic by Kim. Nothing. It was after three a.m. by the time we were done. Less than sixty-six hours to Tatiana's deadline.

"What about his car?" I asked. We were in the kitchen after having gone through every drawer and cabinet.

"The police impounded it."

"Of course." My brain was fuzzy from pain and lack of sleep. "And they searched his office at PRE, right?"

"Yes. They took his computer. I don't know what else. He doesn't have the flash drive, Rick. What are we going to do?" Kim slumped against the kitchen counter. "What are they going to do?"

The "they" didn't need to be named.

They would kill us all. Tatiana's threat had been a promise. The hole in my leg told me violence came easily to her and her surrogates. A reflex. A tool.

A certainty.

"We'll work it out," I lied.

CHAPTER FIFTY

I SLEPT IN one of Kim's spare bedrooms that night. That morning, really. Just for a few hours. She needed someone else in the house with her while she slept. It didn't hurt that I had a gun. And had used it before. I was a shoulder to cry on. Armed security. A friend. She slept just a few feet down the hall, but a lifetime away. She'd pulled me back into her life because she'd needed a friend. Someone she could trust. Just as I had done to her so many times before. I saw a life that was separate from mine and now always would be.

I woke up at six thirty and left a note on the pillow telling her to search Jeffrey's office at PRE. I left without saying good-bye, wearing the sweatpants Kim had lent me out of Jeffrey's closet the night before and my bomber jacket.

The sweatpants were a little long, but had elastic cuffs so they fit fine. The Stanford University logo on the thigh didn't fit, though. Jeffrey Parker and I grew up in the same town. He'd spent his youth in a La Jolla estate, I spent mine in a tract home. Nice, but miles apart in more than geography. All we had in common was Kim and following in our fathers' legacies. His, the most successful realtor in La Jolla. Mine, a disgraced cop who'd been kicked off the force. But Parker was in my world now. The police as enemies, dangerous people wanting something from him or wanting him dead. And his actions pulled his wife and me into the fire with him.

Alan Fineman might save him from prison, but I was the only one who could save his wife's life.

* * *

Peter Stone answered the door on the first knock in full business attire. Like he was about to leave for work, or had been standing by the door. Waiting for me.

"Rick." He looked at my bomber jacket and then down at my borrowed sweatpants. "Morning workout or a flight over Dresden?"

"We need to talk."

"As much as I enjoy such occasions, it will have to wait. I have an appointment to attend."

"Your appointment will have to wait." I flipped open my jacket giving him a glimpse at the holstered Smith & Wesson .357 Magnum I'd transferred from the trunk of my car to the torso of my body.

"Threats don't end well for people stupid enough to direct them at me." The amused smirk morphed into a wolf's snarl. "You of all people should know that."

"This isn't a threat. We're going to talk." I put my hand on the door. "Your choice, either vertically or horizontally."

He eyeballed me for a three-count, then opened the door to let me in. I limped inside.

"That normal altruistic forward lean in your giddyup has been replaced with a hitch. I hope it's only a short-term injury."

I'd left the stolen walking cane in the car and supplanted it with 1600 milligrams of ibuprofen. The cane was weakness. Stone saw weaknesses as a predator would. Something to be exploited. Or killed. A limp hardly showed strength, but I rode it solo without having to lean on something. The ibuprofen had taken the sharp point off the pain, but left the edge. I ate the pain and limped into the living room.

Stone sat down in a massive leather chair, a black monolith above the stark white carpet. The mythic king on his throne. I stood ten feet away in the middle of the room.

"Sit, Rick." Stone swung his hand at a smaller version of the chair he sat in diagonal to him. "Rest your crippled limb."

"I'm fine." I wanted to sit down. I wanted to lie down and take a double dose of the Percocet I'd yet to pick up from the pharmacy. But Percocet would slow my thoughts and sitting would slow my movements if I needed to react quickly. I had a gun, the last resort. Stone had his wits and uncompromising malevolence.

"It's your burden." Stone crossed his legs and rested his hands in his lap. A reasonable businessman. "Now, what is so urgent that you breached my home and are holding me at gunpoint to talk about?"

"Call off the Russians."

"What Russians are you referring to? I'm afraid Vladimir Putin is above even my expertise."

"Stop being clever. Tatiana, the one who stuck a knife in my leg."

"Ouch."

"You didn't tell me searching for Sophia would get me in the shit with the Russian Mafia, Stone." The pain in my leg and my situation stretched my mouth into a raw gash. "You need to tell Tatiana that Jeffrey Parker doesn't have her flash drive and neither do I."

"I don't know who this Tatiana is." Still relaxed. No tell. But lying came as easily to Stone as a knife did to the Russian woman's hand.

"Then maybe I should introduce you to her." I pulled out my phone, took a couple staggered steps toward Stone, and showed him Tatiana's contact information. "Five foot three, goth in matching leather, quick with a knife."

I pulled the phone back and hovered my finger over the phone number. The smirk stayed on Stone's mouth, but something flickered in his eyes before they returned to their normal shark death mask. Fear? He wanted me to call Tatiana even less than I did.

"Let me know if this sounds familiar to you." I put my phone back in my pocket to free my hand and took a step back out of Stone's range. "You and Sophia hooked up when she came here after the Coastal Commission's yes vote on the Scripps sale. A celebration that your bribe through her had made happen. After you two were done, Sophia left, presumably to shower you off of her, and you realized that she took the flash drive that shows you and the Russian Mafia are partners in the Scripps development and maybe other things. Things that neither you nor the Russians want to go public. Or have law enforcement get a look at. Am I getting warm?"

"Not warm." Calm voice, but he slowly rubbed his thumb and forefinger together in his lap, probably unaware of it. "But you seem a bit overheated. Maybe your injury has become infected."

"I'll take that as a yes." I gave him one of his own smirks. "I don't know why Sophia would be stupid enough to steal from you and the Russians. Whatever the reason, you had to get the flash drive back before the Russians knew about it. So, you hired me and probably a couple other PIs to find Sophia. But she ended up dead, so you told me to grab the flash drive from her car. I don't play and turn the scene over to the police, and you have to make a decision. Tell the Russians about the stolen flash drive or hope they don't find out about it. Whether you told them or not, they found out. Maybe one of the other PIs you hired is on the Russians' payroll and told them what you were up to. Doesn't matter. You turned them on me, even though you knew I didn't have the drive."

"Interesting story, Rick. You have quite an imagination." The fingers still rubbed together. "For the sake of brevity, let's say you're right. How would I know that you didn't have the flash drive?"

"Because you know I'm not stupid enough to cross you."

"And how would I know such a thing?"

"Because we had an agreement, Stone. We made one years ago that neither of us has broken. You know you can trust me."

"I suppose I do," he said.

"Then why did you point the Russians at me?"

"What makes you think that I did?"

"Because they knew my weakness." I pulled the gun from my holster and held it at my side. "They knew about Kim. They never would have known about my feelings for her on their own. You did, and you knew you could use those feelings to make me do anything to keep her safe. If you hadn't told the Russians I cared about Kim, they wouldn't have threatened her life. Now you have to convince them to leave her alone."

"I can't convince that little psychopath or her father of anything, Rick. If you don't get them back that flash drive, you and Kim will die. If the information on the drive goes public, I'll be next." Matter of fact like he was talking about the weather. But his fingers still twitched in his lap.

"You don't have to worry about the Russians, Stone. If the clock runs out, I'll kill you first before they get to me."

"We've already discussed the peril of making threats against me, Rick." Stone stood up.

"These are dangerous times." The gun felt comfortable in my hand. A tool, ready if needed. "Ask the Russians."

"Put the gun away and let's figure out a way to extricate ourselves from our unpleasant circumstances."

My threat to Stone had been as certain as the Russians'. A promise. If time expired and the Russians came for Kim, I'd kill them. Then Stone. Or die trying. I'd killed men before. In self-defense. And because someone needed to be killed. From a distance. Up close. I'd seen life leave the eyes and the soul leave the body. Even from a man who didn't have one.

Stone was evil. So were the Russians. I could kill Stone and end his threat, but the Russians would never stop.

I put the gun back in its holster.

"I'm all ears."

Stone looked at his watch. Held up his finger and slowly put his hand inside his coat. I did the same and circled my hand back around the handle of my gun. Stone took a cell phone out of his coat and punched a number. I let go of the gun.

"Tell them I'm going to be late." He put the phone back in his jacket then looked at me. "You say that Jeffrey Parker doesn't have the flash drive?"

"His wife and I searched all over their house last night. The police had already been there with a search warrant. They searched his office at PRE, too. The Russians are convinced that LJPD doesn't have the flash drive in its possession. How can they be so sure?"

"They're sure because I'm sure. The police don't have it." Stone walked over to the glass back wall of the living room and looked out at the ocean a mile away. The marine layer had just started to lift, and the horizon where sea and air separated was visible in a straight line. "Could he have hidden it somewhere else? Somewhere his wife doesn't know about?"

"Anything's possible."

"When's his bail hearing?"

"Today. If Kim can make the bail that's set."

"I'll call Alan Fineman and have a cashier's check ready when the bail is set. All he'll have to do is fill in the amount." Stone turned from the view of the kingdom he rented from the Russians and looked at me. "Tell Mrs. Parker to write me a check for whatever she's accumulated so far, and if it's less than the bail, she can pay me back after the trial."

"If the Russians get hold of Parker, he won't be alive for the trial," I said.

"The Russians are vicious and lethal, but not stupid. They won't kill a man about to be put on trial for a high-profile crime. They're not like the Italians used to be in New York. They do things under the radar, unless they want to make a point. But that's not to say his wife couldn't have an accident."

"What are you going to do when Parker gets out on bail?"

"Nothing. You're going to tell him the situation he's put his wife in and find out where he hid the flash drive."

"What if he doesn't have it?" I asked.

"He has to. It wasn't in Sophia's house or her hotel room. The police—"

"How do you know it wasn't in her hotel room?"

"As soon as I realized she'd stolen it, I had her hotel room searched. The person who killed her must have taken it."

"Why would Parker take it? How would he even know about it? And if he did, what good would it do him? What was he going to do? Blackmail you or the Russians? He's not that kind of guy."

"Sophia conned him out of a percentage of his company with the promise of becoming the realtor for the Green Builders Alliance of San Diego in the Scripps development. That never was in play. He even tried to contact me to verify it, but I never returned his calls." Stone shrugged his shoulders. "Dear Jeffrey was in dire straits. PRE is highly leveraged and payments are coming due. He needed that contract with GBASD to show his creditors that there would soon be a massive influx of cash. When he found out Sophia had played him and he'd soon be in chapter seven or eleven, at the least, he killed Sophia and planned to use the information on the flash drive to blackmail me."

"This is supposition, Stone. Did he contact you after Sophia was dead?"

"No. But I'm sure it would have only been a matter of time. He was arrested before he had the opportunity."

"I don't buy it. I think Jeffrey could have cracked and killed Sophia in a fit of rage. Action without thought. Blackmail takes thought. An understanding of the consequences. I don't think Parker would do it. Especially considering who he'd have to blackmail."

"I take that as a compliment, Rick. However, only a few people in San Diego or La Jolla know of my, ah, decisive actions in protecting my interests. Jeffrey isn't in that select group."

"Okay. I'll talk to Parker." My leg reminded me I'd been standing for ten minutes and that ibuprofen wasn't Percocet. I sat down in the leather chair opposite Stone's throne. "But what if I'm right and he doesn't have it? What if Sophia put the flash drive in a safe deposit box or gave it to a friend for safekeeping?"

"She didn't have a safe deposit box. I checked. And friends?" Stone used his fingers to air-quote the word. "She didn't have any. Her interactions with other human beings consisted of rubbing up against them until they gave her what she wanted. Or until she stole it."

I thought I caught a hint of admiration in Stone's voice. I let it go. We were on the same team now. Partners. Until we didn't have to be anymore or were both dead.

"What about Dina Dergan?" Sophia's kissy-face lady who lunches

"Of course, dear Dina. She may have been the closest thing to a friend Sophia had. More of a mentor, really."

"How do you know Dergan?"

"I used to hire her firm from time to time when I had to deal with the Coastal Commission. That's how I met Sophia. Dina was, ah, mentoring her." Stone winked like Dergan and Sophia's relationship was a secret.

"But you switched to Sophia for the Scripps deal."

"Unofficially."

"What does that mean?"

"Sophia worked strictly on a cash basis." Another smirk.

That would explain why she hadn't filed a tax return in three years.

"How did Dergan feel about Sophia stealing your business from her?"

"She feigned relief. GBASD's business was never quite green enough for Dina, even though our money was."

"If Sophia stole your business from Dergan, why do you think they had lunch together last week?"

"Poor Dina was in love." Stone pursed his lips and tilted his head. "I'm sure she couldn't turn down an opportunity to see Sophia even if she was just there to pump Dina for information on the Coastal Commission. But you're diluting your focus. Jeffrey Parker is your target and you'd better zero in on him like he did on Sophia's nether regions." Stone walked into the foyer and held an open hand back at me. "Now time to go. You have your instructions. I have a meeting to attend."

Stone ever in control even while under the thumb, or leather boot heel, of the Russian Mafia. Or so he thought.

I limped through the living room to the front door. The sixteen hundred milligrams of ibuprofen had already worn off. My leg vibrated pain like a hammered thumb in a Road Runner cartoon. I needed the Percocet, but I needed to stay alive first. That meant paying a visit to Dina Dergan if scaring the hell out of Jeffrey Parker didn't produce the stolen flash drive.

CHAPTER FIFTY-ONE

I LEFT THE La Jolla Courthouse at nine forty-five a.m. Parker's bail was set at $2.5 million, and Kim paid a bail bondsman two hundred fifty thousand dollars of Peter Stone's money to cover the bail. Parker should be home in a couple hours. Kim wouldn't be the only one there to share his homecoming.

My phone rang as I walked back to my car. Blocked.

"Mr. Cahill?" A woman's voice.

"Yes."

"My mother said you wanted to talk to me about my father's murder."

"Callie?" Trent Phelps' daughter.

"Tonya."

"Sorry. Tonya. Could we meet?" Silence. "It would only take about a half hour of your time. I could meet you at UCSD, if that would make it easier."

"I don't really like talking about my father. I called you because my mother asked me to."

"I can understand that. It's a horrible thing to go through." I'd lost my wife to murder, but I wouldn't use that as a way in. It would cheapen Colleen's life. A sad anecdote to pull out when I needed something. I couldn't tarnish her memory that way. "But the person who killed your father may still be walking the streets a free man. Maybe you and I can help bring him to justice."

Unless the killer was my father, who'd spent the end of his life in his own prison. If he was, I needed to know.

"What's justice, Mr. Cahill? Is it going to bring my father back? Or yours?"

My father?

"What do you know about my father?"

"Just what I read in the newspaper when he died."

"He died eighteen years ago. Why would you even be aware of his death? It wasn't front-page news. It was buried in the obituaries."

"I met him a long time ago. I really have to go. I'm sorry I can't help you with your quest."

"Wait. When did you meet my father?"

"When the manager of the Pearl laundromat called the police when he thought someone tried to rob us. Your father and another police officer answered the call."

"What happened?"

"It was a misunderstanding. A friend of my father's was just trying to collect on a debt. I have to go."

"Wait. When was this in relation to your father's death?"

"A few months before. I don't remember. I really have to go." She hung up.

I hovered my finger over the call button. Why had she mentioned my father? Why wouldn't she talk to me about her own father if I was the only person trying to solve his murder? Had the man collecting on a debt really been a mob tough guy? I put the phone back in my pocket. I needed to talk to Ingrid Samuelson again before I made a second run at her daughter.

CHAPTER FIFTY-TWO

I PARKED UP the hill above Kim's house on Calle Del Oro. Far enough away not to be recognized. I used my binoculars to get a good view of the house. Kim's BMW finally pulled into the driveway a little after eleven. She and Parker exited the car and went inside their highly leveraged house. I drove down the hill as soon as he went inside, whipped a U-turn, and parked just below the driveway. I got out of the car and took the steps up to the front door.

This time I had the stolen cane with me. It eased the pain a bit and made walking easier, but that's not why I brought it.

I hard-knocked the door. Parker answered with Kim behind his shoulder. He looked irritated. She looked worried.

"Cahill, I was just let out of jail." His perfect face went tight. "Can't you leave us alone just once so my wife and I can spend some time together?"

"I need less than five minutes."

"I'm trying to keep my temper, but you're not making it easy. Kim is my wife. You can't just drop by here to talk to her whenever you please. In fact, you can't drop by here at all anymore."

Kim grimaced, but didn't say a word. She just stood behind her husband.

"I'm here to talk to you."

"Rick, now's not a good time." Kim finally spoke up.

"It doesn't matter if it's a good or a bad time. We have to talk right now." I looked over my shoulder then back at Parker. "You want to do it out here so your neighbors can listen or are you going to invite me in?"

Parker opened the door and stepped back, bumping into Kim. I three-legged it inside.

"What's wrong with your leg?" Parker asked. The expression on his face said he asked out of curiosity, not concern.

"Somebody stuck a knife in it."

"I guess that's the hazard of the trade when you get paid to spy on people."

"Jeffrey!" Kim raised her voice.

Parker headed into the living room without responding to his wife. Kim followed. I brought up the rear. Parker spun around when he entered the living room.

"Well?"

"We need to talk alone."

"I want to be here," Kim said.

"This is between your husband and me. Go take a drive."

"Don't talk to my wife like that." Parker took a step toward me. I held my ground. Bad leg or not, I relished the chance to lay him out for the way he screwed up Kim's life. He probably felt the same way about me. But I wasn't going to beat a man in front of his wife. Unless I had to.

"Kim, go take a drive." I shot a look at Kim, then zeroed back onto Parker, in case he got brave. Fear in Kim's eyes. She walked through the living room into the kitchen and grabbed her purse off the counter.

"Where are you going?" Parker's voice broke up an octave.

"Just tell him what he wants to know." Kim walked toward the front door. "I'll be back in a half hour." She slammed the door behind her.

Parker turned back to me after he watched his wife leave his four-million-dollar home. "Now what's so damn important, Rick?"

I whipped up the cane and jammed the rubber tip into Parker's chest. He fell backwards, arms windmilling. His leg caught the corner of the couch and he landed on his back. I flipped the cane around, grabbing it by the tip end, and leaped one legged toward Parker. He crabbed backwards. Eyes wide in fear. That's what I wanted. I swung the cane and connected with his right thigh. He yelped. I swung the cane. Ribs. A shriek.

I held the cane over my head and yelled, "Where's the fucking flash drive?"

"What flash drive?" He went fetal, covering up everything vital.

I slammed the cane down onto his shin. The carved handle broke off and shot across the room. A high-pitched wail burst from Parker.

"Where's the flash drive you took from Sophia after you killed her?" I reloaded over my head.

"I don't know what you're talking about!" Parker held his hands up in front of his body to ward off the next blow. "I didn't kill Sophia!"

"They're going to kill Kim unless you give me that fucking drive."

"What? Who?" Terror in his eyes. "I don't have anything!"

I tossed the broken cane onto the couch and reached a hand down to Parker. He covered up like I was going to hit him again. The adrenaline drained out of me and a sick feeling settled into the pit of my stomach.

"I'm done." I continued to hold my hand out to Parker. He slowly reached his hand up and I took hold of it with both of mine and pulled him up. Pain shot through my leg. Not enough. I wanted more to offset what I'd just done. I directed Parker over to the couch and he dropped down into it holding his ribs.

"What the hell's the matter with you?" He rubbed his ribs with his right hand. "I would have told you the same thing if you would have just asked me without beating me with the damn cane."

"I don't have time for interrogation 101. Besides, I know you're a good liar. I had to get the truth fast." I grabbed the broken cane sitting next to him off the couch. "Sophia stole a flash drive from some dangerous people. They stuck a knife in my leg to show me they're serious. They think you have the drive, and I have two days left to find it for them."

"They said they'd kill Kim?"

"Yep. And me. They'll get to you in prison or after the publicity from the trial dies down if you get off. They don't play. They kill."

I limped over to the wall and picked up the cane's broken handle and headed for the front door. I turned back to look at Parker who watched me over the back of the couch.

"You don't tell Kim about the cane, and I won't tell her about what you did with Sophia during your down time."

Parker shook his head. "What are you going to do now?"

"Find the flash drive or kill them all."

"Jesus."

"Yeah. I'll be asking for his help, too."

CHAPTER FIFTY-THREE

I drove north up Interstate 5 to Carlsbad. Dergan Consulting. Dina Dergan. According to Stone, Sophia Domingo's onetime, but no longer, girlfriend. Girlfriend was too strong a word. Sophia didn't have girlfriends or boyfriends. She had hosts. She sucked what she needed from them, then tossed their empty carcasses aside. Again, Stone's perceptions.

I was now taking Peter Stone at his word. I wondered when my car would fall into the sky. My world had turned upside down.

If Stone was right about Dergan, she had a motive to kill Sophia. Jilted lover, who'd been used instead of loved. A knife was personal. Up close. She'd see the life leave Sophia's eyes. Forty stab wounds meant rage. Payback.

But I'd already met one woman who liked knives. And she had plenty of motive, too. Although killing Sophia before she gave up the flash drive didn't make sense. Attaching clear thought to a sawed-off psychopath didn't make much sense, either.

The elevator dinged open into a small foyer, which led into Dergan Consulting. A receptionist greeted me from behind a large wooden desk. Young, millennial five-day growth on his face. Man bun. The new world order.

"May I help you?" Dead voice. Dead eyes. Dead to me.

"Rick Cahill to see Dina Dergan."

"Is Ms. Dergan expecting you?" The "Ms." sounded like a bumble bee hovering in the air. There was life to him, yet.

"No, but you can tell her I'm investigating the death of her friend Sophia Domingo."

"The police have already been here. Are you with the police?" He looked at me like it was an impossibility. It had been twelve years since it wasn't.

"I'm investigating on behalf of Jeffrey Parker." Not a complete lie. I pulled out a paper badge, my California Bureau of Security and Investigative Services license.

The kid looked unimpressed, his default expression, but picked up a phone and gave Dina Dergan the same story I gave him.

"Have a seat. Ms. Dergan will be out in a minute."

I sat on a white leather upholstered bench opposite Man Bun. Behind him, young, casually dressed up-and-comers scurried about. Everyone seemed to have a purpose in the open office area. The back wall was glass and had a view of the Pacific Ocean a half mile away. The vibe was purposeful. True believers. One desk had a Sierra Club poster. Seemed an odd pairing with a consulting firm that helped businesses and wealthy celebrities cut through the Coastal Commission's red tape.

"Mr. Cahill?" The blond woman who'd had lunch with Sophia Domingo the day of the Coastal Commission vote affirming the sale of the Scripps land to GBASD, Stone's and probably the Russian Mafia's green-faced shadow company. Taller than I'd expected from the photos Moira had taken of her sitting at the restaurant. At least five-ten. She wore gray slacks and a cream armless top with a flowing drop collar. She had swimmers' shoulders and arms that a woman in her forties would want to show off. Tan, lean-muscled.

"Yes." I stood up and put out my hand.

"Dina Dergan." She smiled a professional smile that didn't reach her eyes. They looked tired. The only part of her that hinted she was in her late, rather than early, forties. She shook my hand. "What can I do for you?"

"As you heard"—I nodded at Man Bun—"I'm here representing Jeffrey Parker and I'd like to ask you a few questions about Sophia Domingo."

"Parker's the one who killed her, right?"

"Allegedly." I smiled. "Where can we talk?"

"I'm quite busy, Mr. Cahill, another time would be better."

"An innocent man is about to go on trial for his life. This will only take a few minutes."

She frowned and put her hands on her hips. I stood in front of her, the pain of Jeffrey Parker's situation on my face.

"Alright. Five minutes." She spun and walked down a hall to the right. I followed, pain buzzing up my leg with each hurried step.

Her office had the same view as the outer office. A huge satellite photo of the California coast hung behind her raised glass desk. A little statue of a woman sat on the corner of her desk. It looked like Medusa, but a softer rendering. Dina sat down and motioned for me to take the seat across from her.

"Go ahead, Mr. Cahill. *Tempus fugit.*"

"How well did you know Sophia Domingo?" I needed to find a path to ask her about the flash drive instead of just blurting it out.

"Not that well anymore. She worked here a few years ago, then left."

"You didn't keep in touch?"

"No. Not really." A dismissive shake of the head for a woman she'd kissed on the lips a week ago who now rotted in the morgue. "She called for my advice a few times."

"When was the last time you saw her?" I studied her face, waiting for a lie and hoping for a tell I could spot with a later question.

Dina studied me. Intelligent blue eyes that had suddenly discarded ten years. Maybe she spotted a tell in me. That I was lying about working for Jeffrey Parker.

"We had lunch together last week." Eyes steady. No twitch in her lip or anywhere else. Her hands gently clasped together on the desk.

A wedding ring on one finger, a bandage on another. Moira hadn't mentioned the ring when she spied on Sophia and Dina at lunch. Kissy-face with a woman in public when she's got a man or another woman she's married to at home. Open marriage or careless?

"Really?" I scratched my head. "I thought you said you didn't keep in touch. Just an occasional phone call."

"That's right." No panic. No twitch. "And we had lunch together last week."

"Was this social or one of those advice situations?"

"This was having lunch with a former employee." The professional smile again with a hard glint in her eyes. "Is there anything else, Mr. Cahill? I mentioned that I'm quite busy."

"Just a couple more questions then I'll be on my way." I absently picked up the statue off her desk. It was heavy and made to look like it had been cast in bronze. On closer look, it wasn't Medusa. What I thought were snakes coming from her head was hair intertwined with berries and feathers or leaves. The woman held three doves in her arms. I twisted the statue in my hand then looked back at Dina. "Mother Nature?"

"That's one name for her."

"Kind of a strange mascot for a firm that greases the skids for builders who want to develop the California coast."

"You didn't do your research, Mr. Cahill. Dergan Consulting is very discerning about the projects we take on. Almost all of them involve the best option for the preservation of our coast."

"And where did the Scripps sale fall?" I squished up my face. "I'm guessing into the other bucket."

"We weren't involved in the Scripps project." A couple extra blinks. She hadn't been expecting to be asked about Scripps. The police must not have asked her about it. They'd already zeroed in on their suspect.

"That's odd. Because a couple hours after Sophia left your former-employee lunch or advise-and-consent lunch or whatever you want to call it, she went down and watched the Coastal Commission vote in favor of GBASD in the sale of the Scripps land for residential development."

Dina's face didn't change, but the knuckles of her clasped hands turned white.

"That was her client, not ours."

"But she stole them from you."

"We dropped them." A couple blinks.

"Whatever the case, she ended up being a fixer for them." I raised my eyebrows. "Which is strange because I didn't think she even had a business. At least not in the ordinary or legal sense. She seemed like a free agent who did favors for people and got paid in cash."

"I'm not familiar with how Sophia managed her life."

"Then her calls for advice weren't about the business she learned from you?"

"I don't have time to learn the details of former employees' lives, Mr. Cahill." She stood up. "Just as I'm afraid I don't have any more time for you."

"We agreed on five minutes." I smiled and stayed seated. "I think I have about a minute left. So, you weren't in favor of the sale to GBASD? They're green. Aren't they the best option?"

"The only green in GBASD is greenwash." She put her hands on her hips. "It's time to leave."

I didn't move. "Did you see Sophia after the vote?"

"No." She moved her head backwards a fraction.

"And the only time you saw her recently was the lunch last week?"

"Yes."

"Where were you Friday night the twenty-second?"

"Is that the night the police think Sophia died?"

"Yes."

"I was at a business dinner, Mr. Cahill." She swallowed and picked up the phone on her desk. "Now are you going to leave or do I have to call security?"

"I'm done. Thanks for your time." I stood up, tossed a business card onto her desk, and walked to the door, then turned back and looked at her. "The people Sophia took that flash drive from want it back. If you give it to me, I won't tell them where I got it. If you don't, I'm going to tell them who I think has it. Call me. Soon."

Dina's eyes held steady, but the tan faded from her face. She pushed a button on the phone. "Security . . ."

I left the office before she finished her sentence.

CHAPTER FIFTY-FOUR

I LIMPED BACK to my car and eased into the driver's seat, but didn't turn on the ignition. Dina Dergan was lying. She had the stolen flash drive or at least knew about it. Had Sophia given it to her for safe keeping or just told her about it? Or . . .

Despite what she said about Sophia being nothing more than a former employee, the kiss and Stone's claim that she and Sophia had had a fling years ago said she'd lied. And her body language said the same thing about not seeing Sophia aside from the lunch. They'd at least been friends with benefits in the past and had still been friends at lunch the day of the vote. Had that changed after the vote? Dina was clearly not a fan of GBASD. What if Sophia had rekindled their relationship to get information that she could leverage against a couple Coastal Commissioners to swing the vote in GBASD's favor?

Was that enough to make Dina kill Sophia? Not only a scorned lover, but a duped businesswoman. If Dina was a murderer and had the flash drive, was that justification enough for me to sic the Russian Mafia on her? Mine and Kim's lives for hers? I wouldn't have a conscience if I was dead. I looked up at the tinted window of the corner office of Dergan Consulting and could feel, if not actually see, the silhouette of Dina Dergan staring down at me.

I started the car and left the parking lot. Dina had to have watched me limp to my car from her perch on the third floor. I'd rattled her. If she had the flash drive or knew of it, she'd watched me. She'd want to know what car I drove. Following her in my Accord wasn't an option. She knew my face, she knew my car. I needed another one with tinted windows. Or I needed someone else to tail her.

I parked a half block from Dergan Consulting, but with a view of the parking lot. I grabbed my binoculars from the trunk and set up shop in my front seat. With the binos, I could zero in on the front door and spot Dina if she exited the building.

I tapped a number on my cell phone and held it to my ear as I resumed the view through the binoculars. A few rings then voicemail.

"You didn't tell me about Dina Dergan's wedding ring," I said into Moira's voicemail, then hung up.

She'd told me to stop calling her and asking for favors. That was fair, but I needed her help. Lighting her anger would work better than appealing to a broken friendship. Maybe I didn't have to be dead to not have a conscience.

My phone rang. I answered and put the call on speaker.

"What's your problem?" The machine-gun voice on full burst.

"I need your help. Not as a favor. I'll give you a thousand dollars if you can drive up to Carlsbad and tail Dina Dergan."

"I'm working a case."

"Two thousand."

"Shut up, Cahill!" She let out a deep breath. "What did you mean about Dina Dergan's wedding ring?"

"You didn't tell me she was wearing one when she kissed Sophia Domingo. Would have been good to know."

"I don't remember seeing one." Rare uncertainty in her voice. "If she wore one, I must have missed it."

"It happens." Now I felt bad. I shouldn't have called.

"Shut up. Where in Carlsbad? Her office?"

"Listen, you don't—"

"Shut up. Her office?"

"Yes."

"I'll be there in twenty minutes."

* * *

I waited in my car for Moira to arrive. I didn't expect a happy reunion. Moira had earned the right to be mad. I knew how to be a colleague. I knew how to be a friend, even though I didn't have many. I didn't know how to be a colleague and a friend.

Fifteen minutes in, someone came out of Dergan Consulting. Man Bun. I let him walk out of the binoculars' view. I ran my conversation with Dina Dergan in my head over and over while I waited. Something was pecking at the edges, but I couldn't bring it into focus. I'd already figured that Dina was lying. That wasn't it. The statuette on her desk flashed across my internal screen. Medusa, but not Medusa. I'd called it Mother Nature and Dina had said, "Something like that." No. She said, "That's one name for her." Those were her exact words. Another name for Mother Nature.

Gaia.

The name of the trust that owned the home in Point Loma where Sophia had spent the night after leaving The Pacific Terrace Hotel. I wondered if Dina let all her former employees shack up at her million-dollar hideaway in Point Loma. Or was it just for former lovers? Or current lovers about to be former?

My phone buzzed interrupting my thoughts. Moira.

"Where are you staked out?" Businesslike with a trace of disdain. I told her.

"Okay. I'll position myself on the other side of Dergan Consulting."

"No. You can take my spot. You're riding solo."

"What are you going to do?"

"Get a closer look at Mother Nature."

CHAPTER FIFTY-FIVE

THE SUN HAD dropped below the waterline by the time I arrived in Point Loma. Good. I needed the cover of darkness. I climbed the hill that held the Gaia Trust–owned house and drove past it. A floodlight splashed light over the empty driveway, but the house was dark inside. I drove past and parked on the flat street behind the house.

No streetlight on my end. I sat in the car and let the night fall completely. My phone rang. Moira.

"She's on the move—5-South."

"Thanks. She lives in Del Mar. Call me back if she hasn't gotten off the freeway by the time she hits Del Mar Heights."

"Roger. Where are you, Cahill?"

"You don't need to know. Better for plausible deniability."

"Don't make me your one phone call if it goes wrong." She hung up.

The only friend I had left still didn't want to be my friend. I couldn't blame her, but I had to find a way to heal the wound. I didn't want to die friendless.

I turned the car's interior light switch to off, got out, and opened the trunk. The light went on, but I kept the lid low so not much light escaped. I scanned the street. No one out walking a dog. Lights on in the mansion on the raised lot across the street, but no heads in windows that I could see. There were probably security cameras on the property, but hopefully it was dark enough and I was far enough away to not be identifiable if someone looked at the video later. I prayed it wouldn't come to that. I reached into the trunk, pulled up the carpet, and raised the particleboard flooring to expose the spare tire well. I grabbed the duffel bag flattened down against the tire and let the flooring drop back into place.

The duffel was small and colored gray. My black bag. It held the tools I needed to do things I never told my clients about. Plausible deniability. If the cops ever caught me holding the bag, they'd call it a burglar kit or worse. It held a lock pick set, black ski mask, black gloves, small crowbar, a blackjack, and a penlight flashlight. All it needed were handcuffs or a rope to qualify as a rape kit.

I put the pick set in my back pocket, put on the gloves, and grabbed the ski mask and flashlight. Still no one on the street. I closed the trunk and headed toward Dina Dergan's secret crash pad. I turned the corner and headed down the hill. The downward pressure on my leg accentuated my limp and squeezed more pain out of my stab wound.

Still no one else on the street. I put on the ski mask before I cleared the tall hedges bordering the Gaia house. A floodlight attached to the eaves lighted the driveway and caught the walkway up to the house. Under the eaves below the floodlight hung a security camera pointed at the entrance to the house.

The ski mask could hide my face, but not my limp. I'd be pretty easy to identify if I was still limping by the time someone looked at the security video. A Russian goth girl with a knife and her posse with guns didn't allow the option of turning back. I shuffled through a desert garden up to the front door to stay out of the light.

The front door had a dead bolt. I pulled the pick set from my back pocket and took out a tension wrench and a pick. Breaking and entering could get me Jeffrey Parker's old cell in the downtown jail. My father's credo about doing right even when the law called it wrong didn't apply. I was breaking the law out of self-interest. Self-preservation. No moral quandary. I wanted to live.

I slid the wrench into the bottom of the keyhole, applied slight pressure, and worked the tumblers into place one by one as I moved the pick back and forth with my other hand. Even out of practice, I opened the lock in less than a minute. I pushed the door open and listened for the beep of an alarm system. Nothing. Didn't mean there wasn't one there. I went inside and scanned the wall by the front door with the flashlight. Nothing. If I had tripped an alarm, someone at the security agency would call the house to check for a false alarm soon. I closed the door and locked the dead bolt. The sealed house's smell hit me. Clean. Freshly scrubbed. Pine-Sol–scented air.

My phone buzzed in my pocket. I jumped. My leg spat pain. I pulled out the phone. Moira.

"She passed Del Mar Heights and is still headed south on the 5."

"Okay." I whispered. I still hadn't cleared the house. "Thanks."

"Why are you whispering?"

"If she goes all the way down to Point Loma, give me a call, then you can drop off. I'll put an envelope with two grand under your doormat sometime tomorrow."

"Keep your stupid money, Cahill. Just don't get caught." Moira hung up.

I scanned the room with the flashlight. The entrance opened into the living room. No foyer. The money in this house was in the view, not the outdated floor plan. Even that was reduced down to a single rectangle window looking out the front. A modern house would have had glass around the whole living room. The whole room one giant window. The furniture was nothing special either.

I turned to walk down a short hall and bumped the side of the couch with my leg. Right on the wound. Pain. I dropped the flashlight, swallowed a scream, and tried not to grab my leg. That would just hurt worse.

After I stopped hyperventilating, I stooped down and picked up the flashlight. The carpet's smell kept me bent over. I stuck my nose down near it. Medicinal, yet soapy. It had been cleaned recently. A carpet that was at least twenty years old. The Pine-Sol in the air. Why the deep clean now? Was the crash pad for sale? Or had something needed to be cleaned thoroughly and in a hurry?

I limped down the hall and opened the first door on the right. Bedroom. Empty. Musty, unlike the living room. If the house was for sale, why hadn't the spare bedroom been cleaned? I was pretty sure I knew the answer, but needed more evidence.

The next door was on the left. I opened it. Bathroom. Pine-Sol wafted into my nose and irritated my eyes. Like someone had just spilled an entire bottle on the floor. Something else pushed through the Pine-Sol.

Bleach.

The hair spiked on the back of my neck. The ski mask now hot on my face.

Pine-Sol was powerful enough. Bleach was overkill. Unless you were trying to eliminate DNA. I turned on the light. The dated bathroom was immaculate, but something was missing. Towels. Not a single one on either of the two towel racks. No washcloths either. I pulled open the shower curtain to look at the tub and the smell of recently unsealed plastic fought through the cleaning agents. I examined the shower curtain and then smelled it. Brand new. Dina had replaced the curtain, but forgot about the towels. Unless they were in the washer or dryer. The tub shined like new.

Dina Dergan killed Sophia. I was certain now. And I stood on the killing ground. The recently cleaned carpet, Pine-Sol, bleach, missing towels, new shower curtain, plus the feeling in my gut added up to murder. She'd convinced Sophia to meet her at the Gaia house for one last fling, offered her the shower afterwards, then stabbed her in the tub to make the cleanup easy. If I had a spray bottle of Luminol and a black light, the bathtub would probably light up like a blue oil slick.

Dina must have spilled some of the blood left in Sophia when she wrapped her in the old shower curtain and dragged her through the house to the trunk of Sophia's car. Unless she poured bleach in the rug-cleaning solution, there was probably still some blood and DNA in the fibers of the carpet. I walked back out into the living room and turned on a light switch on the wall. The room lit up from an overhead light.

There was a light spot in the mauve carpet just outside the bathroom. She had used bleach. She probably already had a new carpet on order. I found a laundry room in a pass-through to the garage. I checked the washer and dryer. Both empty. Dina had disposed of the towels she'd used to clean up the blood that spattered outside the shower. The rest went down the drain. I wondered if she'd been smart enough to clean the drain cover. If not, there was probably some of Sophia's hair and blood stuck in it.

That was for the police to find. I just had to figure out a way to get them here with a search warrant. I took a picture of the light spot on the carpet with my phone, turned off the light, then went back into the bathroom and took a couple shots of the empty towel racks and new shower curtain. None of this would get anywhere near a search warrant, but it was a start.

I went into the master bedroom at the end of the hall and flipped on the light. Small master. Queen bed. Painting of the Point Loma Lighthouse above the bed. Small bureau. Nightstand. Bathroom. I looked through the bureau and checked the nightstand. Nothing. I searched the closet for a wall safe. None. Bathroom. Counter, drawers, medicine chest. Nothing. If Dina had the flash drive, she'd probably hidden it here away from her life in Del Mar and Carlsbad. It had to be here. And if the drive was here in the crash pad, it was probably in the master bedroom. Somewhere close when she stayed here. If it was here, she was on her way. The normal instinct is to put your hands on your secret when someone has brought its existence to light.

My phone rang on cue.

"She's on Rosecrans heading your way."

"What do you mean my way?" I turned off the bedroom light.

"I'm not stupid, Rick. Don't insult me. Point Loma. The house where you tailed Sophia to after she left The Pacific Terrace Hotel. I know you're there. I just don't know why."

"Plausible deniability, Moira. Go home. And thanks. I owe you. As always." I hung up to keep her from making an objection. I knew she wouldn't call back with Dina closing in.

I figured I had at least five minutes. I hustled-gimped down the hall, through the laundry room and into the garage. I flicked on the light. Small. Would only fit a car and a half.

A few gardening tools on a workbench. A handcart. A tool box. I whipped it open and dug through a few odd tools. No flash drive. Nothing else in the garage. I hustled back into the house and back into the master. One more check of the closet. I shook the five or so pairs of shoes. No flash drive.

I turned off the light to the bedroom and went back into the closet, left the doors an inch apart, and waited.

The sound of a car pulling into the driveway and stopping with a start. Dina was in a hurry. A few seconds later the click of an unlocked dead bolt and a snick of the front door opening and slammed shut. Footsteps down the hall. Light. She flashed by the closet, dropped her purse, kicked off her shoes, and jumped onto the bed.

The painting that hung over it, now in her hands. She pulled something off the back of the picture frame. I couldn't see what it was, but didn't have to.

The flash drive.

CHAPTER FIFTY-SIX

I EYED DINA Dergan through the slit between the two closet doors. She put the flash drive in her jacket pocket and hung the painting back up on the wall. She stepped off the bed. If she left with the flash drive, Kim and I were dead. I whipped open the closet doors and dove at her. She turned toward me. Horror in her eyes. My shoulder hit her chest and drove her onto the bed, landing on top of her. She screamed. Clawed at my eyes, but got only ski mask. I shot my hand into her pocket, grabbed the flash drive, and rolled off her onto the floor.

My wounded leg gave and I banged into the wall, but stayed upright. Dina jumped off the other side of the bed, snatched her purse, and pulled out a small black canister and pointed it at me. Pepper spray. I lunged for the door. The sizzle of spray hit the wall behind me. I hop-skipped into the living room.

"Cahill?" Dina chasing behind me. "I know it's you."

I made it to the front door. She was ten feet behind me.

"Stop or I'll call the police!"

I put my hand on the doorknob. Breaking and entering. Assault and battery. She could even claim attempted rape. If I ran now and got arrested before I gave the Russians what they wanted, I'd end up dead in jail and Kim dead in her home.

"Put the pepper spray down." I kept my head angled away from her.

"Give me back the flash drive and you can go." Dina back in control.

"Put the pepper spray down and we can figure out how to keep you alive." I tilted my head away from Dina.

"Now you're threatening my life?" A chuckle. She was cool. And had already proven deadly. "You just keep tacking on more charges. Don't you ever want to get out of jail?"

"Put the pepper spray down and we can talk."

I heard movement away from me and then the overhead light went on. I peeked over my shoulder. Dina stood next to the wall near the kitchen. She set the canister of pepper spray down on a countertop breakfast nook that connected the living room and kitchen.

"Okay." She remained standing within reach of the pepper spray. "But there's not much to talk about. If you give it back to me, I won't call the police."

I limped a few feet into the living room. I'd already been teargassed once this week. I knew the damage pepper spray could do.

"We both know it's not your property."

"It's mine now." She smiled. It would have been considered a beautiful smile, if she weren't evil. "And if you don't give it back to me, you're going to jail."

"You don't understand the danger you're in. The people who want that drive back will kill you. If you work with me, maybe we can find a way to keep you alive."

"Empty threats, Mr. Cahill." She smiled a death grin and shook her head. "I'm not afraid of the disreputable people Peter Stone's gotten involved with. I've dealt with politicians who are more dangerous. I'm going to screw Stone the way he and Sophia screwed me. Everyone will learn the truth about just how corrupt the great philanthropist really is. You should be concerned with your own freedom."

"You don't really know who those people are, do you?"

"I know that the shell corporations that are helping finance the construction project have been involved in some shady deals."

"The people behind the shell corporation are the Russian Mafia. And they're going to kill whoever took this flash drive. You already saved them one murder when you killed Sophia. They're going to think you were in on it with her if I tell them where I got the drive."

"Is that what Peter told you? That his silent partners are the Russian Mafia?" Her voice wasn't as confident as her words.

"No. I figured it out when one of them stuck a knife in my leg and told me I had seventy-two hours to find the flash drive."

The fear that I'd seen in Dina's eyes when I attacked her returned.

"I didn't steal the flash drive. I found it in Sophia's purse when . . ." She looked at the pepper spray and then back at me. Eyes wide. "I'm not going to tell anyone about what's on the drive. I looked at it once and clearly didn't understand its importance. You have to tell them that."

"Did you make a copy?"

"No. You have to tell them. You said you knew how to save my life." Frantic. "How? What do you want?"

"I'll lie to the Russians about where I found the flash drive." I locked my eyes onto hers and held them. "If you go to the police and confess that you killed Sophia."

"What?" Still scared.

"I know you killed her in this house." I nodded once. "The bleach. The recently cleaned carpet. The new shower curtain. The cut on your finger. She jumped back into bed with you, then stole GBASD and used what you taught her to get the Coastal Commission vote to go GBASD's way. And you killed her. But at this point, I don't care. Make up a story. Self-defense. She attacked you and you went crazy.

Diminished capacity. Any scenario you like. Just turn yourself in and take responsibility. You have until noon tomorrow."

"I'm not going to spend the rest of my life in prison." She grabbed the receiver of her house phone sitting on the counter and hovered her index finger over the keypad. "I'll call the police and report that you broke in and tried to rape me or you lie to the Russians about where you found the flash drive."

I pulled out my cell phone and tapped the phone number associated with Tatiana's text and hit the speaker button.

"Talk." The distant voice with a hint of a Russian accent.

"I've found the flash drive."

"Where?"

I held up the phone to Dina. She hung up her house phone.

"In the hotel room where Sophia had been staying. She taped it to the bottom of the nightstand."

"And how did you find it there?"

"I bribed a maid to let me into the room."

"Really? How clever. Wait for my text on where to meet." Tatiana hung up.

"If you don't turn yourself in to the La Jolla Police Department by noon tomorrow, my story for the Russians will change."

"How do I know that you won't just change the story anyway?"

"How many different stories do you think I want to give to the Russians?" I limped toward her. "Where's the feed from the security camera stored?"

"It doesn't work."

"Where?"

"It's recorded on CDs in the entertainment center."

"Show me."

I followed her across the living room to a large wooden entertainment center. She opened a cabinet below the TV and pointed at a silver and black metal box with the name Lorex on it. It was old technology. Newer models recorded to a DVR or stored in a digital cloud. I popped open the CD tray and pulled out the CD and put it in my back pocket. Then I unplugged the box and detached the cables just in case Dina had thoughts of popping in another CD and recording my exit. It would be useful if she went back to plan A and called the police.

I walked over to the front door and turned back to face Dina. "Noon tomorrow."

I opened the door and left the house where Dina Dergan slaughtered Sophia Domingo.

CHAPTER FIFTY-SEVEN

PETER STONE ANSWERED on the second knock like he'd been expecting me. His security cameras, no doubt, had a wider view than Dina Dergan's.

"Rick. What a pleasant surprise." He stepped back from the door and butlered his arm. "Festus your way on in."

I didn't know what he meant, but let it lie. No need to show my ignorance and tee him up for another insult. I shuffled through the foyer. He closed the door and passed by me in three strides.

"Have a seat." He stood next to his leather throne in the living room and nodded to the mini me version.

This time I sat down immediately. I was tired and sore. I didn't care about showing weakness or having to make a quick move for my gun. I hadn't even brought it with me. Stone was evil and dangerous. But, right now, he and I were on the same team. And I'd learned he had a twisted honor that was real. And that you didn't want to be on the wrong side of it.

"I have the flash drive. The goth psychopath is going to text me where to meet."

"I knew your blue-collar bulldog resourcefulness would come in handy sometime." He smirked to remind me that even though we were on the same team, he was in charge and I was forever lesser than.

"Stone, just for one night, give it a rest."

The smirk creased sharper. Then he let it dissolve and his shark eyes softened to human for only the second time since I'd known him.

"Where did you find it?"

"I can't tell you, but Jeffrey Parker didn't have it."

"That won't be enough for the Russians."

"I lied to the Russians." Probably a mistake. "I don't want to lie to you."

"Why did you come to me instead of just waiting for the Russians to tell you where to meet?"

"I need you to broker for Kim's and my life."

"Hmm." Stone leaned back in his chair and put his hand to his chin. Seemingly in thought as opposed to relishing the situation I was in and the power he had over me. "I'm sorry to say I don't have quite the pull you think I do. At least, not with the Russians. Not after I let inculpatory information be stolen from me."

"You're the only shot I have." I leaned forward. "I'm involved because you hired me to find Sophia. Kim's life is in danger because you gave her name to the Russians as leverage against me. I found your flash drive. I bailed you out. I need your help."

"They'll want to meet somewhere secluded. They'll kill you there." Stone stood up and started pacing. That didn't calm my nerves. "They'll know you lied. Don't ask me how. But, trust me, they'll know you lied. You might be able to save Kim's life if you tell them the truth, but they'll kill you. If you run, you might be able to stay alive for a while. Maybe forever, if they get bored looking for you. But Kim will die."

"So, the only choice I have is me or Kim? Best case is that only one of us lives?"

"There might be one other option."

* * *

Three SUVs were parked in a semicircle, facing forward, in the clearing at the end of the dirt road in the middle of a horse ranch in Harmony Grove. The moon provided the only light. The black Hummer from the other night was the back of the arc. Two black Chevy Suburbans bracketed it. I parked across from the Hummer, thirty feet away, forming the arrow to the other cars' bow. Two men holding Kalashnikov AK 47s stood next to the bumpers of the Suburbans.

I got out of the car and stood in front of it. The headlights of the Hummer flashed on, flooding me in light. I slowly opened my bomber jacket wide to show the armed men and the people behind the lights in the Hummer that I was unarmed.

The passenger door of the Hummer opened and someone got out. Footsteps on gravel, then Tatiana appeared in front of the headlights. Matching black leather outfit to the one last night. The driver door opened and the skinhead I'd headbutted in the Hummer last night appeared next to Tatiana. He had two black eyes and a swollen nose. He held a handgun at his side. The way he looked at me told me he held a grudge.

"Bring me my flash drive." Tatiana held out her hand in front of her. "And tell Mr. Stone to get out of the car."

I looked through the windshield of my Accord and nodded to Stone in the passenger seat. He got out and leaned against the car with his arms folded. The default smirk on his face. For once, it wasn't pointed toward me. I limped toward Tatiana and everyone holding guns pointed them at me. Her mouth was still swollen where I kicked her last night.

I put the two-inch-long Lexar flash drive in Tatiana's outstretched hand. She snapped the fingers of her other hand and the back-passenger door of the Hummer flew open. A man in his early twenties trotted up to Tatiana holding a laptop. He plucked the flash drive from her hand and opened the computer on the hood of the Hummer.

He opened the flash drive like a folding knife and put it in a USB port on the side of the computer.

Tatiana kept her eyes on me, wearing the same insolent smile from last night, as her minion studied the contents of the drive on the computer. He pulled it from the port then closed the laptop.

"This is it," he said, then handed Tatiana the flash drive and got back into the Hummer.

"Did you look at this?" She held up the flash drive.

"No." I told the truth.

"Are there any other copies?"

"That's the only one I found." The words were true if not the intent.

"That's because Miss Domingo taped the flash drive under the nightstand of her hotel room." The smile hardened. "Right, Rick?"

"Right." I doubled down.

Tatiana nodded to her driver. He put his gun in a holster under his coat, threw Stone's smirk at me, and walked toward my car. Tatiana raised her eyebrows and then looked at the driver like I was supposed to watch him. He went to the back of my car on the driver's side and kneeled at the corner of the back bumper and slid his hand under the car. I knew what he'd come out with even before he removed it from the frame. He walked back to Tatiana then turned and stuck out his hand in front of my face. A black device about half the size of a package of cigarettes sat in his hand.

A GPS tracking device. I'd used similar models myself when tailing surveillance targets from a distance. The device connected to an app on your phone or tablet or whatever. You could watch where the subject went from the comfort of your own home, or you could follow in a car out of sight. Tatiana's men must have put it on my car last night when I was inside the Hummer negotiating for my life.

"You went to The Pacific Terrace Hotel and bribed a maid to get into Miss Domingo's old room?"

"No."

They knew I went to Dina Dergan's hidden house in Point Loma. They may have even tailed me there.

The driver pulled something from the pocket of his jacket and dropped it on the ground. A small canister bounced and rolled to a stop in front of me. Pepper spray.

Dina Dergan wouldn't confess to the police tomorrow. She was dead.

My heart redlined and I fought to keep my breath from following.

"Why did you lie to me, Rick?" Tatiana, in a teasing voice. "We had a deal."

"I was trying to keep an innocent man from spending his life in prison."

"The husband of the woman you love? You are a stupid puppy dog. And stupid puppy dogs don't live very long all alone in the wilderness." She looked around at the trees outside the clearing to make sure I got the metaphor. Or just for fun so I could twist on the end of her knife a little longer.

"I got you back the flash drive. That was the deal."

"The deal changed. As you can see we took care of the one loose end you lied for." She kicked the pepper spray with her Doc Marten and it skittered into the dark. "That leaves one loose end left." She reached out and tapped my nose. "You."

I eyed the men pointing guns at me. No escape.

"Call your father, Tati." Stone's voice floated in over my shoulder. I'd never thought I'd be so happy to hear it.

"Don't call me that." Tatiana straightened and eyes and swollen lips went tight. "Are you here to beg for Rick's life? I didn't think you two were that close. I didn't think you were that close with anyone, Peter."

Stone walked over and stood next to me.

"I'm here to make a business arrangement. Call your father."

"My father's not involved in this."

"We both know that's not true. Call him."

Tatiana put her hands on her hips and stared eyes dead enough at Stone to be his own child. He tilted his head and gave her more smirk. Her driver shifted his feet and mean-mugged Stone. Stone looked unimpressed.

"Do you want to call Sergei before he goes to bed or are you going to wait and wake him up?" Stone asked, his head still tilted.

Tatiana maintained her pose for another ten seconds, then yanked her phone from her pocket and stabbed a number on it. She held the phone to her ear and glared at Stone. I wasn't relieved that she'd directed her anger at someone other than me. There were still men pointing AK47s at me waiting for the command to use them. But Stone had gotten Tatiana to make a phone call that might save my life.

"Papa?" Tatiana's tone didn't match the anger in her eyes as she stared at Stone. She turned her back and walked into the dark. She spoke heavily accented Russian that rose in excitement with every fifth word. The only English word she spoke was "Stone." After a minute of arguing or pleading, she walked back in front of the headlights and handed the phone to Stone.

"Sergei?" Stone lost his smirk. "Yes. That was my fault. I had an error in judgment that won't be repeated. The problem has been resolved with no further repercussions."

Stone listened for a full minute before he spoke again.

"I'm afraid Tati has directed her anger and need for reciprocity at the wrong person." He listened and nodded his head a couple times. "The man who solved our problem is very capable. He lives between both worlds." He nodded again. "You're right. My problem. This man and a friend of his should not be held responsible for my error. Particularly after he took care of the problem. For me. For us." He listened again.

Stone handed the phone to me.

"Mr. Cahill." The voice on the other end was heavily accented, guttural. A wolf's bark. "You disrespected my daughter. That cannot stand."

"It was a mistake. I apologize."

"Apology is not enough. I will give you the life of your friend. You will owe me for your life. I will call you. Maybe next week. Maybe next year. I will ask you to do something and you will do it. One favor for your life. You will do it, I will not call you again. If you don't do it, you will die. And your friend will owe me a favor. I think you know the rest. Do you agree to these terms?"

If I didn't, Kim and I died now. If I agreed now but couldn't do what he asked, I died and Kim would have to make the same deal offered me. Not much of a decision.

"Yes."

"Hand the phone to my daughter."

I held out the phone to Tatiana. She snatched it and stomped off into the dark. She spoke into the phone then listened for a couple minutes without saying another word. Finally, "Okay, Papa."

Tatiana put the phone in her jacket and walked over and stuck her goth-painted face up into mine.

"Remember, Rick, I know where you live. And where your girlfriend lives. Enjoy your stay of execution." She whipped around, snapped her fingers, and strode back to the Hummer. Her posse hustled into their SUVs and hit the ignitions. The lead Suburban spit gravel and dirt and headed down the dirt road, the Hummer three feet behind it with the other Suburban riding its tail.

Stone ambled over to my car and got in. I let the dust settle on the dirt road and in my head, then got into my car.

"I guess I owe you a thanks," I said to Stone and started the car.

"You owe me a lot more than that."

I drove out of the clearing wondering what I'd have to do for the two devils to whom I'd just given my soul.

CHAPTER FIFTY-EIGHT

I MET DETECTIVE Sheets at the Brick House the next day. He led me upstairs into the same square white room where he'd interrogated me just a couple days ago. I sat down in the seat that seemed to be reserved just for me.

"You sure you don't want to grab a coffee like I suggested? It's on me." The walls were already closing in on me.

"It's here or nowhere." Sheets sat down diagonally to me and dropped a manila file folder on the table. "I don't want to talk at my desk because I don't want to have to explain to the rest of the squad why I'm talking to you. You're not very popular around here. Or thought of as trustworthy."

I wanted to tell him what I knew and get the hell out of there. But I couldn't tell him everything and stay alive. I could point him at Dina Dergan, but couldn't tell him the Russians had killed her.

"I know someone with LJPD interviewed Dina Dergan. How close did you look at her?"

Sheets let go an irritated sigh and opened the folder. He flipped through some pages and read one for about a minute. "Dina Dergan, founder of Dergan Consulting." He held a piece of paper up that had probably been copied from the three-ring binder Domingo murder book and read from it. "Last known employer of Ms. Domingo. She and Ms. Domingo had lunch in Carlsbad on

Thursday. Ms. Dergan had dinner with a client the night Sophia was murdered."

"Ms.? I thought she was married."

"Separated."

"Where was dinner and what time did she leave?"

"Are you working for the defense, Rick? All of this should be in discovery."

"I'm working for the same thing you are, Detective. Justice." I opened my hands in front of me. "Just trust me for five minutes."

"I'll try." Sheets looked back at the sheet of paper. "They ate at Coasterra and Ms. Dergan left around eleven p.m. She was back home in Del Mar around eleven thirty."

"I've eaten at Coasterra. It's in Point Loma."

"So?"

"Did you know that Dergan owns a home on Lucinda Street in Point Loma under a shell company named Gaia Trust?"

"No. Whether she does or doesn't isn't pertinent to our investigation. Besides, we already arrested the killer."

"The house is probably a five-minute drive from Coasterra."

"With no traffic, the drive from Coasterra to Del Mar is at least twenty-five minutes. And that's just to the Del Mar Heights exit." Sheets put the paper back into the folder. "Are you positing that Ms. Dergan left the Brigantine at eleven, made the five-minute drive to this house, killed Ms. Domingo, stabbing her forty-two times, carried her to Ms. Domingo's car, stuck her in the trunk, drove her to the Parker Real Estate office, left the car there, flew like Mary Poppins back to the house in Point Loma, then drove home to Del Mar, all in thirty minutes?"

"No. She didn't do all that at once. How do you know that she got home at 11:30 p.m. Friday night?"

"We're relying on her word. But we know she was home at 12:45 a.m. when her son arrived after driving down from San Jose State that night."

"Did you know that someone using a Dergan Consulting company credit card rented a car from Hertz in Carlsbad Friday morning, the day of the murder, and it was dropped off at San Diego Airport Saturday morning at 4:27 a.m.?"

I knew whoever murdered Sophia and left her car in the PRE parking lot had to have gotten back to their own car somehow. That morning, I'd played fake cop on the phone and called every car rental business in Carlsbad about rentals by Dina or Dergan Consulting. I got a hit at a Hertz near Palomar Airport. I'd committed a misdemeanor by impersonating a police officer, but my bluff had worked well enough to even get the drop-off information about Lindbergh Field.

"In Dina's name?"

"No. Her assistant, Glen Mathews, rented it."

"Did he drop it off?"

"I couldn't get that detail, only where and at what time, but you probably can. The Hertz by Lindbergh Field is less than a ten-minute drive to the Gaia house. I'm sure you can check taxi or Uber records to see if anyone got a ride at about four thirty that Saturday morning from Hertz to the house on Lucinda Street or somewhere in that neighborhood."

"So, what's your theory?" Sheets folded his arms across his chest. "I have to get back to my real cases. Like who killed Edward Armstrong and Jamal Ketchings. You remember them, don't you?"

"Yes, I do." I leaned into the table. "Here's how I think it went down. Dergan has her assistant bring the rental car to the office. She takes it down to La Jolla and parks it somewhere near Parker Real Estate. She takes the Coaster or a cab or Uber back to the office after hours and drives her car to Coasterra to have dinner with the client. After dinner, she goes to the Gaia house where she meets Sophia. She kills her, probably in the shower. Then she drives up to Del Mar to make sure she's home when her son arrives. She waits until he's asleep, drives back to Point Loma, puts the body in the trunk of the Corvette, drives it to Parker Real Estate and leaves it there—"

"I got the rest. She drives the rental she left there ahead of time to Hertz and takes a cab back to the house and then drives home." Sheets rested his elbow on the table with his hand up like the head of a cobra. "This is a forty-seven-year-old woman carrying around a dead body like it's an empty laundry bag."

"Dina Dergan is five-ten and physically fit. Sophia was no taller than five-two and weighed about a hundred pounds. Not easy, but doable for a woman in Dergan's shape."

"How did you obtain the car rental information?" He gave me the cop look this time, like he knew the answer.

"I found a way, Detective. In the interest of justice, I found a way."

"My partner was right about you, Rick." Sheets stood up and grabbed the file off the table. "You have a hero complex. You do whatever the heck you want, legal or not, to satisfy your sense of justice."

"I don't give a shit what Detective Denton thinks of me." I grabbed air with my right hand. "I'm just trying to keep an innocent man from going to prison. I don't even like the guy, but he didn't do it."

"How heroic. I have to follow the evidence and the law, not a whim or some need for self-aggrandizement." Sheets held the folder out in front of him and tapped it with his right index finger. "Jeffrey Parker's skin was under Ms. Domingo's fingernail. He had a scrape on his face when we interviewed him on Sunday. He lied about leaving Las Vegas on Friday afternoon. Sophia Domingo lied to him about PRE becoming the realtor for the Scripps development and conned him out of ten percent of his business. He was seen leaving The Pacific Terrace Hotel with Sophia on Friday night. He had motive and opportunity. We've got the right guy. Why else would he lie about being in Las Vegas?"

"Because he was cheating on his wife. Hardly original. And the skin under her fingernail could have happened during sex." I pulled out my phone and found the photos I'd taken at Dina Dergan's murder house. "I've got motive, opportunity, and evidence."

I stood up next to Sheets and scrolled through the pictures I'd taken from the Gaia house. The empty towel racks. The new shower curtain. The spot on the rug.

"Empty towel racks? A spot on the carpet? This is evidence to you?"

"The whole house had been cleaned and smells like bleach. Except for one room that is musty and probably hasn't been cleaned in years. No need to, because the killing took place in the bathroom. The towels were used in the blood cleanup and then discarded somewhere. Dergan probably wrapped the body in the shower curtain when she transported it. Except it leaked blood onto the carpet, so she used bleach on that one spot to destroy any DNA."

"What were you doing in the house?" Sheets narrowed his eyes down on me.

"Visiting."

"Really?" Sheets shook his head. "Whatever the case, the one thing missing from your fantasy is a motive. Not that it would make any difference. Like I said, we have our guy."

"Similar to the motive you attribute to Parker, but stronger. Dergan and Sophia had been lovers—"

"Whoa." Sheets smiled and cocked his head. "Where did you come up with that? Ms. Dergan is married. Heterosexual."

"I told you right here a couple days ago that Sophia and Dergan kissed each other on the lips at lunch last week."

"That doesn't mean they were lovers."

"They were, Detective. It wasn't a European touch-and-go kiss. It was on the lips like they'd done it before and it meant something."

"Even if this is true, you're saying Ms. Dergan killed Ms. Domingo over a lover's spat?"

"Sophia used Dergan just like she used Parker. She got enough information to steal the Green Builders Alliance of San Diego from Dergan Consulting in time to grease the skids so they'd get the Coastal Commission's okay for the Scripps purchase. Add on the jilted lover aspect and you have enough motive for two murders."

"All speculation."

"Add everything up. Check with Hertz and Uber and the local taxi companies. If I'm right, you'll get enough for a search warrant at the Gaia house. You're going to find evidence of blood in the bathroom and on the carpet."

"There's nothing here, Rick." He opened the door and held it open for me to leave.

I walked over to him and stopped under the door jam.

"I know you don't want to put an innocent man in prison, Detective Sheets. That's not who you are. You haven't been here long enough to be corrupted. I'm sure your partner must be chipping away at the edges. Maybe it's already starting to take hold. The arrogant certainty that you know the truth and will make the facts match it."

"You mean the way you do, Rick? We're done here."

Sheets walked down the hall to Robbery/Homicide leaving me standing half in and half out of the square white room.

CHAPTER FIFTY-NINE

I PULLED OUT of the Brick House parking lot and headed north on Wall Street. That took me right past Parker Real Estate. I thought of Kim and how I'd failed her. Detective Sheets had tunnel vision on her husband. Sheets probably zeroed his focus on Parker as soon as he found out he'd lied about being in Las Vegas the night Sophia was murdered. I might have done the same in Sheets' position. LJPD had DNA, motive, and opportunity, just as Sheets said. But I had new facts and the truth.

I just couldn't tell all of it.

I called Ingrid Samuelson as I drove up Torrey Pines Road. No answer. I'd intended to ask her to set up a meeting with her daughter for the three of us. Maybe Callie or Tonya would be more comfortable talking to me if her mother was there. I left a message for a call back.

The University of California at San Diego was only a five-minute drive from where I was. I decided not to wait for Ingrid and took Torrey Pines North at the light. The road wound up a canyon that always brought back a bad memory when I drove it.

I was a senior in high school and hadn't saved enough money to go on the Grad Night outing to Disneyland. I earned enough money for the trip working at Muldoon's Steak House on my weekends. I just hadn't been able to save any. All the money I earned went into the household expense fund. Which my father would pilfer for booze money. All while he had an envelope full of fifteen thousand dollars hidden in a safe.

Why hadn't he spent that money? His family was just eking by. He had to steal from his son to pay for his booze. But he left fifteen grand sitting in a safe untouched. If he were still alive, that would be the question I'd ask him above all others.

The night of the Disneyland trip, a couple buddies and I hid in the bushes and egged the Grad Night buses to the amusement of our classmates inside as they went up Torrey Pines North. We'd broadcast our intentions all week and someone had ratted us out. A cop car had been tailing the buses, and I'd been the one who'd gotten caught because I'd run the wrong way.

Unfortunately, the cop who caught me, Officer Martinez, remembered my father and decided to make an example of me once he learned my name. He cuffed me and took me to the Brick House.

Martinez didn't print me or put me in a holding cell. He removed my handcuffs and sat me down in front of the desk sergeant and told everyone within the sound of his voice that he'd caught Charlie Cahill's kid throwing eggs at buses. Blue unis came over one by one to look at me. Some smiled and shook their heads. Some just shook their heads. The desk sergeant, older than the rest, just looked sad.

After the freak show, Martinez picked up the desk sergeant's phone and called my house. My mother was visiting my grandmother in Grass Valley that week. Anything to stay away from my father and, I thought at the time, me. My sister was in college up at Berkeley. That left my father alone in the house.

Martinez held the phone receiver to his ear and listened, then grabbed my jacket and yanked me up. He shoved the receiver into my hand. I put it to my ear.

"Hello? Hello?" My father's voice wasn't slurred, but I could tell from the tone that he was half in the bag. I'd had eight years of experience hearing that voice and the gradations it would change with each new scotch rocks.

"I'm down at the Brick House and I need you to come pick me up."

"What the hell did you do?"

"Just come. Now." I reached over the sergeant's desk and hung up the phone.

My father didn't arrive for another forty-five minutes. The drive from our house to LJPD took no more than ten minutes. I wasn't a perfect kid, but I'd never been taken to a police station before. Most parents would run right out the door and jump in the car if their kid was being held by the police. Not my father. He wasn't trying to teach me a lesson and make me sweat. He'd taken the extra half hour to sober up.

He wore tan slacks, a blue dress shirt, and a tweed blazer. They were all at least ten years old. He hadn't worn them since his last days on the job. I hadn't seen him in anything other than sweats or jeans and stained t-shirts in over two years. The clothes hung off him like saggy skin. He'd lost twenty pounds since he'd been a cop. Compliments of a liquid diet. His wavy, unkempt hair was combed back and tamed by hair gel. He'd shaved for the first time in a couple weeks, memorialized by nicks on his neck, cheek, and chin. Bloodshot raccoon eyes. He looked like a vagrant cleaned up for a court appearance.

He took careful steps up to the desk sergeant's desk. I stood up, ready to grab the car keys from him and drive us both home. Officer Martinez spotted my father from his desk off to the left and walked over.

"Charlie." He smiled and stuck out a hand. My father shook it once and dropped it. He wouldn't make eye contact with Martinez. "I'm afraid Rick here was engaging in some unlawful behavior tonight.

Once I found out he was your son, I decided to cut him a break. But I'm worried about him, Charlie. I wouldn't want him to take the wrong path. That can ruin a man's life and hurt a lot of other people along the way."

"I'll make sure he doesn't do it again." He stooped, staring at the floor.

"I hope so, Charlie. Cuz he won't get another chance." Martinez leaned into my father's space. "Not everyone gets to walk away free after they commit crimes and ruin the reputation of an entire organization."

My father didn't say anything. The man whom I worshipped as a child. The best man I used to know didn't make eye contact. He just took it and stared at the floor. Beaten without a fight. An empty shell of a once great man.

"Fuck you, Martinez." I stood up and slid between my father and the cop. "Charge me or let me go home."

"What did you say?" Martinez grabbed me by my jacket and pushed me against the raised desk. I wanted him to hit me. Not so I could get him for battery. I wanted some physical pain to drown out all the rest. And I wanted him to hit me to keep me from hitting my father.

"I said fuck you, you fucking pig." As a cop's son, a word I'd never directed at someone in uniform before. Or since.

Martinez pulled his right hand off my collar and punched me in the face. I saw it coming. I'd fought Golden Gloves for four years. I could have blocked the punch and countered with a right that would have shut Martinez's mouth until the doctor took the wires off his broken jaw. But I left my chin up and took the punch. The crack told me my nose was broken before the blood started flowing. I staggered but stayed upright. Woozy, but smiling as I tasted blood.

"Martinez!" The sergeant ran from behind the desk, along with a couple of unis from the adjacent room.

My father just stared at the floor.

"Fuck you, Martinez." I spat blood onto his shirt.

Two uniforms grabbed Martinez and pulled him away from me.

The sergeant shoved him in the chest and snapped his head at my father.

"Take your fucking kid and get the hell out of here, Charlie."

* * *

I never spoke to my father again. I put him to bed when he couldn't do it himself and I cleaned up his puke when he couldn't make it to a toilet or a sink. But I never spoke another word to him.

He died a year later.

CHAPTER SIXTY

I PARKED IN the gym parking lot on campus just off North Torrey Pines Road. I didn't know if Ingrid Samuelson's daughter was teaching a class or even where her classes or office were. I pulled out my phone and Googled the UCSD Linguistics Department faculty. I knew Calista Phelps had changed her first name to Tonya, but I hadn't asked her mother about her new last name. Then I found a Tonya on the list.

Tonya King. Tonya. Sometimes short for Antoinette. The name on the checking account at Windsor Bank that paid the monthly fee for my father's safe deposit box.

I called the number listed for the department. A young woman answered.

"May I speak to Tonya King?" The blood pounding in my head almost drowned out the voice on the other end.

"She's teaching a class until two thirty, then she has office hours until four."

I got her office location and hung up.

Calista Phelps was Antoinette King. The daughter of the man whose murder my father was connected to had paid for his safe deposit box for eighteen years after his death? The safe deposit box that held the empty shell casings from the bullets that killed her father. It didn't make sense. King told me she'd met my father when the laundromat was robbed and all she knew about him was what she'd read in his obituary after he died.

She'd lied to me. What did she really know?

Tonya King arrived at her office at two forty-five. I'd been waiting in the hallway for thirty minutes. She looked like her mother. Tall, blond, Nordic beauty. However, she tried to hide it under long bangs and dark, loose clothing. She was in her midforties, but looked younger than me. The only thing that gave away her age was the way she carried herself. Erect, but weary. Small steps for a tall woman.

"Can I help you?" No smile. Flat voice. She put a key into the lock of her office door and unlocked it.

"I wanted to talk to you about auditing a class." I used a southern accent in case she'd recognize my voice from our phone call. Better to talk to her in her office behind a closed door. I didn't think she'd invite me in if she knew who I was.

"You're lying." A statement, not an accusation. She turned from the door and looked at me. "You can drop the accent. You're Charlie Cahill's son. I told you I didn't want to talk to you."

"Stupid of me to try to fool someone who teaches linguistics for a living." I smiled to try to lighten things up.

"You lied to try to get what you want. I've been lied to enough in my life. Good-bye, Mr. Cahill." She pushed open the door and entered the office, flicking the door closed behind her. Except the door bounced off my foot just inside the door jam.

"I've been lied to enough in my life, too." I eased the door open with my hand. "That's why I don't appreciate you lying to me about not knowing my father very well."

Tonya stared at me with cool blue eyes. No fear, no panic, just weariness.

"Tonya." A male voice behind me. "Should I call security?"

I turned and saw a man standing in the doorway of the office across the hall. Late twenties. Scraggly chin hair. Emaciated under a gray cardigan.

"It's okay, Geo." She walked over and opened the door all the way. I walked in and she shut the door behind me without another word to Geo.

The office was immaculate. No messy stacks of papers on the antique desk. Not the way I remembered my professors' offices from college. Dark oil paintings of women wearing blindfolds over their eyes hung on the walls. Actually, all the paintings were of the same lone woman. She looked a bit like Tonya, but more severe. They were captivating but sad. Self-portraits of a broken life.

I looked at Tonya, then back at the paintings. "Yours?"

"You came here to accuse me of lying, Mr. Cahill. Not talk about my paintings."

"I just want to know the truth." I turned back to her. "Why is your name on a shared checking account that funds my dead father's safe deposit box at Windsor Bank?"

"Sit down, Mr. Cahill." She took the seat behind her desk.

"Rick." I sat in a leather armchair opposite her.

"He gave me money to set up a checking account to fund the safe deposit box twenty-five or so years ago."

"Why did he need you? Why not just open a checking account in his own name?"

"He wanted me to keep the box funded in case he died."

"Why?" I asked.

"He said there was evidence from my father's murder in the box that he wanted to preserve."

"What good would it do if no one knew about it?"

"He wanted me to hire a private investigator and investigate the murder."

"Did you?" Why would he want a PI to find the killer he'd blackmailed?

"No." She lifted her chin. "After he died, I didn't care anymore. The two men who were once important in my life were frauds. The safe deposit box was from a life I'd stopped living."

"But you kept putting money into the checking account to keep the box open for eighteen years after my father died. That money must have added up over the years for a life you weren't living anymore."

"I didn't care who killed my father. Your father did for a while before he lost his soul to a bottle. I used money from my father's life insurance to fund the safe deposit box. I figured maybe someday someone who cared would come looking. I guess that's you."

"You said the two men who were important in your life were frauds. My father was the second one?"

"I told you what you needed to know about the safe deposit box and a little too much about me. Good luck in your quest."

"I thought I was done with the life I had with my father, too." I flashed to taking ground balls in the backyard. My stomach hallowed out. "I tried to hide from it for years. Just like you. But we were both fooling ourselves. Look at the self-portraits on your walls. You're still living that life."

"I painted those a long time ago."

"But they're still hanging on your walls. Tell me why my father chose you, Tonya. He pulled away from me after he left the force and got closer to you." My Adam's apple caught in my throat. The scared lonely nights of my childhood pulled at me from decades in the shadows. "Why?"

Tonya looked at me with her blank eyes peeking through blond bangs. A tear appeared at the corner of her left eye. She wiped it away, but more came. A torrent. She gasped and put her head in her hands. I came around the desk, kneeled down, and put my arm around her shoulder. The wound in my leg grabbed me, but I didn't care. I wanted the pain. I slid my other arm across her hands holding her face. I held her. Hard and close. I let her cry. My pain flowed through her tears. Two lost children.

I waited for ten seconds. A minute. Five. I didn't know how long. Time stood still. Tonya lifted her head and patted my arm. She sat straight up in her seat and I went back and sat down in my chair.

"I'm sorry." She wiped the last remnants of tears from her eyes. "I don't know where that came from."

"The same place where it came from for me. I'm sorry I took you back there." I leaned across the desk and opened my hands in front of me. "But I have to go back there and I need your help. Why was my father important in your life?"

Tonya looked at one of her self-portraits. Sadness gave texture to her flat eyes. She didn't say anything for a while. I didn't interrupt her silence.

Finally, "Your father gave a talk about drug abuse at La Jolla High when I was a junior. Some of my friends and I talked to him afterward. I could tell from the talk that he really cared what happened to us. He gave us his card that day and told us to call him whenever we wanted to. Just to talk when life got hard. I didn't call him, but I kept his card."

"Then you found out a couple years later that he was the cop extorting your father and you knew he was a fraud, too. Just like your own father."

"What?" Tonya's head snapped away from her painting and onto me. "Your father wasn't extorting my dad. He and I were trying to find out who was when my dad was murdered."

CHAPTER SIXTY-ONE

"What do you mean?" My breath left me.

Instead of a twenty-seven-year-old weight being lifted from my shoulder, another one piled on. I'd spent most of my life wearing, and believing, my father's shame. Condemning him in my mind and my heart even while I'd held out the flicker of hope that he might be innocent. My father. My blood. The man I wouldn't talk to for the last year of his life. I'd abandoned him. I'd seen his drunkenness as a weakness that exposed his guilt.

It had really exposed a man who held honor and loyalty above all else, broken by betrayal.

"I knew my dad lied to your father and his partner about the attempted robbery. He told them that it had been a friend collecting money on a debt and not a robbery. I'd been at the store before when a man came by and my father gave him money out of the safe in the office. He told me the same thing he told the police later. That he was just paying a friend back some money he owed him. But I knew the man wasn't a friend. I knew he was a criminal."

"Did you tell my father when he came to the laundromat on the attempted robbery?"

"No. I was scared for my dad."

"Did you tell my father about the cop that day?" I asked.

"No. The cop didn't come by until a few weeks after the attempted robbery."

"How did you two try to find out who was extorting your father?"

"I called your father after the cop came by and threatened my dad. My dad wouldn't talk about it and I got scared. I didn't know what else to do, so I called your father. I told my mom I was going to a girl-friend's house and met your father at a coffee shop. I told him about the cop threatening my dad and demanding money."

"What did he say?"

"He didn't believe me at first. Then I showed him the ledger."

"The ledger?" The leather-bound financial records with my father's block writing.

"I did my homework in the Pearl laundromat office every day after school. My mom had taught me bookkeeping before she stopped doing it for my dad. After the attempted robbery by the man my father said was just a friend collecting a debt, I started keeping track of receipts, deposits, and the amount of money in the safe on my own. I knew the safe combination and checked it every day. My father kept a lot of money in there that didn't correlate to the income on the books. That's when I knew he was crooked. A fraud."

"What about the ledger?"

"I kept records of how much money was in each store deposit bag and when the total was different the next day."

"Of course, the total was different because your father was making deposits to the bank."

"No. These were the off-the-books deposit bags. The discrepancies for all the stores always added up to three thousand dollars exactly once a month. Not always the same day of the month, but always the same amount."

"And you gave this ledger to my father?"

"Yes."

"Do you remember seeing him write the store locations on the ledger?" My father's block writing.

"I don't remember, but he might have. I'd just used the store number to keep track. Number one, Grand Avenue. Number two, Cass Street. And number three, Turquoise Street. Number four, Pearl Street. Number five, Genesee Avenue."

"How do you know this wasn't money going to the mob?"

"They took a straight percentage of the gross receipts always on the first day of the month. The total was always different and larger. My father was being extorted by the mob *and* dirty cops. It was all in the ledger that I gave your father."

"Who else knew about this?"

"No one. I didn't even tell my mom. I was afraid she'd tell my dad and he'd do something that would get himself killed." She shook her head. "Maybe I should have told him. Maybe he'd still be alive. Your father was going to try to help my dad and keep him out of jail."

"Did he talk to your father? Did your father tell him who the cop extorting him was?"

"He talked to my father the next day, but my dad told him it was all untrue. That I'd gotten stupid ideas in my head. My dad grounded me for a month." She stared down at the desk. "Didn't matter though. Somebody killed him two weeks later."

"Did you tell all this to the police?"

"No. When I gave your father the ledger, he told me not to talk to anyone about it unless he said it was okay. So, I didn't tell the detective when he questioned me after my father's death. I was afraid if I did, someone would kill your father like they did my dad. I thought he would tell the detectives about the ledger, but he never did."

Maybe he did and they tried to frame him for the murder. When that didn't work, they framed him for taking money from the mob.

Why didn't he take his evidence to the brass or the FBI? Or if he did, why didn't they believe him?

"If you had so much trust in my father, how did he disappoint you? Why was he a fraud?"

"Because he quit. He quit trying to solve my father's murder. He quit on himself. He quit on me." She pushed her bangs out of her eyes. "He quit on you, too."

And I'd quit on him. When he'd needed me most.

"I'm going to find out who killed your father, Tonya. And I'm going to make sure the man who betrayed my father is arrested."

CHAPTER SIXTY-TWO

I CALLED DETECTIVE Sheets' cell phone. The call went to voice-mail. I called again. Voicemail. I called again.

"When you call someone and get voicemail, it means the person is busy and you're supposed to leave a message." Staccato.

"I've got information on a murder case."

"Dammit, Rick. We've already gone over this. I don't have time to hear any more silly theories on the Domingo murder. I'm working the other murders you're connected with and I'm busy."

"This relates to that case."

"Elaborate."

"I have new information on the Trent Phelps murder. I talked—"

"Contact Detective Dixon. He's in charge of all cold cases. Call the LJPD main number and they'll transfer you to him."

"It's the same killer, Detective. Whoever killed Trent Phelps killed Armstrong and Ketchings."

"I told you I don't have time—"

"A cop killed Phelps, Detective. And I've got the gun that killed him."

"You'd better not be playing games, Rick."

"No games." I told him about finding the gun in the safe. And the money. The ledger, the safe deposit box, and Tonya King. I didn't tell him who I thought the murderer was. I wanted first shot before the cops got to him.

Sheets didn't say a word until I was finished. Even then, he was quiet for a few more seconds.

"Where's the gun?"

"In my gun safe at home."

"Do we need a warrant to take custody of it?"

"No. It's yours." It had been in Cahill custody for way too long already.

"Don't touch it again. I'll send a couple uniforms and a lab technician to pick it up. It's too late to get a warrant for the safe deposit box at Windsor Bank. We'll go there tomorrow. Do you have this ledger?"

"No. I saw it once as a kid, but never saw it again. I'm guessing that's one piece of evidence my father or someone else destroyed."

"I'm going to coordinate with Detective Dixon. Wait at your home for the uniforms to get there."

"I'm not home. Give me an hour and a half."

"Where are you?"

"I'm out running an errand."

"Rick, you've done some good work here. Don't ruin it by doing something stupid."

I hung up without answering.

CHAPTER SIXTY-THREE

I PARKED IN front of Judas' house. Bob Reitzmeyer. I squeezed my arm against my side, feeling the butt of the .45 Magnum holstered underneath my jacket. The sun burned out below the horizon. The house's security lights went on. The inside stayed dark. I knocked on the door anyway. No answer. I pulled out my phone and called Bob. No answer there, either. I didn't leave a message. What I had to say needed to be said face-to-face. With a gun as a backup.

Bob Reitzmeyer. My father's best friend. The man who had saved his life in Vietnam. A man he loved like a brother. The cop my father wasn't partnered with on the dates in the ledger when Trent Phelps paid off the cop extorting him. The man who'd claimed the ledger was proof of my father's guilt. The one man my father would do anything to protect. Even remove evidence from a crime scene. The one man's betrayal that could break my father's heart. And his will.

I moved my car down the street with a good view of Bob's house. I didn't want to give him the chance to drive off if he saw my car out front. An hour passed. No Bob. Cops would be arriving at my house in a half hour to take custody of a murder weapon. Detective Sheets wouldn't be happy if I wasn't there to give it to them.

Bob would have to wait. My phone rang before I could restart the car. Unknown caller. I answered.

"Mr. Cahill, this is Detective Dennis Dixon." Cop command voice. "I'm in charge of LJPD cold cases and I just got off the phone with Detective Sheets. We are going to delay collection of the potential murder weapon at your house because we need your help with something else."

"What's that?" Bob would have to wait even longer. But we'd talk tonight. And I still had a gun.

"I don't want to talk too much about it over an open line. However, we need you to verify if the piece of evidence we've uncovered is legitimate before we make an arrest."

"What's the evidence?"

"A leather-bound ledger."

"I can be at the Brick House in ten minutes."

"It's more complicated than that. We need you to come to the site where the evidence is located before we can make an arrest. You'll understand when you get here. Detective Sheets is interrogating a witness right now, but will be on his way here as soon as he's done."

"What's the address?"

He gave it to me. It sounded familiar, then I remembered.

"That's retired Detective Davidson's address."

"Unfortunately, you're right."

CHAPTER SIXTY-FOUR

THE SKY WAS full dark by the time I got out to Ben Davidson's house in East County. Dark enough so you could see the stars. No lights from a city or even a nearby town to dilute the night. A plain-wrap detective car sat in Davidson's horseshoe driveway. No other vehicles. I parked behind it and walked to the front door of the house and knocked. The door opened within five seconds. A man in his early fifties stood in a triangle of light. Fit. Buzz cut. Military bearing. Looked vaguely familiar. He could have been one of the many Brick House cops I'd encountered over the years. Rarely with good result. However, he gave me a polite smile.

"Mr. Cahill?" He stuck out a hand. "Detective Dixon."

I shook his hand and entered the house. He led me into the living room where I'd talked with Ben Davidson a week ago. No one else was in the living room tonight. A ledger sat on a coffee table in front of the chair Davidson had sat in before. I wondered if the retired detective was the person sitting in the square white room with Detective Sheets right now.

"Is this the ledger you saw as a child?" Detective Dixon looked down at the ledger on the table.

"I think so, but I can't be one hundred percent certain."

"Understood." He pulled a pen out of his inside coat pocket and lifted open the ledger. "Do you recognize the handwriting on this page?"

My father's block handwriting. The writing I'd seen on birthday cards as a kid. On a note telling me how sorry he was he'd missed one of my Little League games because of work. And on the envelopes of letters I'd returned to sender unopened the last six months of his life.

"Yeah." I blinked a couple times and swallowed the knot in my throat. "It's my father's."

I looked up at Dixon and the conversation I had with Ben Davidson in that room came back to me. There was a void in the room now. A picture missing from the side table next to the chair where the old man had sat. The back of my neck tingled.

"I'm still not sure why you had me come up here to verify the ledger was my father's."

Headlights flashed through the white-curtained window.

"That must be Detective Sheets," Dixon said. "You'll understand when he comes inside."

A few seconds later the sound of the front door opening and closing came from the foyer. Footsteps and then a man emerged.

Bob Reitzmeyer.

I shot my hand under my coat for the .357. A jab in my side. Dixon won the race.

"Hold it." He pressed the barrel of his gun deeper into my side. "Hands in the air."

My heart machine-gunned in my chest and my stomach dropped down a well. I put my hands up and stared at Bob as he walked over. Flat expression. Dead eyes. Dixon shoved his left hand under my coat just as Bob did the same.

"I got it." Bob pulled out my gun and held it on me. "I never knew exactly why I held onto that ledger for all these years after I took it from your dad's car. I guess I liked having a piece of him close to me."

"The payoff dates in the ledger when you and my father were riding solo wasn't proof of his guilt, but yours."

"Well, I had a partner on those days when I wasn't with your dad." He nodded at Dixon.

"This isn't true confession, Bob," Dixon said. "Let's move this along."

"Sit down, Rick," Bob said.

I sat in Ben Davidson's chair. I remembered the photo I'd seen on the side table now. It was of Davidson's daughter with her arm around a man's waist. Detective Dixon, Ben Davidson's son-in-law.

"There are a couple of uniforms and a crime scene tech knocking on my door right about now." I tried to steady my voice. Shallow breaths made it difficult. "Detective Sheets is going to start looking for me when I don't answer the door."

"No, he won't." Dixon gave me a devil grin. "I told him I'd take custody of the gun when he called me to coordinate."

"When I don't turn up, he'll get a warrant for the gun. He's already getting one for the shells in the safe deposit box. Somebody's DNA is going to be on that gun and ballistics will match the slugs found in Phelps to the Raven .25. The DNA will solve the crime. You're going to have to live life on the run as it is. Killing me's not going to make a difference. It will just ensure that you get the needle."

"Nice speech." Dixon shifted his gaze to Bob. "You get it?"

Bob pulled something out of his coat pocket and set it on the glass coffee table.

The Raven Arms twenty-five-caliber pistol.

"Don't worry, Midnight's fine." Bob's face was still flat, but there was a flicker of humanity in his eyes. "You may not remember this, Rick. When we were having a few drinks the first year you worked for me, you told me the combination to your gun safe was your dad's birth date. You told me some of your fondest memories as a child were your dad teaching you how to shoot and you wanted to always remember those good days. You said the trust and confidence he showed in you was his way of showing love. You were right. He loved you more than anything in the world."

"That's real sweet, Bob." Dixon scowled and shook his head. "He's going to see his dad soon."

"How much does Phelps' daughter know?" Bob's tone was fatherly like the one he'd sometimes use when I worked for him. I guessed he was trying to make my last few minutes on earth as pleasant as possible under the circumstances.

"Just what I told Detective Sheets. I'm sure Detective Dixon has already filled you in." I stared at Bob, a man who I'd once respected like I had my father as a kid, and snapped off each word. "She doesn't know Dixon killed her father because he was going to turn him and you in. Or that Detective Davidson killed the investigation. Or that you tried to set up my father for the murder. He beat you on that setup but you had plan B and it worked."

"If it matters, Buzz Davidson killed Phelps and set Charlie up with the gun." Bob shot a glance at Dixon and rested his eyes back on me.

My stomach settled and my breath came back to me. I didn't want to die, but a whisper within me had been preparing me for an early death for years. The time of my death was in the hands of others. The terms were in mine.

"Why was the gun a setup?" I wasn't stalling for time. Nobody was coming to my aid. If I was going to die tonight, I needed to know the last truth about my father's broken life.

"You believe him about Phelps' daughter?" Dixon looked at Bob. "We shouldn't take any chances. We're almost clear."

"You telling the truth about the Phelps girl, Rick?" Bob asked.

"She's a grown woman now and she gave up caring about who killed her father a long time ago. She's moved on. I haven't." I stared at Bob, man to man. No pleading in my eyes. "Tell me about the gun."

"Let's move this along, Bob," Dixon said.

"He's got a right to know." Bob picked up the .25 off the table and looked at it. "The gun was an accident. Turned out to be a gift to Dixon here and Detective Davidson. Your father was starting to ask questions about Phelps. He showed me the ledger. He was starting to put things together. Anyway, the night of my bachelor party for wife number three, your dad and I got a call about a woman who found a gun in the attic of her deceased father's house. We caught the call and picked up the Raven Arms twenty-five-caliber pistol. Your dad, of course, wanted to run ballistics on the gun when we got back to the Brick House to see if it had been linked to any crimes. I just wanted to get to my bachelor party and convinced him to wait until morning."

Bob smiled the smile that had won him legions of friends and dozens of girlfriends. It bounced off me.

"Anyway, I made a joke at the party about how anal your father was wanting to run the gun instead of going to the party, and Dixon and Davidson saw an opportunity to kill two birds with one stone. They stole the gun out of the trunk of our cruiser and waited for the right time to kill Phelps and frame your father. His prints were on the gun. I never touched it, and Buzz used gloves. Charlie ruined it by covering someone else's shift when Mr. Father and Son-in-Law thought he was home alone without an alibi. You and your sister and mom were up in Northern California for Thanksgiving. But Charlie blew their frame and they had to come up with a plan B."

I remembered the trip. The first one without my dad. He and my mother hadn't been getting along. He must have been already carrying his suspicions about Bob after talking to Phelps' daughter. I hadn't wanted to go on the trip. I didn't want to leave my father alone. I wished I would have been strong enough to hold onto that sentiment later when he really needed me.

"Plan B being the ledger you framed him with. Was it your word against his with the brass, Bob? Did you lie to them like you did to all your ex-wives and girlfriends? You're good at it."

"I don't want you to die thinking your father was a saint, Cahill," Dixon jumped in. "We each pitched in five grand and planted fifteen grand in an envelope in his personal car, but he found it before Internal Affairs searched the car and he never turned it in. So, he had a little grift in him, too."

"You should have checked my desk when you stole the gun tonight, Bob. The envelope is in my desk drawer. He never spent the money."

Dixon shrugged his shoulders, but the color left Bob's face.

"You should have just killed him the night you killed Phelps." I stood up and looked at Bob. "He would have died a hero instead of a broken man. You killed him one day at a time for nine years. And then you had the balls to come to his funeral. Did you spit on his grave while no one was looking?"

"Sit down, Cahill." Dixon shoved his gun in my ribs. "Or I'll turn this white living room red."

"No. Make Bob do it. Make him pull the trigger this time."

Pain exploded in my head and the white living room turned black.

CHAPTER SIXTY-FIVE

I OPENED MY eyes. Pounding head. Liquid dripping into my right ear. Blood. Mine. Arms locked behind me. Hard surface under me. Exposed beams above me. Garage. I moved my hands to try to free them. Plastic cut into my wrists. Something under me crackled when I moved. Plastic. To make the cleanup easy.

"Bring your wife and Buzz out here." Bob's voice. Behind my head somewhere.

"They don't want to see this." Dixon. Out of sight. Maybe in the doorway from the garage to the house.

"You all voted. He has to die. We all have to be here."

"Shit."

Footsteps walking away, then dying. I rolled over and faced Bob.

"How did you get here, Bob? You saved my dad's life in Vietnam only to kill him twenty-five years later. One day at a time. Then you let the world think he was a dirty cop." I tested the flex cuffs around my wrists. No escape. "He once told me my sister and I owed our lives to you for Vietnam. I guess you're reclaiming half that debt tonight. You used his loyalty to break him. He could never betray a brother in arms, but you did."

"He repaid that debt more than once in Vietnam." Bob stared at the ground. The ruddy hue trained from his face. He looked his age for the first time since I'd known him. "He saved everyone in our PBR at least three times, but he never forgot the one time I saved him."

"How many people do you think your partner in there can kill before you get caught? Phelps. Armstrong and Ketchings. Me. Do you think Jules Windsor has figured out that alerting you to the shell casings in my dad's safe deposit box would put a target on his back?"

"He doesn't know anything about the Phelps murder. But he's dirty, just like us. We found out he was laundering money for Phelps and the mob. He's been in our pocket ever since. He knew we'd framed your dad, so when you came snooping around he figured he'd better call us. But you're right, he might start putting things together."

"What happened to you, Bob? There used to be some good in you. I've seen it." I worked my way to my feet. The blood rushing from my head staggered me, and I bumped against the SUV Gina Dixon drove up in the day I questioned her father.

"That good is long gone, Rick." Bob smiled the saddest smile I'd ever seen. "Talk time is over."

He stood by the open door to the house looking inside. The button to the automatic garage door opener was next to his arm. I willed him to push the button. He didn't move.

Voices rolled in from the house.

"Is this really necessary?" Gina's voice.

Dixon came through the door first, gun out.

"Get back on that plastic." He pointed his Sig Sauer at my head.

"Fuck you." My terms.

The inside of the garage exploded. A chunk of Dixon's head bounced off the white SUV. His body crumbled to the ground. A scream muted under the gunshot ringing in my ears. Bob turned toward the open door. Gina knocked over her father trying to run away. Another explosion. She flew three feet and landed in the hall. Still. Davidson crawled toward her in panicked slow motion. Bob walked into the house and stood over him. Another gun blast. A red mist hung in the air, then vanished.

I charged toward the door and banged my head on the garage door opener. The door clanked upward, and I ran toward it. Suddenly, it reversed direction. I dove at the closing gap. No hands to break my fall. I landed on my chest. My chin slammed off the concrete as my head banged against the closed door.

I rolled over onto my back. Blood dripped off my chin. My head throbbed and the pain in my chest made it hard to breathe. Bob stood over me. Two of him vibrated in my eyes. The vibration settled into one.

Dixon's blood pockmarked Bob's face and right arm. He held a gun down on me. My gun. The one he'd taken off me when he entered the house. The gun used to kill Dixon, his wife, and her father. I wondered how Bob would spin it. Would I die a hero or a villain? However he played it, the story wouldn't work if he shot me with my own gun. As loud as the gunshots were, they were contained inside the garage and the nearest house was over half a mile away. Nobody heard the gunshots. Nobody called the police. Nobody was coming to save me.

"I've been preparing for this for a long time, Rick. I knew this day would come."

"To kill me and blame it on someone else? Why? Wasn't my father enough?" I inched my back up the garage door into a sitting position. With my hands cuffed behind me, I had no defense.

"I didn't know they were going to murder Phelps. On my daughter's soul." Bob squatted down like a catcher. Sadness in his eyes.

"What would you have done if you'd been first on the scene? Take the gun like my father had or let the frame stand?"

"I honestly don't know."

The humanity in Bob's eyes evaporated and he stood up. He still loosely held my gun on me. I wanted him to shoot me with my gun and have to explain it to the police. It was the only revenge I had.

Bob raised the gun. I waited for the chance to tell my father I was sorry. For doubting him. For letting him drown alone in his sorrow. For not being at his side when he died. Tears welled in my eyes. For not trusting my father's blood.

Bob cocked his wrist. And pointed the gun barrel at the rafters. Pulled the ejector rod and spun the cylinder. The spent shells and unused bullets clattered down on the concrete floor. Bob spun and stepped over the body of Detective Dixon and walked toward the door into the house. He stopped next to the garage door button, pulled out his pocket knife, and severed the wires. He turned and looked at me.

"I'm sorry." Then he went into the hallway strewn with the bodies of the people he'd murdered and closed the door behind him. Twenty seconds later I heard a car start in the driveway and calmly pull away.

I scrambled to my feet and ran to the door into the house, spun around, and tried the knob with my cuffed hands. Locked. I searched the garage for clippers or a knife that I could maneuver to cut the plastic cuffs off my wrists. Nothing.

My cell phone was in my pants pocket, but I wasn't limber enough to move my cuffed hands from behind my back to get at it. I looked down at the crumpled body of Dixon. His wife was dead inside the house. She wouldn't be able to call the police when he never came home. Someone at LJPD would start looking for him sometime in the next day or two. I could scream all I wanted, but no one would hear me. I'd have to listen for the mailman with my ear to the garage door all day tomorrow when the blow flies started to collect on Dixon's shattered head and lay eggs.

I looked at Dixon again and then at his wife's SUV parked next to his fallen body. I squatted down over his body and found his right pant-leg pocket with my hands. Keys inside. I worked my right hand into his pocket and grasped the key ring. I fingered the key ring with my left hand. Two key fobs and three loose keys. I stepped over Dixon and backed up to the door into the house. I maneuvered each of the three loose keys and tried to fit them into the slot in the doorknob behind my back. None fit. Either Dixon didn't have a key to his father's house or the garage door required a different key.

Didn't matter.

I pushed the buttons on one of the key fobs and heard a car alarm chirp outside. Shit. I pushed the button on the other fob. Lights flashed on Gina Dixon's SUV and the locks clicked open. I ran to the car and spun around and opened the driver door behind my back, then stepped up into the seat. I pushed my nose against the ignition button and the car turned on. I put my foot on the brake, then grabbed the shifter on the steering column with my teeth.

Reverse. Foot off brake. Pound gas peddle. Collision. I banged off the steering wheel, but not hard enough for the airbags to go off. My injured chest throbbed, and I could only take short breaths. I looked in the rearview mirror. The garage door stood in place. I kept steady pressure on the gas. The garage filled with exhaust. The garage door stayed in place. Another minute or two and I'd probably die of carbon monoxide. Maybe I should just wait for the mailman.

I pushed the gas pedal to the floor. Burned rubber. Exhaust. Grinding metal. Bent aluminum. I checked the rearview mirror. The garage door still stood, but had a kink in it. I jammed my foot on the brake, teethed the shifter to park, and nose butted the ignition off.

I stumbled out of the car and saw it. The dent in the garage door had lifted a crooked gap up from the garage floor. I laid down and shimmied through.

Freedom. Fresh air. Bob Reitzmeyer in the wind.

CHAPTER SIXTY-SIX

THE WOMAN WHO answered the door of the house a half mile from Ben Davidson's home reeled backwards and threw up her hand when she saw me after I'd rung her doorbell with my nose.

She locked me outside and called the police. I couldn't blame her. I liked being locked outside better than inside anyway. I waited on her front porch. The police arrived fifteen minutes later. The walk from Davidson's house had taken me twenty minutes with my wounded leg, armless gait, and a probable broken sternum. After I directed Poway PD to the crime scene, they took me to the nearest station and grilled me for an hour until they finally ceded my wishes and called Detective Sheets.

Poway PD didn't put out a BOLO for Bob until after Sheets arrived and vouched for me a half hour later. Bob had told me he'd been planning for this day for years. Not to kill me, but to flee the country. He was probably already on a plane under an alias off to an exotic land.

He'd saved my life and was now on the run because of it. He could have gone along with Dixon's plan and still be living in La Jolla, bedding a different long-legged attorney every night. But he chose to save me and flee a life he could never return to. Guilt for what he'd done to my father? Genuine affection for me? I'd never know.

But now I did know that my father, broken, betrayed, and forsaken, died with the honor he lived by still intact. And I prayed I could uphold the truth of his blood.

EPILOGUE

Jack Anton wrote a freelance article that made the front page of the *Union Trib* two days after the Poway murders. It laid out the whole story, going back to the Phelps murder and cover-up. The truth about my father. A man betrayed and broken. Trent Phelps' daughter, Tonya King, showed up at my house the afternoon the article hit the newsstands. She didn't say much. Just cooked and cleaned and took care of me while I recuperated from a fractured sternum.

Kim visited me the first day I got home from the hospital. She sat next to my bed and held my hand. Her hand was warm and felt right in my own. But I knew it couldn't stay there. And it suddenly felt wrong.

"I'll never be able to repay you for all you did for me . . . and Jeffrey."

"We're even. For all that you've done for me over the years. When it was hard and you didn't have to." I patted her hand, then slid mine out. I thought back on the day I broke a wooden cane over Jeffrey Parker's shin. "I don't remember doing too much for Jeffrey."

"You haven't heard?"

"Heard what?"

"LJPD dropped the charges. They are now calling Dina Dergan a person of interest and are looking for her."

They'd never find her.

"That's great." I meant it. I didn't want any innocent man to be hounded for something he didn't do. I knew the damage it could wreak. For a generation.

"I know it was you, Rick. I know you convinced them that Jeffrey was innocent."

"I think they just finally looked at all the evidence."

"Rick?" Kim looked down at the floor, then back at me. Her green eyes were heavy. The last few weeks had taken the sparkle out of them. The one thing I could always count on. The sparkle of optimism. I already missed it. "I know you were pretty rough on Jeffrey. Did he . . . did he ever tell you that he slept with Sophia?"

Kim had made her choice. She'd chosen one imperfect man who loved her over another. She was about to start a family, but doubt still clouded her joy. Parker had tearfully confessed to me in jail. I took him to be truly remorseful, but he'd betrayed the woman I loved.

"No."

"Do you think he did?"

"No."

Kim deserved a chance at happiness more than anything. Even more than the truth.

* * *

Moira called me the next day.

"You'll do anything to get your name in the paper, won't you, Cahill." The full blast machine-gun voice. I'd missed that voice.

"You're just sorry it wasn't you."

"Next time ask for help. Asshole." She hung up.

Friends.

* * *

I rented a safe deposit box once I was finally healed. In a bank near where I lived, not at Windsor Bank and Trust. Jules Windsor fled to Europe before the news came out that he'd laundered money for the mob three decades ago. His crime was well past the statute of limitations, but there wasn't a statute of limitations for a soiled reputation. My father and I knew all about that.

The one item I stored in my new safe deposit box was a letter envelope. Inside was a flash drive with a copied file from the flash drive I gave back to the Russian mafia. Insurance for when I receive a certain phone call.

I donated the fifteen thousand dollars in the twenty-seven-year-old envelope to the Mount Soledad Veterans Memorial.

A plaque was scheduled to go up in my dad's honor in the spring. Not because of the money, but for his service to our country. I offered to put up my aunt and my sister and her sons when they came down for the ceremony.

Sometimes when I'm sitting in front of the TV at night, I let my eyes drift up to the bookshelf above it and gaze at the shadow box holding my father's LJPD badge.